THE DOORKEEPERS

Recent Titles by Graham Masterton from Severn House

The Jim Rook Series

ROOK
THE TERROR
TOOTH AND CLAW
SNOWMAN

Anthologies

FACES OF FEAR
FEELINGS OF FEAR
FORTNIGHT OF FEAR
FLIGHTS OF FEAR

THE DOORKEEPERS

Graham Masterton

This first world edition published in Great Britain 2001 by
SEVERN HOUSE PUBLISHERS LTD of
9–15 High Street, Sutton, Surrey SM1 1DF.
This first world edition published in the USA 2001 by
SEVERN HOUSE PUBLISHERS INC. of
595 Madison Avenue, New York, NY 10022.

British Library Cataloguing in Publication Data

Masterton, Graham, 1946–
The doorkeepers
1. Horror tales
I. Title
823.9′14 [F]

ISBN 0–7278–5685–5

Typeset by Palimpsest Book Production Limited,
Polmont, Stirlingshire, Scotland.
Printed and bound in Great Britain by
MPG Books Ltd, Bodmin, Cornwall.

There was a Door to which I found no key:
There was a Veil past which I could not see.

Edward Fitzgerald
The Ruba'yát of Omar Khayyám

Six doors they stand in London Town
Six doors they stand in London, too
Yet who's to know which way they face?
And who's to know which face is true?

Traditional nursery rhyme

One

Julia typed *Yours in anticipation, F.G. Mordant*, and tugged the letter out of her typewriter. She slipped the letter into Mr Mordant's red signing folder and dropped the pink and yellow copies into the box file next to her. She returned the carbon paper to her second drawer down.

It was five thirty-two p.m. and the office was bright with the last marmalade-colored light of the day. Julia put the lid on her typewriter, not knowing that this was the very last time she would do it, and that once the sun had sunk below the rooftops of the factories opposite, she would never see it come up again.

Alexandra put her head round the office door and blinked at her through owlish glasses. "Haven't you finished yet? David's offered to give us a lift to Hammersmith."

"David? Oh, yes please! Just give me a minute, will you? I have to take these letters into Mr Mordant."

"You should *complain*, you know. He's always keeping you late."

Julia gave her a dismissive *pff*! The idea of complaining to Mr Mordant was out of the question: especially if you wanted to keep your job. Alexandra had told her that it was highly unusual if any of his secretaries survived for more than six months. Some of them had stayed for only a week.

Julia opened her oak-paneled filing cupboard. There was a mirror on the back of the door and she gave her hair a quick brush. She pushed her tongue under her upper lip. She wasn't sure if she was getting a cold sore or not.

She was a pretty girl, a little plumpish, with a heart-shaped face that made her look much younger than twenty-three.

She had short blonde-streaked hair with a fringe, and wide brown eyes. She had been living in England for ten months now. She had lost all but the faintest ghost of her California tan, and acquired a pale blue twinset, but her accent had hardly changed. Everybody at Wheatstone Electrics called her "Yankee Doodle". Americans were a rarity, except in films, and her friends never tired of hearing her talk about luxuries like washing machines and supermarkets.

She walked along the echoing linoleum-floored corridor to Mr Mordant's office. All through the building she could hear doors slamming and people calling out "g'night" and clattering downstairs. Mr Mordant's door was open but she still gave a little knock. He was sitting at his desk, talking on the phone and cat's-cradling elastic bands between his fingers as he did so.

"Well, I'm sorry, Ronald, you'll just have to buck your bloody ideas up, won't you?" His accent was clipped, like a BBC wireless announcer. "If you can't let me have those insulators by the end of the month, we'll have to start looking for a new supplier. No, Ronald, I don't care tuppence how long you've been dealing with us. *Today* is what counts."

He noisily cradled the phone and said, "Idiot. He couldn't organize a beetle-drive." Then he looked up at Julia and gave her an unexpected smile. "Well, Julia, what have you got for me?"

Frank Mordant was handsome in a sharp, slightly Brylcreemy way. He had a finely chiseled forehead and a straight, thin nose, and his eyes were piercing blue and hooded like a hawk's. His brown hair was brushed straight back, and he sported a thin, clipped moustache. He was always immaculately dressed in gray three-piece suits and starched white shirts with double cuffs and a separate collar. Wheatstone's kept their offices warm and by the end of the day he always smelled faintly of body odor.

Julia put his signing folder down in front of him. He unscrewed his fountain pen, but before he opened his folder he leaned back in his chair. "How long have you been with me now, Julia?"

"Ten months next Wednesday. I started here May eleventh."

"Doesn't time fly! But let me tell you something, Julia, no word of a lie – I've never had a secretary anything like as good as you. Not even a secretary from . . . well, where *you* came from."

"Thank you," she said. "I wonder if you could sign your letters now, please. Some of my friends are giving me a ride home."

Frank Mordant opened the folder and wrinkled up his nose at the letters inside. "These aren't all that desperate, are they? There's only this prospectus to the Air Ministry, isn't there? And if they want that in a hurry you can send it up to Whitehall by taxicab."

"Well, if it's OK with you, Mr Mordant . . ."

He screwed the cap back on his pen. "Of course it's 'OK' with me. But listen, instead of going into town with your friends, why don't you let me take you? I'm going that way myself. I'd enjoy a chinwag."

Julia couldn't think of anything less appealing than driving into Hammersmith with Mr Mordant, especially since she had a severe crush on David and hadn't seen him since Tuesday lunchtime. But Mr Mordant was her boss and it was very difficult to say no.

"I, ah—"

"Fine! That's settled then! Why don't you go and fetch your coat and I'll meet you in the lobby in five minutes."

Alexandra was waiting for her in her office. "Come *on*, Julia! We're going to be late! We're all going to go to the Corner House for tea and cream cakes!"

"Sorry," said Julia. "I'm going to have to take a raincheck. Darth Vader wants to drive me home."

"*Who*?"

"Mr Mordant. He says he feels like a chinwag."

"Oh, God. You poor thing! Can't you faint? Can't you stick your finger down your throat and pretend that you're sick?"

"I wish."

"Oh, well. *C'est la vie*. You can still meet us at the Corner House later."

"I'll try. But if I can't, look, I'll see you tomorrow, OK?"

"All right," said Alexandra. "But just you be careful. You know what they say about accepting lifts from strange men, and you couldn't find anybody stranger than Frank Mordant, could you?"

He was waiting for her in the gloomy hexagonal lobby, with its pale-faced illuminated clock and its polished marble floor and its bronze statue of the goddess Electra. He was wearing a Homburg hat and a long black overcoat, and was buttoning up his black leather motoring gloves when she entered the room.

"Goodnight, Sheila," called Julia to the receptionist, a curly redhead with a high, silly laugh. The lobby rattled with the footsteps of Wheatstone employees going home.

Frank Mordant gave Julia a slanted smile. "You look . . . *splendid*," he complimented her, looking approvingly at the dark brown hooded coat she had bought in Bloomingdale's on her stopover from Los Angeles. "I suppose it would be more circumspect of me *not* to ask where you got it."

They pushed their way through the bronze and glass art deco doors. The sun had set and although the sky was still light there was a nip in the late-February air. Their breath smoked as they walked across the forecourt to Frank Mordant's long navy-blue Armstrong-Siddeley. He opened the passenger door for her, and she climbed into a black leather interior. It smelled of cold cigars and motor oil. Frank Mordant settled himself beside her, turned the keys, and pushed the starter button.

"So, Julia, how do you see your future?" he asked, as he nosed the car out into the rush-hour traffic along the Great West Road. "You're not going to stay a secretary for ever, are you?"

"Actually I was hoping to get into television production."

"Television production?" he said, with obvious surprise.

"What's wrong with that?"

"Well, quite frankly, we don't have much room for women on the television side. Not unless you want to sit on the production line all day, plugging in valves. I suppose I could always have a word with Bill Harvey down at our Bristol plant."

"I was talking about television *programs*, not television sets."

"Oh, I see," he nodded, and thought about that for a while. Then he said, "So that's it, you're thinking of spreading your wings. Goodbye Wheatstone's, hallo fame and fortune?"

"I've had a great time at Wheatstone's, don't get me wrong. It's really helped me to get my head together."

"Well, good. Good. I'm glad about that. I wouldn't like to think of your head being . . . you know. Apart."

They stopped at a red traffic signal and he drummed his fingers on the steering wheel. "Here, do you think, or *there*?" he asked her.

"Oh, *there*, of course. I mean, what do you have here? Black-and-white, seven-inch screens, and less than three-quarters of a million viewers in the whole country. Back there, whole series get canceled if they can only attract an audience of three-quarters of a million."

"I suppose you're right," said Frank Mordant. He pulled out and overtook a crowded double-decker bus. "Still . . . there's a lot to be said for staying here, isn't there? It would be very much easier for you to make your mark in television here, knowing what you know. Having that . . . background, as it were. I mean, look at me. I only got a 'D' in physics, but look at me now. Production director of the second-largest electrical company in Britain. Four thousand pounds a year. Plus perks."

They crawled at two to three miles per hour through the tangle of traffic that would take them in to the Chiswick roundabout. It didn't help that a baby Austin had broken down in the outside lane, and a young man in his shirtsleeves was frantically cranking the starting-handle. Up above them, autogiros swarmed through the evening sky like fireflies, their engines droning, carrying scores of wealthy businessmen home to Windsor and Lightwater and Sunbury-on-Thames.

"Look," said Frank Mordant, "why don't we stop for a quick drink? There's a jolly little pub just along here."

"Really, Mr Mordant, I have to be getting back."

"Come on, one drink won't hurt! You deserve it, after

everything you've done today. All that filing. I know you think I'm a slavedriver, but your efforts don't go unnoticed, you know."

Julia felt desperate, but she couldn't say no. She had refused Frank Mordant's offer of a mint humbug once and he seemed to have taken it as a personal affront, keeping her working till well past six o'clock. "OK, then," she agreed. "Just one drink."

"That's the ticket!" He steered the Armstrong-Siddeley into a side street and did some very complicated parking behind a rusty Wolseley. On the corner stood a small Victorian pub, The Sir Oswald Mosley, with cream-painted walls and maroon woodwork. Frank Mordant ushered Julia in through the engraved glass doors into the saloon bar. It was thick with cigarette smoke but it was almost empty, except for a spotty youth in a green tweed sports jacket playing the fruit machine and an elderly man with a beetroot-colored face and a mournful Staffordshire bull terrier lying by his feet.

The landlord appeared behind the curved mahogany bar with a cigarette stuck to his lower lip, and one eye scrunched up against the smoke. "Your usual, Mr Mordant?" he said, reaching up for a bottle of Glenlivet malt whiskey.

"Thank you, Norman. And what would you like, Julia?"

"Oh, just something non-alcoholic for me. Maybe an orange juice."

A television was flickering on a shelf behind the bar. The sound was turned down but Julia could see what was happening. Hordes of people in sarongs were pulling down barriers and burning British flags. More trouble in Burma.

They sat down at a small marble-topped table and Frank Mordant raised his glass and said, "Cheers, m'dear."

Julia took a sip of her warm reconstituted orange juice and tried to smile.

Frank Mordant looked around. "This isn't a bad little place, you know, especially when it livens up a bit. You should come in here for Gold Cup day. Norman lays on quite a spread. Sandwiches, pork pies. That kind of thing. I call it my secret headquarters."

Julia shook her head to show that she didn't understand.

"Well, all of us have to have somewhere, don't we? *You've* got somewhere, surely, even if it's only a cupboard?"

"I keep some stuff in a drawer, sure. My Walkman, you know, and a whole lot of photographs."

Frank Mordant nodded. He took out a packet of Capstan cigarettes and tapped one on the table top. "I don't miss it, you know. Life's been much too good for me here."

"Don't you miss anything, or anybody?"

"Oh, yes. I was married, you know, believe it or not. Pretty girl, Daphne, met her in Brighton. We had a daughter but she was a spastic and we had to put her in a home. Then I got into trouble with my car business. Cars, that was my line."

He lit his cigarette and blew long funnels of smoke out of his nostrils. "There was a silly business over another woman, too. In the end, I thought, why not? Start all over again. Start afresh, if you know what I mean."

Julia didn't have to say anything. She knew exactly what he meant. It was the chance to start over that had attracted her to stay here, too. She had been halfway through a TV production course at University of California at Santa Cruz when she had fallen for Rex Pittman, and she still couldn't think about Enya's *Orinoco Flow* without a shiver. That was the music he had played when they had first made love: the 48-year-old professional TV writer and the deeply impressionable 21-year-old student. "Whenever you hear this song, you're going to remember this night," he had told her. But *here*, of course, nobody had ever heard of Enya.

It had all ended badly. Rex's neurotic wife Nessa had found out about Julia and deliberately walked through a plate-glass door at Julia's parents' house. Rex had left Nessa and taken Julia to Baja for a week. Swimming, talking, sailing, drinking tequila sunrises and making love. But in the end they had to go back, and when they went back they discovered that Nessa had critically injured their three-year-old son James by pouring scalding water over him. James died two weeks later, in terrible pain.

That was why Julia was here. Mostly, anyhow. It was a way

to begin her life all over again, where nothing and nobody could reach her.

Frank Mordant finished his whiskey and nodded toward her glass. "Fancy another?"

"No, no thanks. I really have to be getting home."

"How is it, your flat?"

"Well, to be honest, it's far too big for just one person. Way too expensive, too. My landlady just put it up to £2.17s.6d a week."

"I say. That's a bit steep, isn't it?"

"Yes, I know. But I don't know if I ever want to share again. I liked Mary, but I always felt like I had to be on my guard. I think she *suspected* me, you know – but of course she never knew what it was that she suspected me of."

"I've got a flat here," said Frank Mordant, quite matter-of-factly, blowing smoke, and nodding his head up toward the ceiling.

"You have a flat *here*? You mean *here*, over this pub?"

"That's right. I've had it for five years now. My secret headquarters. Sitting room, bedroom, bathroom. I suppose an estate agent might call it *bijou*, but I scarcely use it these days so it does for me." He paused, and blew some more smoke, and then he said, "I was wondering, you know. Perhaps you might like to take it over."

"What about you?"

Frank Mordant shrugged. "As I say, I scarcely ever use it. Only when a wave of nostalgia comes over me. I've got a bit of stuff up there but you're quite welcome to use it, too. A color TV with a video recorder and a stereo system and a pile of CDs. Do you like Abba? I used to love Abba. *Dig it, the dancing queen . . .* Those were the days. Oh, and a deep-freeze, too. Not a big one, but it's got fish fingers in it, and pizza, and some chicken balti, too."

Julia couldn't help smiling. "I thought you were so acclimatized. Your accent, you know, and the way you dress."

"Oh, I am. But you know what it's like. If you want to live here happily, you have to edit things out of your mind, and after a while you begin to think that perhaps they didn't happen at all. That stuff upstairs . . . that's just a little reminder that I'm not dreaming, after all.

He stood up and patted his pockets to find his keys. "Why don't you come and take a shufti at it? It's a jolly sight nearer to work than Lavender Hill, and I'd only charge you £1.15s.0d a week."

"I'm not sure . . ." said Julia. "I've already made quite a few friends in Lavender Hill."

"Nonsense, you can make friends anywhere. Personable young lady like you. There's no harm in taking a look, is there?"

Julia glanced toward the landlord. He was polishing pint glasses and watching her with a dull, fixed stare, the cigarette still hanging from the side of his mouth, as if he wanted to remember her for ever. "Well . . . all right then," she agreed. "But then I must get home."

Frank Mordant's flat had a separate front door at the side of the pub. It was painted maroon and it had no number on it, only a small bronze knocker in the shape of a grinning imp's head. Frank Mordant gave it a *rat-a-tat-tat* and said, "Cornish piskie. It's supposed to bring you luck."

Inside, there was a damp coconut mat and then a steep flight of stairs. Frank Mordant switched the light on and said, "Good exercise, stairs. Up and down here a few times a day and you won't need to worry about jogging."

"I don't jog, not any more. People used to stare so much."

"Yes, I suppose they would. Here – watch your step at the top here, the carpet's loose."

At the top of the stairs there was a small brown-wallpapered landing with two doors leading off it. A damp-rippled reproduction of Damien Hirst's *Chinese Lady* hung at an angle between them, and one of them bore a ceramic plaque saying The Smallest Room.

Frank Mordant unlocked the other door and led the way into a narrow corridor. On the left there was a small kitchenette with a gas water-heater and fitted cupboards in lime-green Formica. It was obvious that he didn't use the flat very often: there was a stuffy, sour, closed-in smell, and all of the dried herbs in the spice jars that hung on the wall had faded to pale yellow.

"Needs a woman's touch, really."

The sitting room was surprisingly large and light. It had a high ceiling and all the walls had been painted white and the light gray carpet wasn't luxurious but it was fairly new. There was a plain couch covered in black cotton fabric and a large brown 1930s armchair. A large television stood in one corner of the room, as well as a video player and stacks of labeled videotapes. There was a video camera, too, tilted on top of a tripod.

"A few pictures on the walls," Frank Mordant suggested. "Scatter cushions, that kind of thing. You could really make it quite homey."

A plain white calico blind covered the window. Julia went over to it and tried to release it, but it was fastened to the window frame with thumbtacks. She lifted an edge of it and peeked out. It looked right over Chiswick High Road, still crowded with buses and cyclists and homegoing cars.

"Want to see the bedroom?" asked Frank Mordant. "The bedroom's nice. Only had it redecorated in September."

He opened the door that led to the bedroom. It was just large enough for a double bed covered with a pink candlewick bedspread, a wardrobe and a chair with a leatherette seat. The walls had been stippled with pale blue distemper. Over the bed hung a fan-shaped mirror with two picture postcards stuck in it, and on the pillow lay a defeated-looking golliwog.

"Well . . ." said Julia. The flat wasn't as seedy as she had expected it to be. Frank Mordant was right: one or two colorful pictures would make the whole place look much more welcoming, and she could cover that deadly black couch with the sunflower-patterned throw she had bought from Habitat. Living here would save her more than one pound a week on rent, and nearly as much as that again on bus fares.

She came back into the living room. She found Frank Mordant tinkering with the video camera. He swiveled around like a floorwalker in a department store and wrung his hands together.

"What do you think, then? It's really quite cozy, isn't it?"

"It doesn't get too noisy, does it, with the pub downstairs?"

Frank Mordant shook his head. "I won't lie to you, there *is* a bit of a racket at closing time. Car doors slamming, everybody saying goodnight, things like that. But it doesn't last for long. And here's the secret ingredient." He knelt down and lifted up one corner of the carpet. "Underfelt, double-thick, almost completely soundproof. I had it laid so that I could play my music as loud as I liked. You could scream your head off in here and nobody would hear you."

Julia took another look around. "It's interesting . . . I'd like to think it over, if I may."

"Of course. Take as long as you like. Before you go, though, there is one thing you might like to consider."

He went to the kitchenette. She didn't know whether she was supposed to follow him or not, so she waited. She lifted the edge of the blind again, and looked down into the street. The road was noisier here than her terrace in Lavender Hill, but she didn't really mind the background jostle of traffic.

"Do you know which bus—?" she began; and then she was suddenly aware that Frank Mordant was standing right behind her. She hadn't heard him, hadn't even sensed him approaching.

Without a word he clamped a thick white cloth over her nose and mouth, as thick as a muslin diaper. It reeked with a pungent, chemical smell – a smell that seared her nostrils and burned her eyes. She gave a panicky snuffle and breathed it in. She staggered against him, tried to struggle, and managed to snatch at his wristwatch. But he kept the cloth pressed firmly against her face, and as she tried to pull away from him the room tilted on its end and the floor came toward her like a dark, silently slamming door.

Two

Julia was woken up by a penetrating white light shining in her eyes. Gradually she opened her eyes a little wider, but the light dazzled her so much that she closed them again. Her head was throbbing and there was a biting, astringent taste in her mouth. She felt chilled, and weak, as if she had the 'flu, and she was conscious of something harsh encircling her neck.

"Ah, coming round," said Frank Mordant's voice. "Welcome back to the land of the living."

She opened her eyes again. She was lying on a prickly woolen blanket on the floor and Frank Mordant was looking down at her with a grin. Somebody else was looking down at her, too – a suntanned man with very white hair.

"Got us a beauty this time, Frank," said the suntanned man. "Done yourself proud."

Frank Mordant knelt down beside Julia and helped her up into a sitting position. She felt sick and the floor was slowly rising up and down like the deck of a car ferry. She put her head down between her knees and it was only then that she realized that she was naked.

She looked up, woozy but startled. Frank Mordant was still grinning at her as if she were the victim of a huge practical joke.

"What have you done? What have you done to me?" Covering her breasts with her arm, she tried to get up, but she lost her balance and fell sideways. As she fell, the harsh thing around her neck almost choked her and she reached up to pull it free. Except that it wouldn't come free. It was a thick rope, tied around her neck in a noose.

She tried again to climb to her feet, and this time she

managed to get herself into a kneeling position. "What's happening?" she gasped. "What are you trying to do to me?"

Frank Mordant took hold of the loose end of the rope and pulled it. Immediately, it tightened around Julia's neck, and she looked up. The rope ran through a large hook fixed in the center of the ceiling.

She stared at Frank Mordant in disbelief. Apart from him and the white-haired man with the suntan, there were three other men there, standing in the far corner by the television. They were all middle-aged, wearing respectable suits. A dark-skinned, languid-looking man with a hooked nose. A heavily built man with bushy gray hair. A smaller bespectacled man, who must have been Thai or Malay.

Three spotlights had been arranged around the room so that they shone directly on Julia. And the video camera was now tilted on its tripod so that it was facing toward her, too. There was a smell of hot light bulbs and alcoholic breath, and a taut, expectant atmosphere. *Yours in anticipation, Frank Mordant.*

Julia's head was completely clear now, and she looked at the men and the spotlights and the video camera with increasing horror. She felt almost absurdly weak, and completely defenseless, and she was so frightened that her lower lip was juddering and she couldn't speak clearly.

Frank Mordant and the suntanned man took an arm each and tried to lift her on to her feet. Immediately her knees buckled, but Frank Mordant pulled the rope until it was tight around her neck again, and then she was forced to stand up.

"You're choking me," she pleaded. "Please don't choke me. I can't stand anything round my neck."

"Well, there's one way to relieve that choking feeling," smiled Frank Mordant, "and that's to slacken the rope. Here, Tun," he beckoned the Malay-looking man. "Do us a favor and bring us over that little stepladder, please."

The Malay carried over a small wooden stepladder and set it down right in front of Julia. He paused for a moment, and scrutinized her through his bright shining glasses. His eyes were dark brown and deeply curious, as if he were looking at an exhibit in a natural history museum. He stared into her eyes and then down at her naked body.

Frank Mordant gave the rope another sharp tug. "If you climb the stepladder, Julia, the rope will be slacker. The higher you go, the slacker it will get."

"You can't do this," Julia protested. "You just can't do this."

"And who's to say that we can't?"

"The law! This is assault!"

Frank Mordant thought about that, and then he said, "Yes, you're right. It *is* assault. But I don't think that the law is going to be able to help you, do you?"

"*Let me go*!" she screamed at him. "*You're sick! You're totally sick! If you don't let me go right now, mister . . .* !"

"You'll what?" said Frank Mordant, and the slowest smile broke over his face as he watched her remember what he said about the underlay.

"Let me go," she breathed. "Please let me go. I won't tell anybody what happened here."

Frank Mordant tugged on the rope again. She reached up and tried to force her fingers between the noose and her neck, but it was far too tight.

"Please don't do this. Please let me go. I'll do anything you want me to do. Please."

"You're already doing what I want you to do. Now, why don't you take a step up the ladder and give yourself a little slack?"

He pulled the rope harder and in spite of herself she let out a horrible, high-pitched cackle. He pulled again and she felt as if she was going to choke. She reached out with her right foot and found the bottom rung of the stepladder and climbed on to it: and then, with her left foot, the second rung. The rope relaxed, and she was able to gasp in three or four mouthfuls of air.

"Mr Mordant, I don't know why you're doing this . . ."

"My dear, you don't *have* to know. All you have to do is to play your part."

"Is this personal? Is there something I've done to upset you?

If there is, I'm sorry. I'm really, truly sorry, and I swear to God that I'll make it up to you."

Frank Mordant looked at her with those hooded blue eyes and she thought for a moment that she saw the slightest hint of compassion.

"Mr Mordant, if I did anything wrong, *anything*, I'll put it right. I have people back home who are going to be worried about me. My mother, my father. My brother. They're good people, Mr Mordant, you can do what you like to me but don't make them suffer."

The suntanned man with the white hair turned to the others and spread his hands wide in mock bewilderment. "Why do they always do this? Why do they always get so sentimental? You'd think they'd eff and blind and kick their legs about, wouldn't you? I mean, that's what *I'd* do, if somebody was doing it to me."

The Malay didn't take his eyes off Julia, but he said, with a slight smile, "That's because you're afraid of dying, Roy. You know what the next world has in store for you."

Julia had made a mistake. What she had seen in Frank Mordant's eyes wasn't compassion at all. If it was anything, it was simply a predatory flicker, like a snake refocusing before it strikes. Frank Mordant wound the rope around his arm and took up all of the slack that Julia had given herself by climbing up the stepladder. "Don't," she gargled. "Please don't."

The dark-skinned man with the hooked nose looked impatiently at his wristwatch. In the middle of her terror, Julia realized that he was bored. The thought of that was so awful that her eyes filled with tears. She was naked, utterly humiliated, choking, and he was *bored.*

"*Let me go*!" she screamed. "*I can't stand this any longer*! *Let me go*!"

Frank Mordant yanked the rope hard. "You can't stand it any longer? Then take another step up. Go on! That's the only way you'll get any slack!"

She tried to shake her head and say no, but he wrenched the rope again and this time she saw stars winking in front of her eyes. She climbed up another step, and then another, and now she was only one step from the top.

"You won't get away with this," she whispered. "I swear to God that you won't get away with this."

Frank Mordant pulled the rope one more time. "You wanted to be in television, didn't you?" he asked. He didn't sound sarcastic, or triumphalist. He simply sounded pleased for her. "You wanted to be famous? Well, believe it or not, your wish is about to come true. You're going to be seen by thousands of very appreciative viewers, for years to come! Who knows, you're probably going to be a television classic!"

She took the last step on to the top of the ladder. Her head was only about six inches from the ceiling, but the rope was utterly taut. Frank Mordant knelt down, lifted the black cover on the couch, and tied the other end of the rope around it. He did it so deftly that Julia could tell he had done it before.

For a long moment they all stood in a strange tableau: Julia on top of the stepladder and the four men watching her. The noose was so tight around her neck that she could hardly swallow, and her breath came in thin, distinct whines. She reached up with both hands and clung tightly to the rope, terrified that Frank Mordant would take the stepladder away.

"They'll see this all over the world, Julia. Germany, the Germans love this kind of thing, although they won't admit it. Holland, very broad-minded, we always get excellent sales figures in Holland. Japan . . . well, you know what the Japs are like. They'd pay to see a slug being stepped on. And America, of course. Huge market in America. Perhaps someone will recognize you, you never know."

"*Please*," Julia begged him. Then she couldn't hold it together any longer, and she wet herself. Frank Mordant stepped back a little way and said nothing.

Julia tried to think about her mother and father. She tried to picture their faces, if only to say goodbye to them. She tried to think about her brother Josh. She tried to see the house, and the verandah, and the dogs running out to meet her. But all she could see was the ceiling of Frank Mordant's flat, and all she could think about was choking.

"*Please, don't do this. Please.*"

Frank Mordant approached her and tugged away the step-ladder. Her toes curled, reaching for it – and then, when she realized that it had gone, her legs frantically pedaled in mid-air.

"*Acchhh,*" was all she could manage to say. She held on to the rope but her arms were aching already and she was so close to hysteria that it seemed as if her last remaining strength were ebbing out of her, as if her fingers couldn't grip anything any more.

Her hands slipped down the rope an inch. She managed to cling on a few seconds more and then they slipped another inch. The noose was now so tight around her neck that she couldn't even manage a choking sound. If she could only lift herself up a few more inches. If she could only reach the hook. But she knew it was hopeless. She knew that she was slowly suffocating and there was nothing she could do to save herself.

Frank Mordant and his companions remained quite still, although their eyes were wide and their faces were transfigured by an undisguised hunger, so that they looked more like gargoyles than men. The dark-skinned man repeatedly licked his lips, no longer bored. The Malay had his hand in his pants pocket and his fly was moving rhythmically up and down. The heavily built man had broken out into a glittering sweat.

Only Frank Mordant seemed unmoved, watching Julia spin slowly around on her rope, her legs swimming through the air.

Julia's right hand slipped from the rope above her head. She tried to raise it again, but she didn't have the strength. Almost immediately afterward, her left hand slid another inch down the rope, burning her fingers. Then another inch. She couldn't hold on any longer, and somehow she didn't even want to try. She said *God forgive me* inside of her head, and then she let go.

The last thing she thought of was a daisy that she had once tried to pick, when she was only two years old. She could see it quite clearly, right in front of her. She reached out for it, but before she could touch it the petals flew away, and disappeared for ever into the darkness.

Three

Josh was having an unexpectedly busy morning. After he had cured Mrs Delorme's pedigree Pekinese of its bouts of hysteria last month, word of his healing abilities seemed to have spread from Mill Valley to Corte Madera and Sausalito and even into San Francisco.

Waiting on the verandah outside his kitchen were five assorted people with five assorted dogs and cats, a woman with a cloth-covered birdcage, and a small boy with something in a cardboard box. It was a hot, airless day, and one of his clients was fanning her Siamese cat with a rolled-up copy of the *National Enquirer*.

At the moment Josh was dealing with a mournful black Labrador called Valentino, whose sight was failing. Valentino was sitting on Josh's breakfast table while his mistress stroked him and petted him and chain-fed him with Reese's Pieces. His mistress was a short round woman with greasy iron-gray hair fixed in a bun. She wore dangly hooped earrings, enormous red and yellow shorts and Birkenstocks.

Josh remarked, "You really shouldn't keep on feeding him candy. Dogs get dehydrated by chocolate. Apart from that, you're totally screwing up his reward system. If he gets continuous candy, just for sitting around, how's he going to know when he's done something good?"

"He's like me. He's so much like me. We both need constant reassurance."

"I see," Josh nodded. He didn't argue. So far as he was concerned, dogs were exactly the same as humans. In fact, he thought that all animals were exactly the same as humans, and that was part of the secret of his success. Unlike most veterinarians, he understood that all animals wanted out of life was fun, sleep and food, with an occasional flurry of irresponsible sexual activity.

He peered into Valentino's eyes with an ophthalmoscope. There was no sign of cataracts or any eye disease. Valentino was simply suffering from the effects of old age. "What sort of problems has he had?" asked Josh.

"Bumping into things, mainly. You know, chairs, doors. And he doesn't get the same pleasure out of TV any more."

"Well, him and me both. But there's nothing wrong with his eyes apart from long-sightedness, which happens to most of us when we grow old."

"He's going to need *glasses*?"

"Technically speaking, yes. But, as yet, they don't make prescription glasses for dogs."

"They *should*. I mean, don't you think they should?"

Josh gave Valentino a reassuring pat. "You're right. They should. But there's the little difficulty of getting them to read a sight-chart. All the same, you can still help Valentino to improve his sight. You could try some Bates Method exercises, and see if they sharpen him up."

"How do I do that?"

"Well, Dr Bates was a New York ophthalmologist who invented all kinds of exercises for giving you better sight without glasses. Like splashing your eyes twenty times in warm and cold water every morning; and covering your eyes with your hands for ten minutes twice a day, so that they get a little rest; and blinking as much as possible. You could help Valentino to do all of those things. Oh, yes – and don't let him watch television with the lights off."

He made a quick note of seven Bates Method exercises on a big yellow legal pad. "There . . . if he doesn't improve in a couple of weeks, bring him back to see me."

Valentino's mistress hefted him off the table and on to the floor. Valentino immediately saw himself in an old gilt-framed mirror propped up against the wall and jumped back in fright.

"Try to take him out more, too," Josh suggested. "It helps

your eyes if you keep on varying the distance of the things you're focusing on. Lamp-post one second, street the next. See what I mean? Street, lamp-post. Lamp-post, street. It gets the eyes working." He didn't add that both Valentino and his mistress looked as if they could urgently use some exercise.

He opened the kitchen door and let them out into the garden. Immediately, a tall wiry-haired man in khaki shorts stood up and started to drag a snarling muzzled bull terrier across the verandah, leaving claw marks in the redwood boards.

Josh said, "Wait up a moment. Does this guy bite?"

"Yes *sir*," said his owner, proudly. "Anything from a mailman's leg to a Cadillac's tailpipe. The cable company were digging up the street once, and he bit right through one of their shovels."

"OK, then, bring him on in. But make sure you keep his muzzle on."

"Well, sir, that's going to be kind of difficult. I brought him in for a tongue abscess."

At that moment, a police car drew up in the street outside, beside the white picket fence. A dark-haired deputy climbed out of it, and walked toward the front door, around the corner of the house, where all the bougainvillea hung down. Josh heard the doorbell ring and a door slamming as Nancy went to answer it. He hesitated for a moment, curious to know what was going on, but then the bull terrier began to snap and snarl and chase its own tail and he had to take it into the kitchen.

"He slobbers something awful," said the owner, as Josh heaved it up on to the table. "I wouldn't mind myself but the wife keeps on about the loose covers."

"Have you noticed any change in his motions?" asked Josh.

"Can't say that I have. One leg in front of the other, same as usual."

"Sit," said Josh, but the bull terrier only growled at him. "Sit, damn it," he repeated, and pressed both hands down on its rump.

"He don't sit much," the owner remarked. "Not when people tell him to, anyhow."

Josh lifted one finger in front of the bull terrier's eyes. The bull terrier snarled and shook its head, so that strings of thick saliva flew in all directions. But then Josh slowly brought his finger nearer and nearer to the bull terrier's nose, and then he touched it very lightly on the top of its head.

"You will sit," he said, in a very quiet voice. "You will be calm and well behaved and you will not snarl."

The bull terrier looked up at him wide-eyed. Then it gave a pathetic, throaty whine and obediently sat down.

"How do you do that?" asked the owner, in amazement. "I could break a stick on his back and he wouldn't do that for me."

"Alternative pet management. You use the animal's natural stupidity against him."

Josh was about to unbuckle the bull terrier's muzzle when Nancy came through to the kitchen. Her long shiny brunette hair was tied up in a blue bandanna and she was wearing one of Josh's checkered shirts and a tight pair of white sailcloth jeans.

"Josh – I'm sorry to break in, but there's a cop here to see you."

"Yes, I saw him. Jesus. You run one red light and you never hear the end of it."

"It's not that," said Nancy. "He wanted to know if you had a sister called Julia."

"Julia? What did he want to know that for?" Josh turned to the owner of the bull terrier and said, "Excuse me a minute, will you? Maybe you could finish taking this guy's muzzle off."

The owner stared at him as if he were mad. "Hey, come on now! You're the animal doctor."

Josh went through to the living room. It was long and low-ceilinged, with Navajo rugs thrown over the furniture and naif oil paintings of animals on the whitewashed walls. Pigs, cockerels, cows, dogs and even more pigs. The deputy was standing uncomfortably by the window, in a sharply pressed khaki uniform, his hat in his hand.

"Mr Joshua Winward?" he asked.

"That's right. Is anything wrong?"

"I'm sorry, sir. I'm afraid we've received some real bad news. Do you want to sit down or something?"

"No," said Josh. "Just tell me what's wrong." *Dad*, he thought. *His heart's given out*.

"Well, sir, we had a call from London, England. Your sister was found dead yesterday."

"My sister?" he repeated. "What do you mean, 'found dead'?"

The deputy consulted his notebook. "Her body was discovered in the River Thames near a place called Kew and was picked up by a police river patrol just after five thirty a.m. London time."

Josh reached for the arm of the old colonial rocking chair and awkwardly sat down on the edge of the seat. *Julia*? He couldn't believe what the deputy was telling him. He hadn't heard from Julia in nearly a year now, but he had known why she wanted to escape to England. He had written to her from time to time, with all the latest gossip from Mill Valley, but he hadn't seriously expected her to reply, not till she was ready. He looked across the room and there she still was, in a wooden photo frame, smiling at him as if everything was fine. It was impossible to think that she was dead.

"Do they know—" he began, but then he had to clear his throat. "Do they know how it happened?"

The deputy shook his head. "If they do, they didn't say. All they told me was, they're going to be holding a post-mortem, and they'll e-mail any further information, if it's relevant."

"But what? Did she fall in, was she pushed in, or what?"

"They didn't say, sir. I'm sorry."

"Well, is there anybody I can call? I mean, who did you speak to?"

The deputy copied out a name in his notebook and tore off a page. "Here you are – Detective Sergeant Paul, New Scotland Yard. There's the number, too."

Josh took the note and said, "Thank you."

"If there's anything else we can do, sir, don't hesitate to call the sheriff's department. My name's Rudy Goralnik."

The deputy hovered a little longer, but when Josh said

nothing more, he mumbled an embarrassed goodbye, and left. Nancy closed the door behind him and came back into the living room. Josh looked up at her, stricken. "She's dead," he whispered. "They found her in the river."

Nancy knelt down in front of him and put her arms around him. "Oh, Josh. I'm so sorry. I don't know what to say."

"The British police didn't tell them how it happened. She wouldn't have jumped in, would she? She wouldn't have tried to kill herself? I know she was depressed and everything, but she was very positive, wasn't she? Very self-protective. She wouldn't have taken her own life, ever. She would have worked things through."

"I'll tell your patients what's happened," said Nancy. "You can't do any more animals today."

Josh sat up straight. "I'll tell them myself. They came all this way."

He made his way back to the kitchen, with Nancy close behind him. The man with the bull terrier still hadn't attempted to remove its muzzle, and was waiting for him with an expression on his face that was half-sheepish, half-belligerent.

"I'm sorry, sir," said Josh. "You'll have to make another appointment."

"Hey, listen, just because I happen to own the dog, that doesn't mean I'm skilled in handling him, does it? You think I want my fingers bitten off? I play Hawaiian guitar."

Josh patted him on the shoulder and said, "Never mind. Just make another appointment, will you? The clinic is closed for today."

He went out on to the verandah and told the rest of his clients the same thing. "I'm sorry," he heard himself saying, "but there's been a kind of family tragedy." He paused, and suddenly he couldn't stop the tears from running down his cheeks. "I've just been told that my sister has died."

Everybody came up to him and squeezed his hand or murmured some small condolence. Only the small boy with the box remained behind.

"I'm sorry, kid," Josh repeated. "I can't see any more animals today."

The boy looked up at him in obvious distress. Josh hesitated, and then he went over and said, "Come on then, show me." He took the lid off the box and there was a cricket lying inside, a cricket with only one leg.

"I just wanted to know if you could sew his other leg back on. I've saved it, look." He produced a carefully-folded piece of Kleenex.

Josh bent down and gently prodded the cricket with the tip of his finger. It tried to hop but it succeeded only in falling on to its side. "I'm sorry, kid," Josh told him. "Some things are just beyond saving."

He called the number that the deputy had given him. He was told that Detective Sergeant Paul had left for the evening, but that he could call in the morning, around eight. That meant midnight, Pacific time.

He sorted through his scruffy, higgledy-piggledy phone book, and found the last number that Julia had given him in London, the Golden Rose Employment Agency, in Earl's Court. He called it, but all he got was a nasal answerphone message. There was nothing else he could do until tonight, when the sun came up over London and everybody went back to work.

Nancy came in. "How about some coffee?" she asked him, putting her arm around his shoulders and kissing him.

"I think a Jack Daniel's would go down better. You know what I have to do now, don't you? I have to phone the folks."

"OK. One Jack Daniel's coming up."

She held on to him for a moment, and he was glad of it, because right now he really needed her strength. She had always been strong, which was one of the things that had attracted him so much. Her late father had been a Norwegian-born merchant seaman and her mother was an artist, a full-blooded Modoc, which had given Nancy a startling combination of high cheekbones and dark skin and ice-blue eyes. It had also given her an inner toughness, a very sinewy sense of herself, and even though that often led them to argue, Josh was glad of it. When he lay in bed at night, he knew who was lying next to him.

Nancy was very silent at night, he could never hear her breathing, and he used to wake her up to make sure that she wasn't dead. This had annoyed her, of course, because Josh snored like a riot in a zoo, and she could never get back to sleep again. But Josh had always been noisy and messy and untidy, ever since he was a small boy. He tried his best to be neat. He tried to be organized. But he was always too interested in moving on to the next thing before he had cleared up the thing before.

Josh was tall, like his father Jack. In fact he looked so much like his father that his mother always called him "Jack" – 6ft 2½ins in his long bare feet, and very lean, with chopped brown hair that looked as if Edward Scissorhands had been at it. He had a long, handsome face and very large brown eyes, but he was the only one in his family to have inherited his great-grandfather's large triangular nose. He had also inherited his great-grandfather's extraordinary empathy with animals. The old man had worked with Barnum & Bailey for years before he eventually came to San Francisco and opened up a pet store on Folsom Street, Winward's World of Waggers.

Josh had spent his childhood nursing crushed snails and feeding abandoned fledglings with eyedroppers, and he had always wanted to be a veterinarian. But his approach to animal medicine had been so unorthodox that he and the California State Veterinary College had parted company by mutual agreement. At college he had set up a pulsed electromagnetic field in order to improve the general health and intelligence of cats; and he had taught dogs to meditate.

He swallowed a mouthful of whiskey and then he punched out his parents' number in Santa Barbara. It rang and rang and he could imagine his father saying, "Who the hell is *that*?" and at last climbing testily out of his deckchair and making his way into the house. He could imagine him shuffling down the pale blue-painted hallway and picking up the phone. And right on cue he heard, "Winward residence . . . what do you want *now*?"

"Dad, it's Josh."

"Josh? Well, how about that? I thought you were dead."

"Dad, listen. Something terrible's happened."

Josh called Detective Sergeant Paul dead on midnight. Common sense told him that he would need a few minutes to get to his desk, but he couldn't wait any longer. As it was, it was picked up instantly, and a woman's voice snapped, "Incident room."

"Hallo? I'm calling from the United States. I'm trying to get in touch with Detective Sergeant Paul."

"That's me."

"Oh, I see. I'm real sorry, I expected—"

"I know. You expected a man. Quite understandable. You must be calling about Julia Winward."

"That's right. My name's Josh Winward, I'm her brother."

"Well, I hope you'll accept our condolences, Mr Winward. This is obviously a most distressing time for you."

"It came as a shock, for sure. Do you have any idea how it happened? I mean, Julia went to England to get over a messy romance, but she wasn't the suicidal kind. Not unless something's happened to her that none of her family know about."

"This wasn't a suicide, Mr Winward."

"What does that mean? That somebody else pushed her in?"

"Somebody else *dropped* her in, sir. We haven't had a complete post-mortem, but there's no question at all, she was dead before she went into the river."

"You're sure about that?"

"Absolutely, sir. Yes."

"You mean there was no water in her lungs or anything? I'm sorry – maybe I've been watching too much *Murder, She Wrote*."

"There was no water in her lungs, sir." Pause. "Not as far as we know."

There was something about the way she paused that aroused Josh's suspicion. "You mean you don't definitely know whether there was water in her lungs or not?"

"Not at this stage, sir. I'm afraid there was some degree of tampering with your sister's body."

"Tampering?"

Another pause, and then the word that Josh had been dreading. "Mutilation, I suppose you'd have to call it. I really can't say any more over the phone. But we've initiated a full-scale murder inquiry and I'd like to reassure you that everything possible is being done to find the person or persons responsible for your sister's death."

Josh had to take three deep breaths. He felt as if a huge weight were pressing on his chest.

Detective Sergeant Paul said, "Are you still there, Mr Winward?"

"Yes, I'm still here. I was just a little . . . overwhelmed, that's all."

"I'm sorry, sir. But I can't pretend that it was anything other than a very brutal murder. Whoever did it is an extremely dangerous individual, and your sister's case has absolute top priority. Do you have e-mail?"

"Yes, yes I do."

"In that case, I can send you copies of some of the newspaper reports. But only if you don't think you'll find them too upsetting."

"No, no, please. I wish you would. Right now . . . well, I'm still finding it difficult to get my head around it."

"I do need to ask you some questions, too. Quite a lot of questions."

"Fire away. Anything I can do to help. Anything."

"Well, let me send you the newspaper reports first. I've got one or two things on my plate at the moment. Supposing I call you back in a couple of hours?"

"Sure, please do."

Josh quickly left his number and then let the phone drop. Nancy appeared, bundled up in a white feather comforter. It had been hot during the day, but it was one of those foggy coastal nights when the temperature suddenly drops, and the windows look as if long-drowned mariners have been breathing on them.

"You need some sleep," Nancy told him.

"Not tonight," said Josh. "Not until I know what happened to Julia."

They read the newspaper reports two and three times over. Julia's death had been the lead story in the London *Evening Standard*: RIPPER VICTIM FOUND IN THAMES. Most of the national dailies had carried it as a second lead, and all of them reported that this was the seventh such murder in less than three years.

The Daily Telegraph read: "Police are strenuously trying to deter the media from jumping to the conclusion that a serial killer is at work. Detective Chief Inspector Kenneth Bulstrode pointed out that none of the seven women had been murdered in exactly the same way, and that not all of them had been mutilated as extensively as Julia Winward. Some victims had lost only their eyes or their livers, while Julia Winward had been 'to all intents and purposes, emptied'."

Emptied, thought Josh. Jesus. He couldn't imagine it. He didn't *want* to imagine it.

Julia had been identified only by chance. She had a tiny tattoo on her right shoulder in the shape of a daisy, and a Soho tattooist had recognized it from the pictures that appeared on ITN News. Josh's eyes filled with tears again when he read about the daisy. For some reason, it had always been Julia's favorite flower, and she had told him that it symbolized "something you're not quite capable of reaching, not just yet, but one day you will".

He finished reading the last report and yawned. Nancy was fast asleep on the floor, silently breathing, as if she were dead. He reached out for his half-empty glass of Jack Daniel's and it was then that the phone rang.

"Mr Winward? Detective Sergeant Paul here. Did you receive the newspaper cuttings?"

"Yes, thank you. I read them."

"You don't mind if I ask you some questions over the phone? It shouldn't take more than an hour."

"Listen, I have a much better idea. Why don't you ask me face to face?"

"I beg your pardon?"

"I mean I'm catching the first available flight to London. My kid sister's dead, detective. I'm not leaving her body all alone in a strange country, with nobody to look after her."

There was a pause. Then DS Paul said, "All right. I understand. As soon as you've booked your flight, call me and tell me, and I'll arrange to pick you up at the airport."

Josh put down the phone and shook Nancy awake. "What is it?" she blinked. "Earthquake?"

"Get your things together," he told her. "We're going to London."

Four

Detective Sergeant Paul met them at Heathrow Airport as they came out of immigration, holding up a cardboard sign saying *Winward*. To Josh's surprise, she was a petite Asian woman in a smart black suit and a brown silk blouse, her hair tightly braided on top of her head. Quite pretty, and very delicate, with hand movements like an Oriental temple-dance. "Mr Winward? I'm Indira Paul. I'm so pleased you made the effort to come here. This could be a considerable help, you know."

"Anything we can do," said Josh.

It was a warm, sunny day, unusually warm for March. As they drove along the M4 into West London, Josh saw pink cherry trees blossoming and bushes coming into leaf, and the sun sparkling from the windows of thousands of suburban houses and factories. Up above them, the sky was the clearest of blues, with large white cumulus clouds rolling across it like Nelson's navy.

"You know, I thought it was always raining in London," Josh remarked.

"We get our share," said DS Paul. "But we've been having a dry spell. When your sister was found the river was very low, and her body was caught on a mudbank. Otherwise, you know, she might have been carried a lot further, even back out to sea."

"Who found her?"

"Some anglers, digging in the mud for worms, at a place called Strand-on-the-Green. But we think she was dropped into the river much further downstream."

"*Down*stream?"

"The Thames is tidal, up as far as Teddington Lock. The pathologist estimates that she was in the water for approximately five to six hours, which means that she went into the river just before midnight. At that time, the tide was coming in, and her body would have been carried upstream. We've worked out how far she would have traveled before the tide began to turn, and we think that she was probably dropped into the river somewhere between Southwark Bridge and London Bridge."

"I see," said Josh, although he had no idea of where any of these places were. Nancy, in the back seat, reached forward and touched his shoulder, just to comfort him. The morning sunlight flickered through the car as they drove over a long flyover with Victorian church spires on one side and glittering office blocks on the other. Then they descended into three lanes of solid traffic, and rows of apartment blocks and hotels and shops.

Josh had never visited England before, but he had never imagined that London would feel so foreign. The buildings weren't tall, but they had a grimy Imperial massiveness about them. The traffic was deafening and hair-raisingly fast, and the sidewalks were crowded with hordes of shoppers. The famous red buses didn't drive sedately along, the way they always did in movies: they barged through the traffic at full speed, belching out clouds of diesel smoke, and the black taxicabs were just the same. DS Paul drove around Hyde Park Corner, where six lanes of traffic jostled to go in twelve different directions, and as they narrowly missed a white decorator's van and turned into Grosvenor Place, all Josh could say was, "Jesus."

They arrived at last in DS Paul's office in the bland 1960s office block of New Scotland Yard. It was a large untidy room which she shared with four other officers, with a view of the building next door. Phones kept ringing and people kept hurrying in and out, and in the far corner a detective was frowning at a computer as if he couldn't understand what it was.

"How about a cup of coffee?" DS Paul suggested.

"You have decaf?" asked Nancy.

"Sorry. We've got black or white, with sugar or without. Or tea, if you'd rather. Or oxtail soup."

Josh and Nancy settled for two Cokes. They sat down next to the air-conditioning vent, which was uncomfortably hot, while the sun shone through the dusty windows into their eyes. DS Paul sat down at her desk and opened a file containing interview sheets and glossy color photographs.

"You realize that, now you're here, I'm going to have to ask you to make a formal identification of your sister's body."

"Yes, well, I guessed you would."

"I have some photographs here. I wonder if you could look at them and confirm that it's her."

Josh swallowed and Nancy reached out and held his arm. "OK," he said, his mouth suddenly dry.

DS Paul handed over one color print, and then another. In the first, which was taken from the neck up, Julia lay against a pale green background, her eyes open, her hair wet and bedraggled, her cheeks puffy and pale. It was true what they said about your soul leaving you, when you died. It looked like Julia, but Julia simply wasn't there.

The second print showed her right shoulder, and the tiny daisy tattoo.

"That's her," said Josh. "That's Julia. But I never saw the tattoo before."

"Well, as I said, it was the tattoo that identified her. The tattoo artist called us and said he remembered an American girl who had asked him to do it specially. Apparently she was very chatty. She told him that she had only just arrived in England and that she was looking for a new life. She was trying to find a job as a nanny or something similar, but she didn't have a work permit. So the tattoist put her on to a girlfriend of his who knew an employment agency that didn't ask too many questions about where a girl came from, or what her qualifications were."

"Was that the Golden Rose Employment Agency? That was the last contact number Julia gave me."

"That's right. They found her a position with a Saudi family in Holland Park, looking after two small children. But it seems as if she didn't like the job very much. The mother treated her like a slave, and the father kept making advances. So after three weeks she left."

"What did she do then?" asked Josh.

DS Paul took back the pictures. "I was hoping that you could tell *me* that. Didn't she contact you at all?"

"Not once. Not a word. I tried calling the agency a couple of times, but they just said that they hadn't heard from her, either. I just assumed that she would get back in touch with us when she felt ready. Didn't she go back to the agency for another job?"

"No. She told them over the phone that she was quitting the Saudi job and that was the last time they ever heard from her. She didn't even collect her wages, and they didn't know where to send them."

"They had no address for her?"

DS Paul shook her head. "She told them she was in temporary accommodation at the Paragon Hotel in Earl's Court. It's a very cheap place, fifteen pounds a night, popular with backpackers. But wherever she was, she wasn't there. The management always keep their guests' passports – you know, just in case they try to do a runner – and no single American females have stayed there for over a year."

"And nobody else knows where she might have been?"

DS Paul shook her head. "Nobody. But we've sent her picture out to the media, and we're trying to arrange an appeal for information on *Crimewatch* – that's a BBC-TV program where we ask viewers to help solving crimes. We usually get a very good response to that."

"How can somebody just disappear like that? I mean, totally?"

"People do it every day, Mr Winward. There are eight million people in London and it isn't difficult to get swallowed up, especially if you want to be."

They ate lunch at a pub called The Frog & Waistcoat, around the back of Victoria Station. It was smoky and noisy and crowded with a mixture of office workers and miserable-looking travelers with too many bulging bags.

"I feel like I've walked right into a Dickens novel," said Josh. Everybody around him was talking very loudly but he couldn't understand a word they were saying. He had always assumed that the English spoke English the way they did in movies, clipped and precise, but instead they talked in a mangled torrent, and he couldn't tell when one word ended and another began. He had ordered shepherd's pie, and then the barman had asked him again if he wanted a pie.

"Yes, the pie."

"Pie of what?"

"Sorry, I don't understand."

"Pie of ordinary, pie of best, pie of Guinness, what?"

He was almost reduced to sign language, but even sign language didn't help when the girl behind the food counter asked if Nancy wanted a jacket. He thought that they might have inadvertently offended the pub's dress code.

"Maybe this was a mistake," said Josh, as he poked at his shepherd's pie.

"You think *that's* a mistake, you ought to taste this lasagne."

"No, I mean coming here. The police don't seem to know squat."

"Oh, come on, Josh. You have to give them time. It was a miracle they even found out who she was."

"I guess you're right. But where the hell has Julia *been* for the last ten months? You'd have thought that she'd have left some kind of forwarding address."

"Think about it: if she told her employment agency that she was staying at the Paragon Hotel in the Earl's Court district then she must at least have *known* it, even if she didn't actually check in there. So maybe we should look around Earl's Court, and see if we can find anybody who remembers her."

"You don't think the police are going to do that?"

"I'm sure they will. But where's the harm in us doing it, too?"

Josh took a cautious mouthful of pie. "This is weird," he

said, after a while. "I hate it, but I want some more." He paused, and then he said, "What do you think a 'jacket' is?"

Nancy said, "We could print up some enlargements of a picture of Julia, and stick them on lamp-posts and stuff. You know, 'Have You Seen This Girl?'"

Josh nodded. "That's a good idea." He pushed aside his plate and opened up his newly bought A–Z Guide to London. "I guess we're here, right? Earl's Court is here, only three subway stops away. If we can find ourselves a hotel around there . . ."

They took the tube to Earl's Court, where the sidewalk was crowded with young people waiting for nothing in particular and old people shuffling along with shopping baskets on wheels. There was a pungent smell of hamburgers-and-onions in the air.

They found the Paragon Hotel two streets down, in Barkston Gardens – a red-brick Edwardian building with battered cream paintwork and drooping net curtains as gray as cobwebs. Inside it was gloomy and overheated and the crimson patterned carpet was worn down to the string. Behind the reception desk sat an overweight woman with dyed-blonde hair and a black suit that was far too tight for her.

"If you're looking for a room, dear, sorry – we're full to busting."

"No, no, we don't need a room. We were wondering if you might remember seeing this girl." Josh handed over a picture of Julia standing outside a bookstore. "We're talking about a year ago, last spring sometime."

The woman found a pair of thumbprinted reading glasses and peered at the photograph closely. "No," she said, after a while. "Can't say I do. But, you know, they come and they go, thousands of them, these young people, and they all look the same to me. All looking for something, or running away from something."

"You're absolutely sure you don't remember her?"

"I honestly wish I did. But, no. I'm sorry. Missing, is she?"

"You could say that. She's dead."

"Oh, I'm really sorry. She's not that girl the police were here asking about? The American one?"

"That's right, Julia Winward. She's my sister. She *was* my sister."

"It's a bloody tragedy," said the woman, shaking her head. "So young, too. They come and they go, you know, thousands of them, and sometimes I feel like taking hold of them and shaking them and saying, 'Where are you going? What on earth do you think you're going to find?' But still they come, year after year. So hopeful, you know. Backpacking round God knows where, looking for God knows what."

"We're going to have some copies of this picture printed," said Nancy. "Is it OK if we pin one up in here?"

"Oh, of course it is. You're very welcome. But I'll tell you what you ought to do. Make a big picture like a poster and stand outside the tube station. Just stand there, all day. If she's ever been around here, sooner or later somebody will recognize her."

"Well, thanks, you're really kind," said Josh.

"Don't mention it. I lost somebody once. My only son Terence. He went off to India, that was back in the Beatles days. Can't think what he was looking for. We all end up with two kids and a mortgage and a clapped-out Datsun, don't we? We don't need no maharishi to tell us that."

She found a small lacy handkerchief in her pocket and dabbed her nose. "He died, my Terence. Hepatitis. Such a waste. All those shirts I ironed for him, for school. All those packed lunches. And they cremated him, and scattered his ashes in the bloody Ganges."

They found a hotel overlooking West Brompton Cemetery, a real Victorian cemetery with tilting headstones and weeping angels. In complete contrast, the hotel was a seven-story concrete block with air-conditioning and new blue carpets and crowds of bewildered Japanese around the reception area. It could have been any hotel anywhere at all, and that was what Josh wanted. As they went up in the elevator he saw himself reflected in the stainless steel doors and he thought that he looked like a ghost. His hair was tousled and his eyes were reddened and his nose looked twice as big as normal. His first day in London had left him grimy and depressed and tired, and he was desperate for a cold beer and a shower and some mindless TV.

He showered until his skin was bright pink, and then he lay on the bed in his complimentary Sheridan Hotels bathrobe watching *The Simpsons* and drinking Harp lager out of the can. It was four o'clock now, and the sun was much lower. Nancy came out of the bathroom toweling her hair. "I don't know how you can come all the way to England and watch *The Simpsons*. Apart from that, you hate *The Simpsons*."

"I know I do. But at least I can understand what they're saying. Did you bring any dental floss?"

"I forgot. We'll have to buy some."

"They've probably never heard of dental floss in England. Or they call it something totally different, like 'trousers', and we'll never find out what it is."

"What are you panicking about? You never used to floss at all until you met me."

"Of course I flossed before I met you. You're trying to make me sound like some kind of animal."

"You *are* a kind of animal. You're more like an animal than any man I ever met. Gentle, affectionate, stupid and manic-depressive."

"I love you, too."

Nancy went to the window and drew back the nets, and Josh climbed off the bed and joined her. Six stories below they could see rows of small backyards, some with sheds, some with pink-blossoming trees, some with rusty automobile parts, some with fish ponds. In the distance, in the late-afternoon haze, they could see thousands of chimney pots, and turrets, and spires, and more trees. Josh had never seen a city with so many trees in it.

He picked up his A–Z. "That's south-east we're looking at, toward Fulham."

"They call it 'Fullum'. I heard a woman in reception."

"All right, Fullum. And beyond Fullum is Walham Green, except they probably call it 'Wallum'. And beyond Wallum Green is . . . the River Thames." He closed the book. "I don't know whether I want to see the Thames. I keep thinking about Julia floating along it. Upstream. Empty."

They were still staring out of the window when the news came on the television: "*In the Middle East . . . six Israelis were killed and two seriously injured . . . Police today released a new picture of the murdered woman found floating in the Thames two days ago . . . Miss Julia Winward, twenty-three, from San Francisco, California, could have been the seventh victim of a serial killer who mutilates his victims and drops them in the river at or near Southwark Bridge . . . If you knew Julia Winward or if you saw her at any time in the past twelve months, please contact New Scotland Yard on this special number . . .*"

"You see," said Nancy, curling a finger around Josh's hair. "They're doing everything they can."

"Sure," he said. He couldn't take his eyes away from the picture of Julia on the television screen, smiling at him. He could remember the morning that he had taken that picture. He could remember it as clearly as if it had been today.

That afternoon, shortly before five o'clock, a police car came to collect them and take them to the mortuary at St Thomas's Hospital. The car was so tiny that Josh had to try three different ways of folding himself up before he managed to climb into the front passenger seat. They drove along the Embankment, and for the first time Josh saw the River Thames, shining brilliant gold in the afternoon sun.

Josh peered at it over his knees. "It's a whole lot wider than I imagined it," he told the young constable who was driving them. "I thought it was going to be real narrow. You know, and *dirty*."

"Oh, no, sir, it's much cleaner than it used to be. They've caught salmon, right up as far as Chelsea Harbour. Mind you, I wouldn't swim in it. Too many dodgy currents."

Josh thought of the "dodgy currents" that must have swirled Julia's body upstream, like Ophelia.

Then they were driving around Parliament Square, and he saw Westminster Abbey for the first time, and the Houses of Parliament and Big Ben. He always felt a sense of history in San Francisco, with the wooden houses and the cable cars, but London's history was different: older, darker, much more complicated, much more multi-layered. In a way that he had never expected, he found it threatening – as if the British knew something that he didn't know, and would never tell him what it was.

They drove over Westminster Bridge. "Earth has not anything to show more fair," quoted the young constable.

"I'm sorry?"

"William Wordsworth, that's what he wrote about standing on Westminster Bridge."

"William Wordsworth actually wrote that here?"

"Well, no, sir. I expect he went home and did it."

Josh turned and looked at the constable and said, "Do you mind if I ask your name?"

"Not at all, sir. Police Constable Smart."

"Yes," said Josh. "I might have guessed."

The morgue attendant switched on the closed-circuit TV camera and there she suddenly was. Her face was fluorescent gray, like all drowned people. Her eyes were open and staring straight at him, out of the screen.

"Yes," he said. "That's her."

DS Paul said, "Thank you, Mr Winward," and led him out of the room.

"Is that it?" he asked her.

"Just for the moment, yes. But depending on what response we get from the public in the next thirty-six hours, we may ask you to go on television and make an appeal for witnesses. You wouldn't mind doing that, would you?"

He shook his head. He was beginning to feel badly jet-lagged and the floor kept rising and falling. Nancy said, "Let's go back to the hotel, OK? I think you've had enough for one day."

They walked along a long, antiseptic-smelling corridor. An elderly woman approached them, pushed in a wheelchair by a hospital porter in a turban. She was so old that she was almost transparent: white hair, white skin, even her eyes were colorless. As she was wheeled past them, she whispered, "*Jack.*"

Five

Josh froze, and then turned slowly around to stare at the old woman as she was pushed away.

"Josh?" said Nancy. "What's the matter?"

"That old woman . . . she just said my name. Well, she said 'Jack', anyhow."

"Oh, come on, you're imagining it. How could she know your name?"

"I swear it, Nance. She said, 'Jack'."

DS Paul impatiently looked at her watch. "I'm sorry," she said, "but I'm late for a meeting. Perhaps I can call you tomorrow morning."

"Oh, sure, yes," said Josh, still staring after the old woman. She was pushed through a pair of double swing doors, and then she was gone. Josh hesitated for a moment and then began to hurry after her.

"*Josh*!" Nancy protested, jogging after him with her Indian bead bag slap-slap-slapping on her thigh.

Josh shoved his way through the double doors and there was the woman and her Sikh attendant, silhouetted against the window at the end of the corridor. He called out, "Pardon me!" and hurried after them. He reached the old woman just as the Sikh was about to open a door marked *X-ray Department: Authorized Personnel Only*.

"I'm sorry," said Josh, "but I believe this lady called out my name."

The Sikh porter stared at him impassively. "She is having to go for an X-ray, sir. Excuse me."

Josh hunkered down beside the wheelchair and took hold of the old lady's hand. The skin was thin and crinkly, like tissue paper. She looked down at him and gave him something that could have passed for a smile. She was so old that it was impossible to tell if she had ever been really beautiful, but Josh could see that she had never been ugly.

"You said my name. Back there, in the corridor, you said 'Jack'."

"Jack be nimble, Jack be quick," she whispered. She spoke so softly that he could barely hear her.

"How did you know what my name was? That's what my mother calls me, Jack."

"I know what you're looking for, Jack. But you won't find it, you know. Not unless you look *here*." She tapped her forehead with her long chalky fingernail.

"I don't understand what you mean."

"You won't understand, either. Not unless you're nimble. Not unless you're quick."

"I'm sorry, sir," the porter interrupted. "This lady has to get to X-ray."

Josh slowly stood up. Maybe the old woman hadn't really whispered his name at all. Maybe she was senile, and had simply been babbling a nursery rhyme from the days that she could still remember clearly.

"Take care," he told her, and turned to go. But suddenly she reached out and snatched at his sleeve.

"Come on, Polly, leave the gentleman alone," the porter smiled. "Our Polly, she's one for the men, aren't you, Polly?"

But the old woman continued to clutch at Josh's sleeve and she wouldn't let go. She fixed him with her boiled-cod eyes and hissed at him as loudly as she could manage. "*Six doors they stand in London Town. Six doors they stand in London, too. Yet who's to know which way they face? And who's to know which face is true?*"

"That's enough, Polly," said the porter, and before Josh had a chance to ask her what she was talking about, she was pushed into the X-ray department and out of sight.

"What the hell was all that about?" asked Nancy.

Josh shook his head. "I don't have any idea. It sounded like a Mother Goose rhyme."

The Sikh porter came out again, pushing an empty wheelchair. "I'm sorry if Polly was any trouble to you. She is a very determined lady, even for one hundred and one."

"One hundred and one? That's how old she is?"

"She celebrated her birthday last week. She is very wonderful for her age, you know. But she does like to be grabbing people."

"Do you have any idea what she was talking about? The six doors standing in London Town?"

The porter gave Josh a dazzling smile, full of gold teeth. "I'm sorry. I never listen to anything they say. I nod my head and I say 'yes' and 'no' and 'really' and 'how terrible'. But you can't listen to them all day. You would be going doolally in your head, too."

"It could be a Mother Goose rhyme, couldn't it . . . *Six doors they stand in London Town*?"

The porter didn't stop smiling. "I was brought up in Punjab. I didn't speak English until I was seventeen."

"OK, thanks," said Josh, and together he and Nancy walked back to the front of the hospital, where PC Smart was waiting for them.

"All right, then?" he asked. "Back to Earl's Court, is it?"

"Yes, please." It was nearly eleven o'clock already and Josh wanted to collect the photographs of Julia from the Kall-Kwik print shop.

They struggled their way through the mid-morning traffic. "Is it always as busy as this?" asked Nancy.

"It's not too bad today. At least they're not having a demonstration or a state opening of Parliament. Then it's murder." He sat for a while, drumming his fingers on his steering wheel. Then he said, "It's not getting any worse, though. They just brought out a report that London's traffic moves at exactly the same average speed today that it did in 1899."

"You know a whole lot about London."

"I know a lot about a lot of things. It's my hobby, general knowledge. Here's one for you – do more people die every year from air crashes, or accidents with donkeys?"

"I really couldn't guess."

"Accidents with donkeys. Amazing, isn't it? So when you're going to fly back to the States, make sure you pick an airplane and not a donkey. You'll thank me for it, I promise you."

Josh stared at Nancy in disbelief. He was beginning to feel that he was in the middle of a very long Monty Python sketch. Nancy must have felt the same way, too, because she reached over and squeezed his hand.

"Did you ever hear of a Mother Goose rhyme about six doors standing in London?" Josh asked PC Smart.

"Yes, sir. My nan used to sing it to me. *Six doors they stand in London Town. Six doors they stand in London, too.*"

"Any idea what it means?"

"Haven't the foggiest. Sorry."

"It doesn't seem to make any sense, does it? Six doors standing in London, but six doors standing in London, too?"

"No, sir. Not unless there are twelve doors altogether."

Nancy said, "You don't honestly think it's relevant to Julia, do you? That poor old woman was demented."

"She knew my name was Jack, and who knows that except for you and my mother? And she knew that I was looking for something. Maybe that doesn't mean anything at all. But then maybe it does. Maybe she was trying to give me some kind of a clue."

"Come on, Josh. You don't believe in all that psychic stuff."

"No, I don't. But I *do* believe that some people have heightened perception, the same as dogs."

"But knowing what somebody's thinking . . . that's a whole different ball game than being able to hear them or *smell* them."

"Why should it be? Everybody's brain gives off electric pulses, right? I mean, that's how we think. The pulses are pretty weak, not like radio waves. But if somebody happened to be sensitive enough to pick them up, they could hear what you were thinking, as clearly as smelling you from five miles away."

"That's a monster *if*."

"I know it is. But old Polly knew what my name was and she knew that I was looking for something. So what explanation do you have for that?"

"Josh," said Nancy, "what happened to Julia was terrible. But you mustn't let it push you off the edge."

"No, well, no, you're right. You're absolutely right. But I'd still like to know what that rhyme means. And *Jack be nimble, Jack be quick*. What was that all about? Why do I have to be nimble? Why do I have to be quick?"

"Because we've arrived, sir," put in PC Smart, pulling up in front of their hotel. It was beginning to rain, and a few large spots were measling the sidewalks.

"Have a good evening, sir. Detective Sergeant Paul will be in touch with you tomorrow. Oh, and just a word of advice. I know you've probably seen all these TV programs where an American comes over to London and sorts out a crime that the poor old British woodentops can't make head nor tail of. But the team we've got on your sister's case, they're absolutely shit-hot. So there's no need to try any amateur detective-work of your own. Just relax while you're here, and enjoy the sights, if you get my drift."

"Were you specially instructed to tell me that?

PC Smart nodded. His cheeks were bright pink and he only shaved in two small patches on either side of his chin.

"No amateur detective-work?" Josh retorted. "This is the city of Sherlock Holmes!"

"Sherlock Holmes was a story, sir. This is real. And the point is, if you did find something, you might compromise valuable evidence without even realizing what you were doing."

"All right," said Josh, as he climbed awkwardly out of the car. "Drift got."

All the same, he and Nancy went to collect 200 posters of Julia from the Kall-Kwik copy shop, as well as two boxes of thumbtacks, and they spent over two hours fastening them to fence posts and gates and the scabby gray-green trunks of plane trees. They stopped for half an hour at Pizza Express, and for once the coffee was tolerable and the pizza was marginally tastier than they would have been served in the States.

Nancy said, "I want to make sure that you stay balanced, Josh. I know you have to grieve, but don't let your grieving drive you crazy."

Josh was coping with a mouthful of hot pepperoni. "I wohmp."

"Like, if we find out anything, we tell the police, OK? We don't try to follow it up on our own?"

Josh swallowed, and wiped his mouth. "We haven't found out anything yet, and I don't think we're likely to."

"But if we do."

"Even if we do, how are we going to be able to tell if it's serious or not? They don't speak English here, they speak Sarcastic. 'Wordsworth went home and wrote it' – haw, haw, haw. No wonder they lost the Colonies."

By the time they had finished their pizza it had stopped raining and a sick, watery sunlight was shining down the Earl's Court Road. They fastened their "Have You Seen This Girl?" posters of Julia on to the front of their windbreakers with safety pins and stood against the railings right outside the station entrance. Rush hour was approaching, and every time a train arrived another surge of people came hurrying out, all elbows and umbrellas and grim, tired, determined faces. At the same time there was a sluggish cross-tide of people walking up and down the sidewalk in front of the station, and people stopping to buy copies of the *Evening Standard* from the newsstand, and people just milling around as if they had nothing to do and no place to go.

Josh and Nancy stood there for three and a half hours, until the rush hour subsided and the streetlights came on. They had almost given up when a black mongrel with a pointed nose came trotting out of the station entrance. It wore bells around its collar and a little sheepskin coat. It seemed to be on its own, and Josh immediately stuck two fingers in his mouth and gave it a high, piercing whistle. It stopped and stared at him with bulging amber eyes, one ear floppy and the other pricked up.

"Here," called Josh. He pointed his finger at the dog, and then drew it downward to point to a place by his side. The dog looked around with a querying expression on its face, as if it were asking the crowds of people in the station entrance what the hell this was all about, all this whistling and pointing. But Josh repeated his gesture and the dog obediently walked up to him.

"Sit right there," Josh ordered, and it sat. "I don't know what you're doing, running around on your own without a leash, but that's pretty heavy traffic out there. You try crossing that street in that little coat of yours, you could end up looking like a sheepskin tortilla."

Nancy hunkered down beside the dog and stroked him. "Hi, little fellow! He's cute, isn't he? What breed do you think he is?"

"You mean, what breed do I think he *isn't*?"

Nancy took a bag of dried apricot slices out of her pocket and held one up in front of the dog's nose. "You want some organic fruit? Hmmh? Do you know how to say please?"

Josh pointed at the dog's right leg and gave the animal a curt, beckoning gesture. "Lift your paw. That's right. Lift it right up. Now bark. Come on, woof."

The dog barked, but at that moment a young black woman in a black beret pushed her way out of the station entrance and said, "Hey! What are you doing? That's my dog!"

She came up to them indignantly and tried to open the dog's mouth. "What did you feed him? You shouldn't feed other people's dogs!"

"Come on," said Nancy, confused and embarrassed. "It was only a piece of dried apricot."

The woman stood up straight and looked at Josh and Nancy with a frown of almost ludicrous severity. She was not tall, only 5ft 4ins or thereabouts, but she had extraordinary presence. Josh could sense a kind of *drama* about her, an invisible cyclone of self-possession, as if she were the ringmistress and the world around her was her private circus. Her beret was studded with enamel pins and glittery glass brooches and her hair was plaited with colored beads. She wore a black velvet-collared cape and a very short black dress, with thick black leggings and black boots.

"Dried *apricot*?" she said, wrinkling up her nose.

"Nancy's into . . . organic food," Josh explained.

The woman looked down at her dog, which had finished the fruit and was licking its lips for more. Then she said, "OK. But I have to be careful, you know what I mean? People give him all kinds of rubbish, you know, like bits of old chicken tikka sandwich."

"Sorry," said Josh. He was already learning that "sorry" was a very useful word in England. If somebody bumped into you in the street, you *both* said "sorry", for some inexplicable reason.

"OK, no harm done." She reached down to clip a leash on the dog's collar, and as she did so she glanced at the posters of Julia pinned on to their windbreakers. "You're looking for *her*?"

"That's right," said Josh. "I'm her brother, and this is my girlfriend. We're trying to trace anybody who might have known her."

"I knew her."

Josh stared at her. "*You* knew her?"

"Yeah. Daisy, we always used to call her, because of her tattoo. I couldn't believe it when I heard that she'd been murdered."

"Why didn't you call the police?"

"What was the point? I hadn't seen her for ages. Besides, you know." She gave an eloquent shrug which showed that she didn't like the idea of having anything to do with authority.

Josh said, "For Christ's sake, any little piece of information might help."

"Yeah, well." The woman looked impatient to cross the road.

"Listen, would you mind if we asked you some questions about her? She was missing for nearly a year, and nobody seems to have any idea where she was."

"Well . . . all right, then. But we can't do it out on the street, can we? Come back to my place. It's only just around the corner."

Six

It was too noisy to talk as they walked along Earl's Court Road, but once they had turned into Trebovir Road, the woman said, "I just couldn't believe that anybody would want to do anything like that to Daisy. She was a treasure, you know. A real treasure."

"Did you know her very well?" asked Josh.

"She stayed with me for a couple of weeks, after she walked out on those horrible Arabs. She was supposed to stay in some hotel, but I wouldn't let her. She was too – what d'you call it? – vulnerable, you know what I mean? I didn't want her staying in some crappy hotel room all on her own and cutting her wrists in the bath."

"You think she was suicidal?" asked Nancy.

The woman opened a peculiar black bag that looked like a shrunken head, and took out a set of keys. "She might have been, left on her own. But she wasn't left on her own."

The dog had already trotted ahead of them until it reached the steps of a gloomy red-brick mansion block. They climbed the brown and white tiled steps and the woman opened the front door. Inside it was impenetrably dark until she pressed the timeswitch. The hallway was cold and narrow with an old-fashioned bicycle in it.

"I'm right at the top," she said. "Up in the tower, like the Wicked Witch of the West." She led them up a steep flight of stairs. Halfway up, the timeswitch clicked and they were plunged into darkness again. "Don't move," warned the woman. She found the switch on the next landing and they continued their ascent. Behind every door they passed they could hear music, or the television, or people talking.

The woman opened the door to her flat. It was a wide, open-plan space, right up in the roof, with sloping ceilings, illuminated by an odd collection of spotlights and lamps made out of bottles and seashells and colored glass vases. The walls were painted gray and hung with literally hundreds of charms and mascots and mystical pictures of saints and demons. To the left, under the window, lay a crumpled black futon, with a mobile of sequinned fishes circling over it. To the right, there was a table and chairs in the Mexican rustic style, painted red and gold. Ahead, under another window, was a small kitchen area, with shelves that were crowded with every conceivable kind of spice and herb and seasoning, from cassareep to dry masala. There was a lingering aroma of sandalwood joss sticks and Caribbean cooking.

The dog immediately went to his bowl and started to make a furious lapping noise. The woman dropped her bag on the table and said, "How about a cup of tea? I always have a cup of tea as soon as I get home."

"Sure, that'd be great. My name's Josh, by the way. Josh Winward. This is Nancy."

The woman held out her hand, her wrist jangling with bangles. "Ella Tibibnia, and my dog's called Abraxas. That's a very magical name, Abraxas. It's a pity he's such a plonker. You never think of dogs being plonkers, do you? But he is."

Josh didn't have the faintest idea what a "plonker" was, but he pulled a kind of Harrison Ford grimace to show that he probably agreed. Ella filled a big blue enamel kettle with water and put it on the gas to boil. "You like hawthom flower tea? It's very good for insomnia."

"Sure, whatever you're brewing up." Josh looked around the room. Nancy was inspecting an opalescent glass globe in a decorative bronze base, and a collection of sinister little figurines, like chess pieces, all with their heads covered with hoods.

"When was the last time you saw Julia?" Josh asked Ella.

"I can tell you the exact date." She went across to a bookshelf crowded with an odd assortment of paperbacks and old leather-bound volumes, and brought down a dog-eared exercise book marked DiArY in multicolored pens. She thumbed through it for a while, and then she said, "Here it is. May tenth last year. It was a Sunday. We took Abraxas for a walk in the morning, in Holland Park. Then we had lunch with Wally and Kim in Philbeach Gardens, which is just across the road from here. Daisy was in a really good mood, because she'd found herself a new job. In fact she was almost in too much of a good mood. She kept talking all the time and flapping her hands around. I remember one of my friends asking if she was on something."

"Maybe she was just excited," Nancy suggested.

"No, no, it was more than just excitement. I mean, what are we talking about here, it was only a secretarial job for some electrical company out on the Great West Road. But she was bubbling, you know? And saying that she couldn't wait to start. You'd have thought that she was going off somewhere really exotic."

Josh said, "I don't know the Great West Road. Is that someplace you might get excited about?"

"You're joking, I hope. It's just one boring factory after another. Hotpoint washing machines. Smith's Crisps."

"She didn't leave you her new address?"

"She kept saying that she was going to, but we all got a bit pissed that afternoon and I forgot to ask her for it. *But* . . ." Ella returned to the bookcase and took out a folded letter that was tucked between two books. "I found this under her futon after she'd gone."

Josh angled the letter toward the nearest lamp. It had a black and white illustration of a 1930s factory on the top, with pennants flying from the roof, and the name *Wheatstone Electrics C^o^ Ltd* in elegant, dated lettering. The address was Great West Road, Brentford, Middlesex, and the telephone number EALing 6181.

The letter was addressed to Julia here, at 37 Trebovir Road. It was dated May 6, 2000, and it was signed by somebody called F.G. Mordant, Sales Director. It said: "We are pleased to be able to offer you a secretarial position, commencing on May 11, at a salary of £7.13s.6d a week. Please be at Star Yard as before at 8:15 a.m."

"This was written on a manual typewriter," said Josh. "You don't often see that these days."

"You don't often see somebody being offered £7.13s.6d a week, either," put in Ella. "That's old money, before Britain went decimal, and that was over twenty-five years ago. Apart from the fact that a secretary gets seven pounds an hour these days, not seven pounds a week."

"Did you try calling this number?"

"No point. They haven't had an EALing exchange since 1966. It's all numbers these days. I tried directory enquiries, too, but they didn't have any record of a company called Wheatstone Electrics."

"What about Star Yard?"

"I looked that up in the A–Z. It's just a little pedestrian cut-through off Carey Street, near the Law Courts. Right in the city – nowhere near the Great West Road."

Josh turned the letter over. There was another address, written in blue ballpoint pen, on the other side. He recognized Julia's writing immediately. *53b Kaiser Gardens, Lavender Hill.* And the name *Mrs Marguerite Marmion.*

Ella poured boiling water into a large brown teapot and swirled it around. "Before you ask, there *is* no Kaiser Gardens in Lavender Hill, nor anywhere else in London, and there's no Mrs Marguerite Marmion in the London telephone directory."

"You're sure about that?"

"Look them up for yourself. It's possible that Mrs Marguerite Marmion hasn't got a phone, or else she's ex-directory. But if the street doesn't exist . . ."

Nancy took the letter and examined it minutely. "This is really strange, isn't it? I mean, it's quite fashionable for companies to use a traditional old picture on their letterhead, but they'd put their up-to-date telephone number and fax and e-mail numbers on it, wouldn't they?"

Ella shrugged. "What difference does it make, if there's no such company?"

"Well, none. But if Julia didn't go to the Wheatstone Electrics Company, where *did* she go?"

"My friend Wally thinks she was playing a practical joke. She must have found some old paper and made a copy of it."

"You think so?" said Josh. "You feel this letterhead. It's all embossed, and embossing doesn't come cheap. Why would Julia go to the expense of producing a single sheet of embossed paper, just for a practical joke? And if it *was* a practical joke, what was the point of it?"

"Maybe she found an original sheet of paper from the 1930s," Ella suggested.

Nancy rubbed it between her fingers and sniffed it. "I don't know. It looks new. It feels new. It even *smells* new."

They sipped tea for a while, in silence. Josh thought that it tasted like boiled hedges, but it was strangely soothing, and cleared his sinuses. He passed the letter back to Ella and said, "Did you try going out to the Great West Road, to see if this factory's actually there?"

"No, we didn't. We talked about it, but you know. It looked like Julia wanted to disappear and that she didn't want anybody to find her. We decided that leaving us a letter like this was her way of saying that she was going to start a new life, and that she didn't want any of us to be a part of it.

"But somebody murdered her. We have to find out where she went."

"I don't know. I wish I could help."

Abraxas came up to Josh and nuzzled against his knee. "That dog *likes* you," Ella smiled. "That's *very* unusual. I've always taught him to bite first and ask questions afterwards."

Nancy smiled. "Josh has a certain way with animals, don't you Josh? I think he understands them much better than he understands people. He has a degree in animal behavior."

"Seven-tenths of a degree in animal behavior," Josh corrected her. "I was asked to reconsider my future after I prescribed Prozac for a chronically depressive ragdoll. I happen to believe that there isn't very much difference between animals and people. They're both stupid. But it's amazing what they can do if you encourage them."

"Hey, I don't think dogs are stupid," said Ella. "I think they've got incredible abilities."

"They do, you're absolutely right. But they're far too lazy to use them. Evolution, who needs it, when you've got a nice warm basket and all the food you can eat."

"I don't know. You should see Abraxas whenever I hold a séance. He goes crazy, chasing around the room and barking. It's the spirits, you know. I'm sure that Abraxas can actually *see* them."

"You're a *medium*?" asked Nancy.

"Sort of. I do a bit of fortune-telling and a bit of your spiritual conversation. I learned it from my aunt. She came from Martinique and she was heavily into voodoo and black magic and all that stuff. She taught me how to tell fortunes and how to raise up spirits so that they can talk to their loved ones that they left behind. Well, I make a little pin money doing it. It helps to pay the rent."

Josh lifted both hands. "Whoa, don't look at me. I'm the skeptic around here. I believe that dogs can hear things and smell things that are way beyond human capabilities. But spirits? I don't think so."

"What about that old woman at the hospital?" Nancy challenged him.

"That wasn't anything supernatural. She could sense what I was thinking about, that's all. She tuned in to my anxiety."

Nancy explained to Ella what had happened at St Thomas's.

"Ah!" said Ella. "She didn't just read your mind, though. She tried to *tell* you something."

"She told me a Mother Goose rhyme, that's all I know."

"But that's the way these things work. The spirits always speak in a kind of code, right. They tell you things in messages that you can't immediately understand. Snatches you pick up from the radio. Or a song that you only half-hear. How many times have you come across an unusual word, right, or maybe a reference to something strange, and after that you hear it again and again? That's the spirit world, talking to you, guiding you, *warning* you, when it's necessary, and it's so much closer than you think. The spirit world is totally mixed up with ours. You can't say where one world ends and the other begins. Sometimes you feel as if somebody's touched you. That's not a human hand, that's a spirit."

Josh said, "I'm sorry, I just don't believe in it. I believe in the wind, and I believe in radio waves. They're invisible, too, but they're scientifically measurable."

"But that old woman gave you a message. *Six doors they stand in London Town. Six doors they stand in London, too*. She was trying to tell you something, put you on the right track."

"Well, yes. Maybe she was – although I still can't be persuaded that there was anything supernatural about it. I'm going to check it out. I'm going to find out what that rhyme actually means. Just like I'm going to go to the Great West Road and find the Wheatstone Electrics Company. And I'm going to find Kaiser Gardens, too, and the mysterious Mrs Marguerite Marmion. I don't believe that any of this has anything to do with spirits. Julia's disappearance was pretty damned strange, I admit. But there's a totally rational and scientific explanation for it."

"Which is what, do you think?"

"I don't know. I'm not a scientist. But one day, somebody's going to discover what it is, one day, and then all you mediums are going to have to hang up your crystal balls."

Ella poured them all another cup of tea. She was silent for a while, but then she said, "May I ask you something? If you do all of that, and you still can't find out where Julia went, will you come back here, and ask me to try?"

"So what could *you* do that Nancy and I can't do?"

"I'm very sensitive, Josh," she said, and tapped her forehead just like the old woman in the hospital had done. "If you can bring me a clue – a name, a place, even a piece of clothing – I'll do whatever I can to find out what happened to Julia. If I succeed, it doesn't matter whether you believe in spirits or not, does it? And if I fail, well, there won't be any mischief done, will there?"

She paused, and held up her hands in front of her face, so that only her shining brown eyes looked out. "I was very fond of Daisy. She was your sister but she was also my friend. I don't like to think that any part of her life was lost."

She slowly took her hands away, but she kept staring at Josh as if she could see right inside his head. Abraxas, who was standing close beside Josh's thigh, suddenly shivered; and even Josh felt as if something cold had passed through the room. He looked at Nancy, and by the expression on her face he could tell that she had experienced it, too.

Ella said, "You felt that? You know what that was?"

Josh shook his head.

"That was your fortune. A cold wind, blowing through your life. A cold wind, coming tomorrow maybe; or maybe the day after."

She sipped her tea, still without taking her eyes off Josh. "Better to wrap up warm against it. That's my advice."

Seven

Detective Sergeant Paul rang them at seven thirty the next morning. The response to the television appeal had been disappointing, she said. Only seventy-eight people had called in, saying that they had seen Julia sometime during the past ten months, and already the police had weeded out sixty-two of those as definite cases of mistaken identity.

"But it's early days yet. We're putting a lot of faith in *Crimewatch*."

After Josh had put down the phone, Nancy said, "Why didn't you tell her about Ella, and the Wheatstone letter and everything?"

Josh climbed out of bed. "I don't know. I don't think any of it amounts to material evidence, do you? I'm beginning to think that Ella's friend was probably right. It was just a practical joke."

"I can read you like a book, Josh Winward. You want to investigate Julia's disappearance yourself, don't you? I mean, you're so well qualified. You've served three and a half weeks in the military police and watched every single episode of *Columbo*."

Josh said, "OK. I *do* want to investigate it. But it needs imagination. It needs an alternative point of view. If I give it to the cops, they won't see the wood for the trees."

"But supposing you investigate it, and don't find out anything at all?"

"Then, fine. I'll hand it over to Detective Sergeant Paul. But not just yet."

Nancy knelt up on the edge of the bed and put her arms around him and ruffled his hair. "OK . . . I guess you need to keep busy, to stop you from grieving."

"It's that Wheatstone Electrics that's bothering me. The letter looked so bona fide, and yet it couldn't have been. And there's another thing. Julia was supposed to be starting work as a secretary on the Great West Road, yet her new employer wanted to meet her at a quarter after eight in the morning in the middle of town. I looked up Star Yard in the A–Z and it's miles away from Brentford. It's even miles away from *here*, if she lived around here. Why should he want to meet her someplace so goddamned inconvenient?"

"I don't know. But let's have some breakfast, shall we? And then we'll go find out."

That morning Josh had his first encounter with a traditional English breakfast: eggs, bacon, sausages, baked beans, grilled tomatoes and black pudding.

"Black pudding?" he asked the waitress at the servery. "What's this black pudding?"

"If I told you, you wouldn't eat it."

"Tell me, I can take it. I've eaten hot dogs."

She told him and he left it on the side of his plate until the very last. Then he poked it with his fork and tried a tiny taste of it.

"It's good," he said, after a long and cautious chew. "You want to try some?"

Nancy shuddered. "I wouldn't put that near my lips if I was dying of starvation."

"You used to pick your knees and eat your scabs when you were a kid. What's the difference? This is just a gourmet scab."

They rented a car from the Hertz desk downstairs in the hotel lobby. They were given a red Nissan Primera which was cramped compared with Josh's old 1971 Mustang back home, but at least it was automatic. He couldn't have managed a stick shift in London.

They drove out first to the Great West Road. The sky was wooly gray and the wind was getting up. As Ella had told them, it was nothing but a long string of factories – Rank Audio,

Hoover, and Gillette – mile after mile. Except for its distinctive clock tower, the Gillette building looked remarkably like the Wheatstone Electrics factory: white-painted, with neat rows of trees, the model of 1930s consumerism. But even though they drove up and down the Great West Road twice, they found no sign of Wheatstone Electrics itself.

It began to rain, and as they drove back toward the center of London, Josh began to feel deeply dejected. Even if he never found out who had murdered Julia, he needed to know where she had been for so long, and how she had spent the last ten months of her life. Nancy put a consoling hand on his knee. "She must have been *someplace*, Josh. Nobody just vanishes."

They reached Carey Street, around the back of the Law Courts, and by now it was raining heavily. They had a drink in a narrow old pub called the Seven Bells, elbow to elbow with noisily braying lawyers. Then they walked down to the end of the street, to Star Yard. It was nothing at all – a narrow flagstoned thoroughfare with high soot-stained buildings on either side, and a black-painted Victorian urinal. They walked up to the end but there was nothing to see, only brick walls and dirt-streaked windows, with curled-up law books on the windowsills inside.

At the corner of the yard there was a narrow niche between one wall and another, but it was clogged up with rubbish and somebody had sicked up a curry in it, so Josh didn't venture any further.

He looked around, with rain dripping from the tip of his nose. "This Wheatstone guy arranged to meet Julia here, at eight fifteen in the morning. But *why*?"

With Nancy navigating, they crossed Battersea Bridge and drove to Lavender Hill. Josh had imagined a hill thickly grown with fragrant purple lavender, but instead he found it was just another noisy traffic-blighted road junction with used-car dealers and second-hand furniture shops and kebab restaurants.

He managed to park in a back street, and they walked back

down to the main road and went into D.R. Patel newsagents. It was a tiny shop, crammed with shelves of dog-eared birthday cards and fragrant with Indian spices and children's candies. The bearded newsagent was balanced on a chair, rearranging the adults-only magazines on his top shelf. His wife stood beaming solicitously behind the counter.

"We're looking for Kaiser Gardens," said Josh.

The wife said nothing but shook her head.

"Mrs Marguerite Marmion, of 53b Kaiser Gardens?"

Again she shook her head.

At that moment an elderly man came shuffling in, wearing a damp cloth cap and a pair of rain-spotted glasses that magnified his eyes like oysters. "Gissa packet of them froat sweets, love," he said, digging into his pocket for some loose change.

"These people are looking for Kaiser Gardens," said the newsagent's wife.

The man blinked at them, and sniffed. "Kaiser Gardens? *Kaiser*, like in Kaiser Bill?"

"I guess so, yes."

"You must be joking, mate. You're sure you don't want Hitler Avenue? Or Göring Grove?"

"I'm sorry, I don't quite—"

"Somebody's been pulling your leg, mate. You won't find nowhere in London named after Kaiser Bill. You're a Yank, incher? How many streets have you got in Yankee-land named after old what's-his-face, Hirohito?"

Josh looked at Nancy and raised his eyebrows. "Guess we're on a wild goose chase. I'm sorry."

"Sorry," said the newsagent's wife.

"Very sorry," said the newsagent.

They arrived back at the hotel and it was still raining hard. There was a message from DS Paul saying that all of the seventy-eight people who had responded to last night's television news had been eliminated. Apart from the *Crimewatch* appeal, a new picture of Julia would appear in tomorrow's morning papers.

Josh called DS Paul but she was out of the office. All the

same, he was able to talk to her assistant, Detective Constable Widdows, who sounded as if he were about fifteen years old.

"Yes, that's right, Mr Winward. None of them checked out. Well, that always happens with a murder inquiry – people like to be helpful even if they don't have any useful information."

"So, no leads at all?"

"Nothing that's panned out yet. We've had the full post-mortem report, but I'm afraid that doesn't tell us anything that we didn't know already. Cause of death was asphyxiation with a rope. Pure hemp rope, apparently, with no nylon or other synthetic ingredient, which is quite unusual these days. Obviously we're doing the rounds of chandlers and other rope suppliers. Immediately after death the body was eviscerated and then taken to the river and thrown in. There's very little fingerprint bruising, which suggests that she wasn't roughly handled before death and that her body was probably carried in a sheet or a duvet or something similar."

"She wasn't—"

"Sexually assaulted? No sir, she wasn't. Whatever the motive was, it wasn't that."

For some reason, Josh thought *thank God*. But of course it didn't make Julia any less dead.

"You still have no idea where she's been since she quit that Saudi job?"

"None at all, sir. We've checked with the Inland Revenue and the Department of Social Services and she wasn't registered with either of them. We've checked with every employment agency in West London and none of them had your sister on their books, or even a girl who might have been your sister under a false name. We've checked with hostels, hotels, clinics and hospitals. We've checked with airlines, shipping lines, coach companies and all rail services. Your sister had an American Express Card and a Mastercard, but she made no purchases with either card after six thirty-eight p.m. on the evening of May tenth last year, when she used her American Express Card at Thresher's off-license in Earl's Court Road to buy two bottles of Lanson champagne, a packet of dry-roasted peanuts and a Topic. That's a chocolate bar with nuts in."

Josh pinched the bridge of his nose. "Thanks," he said. "I guess you're doing just about everything that's humanly possible."

"It's only day three, sir. And we've still got *Crimewatch*."

Josh and Nancy went to the Brompton Library. It was a huge, gloomy red-brick building filled with the sour smell of old books, and it was suffocatingly silent, except for the pattering of rain on the windows. They looked up Wheatstone Electrics in the register of companies and found no mention of it. Upstairs, they found an enormous book on the history of London's development in the consumer boom of the 1930s with dozens of illustrations of all the spectacular new art-deco factories that were built along the Great West Road – Smith's Crisps and Hudson Cars and Henly's Garage – but no reference whatsoever to Wheatstone's. Josh couldn't understand it. Wheatstone's was such a distinctive building that it seemed impossible that a definitive study could have omitted it.

He slammed the book shut and a thin man on the other side of the table gave him a look that could have stunned a tortoise. Josh leaned over to Nancy and whispered, "Ella and her friends were right. It was a practical joke. Kind of a weird joke, I have to admit, but a joke all the same. There never was a Wheatstone Electrics, and there never was a Kaiser Gardens, nor a Marguerite Marmion. Julia made up the whole damn thing, and left the letter under her bed just to make absolutely sure that Ella found it."

"But what was the *point* of it?" asked Nancy. She had her hair pinned back and she was looking tired.

"I don't think there *was* any point. She was depressed, she was mixed up, maybe that had something to do with it. Maybe she'd caught a dose of the English sense of humor. Kaiser Gardens, for Christ's sake. She made a fool out of all of us."

"So what are we going to do now?"

"There's nothing else we *can* do. We've checked every possible angle."

"What about the old woman's rhyme?"

"I don't think that meant anything, either. She was senile, that's all. I was still in shock after seeing Julia in the mortuary."

"What happened to all of that stuff about her tuning in to your anxiety?"

"I was in shock, wasn't I? I was subconsciously looking for some kind of meaning in Julia's murder. Some kind of an explanation, I guess."

"The old woman couldn't have known you, but she said your name."

"She was reciting Mother Goose rhymes, that's why she said my name. When I walked past she happened to be saying 'Jack be nimble'. Sheer coincidence."

"Ella seemed to think that it meant something."

"Ella's a . . . spiritualist, for Christ's sake. She reads tealeaves. She talks to dead people."

"Well, let's look up the six doors rhyme, anyway. I mean, just out of interest. I think this British culture is really fascinating."

"I think it's really depressing. It's so *old*."

They found the latest edition of the *Oxford Dictionary of Nursery Rhymes*, but it contained no mention of the six doors. In an older book, however, *Goosey Goosey Gander & Other Rhymes*, by James and Sylvia Wilmott, almost three pages were devoted to it, including a disturbing but beautiful drawing by Walter Crane, the famous children's illustrator.

"Look at this," said Nancy. "This is really strange."

The drawing showed a high brick wall with a door in the middle of it. On one side of the door was a rain-lashed medieval city, with dark overhanging buildings and cobbles strewn with straw. In the near distance, a group of six or seven men were approaching, with high Puritan hats and black capes and buckled shoes. They were all carrying swords. Strangest of all, though, under their hats, their faces were completely covered with rough hessian hoods, with staring black eyes painted on them. A fearful mother was snatching her tiny children out of the Puritans' path; and a bristling black cat was jumping for shelter.

The door was half-open, and a handsome young man with long curly hair was stepping through it, turning around as he did so to see how near the Puritans were. Ahead of him he was pushing a young woman with a baby clutched tight in her arms, presumably his wife.

On the other side of the door, in complete contrast to the grimness of the city, the sun was shining, and there were fields of barley and apple orchards. A small thatched cottage stood in the distance, under a large elm, with smoke rising from its chimney. Two or three laborers were scything the barley, and it looked as if one of them were running toward the door to help, or maybe to shut it; who could tell?

But there was another man, too, who was disproportionately tall, almost as tall as the cottage. His back was turned so that his face was hidden, and he wore a long cloak with a pentagram marked on it.

"Weird," said Josh.

Nancy read out the rhyme. "*Six doors they stand in London Town. Six doors they stand in London, too. Yet who's to know which way they face? And who's to know which face is true?*"

Underneath, the commentary read:

> Although it is less well known than many nursery rhymes, *Six Doors They Stand* is probably one of the oldest, dating back to the early part of the seventeenth century. There are several different interpretations of its meaning, but most historians agree that it was at its most popular in London in 1650, immediately after the execution of Charles I. Samuel Pepys refers to it briefly in the first volume of his diaries in 1659, and says that "Even now, this simple rhyme still excites a quiver of dread, conjuring up as it does such vivid memories of the Hooded Men, hurrying about their terrible business in the name of the Almighty."
>
> In the first years of the Commonwealth, a secret

society of extreme Puritans sent groups of Hooded Men through the streets of London every night, hunting down Catholic and Episcopalian families. Those who refused to deny their popery or their allegiance to the Book of Common Prayer were cruelly tortured or put to death.

Some say that the "six doors" were the doors of six London churches in which the Catholics could seek sanctuary from the Hooded Men. However, this sanctuary was only limited, and by the time the next Sabbath day came around, the Catholics were given the option of renouncing their religion or of being forced back on to the streets. The clerics in some of the churches, however, were thought to have been more tolerant, and assisted the Catholics to escape by river to France. Hence the question, "who's to say which way they face".

Others suggest that the "six doors" were the doors of secret Catholic meeting places, where they could safely celebrate mass together. Yet another interpretation is that they were gaming houses where dice was played for large sums of money. The question about "which face is true" is a reflection on the common practice of weighting dice to change the odds in favour of the house.

Perhaps the most colourful explanation is that the "six doors" were six places in London where it was possible to pass from the world of harsh Puritan reform into a parallel world of tolerance and happiness. The stories go that the location of these "doors" was known only to a select few, called the Doorkeepers, who became extremely wealthy by charging Catholics huge sums of money to escape from Puritan London. The likelihood, however, is that once the Catholics had paid their extortionate "fare" into the next world, they were simply murdered and their bodies dropped into the Thames – their friends innocently believing that they were now living another, Elysian existence, beyond the reach of the Puritans' Hooded Men.

The Doorkeepers were said to practise the very oldest of magical arts, since it was only by the use of certain

> occult rituals that one could safely pass through to the other side. Part of the ritual was probably Druidic. Another part involved the lighting of communion candles and leaping over them, which by 1688 had given rise to another famous nursery rhyme, "Jack be nimble, Jack be quick, Jack jump over the candlestick" – "Jack" being seventeenth-century slang for Jacobite, a Roman Catholic supporter of the Stuart restoration.

Nancy said, "That's some legend. You jump through the door and you're someplace else!"

Jack touched the illustration with his fingertip, tracing and retracing the outline of the door. "Yeah. Wild, isn't it?"

Nancy narrowed her eyes. "I know that look. Just a minute ago you were telling me that the old woman was senile. Just a minute ago, you were telling me that the nursery rhyme was just a coincidence."

"A hundred to one it probably is."

"But?"

"I don't know. I seriously don't know what to think."

"We have a parallel world in Modoc and Klamath mythology, too. A world without white men, where we still hunt, fish and farm without interference from you palefaces."

"Sure. But you've never actually *been* there, have you? And you don't know anybody else who's been there, either?"

"I've never been there because I don't believe in it, I mean not as an actual reality, and anyhow I like palefaces and I've never wanted to fish or farm. Apart from that, I wouldn't have the first idea how to get there."

Josh looked down at the illustration. "But supposing you *did* know how to do it?"

"Josh . . . you don't seriously think this could have anything to do with Julia's disappearance, do you?"

"What? No, how could it? This is nothing but a children's rhyme."

"But?"

"But, like you said, Ella thought that it was important. Ella thought the old woman was trying to tell me something."

"But a parallel world? A *real* parallel world? Come on, Josh!"

"Sure, you're right, you're absolutely right. I'm tired. I'm still jet-lagged. I'm letting my imagination run away with me. It's crap."

"But? Look at you, your whole face is saying *but*!"

"But it really clicked with something I was reading a couple of weeks ago, in the *Chronicle*. They had a scientific convention down in San Diego, and they were talking about parallel worlds. About two hundred of the world's greatest eggheads. And they decided that the likelihood of a parallel world *not* existing was so remote it was almost impossible. In fact, they thought there could be an infinite number of them, because the universe is all about an infinite number of choices, an infinite number of alternatives. It simply wouldn't make sense if there *weren't* any parallel worlds."

"That's easy to say. But where are they, these parallel worlds? And how do you get to them?"

"How the hell should I know? In 1491, they probably used to say that about America. But it's a possibility, isn't it? Julia disappeared for ten whole months, and in all of that time nobody saw her and nobody knew where she was. *Nobody*. She was supposed to be working for a company that doesn't exist, and she left an address that doesn't exist, either."

"This is the great skeptic speaking, remember."

"And I'm *still* skeptical. But that doesn't mean I have to close my mind off altogether, does it? OK, the Wheatstone letter could have been a practical joke. That's the most likely explanation, even if it isn't a very *good* explanation. So what are the other possibilities? Maybe Julia left London altogether. Maybe she left *England* altogether. Maybe she was still in London but she was abducted and kept tied up in a cellar someplace. But then again . . ."

Nancy said, "Go on."

Josh slowly closed the book. "Maybe there *is* a parallel world, where Wheatstone Electrics really exists, and Kaiser Gardens really exists. Maybe there *are* six doors, and Julia found out how to get there, and that's where she's been."

They left the library and walked down the steps. The rain had stopped and the streets were glistening with reflections, an upside-down world of blackness and lights beneath their feet.

Nancy said, "Even if these six doors exist, how did Julia find them?"

"Search me. They can't be easy to find, or everybody would be jumping through them."

"You're not going to tell Detective Sergeant Paul about this, are you?"

Josh unlocked their car, and they climbed in. He switched on the windshield wipers and a parking ticket was dragged backward and forward across the windshield in front of him.

"No," he said. "I'm not going to tell Detective Sergeant Paul. The first thing I'm going to do is find somebody who knows more about these six doors."

Nancy kissed him on the cheek; and then on the lips. "What was that for?" he asked her.

"Because you're always trying to make out that you're such a logical, rational person when all the time you're crazy and spontaneous and you follow your instincts just like one of your dogs."

"Woof," he said, and shifted into reverse by mistake, colliding with the car parked behind him.

Eight

They went back to Ella's that evening, uninvited, but taking two chilled bottles of California Chardonnay with them. Josh didn't think that Ella could really help them any, but they needed somebody else to talk to, and she was the only person who would listen. He knew what DS Paul would think about them if they tried to discuss the six doors with her. His old schoolfriend Steve Moriarty had joined the SFPD and was always griping about the "X-Filers" who pestered him after every unexplained disappearance.

There was the old man whose false teeth had been found in the bottom of the toilet bowl: his wife had immediately assumed that he had been devoured by a giant anaconda that was lurking in the sewer system. Seven months later he was found alive and well and living in Santa Cruz. His wife's cooking had always made him physically sick, and the very last time, when he had lost his dentures, he had walked out and vowed that he would never go back.

Other absconders were said by their relatives to have been sucked off their sundecks by the slipstream of passing UFOs; or to have walked through mirrors, to be trapped for ever in back-to-front land. A parallel world from a Mother Goose rhyme sounded just as insane.

Ella didn't seem surprised to see them. She was wearing a black headscarf and huge silver hoop earrings. "Come on in," she said. "I'm just cooking up some *sancoche*."

Abraxas came running over and threw himself up at Josh's knees. Ella said, "Down, Abraxas! How many times have I told you, you disobedient mutt!" Abraxas barked and kept on bungee-jumping up and down, so Josh popped his fingers and gave him his famous obedience stare. Abraxas immediately whined and hung his head and went trotting back to his basket under the sink.

"How do you *do* that?" asked Ella, shaking her head.

"It's an unarmed combat technique. Eye-karate, they call it. They teach you how to do it in the US Marine Corps. I guess I'm the only person who thought of trying it out on dogs."

"You were in the marines?"

Josh looked up at the ceiling. "Briefly."

"He doesn't talk about it," Nancy explained.

"You don't mind if I carry on cooking?" asked Ella. She went over to her stove and lifted the lid of a large orange casserole pot. A strong smell of meat and peppers and vegetables wafted into the room. Josh went over and peered at the bubbling brown stew inside. "*Sancoche*," said Ella. "It's a traditional Trinidadian dish, with salt pork and beef, thickened up with yam and dasheen and cassava root and sweet potatoes, with coconut cream and hot chili peppers."

"Smells pretty nourishing."

"My grandmother taught me how to cook it. She always used to say that it brought you good luck. Whenever you cook *sancoche*, they can smell it in the spirit world, and it reminds them of the good times they had when they were alive. They gather round close, just to breathe it in."

"You're not expecting anybody to supper, are you?" asked Nancy. "We can always come around tomorrow instead."

"As a matter of fact, I was expecting somebody. Here, I kept the cards to show you."

"The cards?"

Ella led them across to her dining table. Arranged on the purple velveteen cloth were twelve greasy, worn-out playing cards, with a thirteenth card in the center. Seven of the cards had been turned over so that their faces were visible. They bore tiny representations of each of the traditional playing cards in the top left-hand corner, and a large colored illustration in the center.

"These are French fortune-telling cards, *la Sybille*, from Martinique," said Ella. "Handed down by the women in my family from one generation to the next. Whoever uses them gives them a little of her power, so they are very powerful now, very *knowing*. You both carried such a strong aura that I laid them out yesterday, after you were gone. I wanted to find out what would happen to you."

"You're determined to make me into a believer, aren't you?" said Josh.

Ella gave a thick chuckle. "You don't have to believe if you don't want to. You may not believe in tomorrow, but it's coming all the same."

She picked up the center card and showed it to them. It was the three of hearts, illustrated with a woman in a brown silk dress sitting on a chair. "That's me, *la consultante*, the person who's asking the questions. But here, this is also me, the queen of clubs, *une amie sincère*. This means that I'm your friend and that I'm going to help you in whatever is going to happen to you."

Josh picked up the next card, on which a man and a woman were being offered a chair. "*La visite*," he said. "This told you that somebody was coming. But how did you know it was going to be us?"

"Look in the corner of the card. The jack of hearts. A man called Jack looking for something close to his heart. It had to be you."

"Well, maybe it is. My mother always calls me Jack. So what do these other cards mean?"

"Here," she said, and showed him a card with a woman looking startled as a man in a tailcoat and a Napoleonic hat put a letter on the table in front of her. "*Révélations importante*, important revelations. You're going to find out something tonight that will change your whole life."

"I see . . . and what about this fat guy with the pipe, and the fellow behind him carrying all that luggage on his back?"

"*Voyage*, the ten of diamonds. What you learn tonight will send you on a journey to a very different place, where you have never been before."

"And do the cards say what's going to happen when I get to this different place?"

"You will meet two people. One of them is your enemy . . . here, this one." She showed him a card with a man swathed in a cape, waiting around a corner with a club in his hand, while an unsuspecting passer-by walked toward him. "This one, the king of clubs, this is your protector, whoever that is. But you have to watch out for this one, *pièges*." This card showed a man sitting in a field snaring songbirds. "This means that you could walk into a trap."

Josh picked up the last card. "You don't have to tell me what this one means." It depicted a grinning skeleton in a black robe, carrying an hourglass. The nine of spades, *mort*.

Ella plucked it away from him and tucked it back into the pack. "The nine of spades doesn't always mean death."

"Oh, yeah? What else does it mean? I'm going to buy an eggtimer?"

"It can signify mourning. The cards have probably sensed that you're grieving for your sister. Or it can mean that somebody very close to you will try to deceive you."

"On the whole, though, not a great card?"

Ella gave him a long, steady look. "You don't believe in it, so don't let it worry you."

Nancy said, "This card, *révélations* . . . what are we going to find out tonight that's going to change our whole lives?"

"You came back tonight because you wanted to ask me something. That's what the cards are telling me. You wanted to ask me about locks and keys and doors and getting through doors."

"How did you know that? There's nothing like that in any of these cards."

Ella said, "When I turned up the revelations card, all the keys in my key box started to jump."

"I don't understand."

She went over to the bookshelf and brought down a battered black tin box. She shook it hard, and then put it down on the table. "This was something else I learned from my grandma. Never throw a key away. Every time you find a key, keep it. You never know when you'll come across a clock you need to wind up or door that you badly need to open."

Nancy pulled a stool across and sat down next to the table. In the muted light from Ella's lamps, she looked even more Modoc than usual, her hair drawn back into a blue and white beaded headband, her eyes slightly hooded, her cheekbones distinct. She was wearing jeans and fringed suede boots, and a necklace of silver medallions and colored beads. That necklace carried its own magic: it was said to have belonged to the Modoc shaman Curley-Headed Doctor.

Nancy's medallions jingled as she sat down; and there was an answering rattle from the metal box. Josh looked at Ella cautiously.

"This has only happened once before," she said. "And that was when I met a man whose brother was in prison, and he desperately wanted to get him out."

Nancy's medallions shivered again, almost excitedly; and the box rattled again, much more furiously this time. Abraxas lifted his nose over the edge of his basket but he didn't venture out.

"Are you ready for this?" asked Ella.

"I don't know if I'm ready or not. It depends what it is."

"It's the power of artefacts, that's what it is. Like pots and pans. Like keys. On its own, metal's just metal, isn't it? But when we make it into a shape, we teach it something, don't we? In a very spiritual way, the metal learns what we want it to do. The pot understands that it was made for cooking. The key understands that it was made for opening doors. That's why these keys are making such a noise, Josh. They know that you need them."

She unfastened the catch. From inside the box came a clicking, stirring sound, as if a collection of live crabs were trying to climb out. She hesitated for a moment, and then she threw back the lid. In a clattering rush, twenty or thirty keys hurtled out and stuck to Josh's right hand as if it were a magnet. He shouted out, "*Jesus*!" but it was out of surprise, not pain. He lifted up his hand and it was bristling with keys of all sizes and shapes – clock keys, padlock keys, trunk keys, music-box keys and some keys that were so old and blackened that it was impossible to tell what they might ever have opened.

Josh turned his hand this way and that, staring at the keys in disbelief. He shook it two or three times, and two or three of the keys dropped off onto the table, but they immediately jumped back onto his hand again. Ella grinned and shook her head in sheer pleasure.

"You must want those doors opened so bad," she said. "Even that fellow who wanted his brother out of prison, the keys didn't stick to him like that."

Abraxas barked once, but when Josh turned to look at him, he ducked his head below the edge of his basket. Josh said, "This is static electricity, right? This is a trick? Like Uri Geller or something?"

"Perhaps it is. Perhaps Julia's disappearance was a trick. We won't know, will we, unless we find out?"

"And how do you suggest we do that?"

"We do what you really came here for. We ask the one person who knows the truth."

Nancy whispered, "You mean Julia, don't you?"

Ella shrugged.

"You want to hold a séance, is that it?" Josh asked her, sharply.

"*Moi*? Oh, no. *You're* the one who wants to hold a séance. You came here to see me tonight because you need *so* badly to find out what happened to Julia and you didn't know where else to turn. Why don't you admit how overwhelming your need is? Why don't you admit that you're willing to believe in anything and everything? The cards told me you were coming, the keys told me why. You might as well carry a placard."

Josh took a breath. "We went to the library today and found out a whole lot more about the six doors. All kinds of different theories about what they were."

"And?"

"There was one theory that the doors led through to a parallel world," said Nancy. "A kind of alternative existence, like the Happy Hunting Ground."

"So that's why you came here, instead of going to the police? You thought that I might believe you? Or at least, I wouldn't laugh at you?"

"Yes," said Josh.

"And you thought that perhaps I could help you find out what the six doors really were, and if they had anything to do with Julia's disappearance?"

"Yes," said Josh, irritably, even though he knew that Ella was provoking him only because she wanted him to ask for help. "Now how do I get these keys off?"

Ella plucked the keys off his hand one by one and dropped them into the box, quickly snapping the lid shut every time. "When that old lady spoke to you in the hospital, you knew that she was telling you something very important, didn't you? Oh, you tried to think of a rational explanation for it. But sometimes it's dangerous to rationalize. A whole lot of bad things happen in this life because people don't pay any attention when somebody gives them the warning."

She took the last key off the end of Josh's thumb and closed the box and locked it. "If it tells us nothing else, it will tell us if you're right to go looking for the six doors, or if you're simply clutching at straws."

"So what do we have to do?"

Ella took hold of Josh's hands. He could feel all the rings on her fingers, silver and gold and studded with stones. "First of all you have to realize that this isn't a game. You're going to be hearing from Julia, from the other side. You might hear her voice. You might even see her, in some form or another."

"She's my sister. I'm not afraid of her."

"The only thing you have to be afraid of is your own emotions. It's easy to say that you won't be frightened, but we're dealing with the dead here, Josh. We're dealing with people who have lost everything: their loved ones, their friends, the world they lived in. It's the sense of loss that's so hard to deal with. The grief. Even if we can manage to talk to them, they're gone, and they're never going to come back."

Nancy came up and laid her hand on Josh's shoulder. "You don't have to do this, Josh. The chances are that it's only going to hurt you."

"I have to know," Josh told her. "Besides, what else am I

going to do? Sit in that hotel room all day, waiting for Detective Sergeant Paul to call me?"

"We could go back home."

Josh shook his head. "Not yet. Let's try this first."

"And if this doesn't work? If you still don't know what happened to Julia, one way or another?"

"Oh, you'll know," said Ella. "I guarantee it. One hundred and ninety percent."

She switched off all of the lights but one – a standard lamp draped with a beaded crimson shawl – and she lit an odd selection of differently colored candles, some of them scented with vanilla and myrrh and strawberries.

On the table beside her she set a silver dish full of salt.

"In Africa, salt is the sign of deepest friendship," she said. "A bowl of purest salt must always be offered to your guests when they arrive. It is an offering to the spirits, too. A token of affection. It is also a token of grief. Many people believe that we shed tears to dissolve all of the salt that we have accidentally spilt.

"Salt also protects us from evil. You should always keep a bowl of salt by the door or any other entrance that demons might use. When you walk through the house at night, you should always carry a handful of salt. If you see a demon lurking in a corner, you can throw salt in its face to blind the evil eye.

"Tonight I'm using this salt to encourage Julia to come to talk to us. A gift of purity."

She stood in the center of the room and offered a hand each to Josh and Nancy, and told them to hold hands, too. Abraxas stared at them pensively, but didn't make any attempt to join them.

"He's behaving himself," Josh remarked.

"He doesn't like séances. They spook him. If he wasn't a dog, he'd be a chicken."

"Don't you sit around a table for séances?" asked Nancy.

"That's always a mistake. Almost every medium makes it. How do they think a spirit is going to manifest itself in the middle of them, if they're all sitting around a piece of solid wood? Wood is a non-conductor, and spirits are formed of electrical energy. You might just as well have a television with a wooden screen, and expect to get a picture on it."

"Do we have to close our eyes?" Josh wanted to know.

Ella smiled. Her skin gleamed in the candlelight like polished bronze. Her eyes shone white. "All you have to do is relax, and breathe deeply and gently. Think about the times you spent with Julia, the really good times. Try and picture her face. See it as clearly as you can. The color of her eyes, her eyelashes, every detail of her skin. Any freckle, any little wisp of hair. Try to imagine that she's living and breathing, living and breathing, just like you are. Her body's warm and her lungs are going in and out, in and out.

"Her eyes are closed; but her eyelids are fluttering because she's dreaming, Josh. She's dreaming of you. She's dreaming of coming back and talking to you, and telling you where she's been. Can you see her now, Josh? Can you *smell* her now? Remember that perfume she always used to wear?"

Nancy, beside him, took a deep breath, and suddenly said, "Anaïs Anaïs."

"What?" said Josh, with a prickling feeling all around his scalp.

"Anaïs Anaïs. That was the fragrance that Julia always used to wear. Can't you smell it?"

Josh sniffed. He could vaguely detect a light, floral scent, but he couldn't be sure that it was Julia's. "I don't know . . . it could be the candles."

Ella said, "She's close, Josh. The spirits are always close, especially when they've only just left us. She misses you, Josh, as much as you miss her. She wants to talk to you. She wants to touch you. She wants to tell you what happened to her."

Josh glanced at Nancy. He was beginning to feel that they had made a bad mistake, coming back here to Ella's. As if she could really bring Julia back from the dead. Julia had been hung and mutilated and dumped in the Thames and that was all there was to it. Ella was simply fueling his grief, so that she could exploit him. He wondered how much money she would ask him for, once this "séance" was over.

"Nothing," said Ella, without blinking.

"What do you mean, nothing?"

"I'm not going to ask you for anything. This is all about faith, not money."

Josh felt himself flushing. "Jesus. I wish my bank manager could tell when I was thinking about money."

"It's all right," said Ella. "It's all right to doubt. If nobody doubted, then belief would have no value at all. But remember that Julia was more than your sister. She was a friend to many, many people; and she was *my* friend, too . . . Now," she went on, "let's bring her closer, shall we? Let's feel her living and breathing, living and breathing. Let's see her face, the way we remember her best. The way we loved her."

Ella raised her eyes to the ceiling and her grip on Josh's hand tightened so much that her long fingernails dug into his palm. She was hurting him, but he guessed that she was doing it on purpose, to concentrate his mind.

She was silent for a long time. Her breathing was deep, with a slight rasp in it. The candle flames dipped and swiveled and all kinds of distorted shadows danced in the corners where the sloping ceilings met the walls. Outside, in the night, Josh could hear the ceaseless muttering of London's traffic, and for the first time since he had arrived in England he felt very far from home.

Ella released Nancy's hand for a moment and took a pinch of salt out of the silver bowl. She threw it into the center of the room between them, and chanted, "Three angels came out of the east. One brought fire, one brought frost. The third brought the spirit we seek."

She took another pinch of salt and threw it in a criss-cross pattern over the candle flames, which flared up bright blue. "Three maidens once going on a verdant highway. One brought bread. One brought wood. The third brought the spirit we seek."

Now she took hold of Nancy's hand again, and closed her eyes. "Julia Winward, Julia Winward, Julia Winward. Thrice the candles burn by me. Thrice our hearts shall broken be. *Pchagerav monely, pchagerav tre vodyi.*"

Josh took a deep breath, and this time he could smell Julia's perfume quite distinctly. The air in the flat began to grow cold, and somehow everything seemed blurry, as if they were being shaken by a distant temblor.

"Julia Winward, Julia Winward, Julia Winward," Ella chanted, her voice rising every time she called Julia's name.

The temperature dropped and dropped, and the smell of perfume grew so strong that it was almost overwhelming. They heard a creaking sound, too – very faint at first, but gradually growing more distinct. *Creak*, pause. *Creak*, pause. It reminded Josh of Julia sitting on their grandfather's rocker, on the porch in Sausalito. Her hands covering her eyes, to shield them from the setting sun, her bare toes swinging, her blonde hair alight. *Creak*, pause. *Creak*, pause. *Creak*, pause.

Suddenly, they heard a soft, desperate tumbling noise. Something appeared right in front of them, in the air. A pale, flickering shape, like the images seen in an old-fashioned zoetrope. The movement was frantic, but the creaking continued at the same measured pace as before.

Creak, pause. *Creak*, pause.

Ella dug her nails so deeply into the palms of Josh's hand that he almost expected blood to come dripping out. "Julia Winward!" she called, her West Indian accent very strong now. "*Juli-a Win-ward*!"

The tension in the flat was almost unbearable. Josh felt as if the air pressure were increasing as the temperature plummeted, and his eardrums popped. The flickering shape in front of them became brighter and brighter, and at last Josh realized that it was two legs – two bare legs – pedaling like a cyclist in mid-air.

"Julia?" he whispered. Then, much louder, "*Julia*?"

Gradually, the image brightened even more, and grew, and Josh looked up at it in growing horror. Nancy said, "Josh – what is it? Josh, speak to me, for God's sake – *what is it*?"

Ella babbled, "Save us. Name of the Father, name of the Son, name of the Holy Duppy, amen."

They only saw her clearly for a split second, but that split second was more than enough. Julia was hanging naked from the ceiling, her hands clutching at the noose around her neck, her legs wildly kicking. The rope was swinging slowly from side to side. *Creak*, pause. *Creak*, pause. Julia's eyes were bulging and her tongue was lolling over her chin, but there was nothing that she could do to claw it free.

Nine

Josh shouted, "*Ella*!" but Ella was ahead of him. She picked up the bowl of salt and threw it at the struggling vision of Julia in the air. With a sharp *crackle-crackle-crackle* every grain of salt flared into a tiny pinprick of sparkling blue light. The vision vanished immediately, leaving nothing but a thin swirl of bitter-smelling smoke. Abraxas let out a defiant bark, but still didn't venture out of his basket.

"God, that was scary," said Nancy, her eyes wide and her voice shaking. "That was so, so scary. My grandfather raised the spirits. Shadows, invisible finger-writing in the sand. But nothing like that." She pulled out one of Ella's chairs and sat down, while Ella herself leaned against the table, dabbing her forehead and neck with her scarf.

Josh stayed where he was. He still felt freezing cold, unbalanced, and nauseous, as if he were standing on the afterdeck of an Arctic fishing boat. He reached out for the back of the nearest chair to steady himself but he couldn't move his legs. Ice-cold perspiration was trickling down the sides of his face into his collar, and coursing down his spine. He tried to take some deep, steadying breaths but he couldn't. His throat felt congested and his stomach kept flinching in sickening spasms.

"Josh, what's the matter? Are you all right?" Ella asked him, with a frown.

"I'm just . . . I'm just . . . sick," he choked.

He had never felt so bad in his life. His body temperature felt as if it had dropped to zero, and every joint ached. His stomach made a disgusting gurgling noise, and his mouth was flooded with sour-tasting saliva.

"Here," said Ella, taking his arm. "I'll take you to the toilet."

"That was Julia," Josh gasped. "That was Julia, *hanging*."

His stomach contracted as tight as a fist, and he felt a swelling in his throat that he couldn't keep down. He tried to take another step forward, but he couldn't. He doubled up over the table and something huge and slippery filled his mouth. It felt like an oyster, only twenty times larger. He tried to breathe but bile sprayed out of his nostrils and stung his sinuses. The thing inside his mouth was so large that he didn't think he would be able to open his mouth wide enough to regurgitate it. He reached out for Nancy, desperate for breath, his eyes bulging, his whole body wracked with gut-wrenching heaves.

"Ella – call for an ambulance!" snapped Nancy.

"He has to bring it up," Ella insisted. "It's stuck in his throat. He has to bring it up."

"*Call for a fucking ambulance*! *He's dying*!"

"No, no, no! He has to bring it up."

Nancy went to the phone herself and dialed 911. All she heard was a piercing high-pitched tone, and a polite woman's voice saying, "*The number you have dialed has not been recognized* . . ."

"What's the emergency number?" she shouted. "Ella – what do I dial for an ambulance?"

Josh bent so far over the table that his forehead pressed against the velvet cloth. He clutched his stomach with both hands, trying to stop the heaving. The only sound he could make was a tight, supressed cackle, like a man being pressed under tons of concrete.

"*Tell me the number*!" screamed Nancy.

At that moment, however, a greasy, blood-streaked balloon began to emerge from Josh's wide-stretched mouth. He heaved, and heaved again, and more of it slid out. He felt so sick that all he wanted was a huge rush of vomit, but he could only force this thing out of his mouth an inch at a time, and it seemed to take for ever to slide between his lips.

"Oh God," said Nancy. "Oh God, what's happening to him?"

Ella leaned over Josh and rubbed his back. "Come on, now, Josh. You bring it all up. You bring it all up, man."

Josh's face was gray. But slowly the big slippery bulge came out of his mouth, further and further. It hesitated for a while, drooping, and then it dropped silently on to the table, like a monstrous grub. It was immediately followed by a sharp splatter of half-digested pizza.

Josh collapsed on to his knees, almost screaming for breath. He puked up a little more lunch, and some of it came out of his nose. Ella brought over a large box of Kleenex and gently wiped his face.

"What *is* that?" asked Nancy in horror, staring at the bloody yellow bladder on the table. "Is he sick? He's not going to die, is he?"

Ella stood up, her bracelets and her necklace jingling. "No, girl, he's not going to die. But I never saw that happen before, not like that. I've had ectoplasm, just a small blob, enough to fill an eggcup. I've had locks of hair. But I've never had the whole flesh."

Josh tugged out another handful of tissues and wiped his shirt. He was still sweaty and shaking, but his color was coming back and his nausea was beginning to recede. All the same, he looked at the thing on the table and then back at Ella, and he couldn't stop himself from retching.

Ella said, "Sometimes, when you call up a spirit, they want to come back to the physical world so much that they try to materialize. That's when you see ectoplasm. It's usually white, or gray, in clouds, or fingers, or little wisps, like chiffon."

"But what is *that*?" Nancy demanded. "That isn't a cloud, or a finger or a little wisp."

"Well, I trained to be a nurse once, when I first left school, and I would say that's a lung."

"Oh, my God. One of *Josh's* lungs?"

"No, no, it couldn't be." She took hold of Josh's arm and helped him back on to his feet. "If that was one of Josh's lungs, he'd be dead. That's a lung from the other side. A message." She paused, and then she said, "I would guess that's Julia's lung."

"What?" said Josh, dabbing his mouth. He could still taste blood, like rusty iron, and he could still taste the fatty tissue that had coated the lung and made it so slippery. "How can that be?"

"Her spirit is *very* strong, Josh. She knows you're here. She knows that you've come to England to find her. She wants to talk to you, she wants to get in touch with you. But she's been cut to pieces. She can't appear to you whole."

"I can't believe this is happening," said Josh. "How could I bring up my own sister's lung? It just isn't physically possible!"

"It's possible, Josh. Things like this have happened plenty of times before. There was a famous medium in Edwardian times, Marthe Beraud, who called herself Eva C. She was able to bring human hands out of the spirit world, out of her mouth. Hands with nails and bones that investigators could actually touch. And there have been dozens of others. Some mediums have produced whole people out of their mouths."

"I don't understand what it means. If she's trying to tell me something, what the hell is it?"

"You mark my words. She's trying to tell you that she won't be at rest until you find out what happened to her. She can't find peace until every part of her body is brought back together, and given a proper funeral."

"I seriously think we should call Detective Sergeant Paul," said Nancy. "This has gone way beyond playing detectives. If this lung is really Julia's then it's important material evidence, isn't it?"

"You can't tell the *pigs*," Ella protested. "They'll think you're insane. Worse than that, they'll probably think that you had something to do with her murder, even if you weren't in England when it happened. I mean, what are you going to say to them? 'My sister's lung came out of my mouth'?"

"Jesus, Ella. This séance has created more goddamned problems than it's solved."

"Will you trust me?" Ella demanded.

Josh said, "I don't know . . . trust you? I can't even believe this is happening."

"Trust me. You have to trust me, or this isn't going to work."

"But what are we going to do with this *lung*? We can't just—"

"*Trust me.*"

"OK," said Josh, raising both hands in surrender. "I trust you."

Nancy said, "I'm not so sure about this."

"If it doesn't work, then you can go to the police. But you saw what I did before . . . raising Julia out of the air. Now I can get you closer."

She went across to her sink and produced a plastic Sainsburys shopping bag from the cupboard underneath. She picked up the lung and eased it into the bag. It slid to the bottom and hung in a heavy curve, bleeding. She left it in the sink while she folded up the tablecloth and took it into the bathroom.

"I really think that we're messing with things that we don't understand," said Nancy.

Ella returned and then emptied the lung into the sink and washed it. "All right, if you want to call the police, call the police. But you'd be making a mistake. The way this lung appeared, it shows that your sister's remains are not in this world, they're somewhere else. Somewhere close, but different."

"So what you're trying to say is, there *is* a parallel existence, and this is the proof?"

"Where else do you think it came from, man, this lung? You didn't eat it for lunch, did you?"

Ella filled a small copper saucepan with water and put it on the gas to boil. Then she lifted the lung out of the sink and laid it on a scratched wooden chopping board. She used a triangular-bladed kitchen knife to take off three thin slices, which she cut up fine. Then she reached for some of her glass jars of herbs.

"Is this a *spell*?" asked Nancy, coming closer.

"You're an Indian. You should know about spells."

"Yes, yes I do. My grandfather used to make a powder which was supposed to make the wind die down."

"And did it?"

Nancy didn't smile. "Yes," she admitted. "Maybe it was just a coincidence, but it did."

When the water began to boil, Ella scraped the slices of lung into the saucepan, along with angelica, dill, bay leaves, mugwort, pimpernel, marigold, rue and rosemary. She stirred it three times, and then she left it to simmer. She took out a clean white tablecloth and struck it three times with her wooden spoon.

Josh sat in the corner, underneath the sloping ceiling, feeling as bruised as if he had fallen out of a moving car. His common sense told him that he and Nancy should walk out of here right now and call the police. But the image of Julia's legs kicking in the air had been too electrifying; and the trauma of regurgitating Julia's lung had left him emotionally weak as well as physically bruised. Nancy came and sat beside him and took hold of his hand; and after a while even Abraxas hopped out of his basket and came across to sniff at his knees and give him a reassuring whine.

The smell from Ella's potion reminded him of his mother's herb garden when he was young. She used to rub lemon parsley between her fingers so that he and Julia could sniff it.

Ella knelt on the floor close by, fondling Abraxas' ears. "Whatever happened to Julia, it took her spirit to pieces as well as her body. There are so many spirits like that – spirits who can never understand what happened to them, or where they are. That's why they try so hard to find the people they used to know in their previous life . . . and, when they do, that's why they try so hard to take on their previous shape.

"Usually, ectoplasm doesn't last. There's a dried-up shred of it, in a bottle, at the London Society for Psychical Research; and some French professor managed to cut a lock of hair from an Egyptian princess who was raised up by Eva C. But when you're gone, you're gone, no matter how much you want to come back."

She stood up, and took Josh's hand. "Come here," she said,

and led him across to the sink. The remains of Julia's lung had almost completely disappeared, except for a thin twist of white membrane, and even that appeared to be melting away.

She turned off the gas under the saucepan, and strained the contents into three small thick-bottomed glasses. The liquid was pearl-colored, with a strange shimmer to it.

"We're not supposed to *drink* it, are we?" asked Josh.

"Just a sip."

"But, Jesus, this is like cannibalism. This is like the goddamned Donner Party, boiling children's lungs to make soup."

"There's no other way, Josh. Julia gave you a message and this is the only way you're ever going to know what it was."

The glasses were so hot that they could barely hold them. Ella lifted one up herself and said, "Drink to the sights that the body can bring. Drink to the songs that the spirit can sing. Julia Winward, talk to us. Julia Winward, guide us. Julia Winward, we need to hear your voice."

Josh lifted his glass closer to his lips. To his surprise, the steam vanished and the glass felt suddenly cooler. Ella chanted, "Julia Winward, open our eyes. Julia Winward, show us a sign. Julia Winward, Julia Winward, Julia Winward."

Josh felt his gorge rising again, but he swallowed hard, and took a deep breath, and drank. The potion tasted of nothing but herbs, mostly rosemary, although there was something faintly spicy about it, too, like cloves. Nancy hesitated, but then she drank, too, and Ella followed her.

"I don't think I've ever—" Josh began. But then he was walking quickly along a crowded street on a bright sunny day, with cars and buses all around, and the clouds flickering as quickly as a silent movie. He could hear the beeps of car horns and the sharp shuffling of feet on the sidewalk, but nobody spoke. He tried to look around to see where Nancy had gone, but the people behind him were strangers, none of them interested in anything else but pushing their way through the crowds.

"Where am I?" he asked, but his voice sounded deep and

blurred, as if he were talking inside an empty metallic tank. "*N-a-a-nnnnc-y-y-y, where ammmm I*?"

He passed a stone pillar with a rampant bronze dragon on top of it. He passed a church. People wove around the sidewalk in front of him as thick as flies. Gray suits, pale faces, blank expressions. He turned a corner and began to walk beside a long iron paling. He reached another corner, and another. The light came and went, came and went. One second it was sunny and the next it was shadowy and cold.

Now he was making his way up a narrow alley with tall soot-blackened buildings on either side. The sharp shuffling of feet had died away, and all he could hear was his own footsteps echoing, and the distant rumbling of traffic. He didn't feel frightened. In fact he felt almost elated, as if something exciting was going to happen to him. He wasn't worried about Nancy any more. He was sure that she could find him. After all, this was probably a dream and he would wake up in a minute and Nancy would be lying right beside him, as still as death.

He followed the alley until he reached the corner. There was a narrow niche here, cluttered with rubbish and dead leaves. He paused, and peered into it. It was quite deep, as if it had been a space between two buildings, but it was bricked up, leading nowhere. All the same, he stepped into it, and made his way cautiously to the very end, where the leaves and litter were at their deepest. There, on his left, was another niche, just as narrow and just as deep, and equally cluttered with old newspapers and cigarette packets and leaves and broken twigs. That appeared to be a dead end, too, but he turned into it, and trod through the rubbish, until he found another niche, off to his right.

He looked up. The buildings on either side were very tall, with black-painted drainpipes running all the way down their black scaly brickwork, and window ledges clustered with diseased-looking pigeons. It was curiously silent here. He couldn't hear the traffic. He couldn't even hear the pigeons. The sky was gray, completely neutral, so that it was impossible to guess what time of day it was, or even the season. He carried on trudging his way forward, until he reached yet another niche, on his left. This niche wasn't bricked up. At the far end, he could see people walking backward and forward, and he could hear traffic again.

He began to make his way out of it, high-stepping over the rubbish. But before he was halfway to the end, a tall dark figure appeared in the entrance to the niche, wearing a long black overcoat and a tall black hat. He stood facing Josh as if he were waiting for him – as if he had known all the time that he was coming. There was no drumroll, but Josh felt as if there ought to have been.

"Hallo?" called Josh. His voice sounded weak and flat. The figure didn't answer.

Josh came closer and closer. He wasn't sure why, but the figure disturbed him deeply. He was reminded of having to go to his father for a punishment, when he was small. He was reminded of a black robe that used to hang on the back of his door at his grandparents' house – and which, at night, became a vampire. The inaudible drumroll grew more insistent: maybe it was the blood rushing in his ears.

As he came nearer, the figure spoke. Its voice sounded like somebody dragging a dead body over a concrete floor. "*You came? You don't know how delighted I am.*"

Josh said, "Yes." He turned around and looked behind him, wondering if he ought to run back into the niche – *right, left, right* – and back to where he had come from.

But he was too close now. In fact he wasn't even conscious of the last six steps. The figure laid a hand on his shoulder and said, "*Welcome to your new job. And welcome to your new life.*"

Josh looked up at him. His face was difficult to see, because the bright gray daylight was behind him. But then he stepped to one side, and Josh saw that over his head he was wearing a rough hessian hood, with torn-out slits for eyes. Over the slits were painted two larger eyes, black and slanted, like the eyes of a demon or a huge predatory insect.

Josh's fear was so overwhelming that he felt as if his knees were going to give way.

"*Trust me*," said the figure, leaning so close that the brim of its hat almost touched Josh's forehead, and he could see its real eyes inside its hood, glittering and greedy.

Ten

"Trust me," Ella repeated, and there was a sudden rumble of thunder.

Josh blinked and stared at her. The three of them were still standing facing each other in her Earl's Court flat. Outside it was raining hard. The window was open a few inches so that they could smell the ozone, and hear the clattering of water down the drainpipe.

"That was . . . unreal," said Josh. He reached out for Nancy's hand, and squeezed it. Nancy looked as bewildered as he did.

"You thought you were somewhere else?" asked Ella.

"That's right. I thought I was back at Star Yard. The place where Julia was supposed to meet the man from Wheatstone Electrics."

"I was there too," said Nancy. "It was so clear . . . I believed I was really there."

"Didn't *you* see it?" Josh asked Ella.

"No . . . I stayed here to make sure that you both came back. You have to be careful, when you start messing around with potions like that."

"I went to Star Yard and then I went through a kind of a narrow alleyway and found myself someplace else."

"You actually went through the alleyway?" said Nancy. "I didn't. I just stayed in Star Yard. I guess I was too frightened to go any further."

"So what does it all mean?" Josh wanted to know. "I went through the alleyway and met some guy with a hood over his face . . . just like the Hooded Men in the nursery-rhyme picture."

"Do you know what you were seeing?" said Ella. "You had Julia's ectoplasm flowing through your bloodstream, and what you were seeing was what Julia wanted you to see. She was showing you the way to discover how she died. She was showing you the way through."

"So that alleyway in Star Yard . . . that's one of the 'six doors'?"

"Perhaps. It's certainly the way through to *somewhere*."

"But we checked it out. It's nothing but a blank wall."

"You need a ritual. You need some way to get through. Jack be nimble. Jack be quick. Perhaps you don't need to do anything more than light a candle."

"Supposing that's nothing but a children's song? Suppose that alleyway doesn't lead to anyplace at all?"

"Then I don't know, Josh. I've done my best for you. When it comes to the spirit world, there aren't any tour guides. *The Hereafter on Five Dollars a Day*. You have to find your own way."

Another extravagant burst of thunder made the lamp shake and the ornaments rattle. There was a few seconds' pause, and then the rain began to beat so furiously on the roof outside the window that spray came through the open window and sparkled on Ella's geranium plants.

Josh said, "You're right. You've been a great help, Ella. But I guess we're on our own, from here on in." He took his billfold out of his back jeans pocket and took out a twenty pound note. "Listen . . . we have to give you something for doing this. You don't normally hold séances free of charge, do you?"

"I can't take your money, Josh. I did this for Julia."

"Come on. Buy something for Abraxas if you won't take it for yourself. I'm sure Julia would have wanted you to have it."

"You don't know yet, what Julia wants. When you find out, come back to me."

"You're sure?" said Josh, offering her the note again.

"If you've really discovered one of the six doors, there's a chance that I won't ever see you again, not in this life. So try to remember that you owe me twenty pounds. It'll give you one more reason for coming back."

Nancy came up and took hold of Josh's arm. "Josh . . . it's getting late. I think it's time we left."

"Yes, you go on and catch up on some sleep," said Ella, kissing Josh on the cheek.

"I'm sorry I made such a mess. Puking and all."

"That wasn't your fault. Anyway, puke is easier to clean up than ectoplasm."

It was still raining hard so Ella lent them a large yellow umbrella. She took them down to the front door, and kissed both of them again.

Josh said, "What happened up there, that was real, wasn't it? I didn't dream it?"

Ella's eyes shone white in the gloom of the porch. "What happened up there, Josh, was the realest thing that you've ever experienced in the whole of your life. I swear to you."

Josh's throat was sore and swollen, and even though he gargled with dispersible aspirin before he went to bed, he hardly slept.

When he did manage to doze off, he had endless unraveling dreams about walking down narrow London alleyways, left and then right and then left and then right and never reaching the end. In his dreams it was raining hard and he was forced to wade knee-deep through wet leaves and trash. He saw something that looked like a note or a letter, and he bent over to pick it up. It turned out to be a cream-colored cigarette packet called Player's Weights. Josh briefly wondered what kind of cigarettes would be referred to as "weights"; he dropped the packet and carried on wading through the rubbish.

A nagging voice kept saying, "You lost something, mate? You lost something, mate? You want to watch yourself, mate. You're looking for trouble, you are. You want to watch yourself."

He tried to reply but his lips felt as if they had been anesthetized.

"You want to watch yourself, mate," the voice persisted.

"You're going to get yourself in *shtoock*, you are. You're going to end up brown bread."

Nancy slept soundly and silently as she always did. Just after seven o'clock, a warm sun began to shine through the open-weave drapes, and Josh drew them back to look out over a bright cloudless morning in West London, with the sparrows chirruping and the traffic already busy. Down in one of the gardens below, a man in a grubby undershirt and gray pants was admiring a row of beans and smoking a cigarette. Josh sat down on the bed next to Nancy and stroked her tangled shiny hair. Eventually he bent over and kissed her on the forehead and the tip of the nose and she opened her eyes.

"Wake up," he told her. "It's a beautiful day."

She turned over and smiled at him. "I was having such an amazing dream. I was back home, in my mother's house, and all of my relations were there. My grandfather and my grandmother, my aunts and my uncles, my nieces and nephews, everybody."

"It's good to have your family reunions in dreams. It sure saves on air fares."

"I could never have had *this* reunion anyplace else. My grandparents are dead, remember? So are three of my uncles."

"So what was the occasion?"

"I'm not really sure. It was kind of a farewell party."

"A farewell party? For who?"

"For me, I guess. Everybody came up one by one and kissed me on the cheeks and gave me a little gift."

Josh couldn't fully understand why, but Nancy's dream made him feel worried. He switched on the television news while he showered and dressed. A car bomb in Ulster had killed a well-known woman lawyer. The European Commission had imposed a ban on British-cured prosciutto. American warplanes had attacked Iraq and accidentally blown up a school, killing twenty-three children.

He put on a plain blue shirt and a pair of blue jeans. Nancy wore a simple maroon dress with a matching headscarf and all of her Modoc jewelry, silver and turquoise and red enamel.

They went down to the hotel restaurant. The rosy-cheeked girl behind the counter asked Josh if he wanted his "full English" again, but he contented himself with a peach yogurt. He still felt sick at the thought of bringing up Julia's lung.

"You're quiet," said Nancy during breakfast, laying her hand on top of his.

"I was thinking about that old woman in the hospital. I mean, do you think that was a *coincidence*, her telling me that rhyme about the six doors? It's almost as if she was planted there."

"Planted? An old woman like that? Who would do that? And why?"

"We never would have known about the six doors otherwise, would we? It's like that movie about the Twelve Monkeys. I just get the feeling that somebody *wanted* us to find out about them."

"Then they would have called us up or left us a note, wouldn't they? Not sent a hundred-year-old woman to tell us a Mother Goose rhyme."

"It's the kind of thing that spies used to do. Like the SOE, during World War Two. They sent all their messages in poems."

"But this isn't wartime, is it?"

On the far side of the restaurant Josh could see a television silently showing the twisted Vauxhall of the dead Irish lawyer. "It's always wartime, someplace or another."

They drove to St Thomas's Hospital, and walked through the automatic doors into the sunny, white-tiled reception area. A middle-aged woman with gray bouffant hair and a strident blue suit kept them waiting while she finished a conversation with one of the hospital porters about her holiday in Kos. "Mosquitoes! You should have seen me. I was all blown up like a balloon."

Josh emphatically cleared his throat. When the receptionist didn't take any notice, he did it again. She swiveled around in her chair and peered at him through fishbowl glasses. "Nasty cough, dear. ENT, is it?"

"I haven't come here for treatment. I've come to visit a patient."

"Ward?"

"I'm sorry, I don't know which ward she's in. But she's a very old lady, a hundred and one years old, and her name's Polly."

"I'm sorry, if you don't know the ward."

"How many old ladies of a hundred and one do you have in this place?"

"I'm sorry, I couldn't honestly tell you, offhand."

"Well, how many old ladies of one hundred and one called Polly do you have?"

"We're not allowed to reveal patients' ages. It's against policy."

"But the policy about knowing her age is irrelevant if I know it already."

"Ah, but you don't know who she is, do you? If I told you who she was, that would be the same as revealing her age."

Josh was just about to shout at her in sheer exasperation when he caught sight of the hospital porter who had been pushing Polly into the X-ray room. He said, "Hold on," to the receptionist and pushed his way through the crowds of patients. He managed to catch the porter just as he reached the elevators.

"Hold up a minute! Please!"

The porter gave him a gilded grin. "It's all right. This lift takes a very long time coming. I didn't have a beard when I first pushed the button . . . That's a joke," he added, with the pedantic care of somebody who looks after the elderly.

"Polly," said Josh. "The old girl, one hundred and one years old."

The porter kept smiling, but his eyes were no longer focused. "I'm sorry."

"What do you mean, you're sorry? Yesterday morning we met outside the X-ray Department. You were pushing this very old woman in a wheelchair. She called out my name, so I stopped you and I talked to her for a couple of minutes. You told me her name was Polly and that she had just celebrated her hundred-and-first birthday."

The porter kept on smiling at him blankly.

"You don't remember that? That was less than twenty-four hours ago."

"We asked you about the Mother Goose rhyme," put in Nancy. "*Six doors they stand in London Town.* Don't you remember that?"

"I'm sorry, madam. I was born in Punjab. I didn't speak English until I was seventeen."

"That's what you said yesterday, too."

"I don't think so, sir. You must be making a misidentification."

"It was you, God damn it. You were pushing this white-haired old lady called Polly. You told me how she kept on grabbing people."

The elevator arrived, and the door opened. A man on crutches pushed his way between them. "I'm sorry, sir," said the porter. "But I am very busy now. So, please."

Josh snatched his lapel and pulled him quite violently away from the elevator doors. "You listen to me, my friend. I don't know why you're lying to me, but I need to find that old lady and that's exactly what I'm going to do. Either you take me right to her, right now, or else I'm going to drag you around this hospital, ward by ward, until I do."

"I'm sorry, I shall have to call security."

"Go on then, call security," Josh challenged him, although he didn't have the faintest idea of what he would do if he did.

The porter looked at him for a long time, saying nothing.

"Well?" Josh demanded.

"It is the best plan for you, sir, if you leave quietly. There is no woman called Polly."

"What are you trying to say to me?"

"I am saying that there is no woman called Polly. Enough that you know the rhyme. Now, please release me. There could be somebody watching."

Josh released his grip on the porter's lapel and slowly looked around. He didn't know what he was looking for. Men in hoods? But all he could see was people in plaster and people in wheelchairs and people with an almost comical assortment of exaggerated limps. When he turned back, the porter had gone.

"Something's wrong here," he said, taking hold of Nancy's hand. "Something's very, very wrong."

"This is beginning to frighten me," said Nancy, as they left the hospital and walked back across the parking lot. The sun was dazzling and the wind fluttered her scarf. "What happened last night . . . that was so gross. And now this. That porter was telling us a barefaced lie."

Josh unlocked the car. "First I want to go back to the alleyway in Star Yard. We both saw it, didn't we, and theoretically that's impossible, two people having the same hallucination. So it must have some kind of significance. If there's nothing there, then OK. We'll have to admit that somebody's playing us for mugs. We'll tell Detective Sergeant Paul everything that's happened and leave it to her to go figure. That's a promise."

DS Paul had left them a message to call her. When Josh managed to get through, she sounded brusque and busy. "*Crimewatch* was a washout, quite frankly. Very disappointing. We had only twenty-seven calls, which must be their worst response ever."

"Any leads at all?"

"We're still checking two of them, but I'll have to be candid with you and say that they don't look hopeful."

"You mean you're stymied?"

"That's not entirely accurate. We still have quite a few avenues of inquiry left open to us."

"Avenues of inquiry? That sounds suspiciously like official speak for sitting on your butts scratching your heads."

"Mr Winward, you're an American. You're probably not used to the way that police investigations are conducted in Britain. They're extremely low key, as a rule. No car chases, no gunfights. Just steady, solid policework."

"Resulting so far in what we Americans call squat."

"You don't have to be shirty, Mr Winward. I assure you

that we're doing everything possible to find the people who murdered your sister."

"Tell me the truth. She was my sister. I think I deserve the truth."

"All right. But if you quote me on this, I shall deny it. We have interviewed more than two and a half thousand people in two days. We have checked every single working CCTV camera in central London, every single one, and inspected the CCTV systems of more than four hundred restaurants and nightclubs. We have carried out DNA tests on forty-three different men of seven different ethnic origins. We have contacted every single employment agency in the Greater London area, as well as every hospital and clinic, private or NHS. We know a lot of people who *didn't* kill your sister, but so far we're no nearer to discovering who did."

Josh was silent for a while. Then he said, "I see. OK. Well, thanks for being upfront. I didn't mean to embarrass you or anything. Perhaps you'd check with me tomorrow."

He put down the phone. Nancy looked up and said, "Why do you talk to *everybody* as if they've brought you a molting cockatiel to look at?"

"The police haven't gotten anyplace at all."

"What about that *Crimewatch* program?"

"Nothing. It's supposed to have the biggest audience of any crime-prevention program in Britain. You'd think that at least *one* person would have remembered seeing Julia. Shit, she was *pretty*. You'd think that *one* guy would have noticed her, walking along the street. Well, maybe not. There's supposed to be more gays to the square inch in Britain than there are in San Francisco. Maybe they just don't notice women."

He paused, and massaged the back of his neck with his hand. "Unless, of course, she wasn't here to be noticed."

It was two thirty-five p.m. when they found a spare parking meter on Carey Street, less than a hundred yards away from Star Yard. The day was still sunny, although the traffic fumes had created a faint haze everywhere, as if the Gothic buildings and the brightly dressed people who were hurrying around them were slightly out of focus. Nancy was carrying six candles and three metal candleholders in her bag, which they had bought at the Roman Catholic shop behind Westminster Cathedral. Neither of them were Catholics, but Josh thought that Catholic candles might carry more mystical authority. It was all that Nancy had been able to do to prevent him from buying a vial of holy water and a genuine palm crucifix from Jerusalem.

"For that price, they should at least have given you a guarantee that it was trodden on by Jesus' personal donkey."

They turned into Star Yard. It faced south, so the sun was shining into it, but somehow the sun fell short of the corner where the niche was. Josh peered into the shadows. The niche still looked like a complete dead end. It was still cluttered with rubbish and it still stank of rotten leaves and urine. "This isn't the way I saw it last night," said Josh. "It was deeper, then. What do you think?"

"You're right. It was definitely deeper."

"So what do we do? Light the candles, and say a few words, and hope that it mysteriously changes?"

"Why not?"

Josh opened the box of candles, shook out three of them, and stuck them on to the spikes of the candleholders, in front of the niche. Several passers-by glanced at them curiously, but nobody stopped to ask them what they were doing. That was one thing that Josh liked about England: at least people pretended that they were minding their own business.

He lit the candles and stepped back. "Still doesn't look any different," said Nancy, shading her eyes with her hand.

"Maybe there's a special ritual."

"Maybe we should just recite the rhyme."

"OK," said Josh. He stood in front of the niche, with the three candles flickering at his feet, and raised both hands, palm outward, as if he were giving the benediction.

"*Six doors they stand in London Town. Six doors they stand in London, too. Yet who's to know which way they face? And who's to know which face is true?*"

He repeated the rhyme three times. Nothing happened. The niche remained solidly bricked up.

"I'm beginning to feel a little stupid here," said Josh.

"Let me try," said Nancy. She stood in front of the niche in his place. She crossed her arms high in front of her, closed her eyes, and repeated the rhyme three times. Then she said, "Great Spirit, if there is a way through here, show it to me, guide me, that I may discover the white man's Happy Hunting Ground. Show me the way, so that I may find answers for my questioning mind, and peace for my anxious heart."

She recited something else, in Modoc. Then she bowed her head and stepped back.

"What did you say?" asked Josh.

"I appealed to the Great Spirit's pride. I said that He could open any door, even a white man's door."

Josh waited beside her, but still nothing happened. Five minutes passed, and the sun went in.

"Nothing," said Nancy.

"Well . . . I guess that's it. No door. No parallel world. I never really believed in it, did you? Not in my heart of hearts. Not one hundred percent. All I can say is, it was better than thinking that some sadistic bastard had her locked up in a basement all that time."

Nancy looked down at the candles. "What are we going to do with these?"

"Leave them there. It's not much of a shrine, but it's better than no shrine at all."

They waited for a moment longer, and then they began to walk back down Star Yard toward Carey Street. A gray cat came around the corner, a gray cat with green eyes and sharply pointed ears. It had a black leather strap around its neck and a small silver cylinder was dangling from the strap. It walked up the yard at an odd diagonal, crossing in front of them.

"Here, puss," said Josh. It glanced up at him disdainfully and went on its way.

"That must be a first," said Nancy. "An animal that ignores you."

Josh stopped to watch the cat go on its haughty way up Star Yard. "What does it mean when a *gray* cat crosses your path? You're only going to have moderately bad luck?"

"Maybe it's lost," said Nancy.

"It didn't look lost."

"You never know. It had something around its neck. Maybe we should check it out."

Josh stuck two fingers in his mouth and let out three slurred whistles, like a California quail. "Here, boy! Here, Smokey! Let's take a look at you!"

"How do you know its name?"

"Because I know owners. Black cat, Lucifer. Tabby cat, Tabitha. Gray cat, Smokey. And for some reason, stick insects are always called Randy."

The gray cat ignored him and continued to walk up the yard. When it reached the candles, however, it stopped for a moment and regarded them with narrowed green eyes.

"Here, Smokey!" Josh called it. But without any warning the cat jumped over the candle flames and disappeared into the niche.

Josh and Nancy waited for a moment. "What the hell is that animal up to?" said Josh.

"It's probably doing its business."

"Great. So what I thought was the door to a parallel world was nothing more than a cat's toilet?"

All the same, Josh waited a little longer. Nancy said, "Come *on*, Josh," but Smokey still didn't reappear.

"So what's taking him so long?"

"How should I know? Maybe he's found something interesting to read."

"Jesus, Nancy, I'm being serious."

He walked back to the corner and looked into the niche. He turned back to Nancy and shrugged. "He's not here. He's vanished."

"You're sure he's not hiding under all of those leaves?"

"No. He's vanished."

Nancy looked up. On all three sides of the niche, the soot-stained walls rose more than seventy feet, up to roof level. Josh said, "He couldn't have climbed up there. Not without ropes and pitons."

"So where did he go?"

"I don't know. He just jumped over the candles, and he—"

They looked at each other. "*He jumped over the candles*," Josh repeated.

"*Jack be nimble, Jack be quick, Jack jump over the candlestick*. You didn't do that, did you? You didn't jump."

Josh looked around. Star Yard was quite busy now with people walking through it on their way to Chancery Lane – solicitors' clerks and secretaries and superior-looking barristers with their book-bags slung over their shoulders. The last thing that he wanted to do was hurl himself over the candles and collide with a solid brick wall, right in front of an audience. Especially such a stiff-upper-lip audience.

"Are you going to try it, or what?" asked Nancy.

"Sure. Sure, I'll try it."

"Well, go on then. Try it."

"What if I'm wrong?"

"Then you're wrong, that's all. Look – if you don't want to do it, I will."

"Maybe I ought to say the rhyme again."

"The cat didn't say the rhyme, did it? The cat just jumped."

Josh took a step back, ready to jump, but before he could do so, Nancy said, "For God's sake, Josh," and jumped herself.

"Nance!" Josh shouted. But Nancy didn't hit the wall. She landed on the other side of the candles, among the leaves, and in some extraordinary way the wall seemed further away, even though it wasn't. She turned to him and smiled. "*It's all right*," she said, although her voice sounded watery and strange, as if she were trying to talk to him through a diving mask. She started to make walking movements toward the wall even though she must have already reached it. She walked six or seven paces before she turned around again.

"*It's here*!" she called. Her voice sounded even more distorted. "*There's another alleyway, here to the left*!" She lifted her arm and pointed and her hand disappeared from sight, right into the brick. "*It's here, you can make your way through*!" With that, she took a step sideways and disappeared too.

Eleven

Josh shouted out, "Nancy! Nance! Wait up, will you! Nance!"

Several passers-by stared at him. He was shouting at a brick wall, after all. Three young secretaries in short skirts looked at him and burst into fits of giggles.

There was nothing left to do. He prayed to God that his faith in the jumping-over-the-candle ritual was as strong as Nancy's, and jumped.

He landed in the leaves on the other side, holding out his hand to balance himself. Nothing seemed to be different, except that the wall at the end of the niche appeared to be much further away than it was before. He turned around and looked back, and Star Yard was just the same. He could hear the shuffling of feet and the bustle of traffic and he could even feel the warm morning breeze.

He turned back and started to walk to the end of the niche. Nancy was right: there was a turning on the left, which seemed to lead to another dead end, just as it had in his hallucination. But he could hear Nancy's footsteps through the leaves ahead of him, and when he called out, "Nancy!" she called back, "Hurry up, slowpoke!" and her voice sounded normal once again.

He went to the end of the next section of alleyway, and there was another alleyway, on the right. He went down that, and turned left. As he turned the corner, he made a point of looking up. The sky was uniformly gray, just like his hallucination, and there were scores of pigeons clustered on the window ledges of the buildings on either side. His sleeves brushed against the dirty brickwork.

Nancy was waiting for him at the end of the last section of alleyway, the back of her hand lifted against her forehead. The sun wasn't shining here. In fact, it looked like rain. But as they stepped out of the niche, they were still in Star Yard, exactly where they had been before. People were still hurrying through it, swinging their briefcases, and at first the noises of a busy day in the City of London sounded just the same.

As he stood and listened, however, Josh gradually became aware of a difference in pitch. The traffic seemed to whine more; with a chug-chugging undertone; and he heard two or three motor-horns make an old-fashioned regurgitating noise, instead of the nasal beep of most modern cars. And there was a mixture of other unfamiliar sounds, too. The rumbling of cartwheels, and the clopping of horses.

Up above the rooftops he heard an abrasive droning, like a circular saw. It grew louder and louder, and he looked up to see a small stubby-winged airplane fly overhead, with a huge, idly rotating propeller, closely followed by another, and then another.

The effect was astonishing. Wonderful, and frightening, both at the same time. Josh took hold of Nancy's hand. "Jesus, Nance. We've done it. We've come through, haven't we?"

He looked back at the niche. It was exactly the same, except that there were no candles burning in front of it. "It's one of the six doors. No doubt about it. We're through. This is the parallel world."

The people who walked past them were dressed in heavy, formal clothes. Everybody wore a hat: the men in bowlers or trilbies or pork pies, the women in berets or cloches. They all wore overcoats. Nobody wore sneakers and it was noticeable how well polished their shoes were.

"Do you think we've come back in time?" asked Nancy. Several people slowed down and stared at her, in her fringed buckskin coat, her short white skirt and her knee-high buckskin boots.

"I don't know. Maybe we have. It doesn't look like anybody ever even *heard* of Adidas."

Nancy glanced anxiously back at the niche. "I just hope we can find our way back OK."

"We must be able to. If Julia was here, and they dumped her body back in the real world, then the doors must work both ways."

A young lad with a cloth cap went past, carrying a large basket heaped with loaves of bread. When he caught sight of Nancy he turned around and gave her a piercing wolf-whistle. "'Ere, miss! Left your frock at 'ome?"

"This is *so* embarrassing," said Nancy. "Even if we haven't come back in time, I don't think anybody's seen a miniskirt before."

"You could button up your coat."

"I have a *much* better idea. Let's go back and find some clothes that don't attract so much attention."

"We'll have to find some candles first."

"What? I thought you bought a whole box."

"I did, but I left them behind on the sidewalk."

"God, Josh. You're a genius. How did you think we were going to get back?"

"I didn't. I didn't really believe that we'd get here at all."

"Well, we must be able to *buy* some candles."

They walked down to the bottom of Star Yard. Most of the people who passed them were in too much of a hurry to notice them, but a rowdy group of office girls and their bowler-hatted boyfriends all stopped and stared and said, "Blimey, look at *'er*!"

When they reached Carey Street they began to realize what a different world they had walked into. The older buildings were almost all the same, except that they seemed much more heavily blackened with soot. But the road was cobbled, even if the cobbles had been covered over with tarmacadam, and the traffic that snarled it up looked as if somebody had emptied a 1930s motor museum. Rileys, Bentleys, Wolseleys – all with huge chrome-plated headlamps and sweeping mudguards and running-boards.

They made their way down Chancery Lane, past the dark Gothic windows of the Law Society building. The sidewalks on both sides of the street were crowded with people, all dressed in overcoats and hats. Josh was beginning to think that he must be the only person on the planet who wasn't wearing anything on his head. An old gentleman with a red carnation in his lapel stopped and took off his bowler hat and stared at Nancy with his mouth open, as if Mary Magdalene had just walked past him.

Fleet Street was even more crowded than Chancery Lane. The traffic was at a standstill, all the way down the hill to Ludgate Circus. A steam train crossed the railway bridge on the other side of the circus, chuffing thick brown smoke and orange sparks into the air. Through the smoke Josh could make out the dome of St Paul's Cathedral.

They crossed Fleet Street, weaving their way between buses and taxis. On the opposite corner there was a news-stand, with scores of magazines and newspapers on display. The posters for *The Evening News* announced ZEPPELIN ACCIDENT: SEVEN KILLED and RANGOON RIOTS: REBELS QUELLED. The news-vendor wore a flat cap and a long shabby coat and had a burned-down cigarette stuck to his lower lip. Every now and then, without warning, he whooped out, "'Orrible hairship haccident, seven day-ead!"

Josh offered him a fifty pence coin and said, "*News*, please."

The vendor looked down at the coin as if a pigeon had blessed the palm of his hand. "What's this, then? Bloody American, is it?"

"It's a fifty pence piece. A *British* fifty pence piece."

The news-vendor turned it this way and that, and then handed it back. "Sorry mate. Tuppence-ha'penny in real money or nothing."

"This *is* real money. Look, it has the queen's head on it."

"'Oo, the queen of Sheba?"

"The queen of England, of course."

The news-vendor turned away and served another customer, and then another, tossing their coins into the upturned lid of a biscuit tin. Nancy tugged Josh's sleeve and gave a meaningful nod of her head toward the money. There were heaps of large brown pennies, as well as small silver coins the size of dimes, and some little gold-colored ones, too, with seven or eight sides. None of them bore a likeness of Her Majesty Queen Elizabeth II.

They walked away from the newsstand, past the half-timbered frontage of The Kings Head pub, and the Wig & Pen Club. The traffic noise was so loud that they could hardly hear each other speak. On the opposite side of the road stood the Law Courts, with their wide Gothic arch and their complicated spires. As far as Josh could see, they were the same as the Law Courts in "real" London. But as they walked past, a flood of people came hurrying out, almost as if they had been cued by a movie director, all shouting at each other. Men in trilby hats and long heavy coats; women in a whole variety of hats, with ostrich feathers and veils and trailing ribbons.

A pale-faced woman in an ice-blue suit stood in the center of the crowd, and dozens of photographers clustered around her, taking pictures. They had old-fashioned flashbulbs, which Josh could hear popping, even over the traffic. One man held a heavy cine-camera on his shoulder, while his companion carried a tape recorder the size of a suitcase, and brandished an enormous black microphone.

"We *must* have traveled back in time," said Josh. "Look at this place . . . steam trains, autogiros, disposable flashbulbs, everybody wearing hats. This is more like the 1930s or thereabouts."

A stray newspaper tumbled across the sidewalk in front of him. He tried to step on it, missed, but then he stepped on it again and caught it, and picked it up. At the top of the page a large headline announced PROTECTOR GREETS PRESIDENT. There was a photograph of a black-suited man with a deathly-white face shaking hands with a tall gray-suited man with bouffant hair. In the background there was a gleaming railroad car and a station sign saying *Naseby*.

But above the headline was the date *March 17, 2001*.

"Look at this, we're still in today, leastways as far as the *date* is concerned. We're still in the same place, too, pretty much. But everything's so out of date. Like the past seventy years never happened."

Nancy was reading the crumpled-up newspaper. "Listen to this: 'Lord Pearey of Richmond Forest died at the weekend at the age of thirty-four. He contracted tuberculosis on a visit to Vienna late last year and failed to respond to a convalescence in the Scottish Highlands. His personal physician, Dr John Woollcot, described him as a brilliant young man, full of glittering promise, and called for renewed Government efforts to find a chemotherapeutic cure for tuberculosis as a matter of the gravest urgency.'"

"And look at the headline: KING'S EVIL TAKES PEER. That's a pretty quaint way of describing TB, wouldn't you say?"

Josh stopped on the corner of Arundel Street and looked around. He was trying to imagine what Julia was looking for, when she came here. It was noisy and it was smelly and it was old-fashioned but it must have appealed to her for some reason.

"You're thinking of Julia," said Nancy.

Josh nodded. "She always did have a quirky sense of humor. Do you know something, when she was a little kid, she used to pretend that she was a puppet and that she was made out of wood, and I had to tie string to her wrists and the bow on top of her head, to make her dance."

He suddenly pictured Julia's appearance at Ella's séance, her feet wildly pedaling frantically in the air. Nancy caught the sudden look of distress on his face and squeezed his hand.

They crossed over the Strand and began to walk westward toward Trafalgar Square, past dark, sour-smelling wine bars and men's outfitters with faded tropical suits and topis in the window. The sidewalks here weren't quite as crowded as Fleet Street, but everybody seemed to be walking very fast, and Josh had several irritating collisions with people who refused to deviate from their chosen path.

He found the photographic grayness of the sky more and more oppressive. It was like walking through a 1950s newsreel. The air was so polluted that he had to keep clearing his throat with a sharp, repetitious cough, and he was beginning to develop a headache.

He was struck by how dirty everything was. The "real" London was a grimy city, but this London was even worse. Very few passers-by looked as if they bathed very often. He saw clerks with soiled white collars and pimples and girls with greasy hair pinned up with criss-cross patterns of grips. Whenever they were jostled in tight with a knot of people, Josh could smell sweat and stale tobacco and a cheap, distinctive perfume like lily-of-the-valley. And almost everybody seemed to be smoking. There was no gum on the sidewalks, but the gutters overflowed with cigarette butts.

A third of the way down the Strand they found a red telephone booth, and there were two fat well-thumbed directories hanging inside it. They squashed themselves side by side into the booth and Josh hefted up one of the directories and searched for Wheatstone Electrics. Nancy peered in the mirror and said, "I don't look any different. But I *feel* different."

"Maybe you're suffering from door lag."

"Maybe I'm frightened I'm never going to get back home again."

"Here it is," said Josh at last, and he was almost sorry that he had found it. "Wheatstone Electrics, Great West Road, Brentford. Julia must have been here."

"Why don't you see if Julia's listed? She was here for ten months, wasn't she? She might have installed a phone."

Josh thumbed through residential numbers, under Winward, but there was nothing there. Then he looked up Marmion, of Kaiser Gardens, Lavender Hill, and he found her almost immediately. "She's here, look. LAVender Hill 3223. But we don't have any money to call her."

"We could try calling collect."

Josh lifted the receiver and dialed 0 for the operator.

"*Number please.*"

"I want to place a collect call to LAVender Hill 3223."

"*You mean a reverse charge call? Who shall I say is calling?*" The operator had such a clipped accent she pronounced it "kulling".

"Mr Josh Winward. No, no – tell them it's Julia's brother."

"*Hold the line, please.*"

He waited while the phone rang, and rang. Eventually, he heard a quavery woman's voice say, "'Ullo? 'Oo is it?"

"*Is that LA Vender Hill 3223? I have Julia's brother on the line. Will you accept the charges?*"

"Will I what?"

"*The caller is asking you to pay for the call.*"

"'Oo did you say it was?"

Josh broke in and said, "Tell her it's urgent, for Christ's sake. It's a matter of life and death."

"*I can't pass on any more information, sir. I'm sorry. Otherwise you could have a whole conversation, couldn't you, and you wouldn't be paying for it.*"

"Look, I have to speak to this woman. It's desperately important. My sister's been murdered, and this is the only way I'm going to find out who did it."

"*Hold on, kuller.*"

There was a pause, and then the quavery woman's voice asked, "Did you say Julia's brother? Yes . . . all right. I'll talk to him. Only for a moment, mind. I'm not made of money."

Josh said, "Mrs Marmion? Mrs Marguerite Marmion? Yes! This is Josh Winward speaking, I'm Julia Winward's brother from San Francisco."

"You are, are you? And 'oo's Julia Winward, when she's at 'ome?"

"You don't know her? I found your address amongst her belongings."

"That must've been a mistake. I've never 'eard of anybody called Julia Winward. I don't know anybody called Julia."

Josh was just about to shout at her, *Why did you agree to pay for the call, if you don't know anybody called Julia?*, when it dawned on him what Mrs Marmion was trying to tell him. She *must* have known Julia – otherwise she wouldn't have agreed to talk to him at all. But she didn't want to admit it over an open telephone line.

"So nobody called Julia ever stayed with you?"

"No. I've got a big two-bedroomed flat upstairs in my house. I wouldn't go renting it out to some chit of a secretary, would I?"

"I guess you wouldn't. How long has the flat been empty?"

"Ten months, just over."

"Do you think I could take a look at it?"

"It's full of stuff. Nobody's been round to collect it all yet."

"I see. Do you think I could just come down to Lavender Hill and talk to you, then? I'm pretty interested in renting a flat myself."

"I'm afraid that's impossible. I'm afraid. That's impossible. I really 'ave to go now. Goodbye."

Mrs Marmion hung up and Josh was left with a long disengaged tone. He replaced the receiver with a frown.

"What's the matter?" asked Nancy. A small man with a bristly moustache was standing outside the phone booth glaring at them impatiently.

Josh said, "Julia was staying with Mrs Marmion the whole time she was here. Mrs Marmion said that she didn't . . . but she knew that Julia was a secretary. I think she was saying the *opposite* of everything that was true."

"Why would she do that?"

"Maybe she suspected that her line was tapped. Maybe she's frightened. She *said* the flat was full of stuff, but I think she *meant* that somebody had been round to clear away all of Julia's belongings. When I asked her if I could go visit her, she said 'I'm afraid that's impossible'. But then she said '*I'm afraid*', like she was really afraid. And a pause, and then '*That's impossible*'."

"You're not reading something into this that wasn't there?"

"She said she didn't know anybody called Julia. But if that was true, why did she agree to talk to Julia's brother?"

"So what are we going to do now?" asked Nancy.

"We're going to go see her, of course."

"In Lavender Hill? How? It's miles away, and we don't have any parallel-Londonish money."

"I don't know . . . maybe I could hock my watch."

They were still discussing ways to get to Lavender Hill when the man with the bristly moustache rapped a coin very sharply on the window. Josh gave him a wave to show that they were nearly through.

"I still think we ought to go back and change our clothes and work out a way to pay for things," said Nancy.

"Oh, yes? Supposing we do that, and then we can't find our way back here, ever again?"

"Josh, this place is real. I can feel it. I can hear it. I can certainly *smell* it. If it's real, we can get back to it."

"What about candles?"

"There's a church on the way back to Star Yard. They must have candles in there."

Josh thought for a moment. He knew Nancy was right. They wouldn't get far without money, or suitable clothes. What would happen tonight, when they needed someplace to stay? And apart from that, he didn't think it was a good idea for them to look so conspicuous. Whoever had taken all of Julia's belongings away from her flat at Mrs Marmion's house obviously didn't want anybody to discover that Julia had ever been here. And Mrs Marmion was plainly frightened of them.

The man with the moustache rapped on the window again. Finally he tugged open the door and demanded, "Look here! Are you going to make another phone call or not? Some of us have trains to catch."

"Sure, I'm sorry," said Josh, and they stepped out of the booth and back into the crowds.

They started to walk back toward Fleet Street. The wind began to rise, and sheets of newspaper blew across the sidewalks, catching against the legs of the passers-by. A speck of grit flew into Nancy's eye, and they had to stop for a moment while Josh carefully extricated it with the dampened tip of her headscarf.

They walked as far as Kingsway, jostling their way through the crowds. As they reached the zebra crossing, however, they realized that they were the only people heading eastward, and that everybody else was hurrying west. Not just hurrying – they were walking as fast as they could possibly go without actually breaking into a run.

Josh stopped again and turned his head. "What the hell's going on here? What's the goddamned rush?"

As they crossed over the road, he looked into the faces of the tide of people coming toward them. They weren't panicking, but there was a kind of determination on their faces that was even more unsettling than panic. When he was a boy, he had seen an audience trying to escape from a burning movie theater in Santa Cruz, and these people had the same grim look. *Me. I have to save me.*

Nancy caught hold of Josh's hand to prevent herself from being jostled away. "This is so weird," she said. "Where are all these people going?"

Josh was buffeted by a large man in a flapping camel-hair overcoat. "Hey – watch it, fellow!" he called, but the man stared at him and hurried on.

"They definitely know something that we don't," said Nancy.

They reached the wide area of paving in front of the Law Courts. Only a few minutes before it had been crowded with reporters and lawyers and curious bystanders. Now it was almost deserted, except for two barristers who were hurrying into its vaulted interior as fast as they could, with their black gowns flapping.

The eastbound traffic was still solid, but dozens of people were making their way between the cars and taxis, their briefcases and umbrellas held high, as if they were wading waist-deep through water. Passengers were abandoning buses, laden with shopping bags and briefcases, and joining the throng on the sidewalks.

"I don't like this," said Josh, looking around. "Something has seriously spooked these people. It looks like Godzilla's arrived in town."

He tried to catch a man's sleeve. The man jerked up his arm, as if he expected Josh to start beating him.

"Hey!" Josh demanded. "I'm not going to hurt you! Just tell me why everybody's running!"

The man fled away without answering, colliding with a young woman pushing a large baby carriage. Josh watched him go, shaking his head. "That's one terrified dude."

"Whatever's happening, we still have to get back to Star Yard. And we still have to find some candles."

They pushed their way through the crowd until they could see the grimy facade of St Osbert's Church, which fronted directly on to the street. The traffic was still deafening, but as they came nearer, Josh thought he heard a muffled drumming sound, with a sharper *rat-a-tat-tat*! on top of it that echoed and re-echoed all the way up Fleet Street.

Nancy reached the church door and twisted the handle. "It's locked," she said. "I thought churches were always supposed to be open."

Josh gave the handle a hefty tug. The door was definitely locked and bolted, and it was made of studded black oak. There was no possible way of forcing it open.

"What do we do now?" asked Nancy.

"I saw a couple of stationery stores around the corner. Maybe they have candles. I don't know. Maybe we can improvise something out of sealing wax. In any case, I think the best thing we can do is get the hell out of here."

They had almost reached the lower end of Chancery Lane. The muffled drumming grew louder and louder, and the *rat-tat* rhythm was bouncing off the windows all along Fleet Street like hailstones. It was then that they saw what everybody was hurrying away from.

It was frightening because it was so solemn, and so out of place, like a funeral being held in the street. A procession of men all dressed in black, old-fashioned clothes, cloaks and britches and tall black hats were making their way up Fleet Street, past the Olde Cheshire Cheese pub, led by two dog-handlers with four black dogs between them, straining at their leads. Behind them came six or seven drummers, also dressed in black, with wide triangular black caps that looked like rooks' beaks. The larger drums were beating a dead-slow march time, *poom* and *poom* and *poom*. The smaller drums were rattling out an aggressive volley of noise that made it almost impossible to think.

Behind the drummers came a group of ten or eleven men, all wearing tall black hats and black capes that trailed along the sidewalk. They carried drawn swords, which Josh could see glinting in the gray daylight. Their faces looked gray, too, until Josh realized that they were wearing hoods over their heads . . . hoods with exaggerated black eyes painted on them.

"The Hooded Men," said Josh. "This may be London, 2001, but they still have those Puritan guys patrolling the streets."

"Come on, Josh, I think we ought to stay *way* out of their way."

"You're right. Let's get back to Star Yard. Maybe we won't need candles for the trip back."

They jogged up a Chancery Lane whose sidewalks were increasingly deserted. A few spots of rain began to fly in the wind. They reached Carey Street and crossed over to Star Yard.

As they entered it, however, two young men came toward them. One of them was dressed with almost ridiculous elegance in a long gray coat with a black velour collar. The other was much more bulky, with a round brown face that looked half-Burmese.

Josh took hold of Nancy's arm and drew her to one side of the yard, so that the two young men could pass them. But the thin young man stopped right beside them and the larger one moved himself in front of them so that they couldn't go any further.

"What is this?" said Josh. "A mugging, or what?"

"Depends what you've got to offer, guvnor. We're always on the lookout for novelties. Especially if they come from *over there*."

"I don't know what you're talking about."

The thin young man leaned forward and looked into Josh's face so closely that he could smell the cigarette smoke on his breath. He was elegant, he was so handsome that he was almost beautiful, but he was a wreck.

"Jack be quick?" he ventured. "*Now* do you know what I'm talking about?"

Twelve

"What do you want?" asked Josh. "If you're thinking of mugging us, you're out of luck. We don't have any money at all."

"You're a Yank," said the thin young man, cocking his head on one side like a parrot. "How about that, then? We don't often get Yanks."

"Look, we're just tourists."

"*Tourists*? You're taking a chance, ain't you?"

"What's wrong with being a tourist?"

"What's wrong with being a gob of spit in a hot frying pan? You ought to thank your lucky moons that the Hoodies didn't catch a hold of you first."

The Burmese-looking youth had his eyes half-closed in concentration and his hand cupped to his ear. "They've just turned the corner, Sy. We'd better get weaving."

The thin young man took hold of Josh's arm with a bony hand covered in silver rings. "Come on . . . let's scarper before the dogs pick up the scent."

"Listen, pal, we're not going anyplace. Especially with you."

"You ain't got much in the way of viable choices," said the thin young man. "You can't get back through the door, not today. So it looks like the dogs'll have you, less'n you follow us along. You ever see a man noshed on by dogs? Not an appetizing sight."

"You know about the door?"

"What door?"

"You said we can't go back through the door, not today. So you know about the door."

"I know where you and your good lady come from, guvnor; and I've got a good guess where you're going now. But it's no use your trying to get back there, not till the same time tomorrow. Surprised you didn't know that."

"What are you talking about?"

"It's as plain as mud, guvnor," he said, and slowly spun his finger in the air. "You can only go through the door once in every turn of the earth. Don't matter which way. Once only *per diem* and that's your lot."

"So we can't go back until the same time tomorrow, at least?"

"Not now, guvnor. And if you and your good lady don't want to end up as two matching dogs' dinners, you'd better come along with me and San here, quickish."

Josh hesitated. With the Hooded Men bearing down on them, he badly wanted to get them both back to the "real" London. But it looked as if they had run out of time. The dogs were barking and the drummers were drumming, and even if the thin young man weren't telling the truth, they still didn't have any candles.

Josh could hear the high excitement in the dogs' voices, and he knew exactly what they were yapping about. These were dogs who could smell that their quarry was close. These were dogs who smelled blood.

"How did they pick up our scent?" asked Nancy.

"Simple, missus. You lot always smell different. I can smell you myself. Soap and scent and death, that's what you lot always smell of. Even the geezers."

The drums came racketing nearer. The Hooded Men reached the corner of Carey Street and began to ricochet like grapeshot off the Bankruptcy Court buildings.

"*Josh*," said Nancy, urgently.

Without warning the dogs came sliding and snarling around the corner with their handlers barely able to hold them back. As soon as they saw Josh and Nancy and the two youths, however, the handlers let out whistles of encouragement and snapped the dogs off their leads. Josh didn't recognize the breed, but he could see that they had the barrel chests and unlockable jaws of pit bull terriers. They came bounding across the street barking insanely – spit flying, claws scrabbling on the cobbles. One of them launched itself toward Nancy as if it had been shot out of a catapult. It knocked her down to the sidewalk and started to tear at the fringes of her leather coat.

The Burmese-looking boy turned and ran up Star Yard as fast as he could; but the thin young man stayed where he was, drawing out a triangular-bladed craft-knife and crouching down in front of the dogs, daring them to go for him. "Come on, pooches! Who wants their lights cut out?"

Josh twisted around and seized the collar of the dog that was raging on top of Nancy. He wrenched it clear off the ground and slapped it across the side of the head, twice. The dog went into a frothing fury, snarling and clawing and whipping its body from side to side, but Josh raised it right up to eye level and pointed his finger at it and said, "*Stop*."

He had no idea if his usual dog hysteria management was going to work. Most of the dogs that he had dealt with before had been the neurotic pets of frustrated middle-aged women from Marin County. They hadn't been trained to rip people's hearts out, the way this animal obviously had, and he had never in his life encountered any animal in such a rage.

"*Stop*," Josh told it. But the dog kept on snarling and twisting and trying to take a bite out of Josh's forearm.

"*Stop*!" Josh yelled at it; and quite unexpectedly, it stopped, even though it was still swinging around in the air and half-strangling in its collar. "*Stop*," Josh said again, much more quietly. He turned around, stretching out his right hand, and pointed one by one at the jumping, barking animals.

"*Listen to me*!" he yelled at them. "*You are going to be calm*!" Then, as their barking diminished, "You are going to be calm. You are going to be reasonable. Listen to me. *Don't move*. You are going to think this through."

The thin young man came backing toward him, his knees bent, still waving his craft-knife from side to side. He glanced at Josh but he obviously couldn't think of anything to say. The eight attack dogs were now milling around in front of them, their tongues hanging out like red neckties, confused. Their handlers were walking across the street now, their black capes billowing, snapping their leads.

The drummers beat a long, savage roll and then they were silent. They opened their ranks so that the Hooded Men could walk between them, with their swords raised.

"Go on, Max!" shouted one of the dog-handlers; and the other one shouted too, and whipped his dogs across their backs with his lead.

Josh kept his hand raised. In spite of the noise, in spite of the confusion, he tried to radiate calm, as if he were the center of all tranquility. "You are going to stay where you are until I tell you to move. You feel happier, being calm. You feel much more fulfilled."

Strangely, he could feel the same rapport that he felt with the overfed lapdogs of Marin County, but this was even stronger, in a way. These were *real* dogs, little more than wild, and they had never been treated as if they were human – as if they were capable of thinking for themselves. It was a new experience for them, and they were bewildered.

"They're bewildered," he told Nancy.

"*They're* bewildered?" said the thin young man. "I'm bleeding *mystified*."

Josh dropped the dog that had attacked Nancy and it shook itself and trotted back toward its handler. The man threw back the hood of his cloak. He was shaven-headed and scarred, with a heavy gray moustache, and half of one of his ears was missing. Without taking his eyes off Josh, he reached down and looped the dog's lead around its neck, and twisted it tight. Then, with a grunt, he started to throttle it.

The dog made a thick choking noise and struggled wildly, but the handler kicked it in the stomach. He kicked it again and again, until the animal was limp, and then he picked it up by its hind legs, swung it over his head, and smashed its skull against the granite curb. There was a hollow *crack!* and bright red blood and bright beige brains were spattered all over the other dogs, who visibly flinched. "*Go*!" the handler screamed at them, "*Go*! Or the same thing's going to happen to you!"

The dogs hesitated, confused, yipping and yapping and thrashing their tails.

"*Go*!" screamed the handler; and it was now that the Hooded Men approached, their sackcloth faces blank and threatening, their swords held high.

"*Take them*!" ordered a harsh, thick voice. Josh couldn't tell who it was, but one of the Hooded Men kicked the dog's carcass to one side and deliberately stepped on its shattered head, so that its one remaining brown eye was squeezed out of its socket.

The thin young man took two or three steps back. "I hope you're light on your feet, missus," he told Nancy.

"Let's just get out of here, shall we? You direct us, we'll follow."

"They'll have you, if they catch you. You'll wish you was dead, believe me."

The Hooded Men were beginning to circle them now, but they were playing their attack very cautiously. Their swords were very long, thin-bladed, with plain cruciform handles, and they looked extremely sharp. Because of their hoods, their faces seemed even more threatening, like scarecrows that had come to life, to seek their revenge.

One of them said, in a muffled voice, "In the name of the Lord Protector of the Commonwealth you are detained for trespass. Come quiet, and you will have nothing to fear, so help me God. Resist, and your fate will be the talk of all damnation."

Josh kept his hand raised and his eye on the dogs. Their handlers were whipping them now, and cursing them, and he knew that he couldn't control them for very much longer. "When I say 'run'," said Josh, "don't even think about it – go like hell." He paused for two or three seconds, and then he shouted, "*Run*!"

Nancy galloped up Star Yard with her buckskin fringes flying, and even though she was wearing high-heeled boots Josh found it almost impossible to keep up with her. The thin young man was right behind him, his coat whirling up. The dogs were so close that they were almost biting at their heels, barking hysterically, but all the barking and the shouting of their handlers and the jingling of swords and scabbards were drowned out by a shattering drumbeat. *Ratta-tatta-ratta-tatta-tat*!

As they rounded the first corner, the thin young man said, "In here!" and pushed open a flaking, black-painted door. Nancy had run so far ahead that Josh had to give her a sharp dog-whistle to call her back.

The thin young man slammed the door behind them and jammed it with a broken chair. "Where does this lead?" asked Josh, as he stumbled along a hallway stacked with faded rolls of floral wallpaper, paint-caked buckets and stepladders.

"Upstairs, guvnor," panted the thin young man. "Upstairs and over the roof. Dogs can't follow you through thin air."

Gasping for breath, they climbed up one bare-boarded flight of stairs after another. There was a strong smell of damp and mildew in the building and as they climbed higher, Josh could see that half of the slates were missing, and the attic was open to the sky. On either side they passed derelict rooms with no floorboards, still decorated with faded wallpaper, their fireplaces clogged with ash.

Four floors below them, they heard the front door being kicked open, and the wild barking of dogs. The thin young man said, "Follow me," and led them up a narrow staircase into the attic. Again, all of the floorboards were missing, and they had to cross the attic by balancing from one joist to the next, taking care not to catch their feet on any protruding nails. They could look down and see the rooms two and even three floors lower down, and hear the clattering of dogs coming up the stairs.

The far side of the roof was already stripped of tiles, and the wind made gusty, fluffing noises through the rafters. The thin young man led them out on to the narrow parapet, ninety feet above Chancery Lane. "Oh God, Josh," said Nancy. "You know how much I hate heights."

"You climbed up Spirit Rock, didn't you?" Josh reminded her. "That was three times higher than this."

"That was different. I had my ancestors around me then, to catch me if I fell."

Josh gripped her hands and kissed her forehead. "I'll catch you, if you fall."

They stepped out on to the parapet, one after the other, with the thin young man leading the way. There was nothing between them and the street below except for a low wall of sooty bricks, and they didn't look very safe. They could see the tops of buses and taxis and people hurrying along the sidewalk. Although it was such a pearly, overcast day they could see right over the rooftops of the Public Record Office toward the misty dome of St Paul's, and the twin Gothic towers of Tower Bridge. Josh was surprised to see that there were no tall buildings in the City – no NatWest building, no Canary Wharf.

"Hurry up," snapped the thin young man. "We ain't got time for seeing the sights."

He balanced along to the very end of the parapet, and Josh and Nancy followed him, their arms spread wide. "Eat your heart out, Blondin," said Josh, his heart thumping. Nancy gave a nervous, hysterical laugh.

When the thin young man reached the corner of the building, he crouched down behind the parapet and beckoned them to join him. They looked over the edge and saw the Hooded Men gathered in Star Yard, directly below them. A few curious people were standing around, but only a few, and when the Hooded Men turned their heads toward them they covered their faces with their hands and hurried off.

"Who *are* these characters?" asked Josh. "Are they like cops, or what?"

"Cops?"

"Policemen. Bobbies. Is that what they are?"

The thin young man didn't answer him, but stood up, and pointed to the parapet of the building opposite. It was about a foot higher than the building on which they were standing, and it had a curved coping on top of it, encrusted with pigeon-droppings. In fact there was a matronly pigeon sitting on it not far away, blinking at them with suspicion.

"We've got to jump," said the thin young man.

"You're kidding me," Josh retorted.

"It's the only way, guvnor. It's jump, or give yourself up to the Hoodies. Do you know what they do? They eat the pancreas out of you, while you're still alive. Or else they make you play the Holy Harp."

"The Holy Harp? What the hell's that?"

"I'll give you the SP later, guvnor. But, believe me, you don't really want to find out. Not first-hand, anyway."

Nancy gripped Josh's arm. "I can't do this, Josh. I can't jump across there. It's much too far."

They heard shouting inside the derelict building, and the noise of doors being broken and loose floorboards tossed aside. And above it all, the dogs barking. Josh could hear that their handlers had worked them up into a frenzy of fear and anger. They knew that if they didn't catch their quarry, they would be beaten or even killed. They were hunting for their own survival and nobody could pacify them now.

"Come on, Nance. Those dogs are going to rip us apart."

"Can't we just give ourselves up? We haven't *done* anything, after all."

"Ha, ha," said the thin young man. "You don't think that you have to *do* anything, do you? The Hoodies will carve you up, guilty or innocent."

"Nance," Josh urged her. "You have to make this jump, whether you're scared out of your mind or not." He lifted his finger to her. "Concentrate. That's all you have to do. Concentrate on the wall at the other side."

She stood up on top of the parapet, on the very edge. The wind lifted her hair and made her bandanna flutter. Josh heard a banging sound inside the attic, and a handler appeared with two dogs shrieking for breath on the end of a leash.

"*Jump!*" he shouted at Nancy. She stumbled in her boot-heels and jumped. She managed to catch the top of the parapet opposite, but only just, and she almost lost her grip altogether.

"*Josh!*" she screamed.

Josh shouted, "I'm coming! Find yourself a toehold!"

"What toehold?" she said, her boots scrabbling at the brickwork. "Josh, there isn't a toehold!"

"Listen, I'm coming across. I'm coming across and I'm going to take hold of your hand and pull you up."

The thin young man stared at Josh with his wild blue eyes. "You're going to have to jump right over her," he said, in horror. "How are you going to do that?"

Josh looked at the roof behind him. There were no tiles left on it, but the rafters were intact and still studded with large rusty nails. He stood up and started to climb the nearest rafter, hand over hand, using the nails for toeholds.

"Josh!" screamed Nancy. "Josh, my hands are slipping!"

Josh climbed halfway up to the apex of the roof. He could see the dogs now: they were scrambling along the narrow gutter with their handlers close behind. The thin young man had picked up a heavy piece of rafter and was swinging it from side to side, ready to defend himself.

Josh turned, and stood up. He was caught by a sudden gust of wind, and for an endless three seconds he was desperately trying to stop himself from falling.

"*Come on, Winward*!" He could almost hear his instructor in the Marines, screaming at him in frustration. "*Whatever the fuck you're going to do, don't just stand there – do it*!"

He found his balance, and paused. Then he shouted out, "*Yaaahhhhhhh*!" and ran down the sloping rafter, jumping between the nails like a gazelle. It was mad, but he was running so fast that he didn't fall over. He reached the edge of the roof and gave one last hop, skip and jump, which took him right up into the air. And in that split second he thought: Jesus, I'm not going to make it. The parapet loomed up in front of him, much higher than he had expected it to be.

"*Hold on*!" he screamed at Nancy, because he was sure he was going to hit her, and drag both of them down to the flagstones ninety feet below. But he cleared the parapet by less than an inch, his left heel actually clipping it, and he fell heavily on to the gray shingled roof of the building opposite, rolling over and hitting his shoulder on a chimney stack.

Immediately, he stood up and hobbled back to the parapet. He leaned over and took hold of Nancy's hand. "Here! Pull yourself up! Quick!"

He heaved her up, inch by inch, and at last she was able to grip the top of the brickwork and pull herself over.

"God, I thought I was going to meet my ancestors then, for sure!"

Back on the other side, the thin young man was lashing out at the dogs with his nail-studded rafter. One of them managed to dodge around his feet and jump up on to his shoulders, biting at his neck. But he swung the rafter right over his head and hit it in the back with an audible crunch. He twisted the rafter around and the dog dropped over the side of the building and into the yard below.

He climbed up on the edge of the roof, swaying. Josh shouted, "*Jump*! *I'll catch you*!"

Nancy said, "Why, Josh? He was out to mug us!"

"He helped us escape, didn't he? And he knows a whole lot more about this world than we do. He can help us, Nance. We can't just leave him here!"

Nancy shook her head. But whatever she thought, it was too late, because the thin young man suddenly launched himself toward them, his arms outstretched. At the same instant, one of the dogs jumped after him, and caught his coat in its teeth.

Josh stretched out with both hands and snatched at the young man's wrists as he stumbled against the parapet. The dog, still clinging to the hem of his coat, was thrown against the wall. It didn't yelp, though, or open its jaws.

There was a moment when Josh thought he was going to let the young man fall. He was holding his full weight, as well as the weight of the dog, and the young man's wrists were gradually sliding between his fingers. But then he looked down at the dog, and the dog looked balefully back up at him, and their eyes locked.

"Let go!" Josh ordered.

The dog growled and swung from side to side on the tails of the young man's coat, but it wouldn't release its grip.

"Didn't you hear me, you disobedient mutt? Let go!"

On the edge of the building opposite, the dog-handler shouted out, "Goethe! Hang on! You hear me, Goethe? Hang on, you miserable cur, or I'll have your coddled brains for breakfast!"

"Christ, I'm slipping," said the thin young man. He glanced

down at the paving stones far below him and then he looked back up at Josh in desperation. "God save me! Please, God, I won't ever steal again."

At that moment, the dog-handlers started to throw lumps of timber and broken slates at them. One piece of wood hit Josh on the arm, and a slate hit him on the side of the head, cutting his ear. Blood ran down the side of his cheek and dripped on to the young man's face.

A heavy piece of rafter hit the thin young man on the back. He shouted out in pain, and lurched around, and his right hand broke free from Josh's fingers. Josh clawed the air, but he couldn't reach his wrist again. The young man was dangling now from one wrist only, with a dog hanging from his coat, and Josh knew from experience that it could take two men and a crowbar to pry that dog's jaws open.

Josh ducked his head as he was again pelted with slates and lumps of asphalt. Nancy, crouched behind the parapet, said, "Josh! You're going to have to let him go!"

"How can I?" said Josh, one eye closed against the blood. "Jesus, Nance, if I let him go he's going to die!"

He shouted down to the dog again. "Goethe! Are you listening to me, Goethe? You're a great dog, Goethe, you've done real good! Why don't you bark for me, Goethe? How about barking for me? Come on, Goethe! Bark!"

"Goethe! Silence!" his handler retaliated.

But Josh and the dog were staring at each other, and Josh knew that he had captured its complete attention. "Bark, Goethe," he repeated. "Bark and show me what a good dog you are."

The dog hesitated, but then it barked, just once – and once was enough. It tried to snap at the thin young man's coat-tails again, but it missed, and it dropped howling all the way to the ground, its paws still scrabbling for something to cling on to. It hit the flagstones with a flat, barely audible thud. Josh saw its blood running across the paving and felt worse than Judas.

He tugged at the young man's wrist, and pulled him up far enough to grab his other hand. Nancy seized his coat collar, and between the two of them they managed to heave him up over the parapet and on to the roof. He lay on his back for a moment, saying, "God, oh God. I thought I was ready for the cold cook then. I swear it. I really thought I was brown bread."

"They're breaking into the building downstairs," said Josh. "We have to get out of here pronto."

The thin young man sat up, and he was immediately showered in fragments of broken slate and pieces of brick. "Right, then. Let's go. It's not so difficult from here. We'll be in Lincoln's Inn Fields before the Hoodies even reach the second floor."

Keeping their heads down, they negotiated their way between the chimneys and crossed the roof to the other side. The dog-handlers carried on pelting them with slates and rafters. A dead pigeon came cartwheeling across, thumping against Nancy's back. But when the dog-handlers realized that they were getting away, they turned back from the building's edge. They began to run downstairs again, shouting out to the Hooded Men to hurry.

Josh and Nancy jumped across to the next building, which was lower; and then to the next, and the next. A whole row of rooftops were connected by iron ladders, and then there was some more jumping, and a climb down a fire escape. By the time they reached the corner of Serle Street, the shouting and the drumming were nothing but echoes in another street.

The thin young man led them down the dusty, neglected staircases of another old building, and then they were out in Lincoln's Inn Fields and across the gardens, just as it started to rain.

Thirteen

"If I can trust you with my life," said the thin young man, lighting the gas under a battered kettle, "I think I can probably trust you with my name." He came back into the junk-filled living room and held out his hand. "Simon Cutter. The *famous* Simon Cutter, of the Clerkenwell Cutters. Like, if you get into an occasional spot of bother anywhere in Clerkenwell, or Holborn, or Finsbury Park, all you have to do is say the magic words, 'I'm a mate of the famous Simon Cutter,' and all your problems will melt away like . . ." He thought for a moment, his hand still extended, and then he said, "Margarine."

"Well, that's good to know," said Josh. "But I'm doing my best not to get into any spots of bother anyplace at all. Even occasional spots of bother."

"Ah, but you never know, do you? Bother is one of those unpredictable things. Like you're walking along the street minding your own business, tooty-too, tooty-too, and *whallop*!"

Josh looked around the room. "You lived here long?"

"Three years. I've been wanting to move, but you know . . . it's all my *stuff*."

From Lincoln's Inn Fields, Simon had led them through the backstreets to a two-bedroomed apartment on top of a brown-painted furniture shop in Gray's Inn Road. It was a gloomy, crowded place to live, its windows covered with amber blinds and its floors stacked with every conceivable kind of clutter: suitcases, chairs, empty fishtanks, umbrellas, typewriters, stags' heads, gramophones, boxes of gramophone records and teetering stacks of books. There was more bric-à-brac in the bedrooms, including a mahogany washstand

and the front wheel from a penny-farthing bicycle. In the bathroom there was a stuffed ocelot and a Zulu spear. The kitchen overlooked a shadowy ventilation shaft, where, against all odds, a sycamore tree had managed to grow out of a crevice in the bricks, twenty-five feet above the ground. Every available shelf and counter in the kitchen was crammed with jars and pots and coffee percolators and cheese graters and extraordinary patent devices for coring apples.

San was there, too, standing in the corner in a bronze satin bathrobe with dragons embroidered on it, ironing a black silk shirt and listening to the radio, which was turned down to a mutter, interspersed with occasional bursts of laughter.

"You're quite a collector," said Josh, picking up one of the books and leafing through it. *A British Traveller's Guide To Far-Flung Destinations*, published 1971.

"Well, yes, but I don't collect it conscious-like. It just a-coomalates. Every time I walk out the door I seem to a-coomalate more and more stuff. I've just got so much . . . a-coomalated stuff."

"So, what, you're a dealer?"

"You could say that. Somebody wants something, I can usually oblige. And they're always crying out for anything from Purgatory. Watches, pens, perfumes. They'll even buy those mobile phones, not that they ever work."

"Excuse me? What did you say? Purgatory?"

Simon looked embarrassed. "I'm sorry. I didn't mean to offend. I know you people don't call it that."

Nancy said, "You think we came from *Purgatory*?"

Simon gave her a cautious shrug.

"You think we're *dead*? You think we're spirits, who didn't quite make it to heaven?"

Simon shrugged again, and in the kitchen the kettle began to whistle like a crushed canary. Nancy lifted Simon's hand and pressed it against her cheek. "Do I feel dead to you?"

"I don't know. I never really touched nobody from Purgatory before. Not intimate-like."

"But we're walking around and talking to you," said Josh. "Dead people don't normally do that, do they?"

"Ah! Yes! But there's dead, ain't there, and then there's *gone beyond*. You people from Purgatory, you're not the same as your run-of-the-mill cold meat, are you? You've been sent back to give it another go. Too bent for heaven and too straight for hell, that's it, isn't it?"

"Well, it's a great idea. I only wish it was true. The trouble is, that particular description would fit seventy-five percent of the population of Marin County."

Simon took the kettle off the gas. "So you didn't come from Purgatory? You *look* like all the other people I've seen, what come from Purgatory. Same kind of clothes."

"Have you seen many others?"

"Not a lot. Six or seven every year. Sometimes only one or two. One year none. And if I'm not sharpish, the Hoodies get to them first, and then they scuttle them off before I get the chance to . . . well, you know. Before I get the chance to say 'how-d'you-do'."

"You mean before you get the chance to rob them?"

"I take umbrage to that, guvnor. I'm a collector, not a foin."

"Oh, a collector. I see. But is that what the Hoodies tell you, that these people come from Purgatory?"

"The Hoodies don't tell nobody nothing. The Hoodies is the Hoodies. Everybody learns about Purgatory, from school. *A Child's Book of Simple Truth*."

"So you've *always* believed that people who come through the door come from Purgatory? Since you were small?"

Simon poured out tea, and nodded.

"Haven't they ever told you any different? The people themselves?"

"I never talked to a Purgatorial before. Not conversational."

"You mean you just robbed them and that was it?"

"Be fair, guvnor, I didn't have time for the finer points of parlary, did I? It was touch-and-go to fleece them before the Hoodies showed up. And oftener than not, the Hoodies got there first. Or some other chancer."

"Tell me something about the doors. Is there any way that you can tell that somebody's just about to come through?"

"It's like dowsing for water, guvnor. You got to have the feel for it."

"So you *can* tell? And that means you can be lying in wait for anybody who steps out?"

"It's possible, yes, guvnor. There are ways and ways. But it ain't all that easy. The only guaranteed way to catch the Purgatorials one hundred percent is to stand by the door twenty-four hours through the day and never get no kip. But – if you know what you're looking for, you can see the door change. Something in the *substance* of it, like that wobbly air you get, when the roads are hot. *You* came through it: you must have seen it for yourself. Me and San, we walked through the Yard today, and we saw the door was different-like, just the faintest of wobbles, and that's when we knew that somebody had opened it. That's why we was hanging around, waiting for you. Purgatorials generally come back to the door they come through, given an hour or two, although I never know why."

"The Hooded Men . . . were they aware that we had come through, too?"

"Oh, yes. They always know. That's why they was coming after you. Don't ask me *how* they know. But nobody comes through them doors without the Hoodies being there in five or ten minutes at the most. Then *phwwitt!* that's it, they're catched and off to wherever they take them."

"But if the Hoodies don't want us here," said Nancy, "why don't they simply close the doors off? Brick them up, so nobody can get through?"

"Because bricking them up wouldn't make no difference. The doors is always there, even if you build a church on top of them. I know for a fact that one of the doors is right slap bang in the middle of the river these days, even though it must have been on dry land, when it was first opened up."

"You know where all the other doors are?" asked Josh.

"I wish I did. There's one at Southwark, I do know that, on the corner of Bread Street and Watling Street. My old china Crossword Lenny looks after it, so to speak. I heard there was some up west, too, but as for their precise whereabouts, you'd have to ask an expert on doors and their precise whereabouts, if there is such a person."

They cleared books and magazines out of the seats of the huge sagging armchairs and sat back and sipped their tea out of thick British Railways cups. Josh was beginning to feel exhausted – not only from their chase across the rooftops of Chancery Lane, but because this world in which he and Nancy had found themselves was so familiar, and yet so disturbingly different. It *felt* different. There were different noises, different smells, different sounds; and when Simon and San talked together, they used words that Josh had never heard of, and referred to events that had never happened. Not in the "real" world, anyhow. He thought, even if you went to Beijing, you could say "McDonald's!" or "Julia Roberts!" and people would know what you were talking about. Here, they simply didn't exist, and never had.

"What if I said to you, 'the Beatles'?" Josh asked Simon.

Simon looked uneasy. "The beetles? I don't understand."

"The Beatles. The 1960s pop group."

"Pop? Group? What's that?"

"You've never heard of the Beatles?"

"Never."

"The Rolling Stones? Glenn Campbell? Hootie and the Blowfish? The Doors?"

"I don't understand."

Nancy said, "All right . . . let me ask you something more serious. What is the name of the current President of the United States?"

"The United States of what?"

"The United States of America, of course."

"Oh, America! Well, America doesn't have a *president*. They have a Lord Protector, like us."

"No President? No White House?"

Simon was completely bemused. "Why don't you have some more tea?" he asked them.

"Don't you British have royalty any more?" Josh wanted to know. "What about the Queen and Prince Charles and the Duke of Edinburgh?"

"The last king was Charles I. Sixteen-something. Chopped his bonce off, didn't they?"

"So who ruled England after him?"

"The same people that run it now. The Commonwealth."

"And America is being run by the Commonwealth?"

"Of course."

Josh said, "What about World War Two?"

Simon shook his head.

"You've never heard of World War Two? When America and Britain got together and fought against the Germans?"

"We never fought the *Germans*," said Simon, as if the very idea of it was totally ridiculous.

"What about the Japanese? Did you ever hear of Pearl Harbor? How about Hiroshima, and the atom bomb?"

"Sorry, guvnor."

"All right, then, let's go back a bit. World War One? No? Fighting in the trenches? No? How about the *Titanic*? No? You must have heard of the American Civil War, north versus south. You must have heard of Abraham Lincoln."

"No . . . I don't think so. I've heard of Lincoln cars, they're American, aren't they?"

Josh sat back. "OK, tell me. What was the most important worldwide event of the past decade? In your opinion?"

Simon sucked in his breath. "Whooo . . . that's a tough one."

"You know what it was?" put in San, still meticulously ironing, and hanging up his shirt. "It was Miss Burma, winning the Miss World Competition."

"Listen to him!" said Simon, in mock disgust. "No . . . I reckon the most important thing that happened was them two geezers flying round the world in a Zeppelin. It won't be long before anybody can fly practically anywhere they like."

"How about that?" said Josh, turning to Nancy. "No World War One . . . no World War Two. I guess that's why everything's sixty years out of date. No jet engines. No antibiotics. There's nothing like a war to speed up new inventions."

"It's all wars, is it, where you come from?" said Simon.

"Not entirely. There hasn't been a major war in over half a century. And at least we don't have Hooded Men."

"You don't? What do you do about the Catholics?"

"We don't do anything about the Catholics. Being a Roman Catholic isn't a crime, where we come from."

"Blimey." Simon rummaged in his coat pocket and took out a small cream-colored pack of Player's Weights cigarettes. He lit one and blew a series of smoke rings. "Seems like a bloody dodgy kind of place to me. All wars and popery."

Josh looked down at the dog-torn hemline of Simon's overcoat. "Depends on your definition of bloody dodgy."

San finished his ironing and went into the kitchen. "I hope everybody's hungry," he said; and without waiting for an answer he started chopping onions.

"You'd better kip here tonight," said Simon. "The Hoodies'll be out looking for you still. Tomorrow you can go back through the door and find yourselves some decent clobber. Bring me some pens and some watches and anything else that you can think of and I'll get you some dosh and anything else you need. Maps, tube passes, little black books."

"Little black books?"

Simon reached in his pocket and produced a small, worn-out, leather-bound book. "*The Sayings of Oliver Cromwell.* Everybody has to carry one. Do you know what my favorite saying is? 'Necessity hath no law'. In other words, guvnor, what you has a need of, you furnishes yourself with."

"Tomorrow I want to go to Kaiser Gardens and Wheatstone Electrics," said Josh. "Maybe you'd like to come along and help us. You know, act as our scout."

"Fair enough. So long as you make it worth my while."

Josh took off his gold-plated Polo wristwatch and handed it over. "How about this, for a down payment?"

Simon held it to his ear. "It ain't going to croak on me, is it? Some of them do, and you can't wind them up."

"The batteries probably ran out. I'll bring you some spares."

Simon stood up and climbed through the junk like a mountain goat. He noisily dragged the top drawer out of an antique bureau, and carried it over to the table in the center of the room.

"You must tell me how this works," he said, and produced a Nokia mobile phone. "I know it's a telephone, of sorts, but I can't get a squeak out of it."

Josh shook his head. "It won't work here. It needs a communications satellite, and I don't suppose you have communications satellites, do you?"

Simon looked baffled. Josh pointed to the ceiling and said, "In orbit? In space? You've never sent up rockets or anything like that? You've never sent men to the moon?"

Nancy was sifting through the contents of the drawer. "Look at this stuff, Josh. How many missing people do you think *this* represents?"

The drawer was crammed with credit cards, driving licenses, checkbooks, passports, letters, pens, diaries, theater tickets, restaurant receipts, combs, buttons and photographs of children. Josh picked up an ID card from the University of Michigan. A podgy, bespectacled face stared up at him. David L. Burger, Professor of Applied Physics. How had *he* wandered into this parallel London, and where was he now?

Josh held the passport up so that Simon could see it. "When did this guy come through?"

Simon shrugged. "I don't know. I can't remember."

"Roughly when?"

"I don't know, six months ago, something like that."

"He came through the Star Yard door?"

Simon looked shifty, and shrugged again.

"Come on, Simon. You must know which door he came through. Jesus, you were waiting there to jump on him!"

"We wasn't. We bumped into him round the back of Oxford Street, that's all. We didn't even know he was a Purgatorial, until we rooked him."

"So you don't know how he got here, or how long he'd been here, or which door he used?"

"No, guvnor."

Josh carefully laid the ID card back in the drawer, as if he were laying Professor Burger to rest. "So what happened to him afterwards? After you 'rooked' him?"

"How should I know? He hit his head on the curb and there

was lots of ketchup. I never heard no more about him. The Hoodies got him, more than likely."

"How come they hadn't got him before?"

"I can't guess, guvnor."

In the kitchen, San was busy chopping and frying, and the flat was filled with the aromatic smell of chicken and garlic and lime leaves.

Nancy picked up Professor Burger's passport, too. "What are you getting at, Josh?"

"How does a professor in applied physics from the University of Michigan find out how to pass through to a parallel world in London, England? And when he does find out, why does he do it? And *when* did he do it?"

"What does 'when' matter?"

"If he's been here only a matter of minutes, or hours, then he's simply been lucky, and the Hooded Men haven't caught up with him yet. But what if he's been here longer? Like days, or weeks, or even longer than that? Supposing he's been here ten months, like Julia? How come the Hooded Men haven't picked him up? How come they didn't pick *her* up?"

"I still don't understand what you're driving at."

"Suppose he's been here for months, how does he survive? What does he live on? If he's openly walking around Oxford Street, presumably he's not too worried about being caught. He must be here by arrangement, like Julia. He must have a job of some kind. My guess is that some people stray here by accident, or because they find out about the Mother Goose rhyme, the way we did. But other people come here by invitation, like Julia. And maybe like Professor Burger, too. For all we know, there could be hundreds of people from the 'real' London living here. People who just wanted to escape, the same way Julia did. People looking for another chance."

San cleared a space on the coffee table and set out four plates of Burmesc fried chicken and rice, with chunks of canned pineapple and dandelion-leaf salad with a chili dressing. They all sat cross-legged on the floor and ate with an assortment of spoons. Josh's had a horn handle and a silver Scottish crest on it. He hadn't realized how hungry he was until he actually started to eat.

Nancy said, "This parallel world could explain so much. It could explain where people disappear to. You know, like those schoolgirls in *Picnic at Hanging Rock*."

"That was in Australia."

"Sure . . . but who's to say that there aren't hundreds of doors, all over the world? I'll bet you if you look into every single mythology there's some kind of reference to parallel worlds, and how to get through to them. There are so many references to 'spirit gates' and 'ways through' in Modoc legend; and the Irish have their land of the fairies, don't they?"

Josh helped himself to more rice. "I don't know what to think. Right now I feel like I'm right on the edge of going crazy. If I wasn't sitting here, eating this chicken, I wouldn't believe it, any of it."

Nancy said, "You've cooked a great meal, San."

"Thank you," said San, bowing his head politely. "My mother taught me. She believed that every man who calls himself a man should learn to cook."

"My compliments to your mother. Is she still out in Burma?"

San nodded. "My family, too. My sisters, my cousins. But I don't hear from them any more."

"Is there some kind of trouble in Burma?" Josh asked him. "Where we come from, Burma isn't called Burma any more. It's called Myanmar, and it's run by a bunch of generals."

"Burma is still Burma, but Burma is British. The Puritans tried to convert the Buddhists to Christianity, and there was bad fighting. Much ketchup. Many Burmese martyrs. That was why I came here, to London. I thought that I could talk to the Puritans. I thought that I could persuade them to change their minds, and let us worship Buddha in our own way."

"And?"

"And he nearly got skinned alive for being an impertinent wog and he ended up with me," Simon explained.

"So what now?" said Josh.

"Nothing in particular," said Simon. "If he goes back to

Burma, he'll be hung up by his heels and his tongue cut out. If he stays here, he'll have to keep away from the Hoodies and go on scavenging for a living with yours truly. Not a pretty choice. But I think he'd rather scavenge than swing, wouldn't you, San?"

San smiled, and nodded. He had such grace that Josh found it hard to believe that anybody would want to persecute him.

"I'll tell you something," said Simon. "He's got the lightest fingers that I've ever seen. He could be halfway to Holland Park with your best braces before your trousers fell down."

"You must miss your family so badly," said Nancy.

"Love always brings pain," San told her, with candle flames shining in his dark brown eyes. "If a thing doesn't hurt, then what is its value?"

By the time they had finished their meal, it was growing dark outside, and the small square of sky that Josh could see from the kitchen window was the color of royal blue ink. San washed the plates and Nancy dried them, while Josh and Simon talked about tomorrow. Josh was worried that once they had gone back through the door to find themselves some suitable clothes, they wouldn't be able to find their way back again.

"You still don't believe this is really real, do you, guvnor?" said Simon. His pronunciation was almost Dickensian – "veely veel".

Josh leaned back in his armchair. He was so tired that he felt that he was hallucinating. "No . . . I guess that's the problem. It's more like a dream. I keep thinking that I'm going to wake up and none of this has happened."

"You wait till you find the toe-rag that killed your sister. Then it won't seem like a dream."

They were still talking when they heard dogs barking outside; and doors slamming; and windows slamming, too.

"What's the matter?" asked Josh. San went to the window and peered through the split-bamboo blind.

"I can't see nothing. Whoever it is, they're staying well out of sight."

There was more banging, more barking. Then suddenly,

within the building, they heard the tearing, creaking sound of a door being forced off its hinges, and glass breaking, and men shouting. Footsteps came running upstairs. Another door broke, and Josh heard a flat, uncompromising bang as it dropped to the floor.

"They've found us," said Simon. "God knows how, but they have."

"How the hell did they find us here?"

"Grasses," said Simon, contemptuously. "The Hoodies only have to offer them a couple of quid, and they'll sell their maiden aunts."

San said, "I'll hold the door. You get out on the roof."

The access to the skylight was tiny: a small window not more than two feet square, in the center of the living-room ceiling. Simon dragged the coffee table underneath it and then balanced a chair on top. He mounted the chair and banged at the tiny window with his clenched fist until he managed to dislodge it. A shower of rust and leaves came down, as well as a tiny fledgling, no more than two days old, already green with decay.

"You first," said Simon, taking Nancy's hand. "Climb out on the roof and keep your head down. Wait by the chimney stack."

Josh said, "You don't have to come with us, either of you. You haven't done anything wrong, have you?"

"You're joking, guvnor. San's a political fugitive and I've got a drum full of other people's property. They'll Holy-Harp us without a blink."

Heavy footsteps reverberated on the landing outside. San locked and bolted the door and stood with his back to it. Nancy climbed on to the coffee table, and then on to the chair, and climbed awkwardly out of the skylight, her boots kicking behind her. There was a violent knocking on the door, and the handle was shaken so furiously that it dropped off on to the floor.

"*Open up, in the name of the Commonwealth*!"

"Hurry," Simon urged; and Josh climbed out on the roof, too. Nancy was already waiting by the chimney stack, but he knelt down beside the skylight and held out his hand to help Simon climb up after him.

There was a devastating crash as the Hooded Men tried to force down the door – then another, and another. The door frame cracked and plaster sifted on to San's shoulders. He kept his back pressed against the woodwork, his knees braced, and there was a look of grim determination on his face.

Josh climbed up on to the coffee table. "Come on, San! Before they break the whole goddamned door down!"

"Just go!" San told him.

There was another crash as the Hooded Men kicked against the door panels, and one of the lower panels split. San stood with his arms outspread, his teeth gritted, his heels digging into the threadbare carpet.

"Come on, San!" Simon shouted at him. "You can't hold them back for ever!"

San braced himself, ready to abandon the door and make his escape through the skylight. But as he did so, the point of a brightly shining sword came darting out of the middle of his chest. Another came out of his left shoulder, and a third penetrated his right thigh. He opened his mouth wide, as if he were going to scream, but before he could do so, another sword-blade leaped out from between his lips, like a shining steel tongue.

Fourteen

Two more swords came through the door – one of them jabbing out of San's stomach and the second out of his upper arm.

San stared up at Simon and Josh in helpless agony, the sword-blade still sticking out of his mouth, with blood dripping from the tip of it. "Aaarrghhh," he gargled, and reached out with one hand, but that was all he could manage.

Simon shouted, "Hold on, San! I'm coming to get you!"

"Are you out of your mind?" said Josh.

"He's my mate," said Simon, his face gray and his eyes aglitter with shock.

"Simon – there's nothing you can do. He's as good as dead already."

San stared back at them, unable to move. The door shook again, and again, and San's knees began to buckle.

"Sod this, I can't just watch him die!" said Simon, and swung his legs back down into the skylight.

Josh seized his arm. "Don't! You'll only make it worse!"

"What could be worse than watching this? Tell me? What in the whole of God's creation could be worse than watching this?"

The door repeatedly shook as the Hooded Men kicked and battered against it, and with each shake, San sank a little lower. His bathrobe was covered in rapidly widening maps of blood, and blood was running down his ankles and spreading across the carpet.

"Simon, we ought to go," Josh persisted. "I've got Nancy to think of now."

Suddenly, the door burst open, and San was temporarily

swung out of their view. The dogs came bursting in, followed by the dog-handlers, and close behind the handlers came four or five Hooded Men. For a moment, Josh could see the handles of their swords protruding from the other side of the door. He couldn't even guess what unnatural strength it had taken for them to drive their blades more than ten inches through an inch of solid pine, even if they were incredibly sharp.

The door swung back again, revealing San's body pinned to the paneling. Two of the Hooded Men saw the coffee table and the chair balanced on top of it and the open skylight, and one of them immediately shouted, "Here! They've escaped to the roof!"

Josh dragged Simon away.

They made their way around the chimney stack, down a fire escape, and across the flat asphalt roof of a primary school building. By the time the Hooded Men were out on the roof of Simon's flat, they were nearly half a mile away, well hidden by a forest of chimney pots. They came down to street level by Gray's Inn itself.

"Where do we go now?" asked Josh.

Simon still looked waxy and shocked. He held on to the wrought-iron railings for support and he had to take five or six deep breaths before he could answer. "I know some people at the British Museum. They don't like me much, but they don't like the Hoodies, either, so they'll probably give us a letty for the night."

They walked by a devious route to the British Museum, mostly using backstreets and alleyways. It was a warmish night, but there was a light breeze blowing from the south-west, and clouds kept smudging the moon. Bloomsbury was almost deserted, except for an occasional bus. Every now and then they heard dogs barking in the distance, but Simon was confident that the Hooded Men would have lost the scent. They saw two or three police cars – navy-blue Wolseley saloons with shining chromium bells on their front bumpers – and when they did they stayed well back in the shadows.

"I don't get it," said Josh. "You have cops here, but you have the Hooded Men, too."

"Simple, guvnor. The police take care of natural criminals. The Hooded Men take care of *unnatural* criminals."

"Such as?"

"Catholics and Muslims and anybody else who's got funny ideas about who to pray to. They sniff out faith-healers, too, and mediums, and spiritualists."

"And they make sure that no Purgatorials come through the 'six doors', unless they want them to."

"That's right, guvnor."

"Do they ever put people on trial?"

"Trial? You must be joking. Once they've got you, they've got you. They're judge and jury, both, and nobody dares to cross them. They don't even answer to Parliament. It was Oliver Cromwell who brought them together; and the saying is that Oliver Cromwell is the only man who can ever disband them, and he's been dead for three hundred years. *Hooded Men! Hooded Men!/Hide in cupboard, hide in bed/Old Noll will only pay them when/He sees them playing with your head.*"

"So who appoints them? I mean, supposing *I* wanted to be one? Kind of an odd career move, I know, but supposing I did?"

"You couldn't, you're a tourist."

"What's wrong with being a tourist?"

"Too bloody high church, ain't you? The Hoodies hate your lot."

"I'm a tourist who tours around. A traveler."

"Oh! In that case, beg your pardon, guvnor. Thought you meant you came from the Church of Tours. But I still don't know what you'd have to do, to be a Hoodie. Maybe John will know."

"Who's John?"

"John Farbelow. You're just about to make his acquaintance."

"He's your friend at the British Museum?"

"Um, 'friend' isn't exactly the word that I'd use. Let's say we dislike each other so much we almost enjoy it."

* * *

They reached the basement of the British Museum by way of a narrow iron staircase in Montague Street. Simon knocked at a dark green door with a small window in it, and waited. At last a pale face appeared and stared at them for a while. Then the door opened a little way.

"I need a place to kip," said Simon.

"Who've you got with you?"

"Omee and a donah. Couple of Purgatorials. The Hoodies were after them."

"Hold on."

They waited even longer. A blind man came tapping along the sidewalk next to them. He stopped quite close to the staircase, as if he were listening. Josh and Nancy and Simon stayed perfectly still, suppressing their breath.

"Somebody's there," said the blind man. "I can hear somebody alive down there."

"No, mate," said Simon. "We're all deader than doornails."

The blind man thought about that for a while, and then said, "God have mercy on your souls, then," and went tapping on his way. Josh was uncomfortably reminded of Blind Pew, especially when three or four horses suddenly burst around the corner from Gower Street, dray horses, being run to their stables.

The basement door opened wider and they were admitted by an unsmiling girl with black curly hair. She looked partly Chinese, especially since she was wearing a plain black satin dress with a Mao collar. She was smoking a cigarette in an ebony holder. "How's May, then?" Simon asked her, as she closed the door behind them. "What about a smile for your old mate Simon?"

The girl contemptuously turned her back and led them along a gloomy corridor stacked with wooden crates, her shoes tapping on the concrete floor. There was a strong smell of cleaning fluid and varnish, and something else. A bitter, herbal scent that put Josh in mind of something, but he couldn't think what it was that he was trying to remember.

They reached another dark green door. The girl opened it up and led them through. They found themselves in a large windowless room filled with a fog of cigarette smoke. A motley collection of couches and chairs had been gathered together beneath a single naked light in the center of the room, and in these sprawled a number of pale young people, all of them overdressed in overcoats and embroidered vests and sweaters and scarves and baggy pants. Some of them wore hats and one or two of them wore knitted mittens, too. Josh got the picture immediately: these were the hippies of parallel London, the young rebels, the new Bohemians.

In the largest armchair with one leg slung over the side of it sat a big round-faced man with white hair that stuck up on top of his head like a king's crown made of thistledown. He had probably been handsome once, but now he had bags under his eyes and his jowls had thickened. He was dressed in a black fur-lined coat of the type that used to be called an Immensikoff, and a gray three-piece suit, and a black silk cravat that had been tied to make an enormous bow the size of a dahlia.

"Well, well," he said, coughing and lighting a cigarette. "Look what the cat's dragged in. Haven't seen you for a very decent interval, Cutter." His voice was very deep and suave, like George Sanders with a head cold.

"Didn't want to trouble you, guvnor," said Simon. "But the Hoodies turned over my drum on the Gray's Inn Road. San's dead. You remember San. The Burmese geezer."

"San? Of course I do. He was a good sort, San. Believed in something, unlike you."

He looked past Simon to Josh and Nancy, and blew out a very long stream of smoke. "So who are these two? Purgatorials, are they? You're punching above your weight, Cutter, mixing with Purgatorials. No wonder the Hoodies are after you."

Josh stepped forward, into the light. "Josh Winward – and this is Nancy Andersen. You must be John Farbelow."

"That's right, Josh. Pleased to make your acquaintance. This is quite a novelty, meeting a pair of Purgatorials that Cutter and his ilk haven't robbed and cobblestoned, or the Hoodies taken off for their own particular requirements."

"Well, the fact of the matter is that we didn't really come

from Purgatory," said Josh. "We came from London . . . only it's kind of a different London."

"Oh, I know that," grinned John Farbelow. "Only children and idiots believe in the Purgatory story. You found one of the six doors; and you found out how to jump through it. People do, from time to time. Scholars, usually, who think they're the first people who ever found out what the nursery rhyme referred to. Or people looking for somewhere to hide, because of something rascally they've done in that different London of yours. Which are you two then – scholars, or rascals?"

"Neither. We're looking for the people who murdered my sister. We think she was strangled here and then taken back through one of the doors and her body dumped in the Thames."

"Well, that kind of thing happens," said John Farbelow, with a casual wave of his hand. "Unfortunately, you can't legislate from one world into the other."

"I still want to know who killed her."

"You're taking a very considerable risk, you know. The Hoodies won't hesitate to do their worst with you, if they catch you. They'd do some nasty things to all of us here, if they ever caught us."

"What's their beef with you?"

John Farbelow sucked deeply at his cigarette, and then crushed it out. "You'll forgive me, but I don't know who you are, and I think I've already said more than it's prudent to say."

"They're bona, guvnor," put in Simon. "I can vouch for them myself. Up on the roof at Carey Street, they saved my bacon when the dogs were on me. They didn't have to, and if I had been them, I would've let me drop, and scarpered."

"I see," said John Farbelow. "But how do I know that the Hoodies haven't paid you to bring these two here? How do I know that San is really dead, and that you're not just stringing me a line?"

"Because I'm the famous Simon Cutter, and everybody knows that the famous Simon Cutter would rather poke his eyes out with a pin than run errands for the Hoodies."

There was a very long pause. Then John Farbelow took out another cigarette and said, "Your older brother, wasn't it? Caught breaking into a television shop."

"I don't talk about it."

"They made him play the Holy Harp, didn't they? And he grassed up all of his friends. Seven people hanged because of him, and eight more in prison."

"Why are you asking me, if you know?"

"Because I want to look in your squinty little eyes and see that you're not deceiving me. The Hoodies can make anybody turn. I think they could even make *me* turn, if they ever caught me – which I hope to God they never will."

Josh said, "Listen, for what it's worth, we're just two people looking for someplace safe to sleep tonight. If you don't want to confide in us, it's fine by me. Tomorrow we'll be out of here early and you won't have to see us again."

"So what are you doing tomorrow?" asked John Farbelow, lighting his cigarette with a shocking-pink butane lighter that must have been brought into this world by some unfortunate Purgatorial.

"First, I'm going to visit the house in Lavender Hill where my sister was lodging. Then I'm going to go to Wheatstone Electrics where she used to work."

"Wheatstone Electrics? You're not talking about Frank Mordant?"

"That's the man. He was the one who offered my sister a job."

John Farbelow slowly shook his head. "Frank Mordant . . . there's a man I'd like to see again. Nailed to the floorboards, preferably."

"You know him?"

"Oh, yes, I know him. He's a Purgatorial, like you. Well, let's not use the word Purgatorial any more, but he came through one of the six doors, like you. He's been here for years, running various little enterprises."

"How come the Hoodies leave *him* alone?"

"Because like all of his kind, he's come to some kind of arrangement with them. I imagine that he supplies them with all manner of goods and services which the rest of this godforsaken world have to do without. He comes and he goes, from your world to ours, wheeling and dealing. There are six or seven like him, that I know of, but he is definitely the slimiest of all of them."

Nancy said, "Did he hurt you, personally?"

John Farbelow waved the clouds of smoke away from his face. "Well, well. You're the perceptive one."

"My grandmother taught me how to read people's auras. When you started to talk about Frank Mordant, yours grew very dark."

"You can read my mind?"

"No, but I can see your sorrow. It's all around you. You look like you're wearing a muddy cloak."

"A muddy cloak . . . That's poetic. But yes, you're right. I do bear Frank Mordant a very great deal of ill will."

"It's to do with a woman, am I right?"

The young people in the room began to shuffle restlessly in their chairs. They weren't bored: they were showing their support for John Farbelow; and that they didn't approve of any questions that might hurt or embarrass him.

John Farbelow turned to a pretty gipsylike girl sitting closest to him and said, "It's all right, Siobhan. Don't get upset about it. These people may need our help." Then he turned back to Nancy and said, "Why don't you sit down? You look tired, both of you. What about a cup of tea, or something a little stronger?"

"A glass of water would be fine."

John Farbelow nodded to Siobhan and she went off to fetch them a drink. Simon dragged over a sagging couch and an armchair and they all sat down. A gray cat suddenly appeared, and jumped up on to Josh's knee. It peered up at him, sniffing, and purring as loudly as a wooden rattle.

"That's not the same cat we saw in Star Yard, is it?" asked Nancy.

"Couldn't be," said Josh. But the cat rubbed its head against him and kept patting his hand with its paw as if it was encouraging him to stroke it.

John Farbelow said, "That animal seems to have taken a shine to you, Josh."

"Animals always go for Josh," said Nancy. "He treats them like human beings, that's why."

"You think they have souls?"

"Sure," said Josh. "Just because they have fur and fishy breath, that doesn't make them any less spiritual than we are. I know a lot of old women with fur and fishy breath, and nobody ever suggests that *they* shouldn't go to heaven."

"That's Ladslove. She used to be Winnie's cat. Winnie was the woman that I have such a muddy aura about."

"What happened?" asked Nancy. Josh had heard her use this tone of voice before: calm, coaxing, and oddly dreamy. She had used it on him when they first met, and it had cast a spell over him immediately. It was like having your temples lightly massaged.

John Farbelow said, "I met her on a number fifteen bus, of all places. I was going to work. I used to be respectable then. Conformist. Collar-and-tie. She was bright-looking. So bright. I remember she was wearing a red coat with bright gold buttons. But she couldn't work out her bus fare. It was only 7½d, but she was like a child, or a foreigner. She just held out a handful of coins and asked the bus conductor to pick out the right money.

"She spoke in a normal South London accent, but right from the beginning there was something about her that struck me as strange. She used peculiar words, and odd sentence constructions, and when she talked she would make references to things that I had never heard of.

"I met her again the next day, and we carried on talking where we'd left off the day before. I loved listening to her. She'd be chattering on about something perfectly ordinary, like her holiday, and then she'd suddenly drop in something so – *fantastic* – that you couldn't believe your ears. I don't know . . . something like 'I went to France last year. I love Calais. I don't like the Channel Tunnel, though. I keep thinking about all that water up there.'

"It was breathtaking. I thought she must be suffering from

some kind of brain damage. But I didn't interrupt her. I let her prattle on about famous actors that I didn't know and television comedies that I had never heard of. It was like talking to a madwoman except that everything was so logical. No matter what questions I asked her, she always had an answer. She kept talking about 'Princess Di' and saying. 'Wasn't it sad?' as if I was supposed to know who Princess Di was, and all about this sad thing that happened to her.

"I asked her where she came from, and she said Bromley. Her mother had died of cancer and her father had committed suicide two weeks later. She had suffered from terrible depression herself. Then she answered an advertisement in the paper for a new job somewhere completely different. Escape, that's what it said. If your life is getting you down, come and work somewhere completely fresh. New job, new friends, new place to live. And that's when she met Frank Mordant.

"She didn't talk much about Frank Mordant. Eventually – after a great deal of persuasion – she told me that one of the conditions of her job was that she didn't tell anybody how she had got it and where she came from. But . . . she and I saw each other every day on the bus, and then every evening after work and then we fell in love.

"And one night, in a hotel on the Hog's Back, in Surrey, after we had made love for the first time, she told me where she came from."

"Purgatory," said Josh.

"Well, the Hooded Men want us to believe that it's Purgatory, to discourage us from trying to visit it, and to give them an excuse for capturing and killing everybody who accidentally makes their way through. It's a mystical explanation for a place that actually exists. Not in the mind. Not as a myth, or an ancient legend. It's a parallel world, similar but critically different, that actually exists. As I now believe that heaven does, and hell. They exist. They can be reached. They are other worlds, so close to our own that we can reach out and touch them."

"That's what I thought," said Josh. "What you've done is . . .

taken the words right out of my mouth. Similar but critically different."

John Farbelow lit yet another cigarette. "I felt as if I had been struck down by a thunderbolt. I couldn't believe it. I *wouldn't* believe it. How could there be another world where people went by train under the Channel and people flew to New York in three hours and there was color television and cures for tuberculosis and almost everybody was connected to almost everybody else by computer? And much more than that, another world where people were free to worship in any way they chose? Or not at all, if they didn't want to?

"I couldn't take it in. It almost drove me out of my mind. Winnie told me that it wasn't all nice and that there was pollution and wars and overcrowding, but I knew that I had to go there, I had to see it. I felt as if I had spent my whole life inside the grounds of a lunatic asylum, never realizing that there was a world beyond the walls. A world where men weren't hunted down with dogs because they wanted to worship with the Book of Common Prayer, or because they believed in the power and the purity of the Holy Virgin, or because they lit candles to Shiva."

"So what did you do?" asked Josh, stroking Ladslove's ears. The cat looked up at him as if he should have known already.

"I couldn't go back to work, could I? I was working for Hoover, selling vacuum cleaners. And Winnie told me that where she came from, there were vacuum cleaners made of light colored plastic that were fifty times more powerful and didn't need bags. Knowing that, how could I possibly go back to work? What was I going to tell my customers?

"Maybe it sounds ridiculous to you. But once I knew that better things existed, I couldn't pretend that they didn't. There was a cure for TB, for God's sake! There were cures for cancer! Apart from that – much more serious than that – I knew that if men and women were free to worship somewhere in this universe, then they should be free to worship everywhere."

Nancy reached out and – uninvited – touched his hand. Josh glanced at her with a slight tinge of jealousy, but she gave him a tiny shake of her head to indicate that John Farbelow needed closeness now, and personal warmth, if he was going to tell them what had happened to Winnie, and why he hated Frank Mordant so much.

"I went to Winnie's flat early the next morning. She wasn't there and her bed hadn't been slept in. I went to Wheatstone Electrics and asked to see her. Frank Mordant came down himself and told me that Winnie had left Wheatstone's of her own accord; and that she had left no forwarding address; and that nobody had any idea where she was.

"I stood and I looked him in the eye and said, 'What about the Channel Tunnel?' And he knew then that I knew what he had done; and who he was; because all he said was, 'What about the Commonwealth? And what about the Hooded Men?'

"I knew then that my life was in danger, and I left as quickly as I could. I stayed with some friends in Kennington for a few days, and then I came here. To study."

"Did you find out anything about the Hooded Men?"

"The Doorkeepers, yes. As you have plainly discovered, there are six doors between one London and the next. Into infinity. There are more Londons than you could ever imagine; and more New Yorks; and more Los Angeles. Some of them are so similar that you could never tell them apart, except for the color of their taxis and certain inflections in their speech. One London is flooded, and has gondoliers, like Venice. Another London is like a garden, with nothing but pagodas and summer houses, and firework displays almost every night.

"The Hooded Men guard the doors between these different Londons and patrol them and control any traffic between them. They keep them secret, of course, from the general populace. In this London, if anybody tries to say that they have come through the doors, the Hooded Men simply say that they must be dead people, returned from Purgatory, rejected by God and rejected by Satan. Nobody questions them. After all, they learned it all at school."

"*A Child's Book of Simple Truth*," said Josh, and John Farbelow bowed his head in acknowledgement.

"Some people in the other Londons have discovered the existence of the doors and tried to trade with the Hooded Men. After all, the doors are ideal for all kinds of illegal trafficking: whatever one London lacks, another London can supply. Drugs, women, antibiotics, luxury goods. The Hooded Men are very murderous and will travel through the doors to find anybody who crosses them or tries to cheat them.

"The only real answer is to close the doors, and to close them for ever." John Farbelow paused, reflective.

Josh took a sip of water. "Can that be done?"

"I believe so. The doors are not a physical phenomenon. They are a *psychic* phenomenon. I am convinced that the six doors in London were created by somebody with exceptional psychic powers, and that they have been kept open for centuries by a succession of people of equal psychic ability – each one, perhaps, trained by the one before."

"So if you find the person who's keeping them open . . . ?"

"Exactly," said John Farbelow. "You kill that person, and the doors vanish."

"Do you know who first opened the doors?" asked Josh.

"I believe that the doors were first opened in AD 61, in London, by Queen Boudicca. Also known as Boadicea. She was the wife of King Prasutagas who ruled over the Iceni people in East Anglia, during the time of the Roman invasion of Britain. When Prasutagas died, he made their daughters joint heirs to his property, along with the Roman emperor Nero. He probably had the mistaken idea that this would save them at least some of his possessions.

"But the imperial agent seized everything. Boudicca was flogged and her daughters were raped. Because of this insult, and because of Roman oppression, the Iceni rebelled against the Romans and Boudicca led an armed uprising against Suetonius Paulinus and his legions. The Iceni slaughtered the Roman garrisons in St Albans and Colchester, and then they attacked London and razed it to the ground.

"Boudicca had six or seven Druid advisers – one of them a very mystical senior Druid whose name nobody knows. In AD 61 the Romans were hunting down and killing the last of the Druids and these Druids had come to Boudicca looking for protection. They were very educated, the Druids. They had a written language and they believed in the immortal soul.

"Boudicca's Druid advisers predicted by the entrails of their victims and by the flight of ravens that she and her army would be annihilated. So the senior Druid taught Boudicca how to open up doors to other existences."

"How do we know this?" asked Josh.

"Because one of the Druids wrote it down. They wrote something like, 'Boudicca lit three tapers. She consumed henbane and passed into another world.'"

"That sounds more like suicide to me."

"That's what historians have always assumed. After all, henbane is even more poisonous than opium. But the Druidic word for 'consumed' is almost the same as the word 'burned'. And we know that the Druids used to burn henbane and breathe in the fumes to put them into a hallucinatory trance. In the Middle Ages, dentists used to burn henbane to dull their patients' toothache. It's very dangerous indeed. But it seems to have worked for Boudicca. It put her into a trance and she opened the six doors, so that she and the Druids and some of the Iceni could escape into the next reality."

Josh said, "I have to tell you, this is a pretty hard story to swallow."

"Why? You've been through a door yourself. The doors don't obey any of the laws of space and time. They're not a place, they're a sustained state of mind, and for that state of mind to be perceptible, somebody somewhere has to be experiencing it."

Josh put down his cup. "What about the Hooded Men? Where do they come into it?"

"They were the elite of the Puritan army which defeated the royalists. Over the centuries – in this particular London – they developed into something very much more than religious enforcers. They became what they are today. In your reality, I suppose you would describe them as a kind of Gestapo."

"So what are you going to do now?"

"Somebody will have to find the person who is keeping the

doors open, enter that building and make sure that the doors are closed for ever."

"Like an assassin, you mean?"

"Exactly."

"That's all very well, but your assassin is going to be trapped in this reality for ever, isn't he? Once the doors are closed, he can never come back."

"This is our home, Josh. We aren't going anywhere else." He looked around at all of the young people sprawled on their chairs, and smiled. "This lot didn't know anything about parallel worlds when I first arrived. They were all brought up on *A Child's Book of Simple Truth*. But they knew that something was wrong with the world they lived in, even if they didn't understand what. So I told them as much as I had discovered, and here we are. A sort of fledgling resistance movement, I suppose, although I didn't mean to tell you that, not at the start."

"And Winnie?" asked Nancy, in a voice as soft as a rubbed-out word.

John Farbelow shrugged. "Winifred Thomas. I never found out what happened to her. I pray that she didn't meet the same fate as your sister, Josh; but I suspect very much that she might have done." He was silent for a moment. His mouth puckered and his eyes filled with tears.

"Do you know something?" he said. "I don't even have a picture of her. Not one. And I'm beginning to forget what she looked like."

Fifteen

The next morning it was raining hard. They sat in a gloomy side room using a museum packing-case as a table, and shared a breakfast of Force wheat flakes and dry crackers spread with marmalade, and mugs of tea. Josh had never drunk so much tea in his life. It seemed as if every half an hour or so, somebody would put the kettle on. Having a cup of tea was their response to everything: shock, tiredness, elation, boredom, going to bed and waking up again.

John Farbelow came up to them dangling a set of car keys. "I'm going to let you borrow my Austin. Simon will drive you. You can go down to Lavender Hill and talk to your sister's landlady. Then you can make some inquiries at Wheatstone's. But be very careful when you go there. Frank Mordant's as sharp as a tack."

Simon took the car keys, tossed them up and caught them. "Not like you to trust me with anything, guvnor."

"I'm trusting you because you owe these people your life. You take very good care of them, d'you hear, otherwise you'll have me to answer to."

Simon tried to look nonchalant, but it was obvious that he was frightened of John Farbelow. Josh had the feeling that John Farbelow might have caught Simon in some petty act of theft or betrayal, not so long ago, and that Simon considered himself lucky to have been let off lightly.

"Just remember," John Farbelow warned him, as they prepared to leave the basement and go out into the rain, but from the look on his face Josh guessed that Simon didn't need to be reminded of what he was supposed to remember.

They pushed their way out of the British Museum basement

and climbed up the wet stone steps to the street. The rain was heavy and gusty, but every now and then it would ease off. The clouds rolled so quickly across the sky that one second the day was dark, corroded green, the next it sparkled as if diamonds had been strewn all over the sidewalks. A rainbow appeared in the sky over Broadcasting House – then another rainbow, a double. The air smelled fresh but the roar of traffic was already deafening, and the sidewalks of Great Russell Street were crowded with pedestrians – businessmen, office girls, porters, delivery boys, policemen and flower-sellers.

"John's motor is parked round the back here," said Simon, and led them into a narrow alley at the back of the Museum where six or seven automobiles were parked outside rows of peeling garage doors. He unlocked a large brown Austin and they climbed in. The brown leather seats were cracked with wear and the windows were so filmy that Josh could hardly see out. Simon tried to turn the engine over but it gave him nothing but a weary chug.

"Starting-handle!" he said, and rummaged under the driver's seat for a long crooked metal rod. He went around to the front of the car, inserted the handle, and gave it two or three vigorous turns. The Austin's engine coughed and blurted and a cloud of black smoke billowed out of the exhaust pipe. He climbed back in again, and engaged the gears with a deafening crunch.

They crept down St Martin's Lane in solid traffic. As they waited, a delivery-boy on a bicycle leaned against the Austin's roof, whistling. Simon wound down the window and said, "You! Nanty that leaning on my motor!"

"Oh, yeah, and 'oo's going to make me?"

Simon didn't say a word, but abruptly opened his door, knocking the boy and his bicycle flat on the road, right in front of an oncoming bus. Fortunately the traffic on the opposite side of the road was going slowly, too. The bus ran over the bicycle's front wheel and crushed its basket filled with eggs and groceries, but managed to slide to a stop just before it hit the boy's head. The boy shrilled in terror, his eyes shut, his fists clenched. Simon slammed his door shut and carried on driving.

"What the hell did you do that for?" Nancy demanded. "He could have been killed!"

"Teach him not to lean on other people's motors," Simon replied. "You know what it says in *A Child's Book of Simple Truth*. 'The property of others is God's property, held in trust. Treat it as sacred.'"

"I've never had the pleasure of reading *A Child's Book of Simple Truth*," snapped Nancy. "Besides, it seems to me like you're the last person who should be giving lectures on the sacredness of other people's property."

"That's different. I'm a revolutionary, like John Farbelow."

"You're a goddamn opportunist, more like."

"That's right. I'm a revolutionary goddam opportunist. What else do you want me to be, in a world like this?"

They reached a wide, open square, paved all over, with fountains and statues. The paving stones were shiny with rainwater and the wind blew the fountains into white mares' tails. In the center of the square stood a tall stone column with a statue of a man on top of it, wearing a Puritan hat and knee-britches.

"Isn't this . . . Trafalgar Square?" said Josh, dubiously. "It kind of looks like it, from all of those 1960s movies I used to watch."

"Santa Cruz Square," said Simon, as he steered his way around it, and headed down Whitehall. "That's Robert Blake, standing on the top, pigeons and all."

They drove down Whitehall toward Parliament Square. Josh had never been down Whitehall before, so he didn't realize that the Cenotaph, the British war memorial, was simply not there; and that there were no security gates across the entrance to Downing Street.

The Houses of Parliament looked the same to Josh as they had in "real" London, except that there were noticeably different trees in Parliament Square, and no statue to Winston Churchill. They crossed the Thames again, but Josh didn't look at it, and Nancy, grasping his hand, knew why.

The Austin whinnied its way southwards along the Fairfax Embankment. The rain grew heavier and drummed on the roof like the drummers who preceded the Hooded Men. The windshield wipers could barely cope with the downpour, and Simon kept smearing the glass in front of him with his sleeve, so that he could see where he was going.

At last they reached Lavender Hill. In this parallel London it looked just as dreary as it had in "real" London, except that there were no Indian takeaways and no used-car lots. Simon had a map penciled on the back of a brown envelope, and he steered them slowly toward Kaiser Gardens. It was a short, sloping street, with scabrous plane trees on either side. The houses were small and cramped, with cheap nets hanging at their windows, and front gardens crowded with irrationally cheerful gnomes. They crept along the curb until they found 53b, and then Simon pulled on the handbrake.

They climbed out of the car and pushed open the gate to 53b. Up and down the street Josh could see nets being drawn back and pale anxious faces looking out. Nancy said, "You couldn't even drop a gum wrapper around here without everybody knowing about it."

Number 53b was a pebble-dashed semi. Its bright green door had an oval stained-glass window in it, depicting a galleon under full sail. The tiny front garden had been laid with crazy paving, but there were no gnomes here, only a diminutive wishing-well cluttered with wind-blown candy wrappers.

Simon went up to the door and pressed the button. He waited for a while, then he pressed it again. "Nobody home. Either that, or the alex doesn't work."

"Try knocking," Josh suggested. Simon rapped on the stained-glass window with his knuckles, and listened some more. As he did so, however, they heard a grinding, droning noise in the distance somewhere.

"Do you hear that?" asked Nancy, frowning.

The droning grew louder. Within less than a minute, it was so deafening that they could hardly hear themselves speak. The windows in number 53b began to rattle and a dog started barking in the garden next door. "Simon – what the hell is that?" shouted Josh.

Simon prodded a finger up toward the sky. "The ten o'clock

from New York, that's what. It's coming in low because of the weather."

At that moment, an immense gray shape appeared over the rooftops, no more than two hundred feet above their heads. It was ten times the size of a whale, although it was almost the same shape. It had eight propeller engines suspended underneath it, which accounted for the grinding noise, and a large pale cigar-shaped gondola, with windows all the way along.

It seemed to take an age to pass over their heads, and all the time the dog kept on barking and the windows continued to rattle. Josh watched it with his hand cupped over his eyes to keep out the rain. He felt an unexpected sense of dread, as if he were watching aliens landing in *The War of the Worlds*. At last it turned north-eastward, over the Thames, and gradually disappeared behind the clouds.

"Wouldn't get me up in one of those," said Simon, giving another sharp knock at the door. "Full of toffs and hydrogen."

There was still no answer. The rain made a prickling noise in the nettles.

"Maybe she's out," Josh suggested. "Looks like we'll have to come back later."

Simon lifted the letterbox flap, and peered inside. "I don't know . . . I think I can hear a television. She wouldn't go out and leave a television on. Besides, there's nothing on at this time of the morning. Only the test card."

He tried the door, but it was locked. Josh said, "Let's take a look around the back. Maybe she simply can't hear us."

Simon went up to the side gate, reached over the top and pulled back the bolt. They walked along the narrow path at the side of the house, negotiating three overflowing trash cans, until they found themselves in a small sloping backyard, with a scrubby patch of wet green grass and a lineful of washing hanging up to dry – frayed towels, socks, and a brassiere.

"What woman leaves her washing out in the pouring rain?" said Nancy.

Simon went up to the back door and rapped his ring-covered fingers on the frosted glass. "Mrs Marmion! You in there, Mrs

Marmion?" He rapped again and this time the door swung open. He ran his fingers down the left-hand side of the frame. "Somebody's had a jemmy to this."

Josh came up behind him and opened the door a little wider. Inside he could see a small scullery with a floor covered with green and cream linoleum. There was a heavy china sink with a single cold faucet dripping into it, and a knocked-over bucket with a mop. In the background, he could hear the high-pitched whining of a television set.

"Hallo?" he called. "Mrs Marmion? Are you there? It's Josh Winward, I called you yesterday!"

Still there was no reply. Simon said, "Something's wrong here, guvnor. Let's hop the Charley before we get caught."

"Let me take a quick look inside," said Josh. "It'll only take a minute."

"Entering somebody's house, that's chancing it."

"I have to see Julia's room. Mrs Marmion tried to tell me over the phone that somebody had been here to take all of her things away. But you never know. She might have left some kind of clue behind. A note. A letter. She always kept a diary, too."

He stepped into the scullery. It smelled like old damp floorcloths and it was crowded with buckets and brooms and shelves full of firelighters and Brasso and tins of shoe polish. There was a coal-burning boiler at one side of the room, but when he laid his hand on it, it was stone cold. Josh hesitated for a moment and then he made his way through to the kitchen. This wasn't much larger than the scullery, with a view of the side wall of the house next door, a small enamel-topped table, and a cream-painted hutch stacked with yellow tins of Colman's mustard and brown jars of Marmite and boxes of Shredded Wheat.

Simon said, "We really should get out of here, guvnor. Half the street knows we're in here, and it only takes one old busybody to call the Old Bill."

"I'll be quick, I promise you," said Josh. He opened the kitchen door and found himself in a narrow corridor that led to the front door. Beside the door was a mahogany hat-stand with a mirror in it. Josh caught sight of his own face: the stained-glass galleon cast a green-and-yellowish pattern across his cheeks, so that he looked as if he were dead and decayed.

He opened a door leading to the right. There was a small living room with a dull brown carpet. It was here that the television was still switched on: a black-and-white set showing a test card from the BBC. Josh went into the room and switched it off. Nancy came in close behind him and looked around. She picked up some framed black-and-white photographs from the mantelpiece: one of them showed a group of people at the seaside, paddling in the water in long one-piece bathing costumes. Another one showed a white-haired old lady sitting in a sunny room somewhere, with a cat nestling in her lap.

"*Josh*," said Nancy, and passed him the picture.

Josh angled it so that the gloomy light from the window fell across it. "It couldn't be, could it? But it looks so much like her."

"I'm sure it's her. Look at the way she's sitting. And that smile."

"But what's her picture doing here?"

Nancy took the picture frame, turned it over, and unfastened the clip at the back. She took out the photograph and held it up. "Mother. Iverna Court. 16/08/99."

"So the old lady in the hospital was Mrs Marmion's mother. That's deeply weird."

Simon was growing agitated. He kept peeping out through the net curtains into the street to make sure that the police or the Hooded Men hadn't showed up. "I dodged them once. I don't think they'll let me dodge them again."

Josh clapped him on the shoulder. "Don't lose your nerve, kid. Be calm. Think about something soothing, like the sea."

"The sea makes me sick."

Josh slipped the photograph of Mrs Marmion's mother into his coat pocket. Then he went back out to the hallway and climbed the steep flight of stairs that led up to the first-floor landing. There was a bedroom immediately on his right and another on his left. Ahead of him was a door with a ceramic plaque on it marked *Bathroom.*

He went into the right-hand bedroom. It was wallpapered with pale pink flowers, and there was a cheap oak-veneered double bed with a pink satin quilt on it. Behind the door stood a 1950s-style wardrobe and under the window stood a chest of drawers with a crochet cloth on top of it. An electric alarm clock chirruped loudly on the nightstand.

Nancy went through the chest of drawers. "Nothing, only two buttons and a light bulb."

Josh opened the wardrobe doors. There was nothing inside except an odd collection of wire hangers, the kind that Joan Crawford detested so much, and two pairs of women's flat-heeled shoes, right at the bottom. Josh picked up one of the shoes. Inside, faded gold lettering said *Steps, San Francisco.*

"This is Julia's," he said, holding it up. "She always bought her shoes at Steps."

"Well, that proves that she was here. But that doesn't prove who killed her," said Nancy.

"She was killed in *this* world, I'm sure of it."

"By this guy Frank Mordant, from Wheatstone Electrics?"

"It looks suspiciously like it, don't you think?"

"I think you should be very careful. Just because the love of John Farbelow's life disappeared when she was working for Frank Mordant, that doesn't necessarily mean that he murdered her, and it certainly doesn't prove that he murdered Julia. I've met guys like John Farbelow before. They're charismatic, they're revolutionary, but they're usually full of shit."

Josh picked up the other shoe. It was blue suede, stained with grit and rainwater, as if Julia had been wearing it when she walked through a park. Its toes were packed with newspaper to stop them from curling up. Josh wormed his finger into the toes, pulled out the newspaper and spread it flat on the bed. It was a page from the appointments section of the London *Evening Standard.* Circled in red was a small display ad which read:

Looking For A New Job? Looking For A New Life? If

> you're looking to leave your old job and your old life behind you, if you want to work somewhere totally fresh and totally different, our international electrical company has vacancies for young and enthusiastic secretarial staff. Above average pay. No computer or w/p skills required. Apply Box 331 for details.

"There's no date on it," said Josh. "But I can guess."

"So what do you think this man Frank Mordant is doing? Hiring girls in our world, bringing them through to this world, and murdering them?"

"The ideal crime, isn't it? Nobody misses them in this world, because they never existed. No birth records, no school records, no social security number. And nobody in our world can find the murderer, because he's here."

"But why is he murdering them?"

"Why does anyone murder anybody else? Maybe Frank Mordant is a psychotic serial killer who has found a way to kill as many women as he likes and get away with it, and maybe that's good enough for him."

"So what do we do now?"

Josh folded up the paper. "What I've seen here today . . . that's proof enough for me that Julia was living here. All we have to do now is go see what Frank Mordant has to say for himself."

He crossed the landing and opened the door to the second bedroom. It was similar to Julia's room, except that it had a bay window, and there was a small brick fireplace with a damp patch beside it. He opened the wardrobe but it was stacked with neatly-folded blankets, a hot-water bottle, and an old electric fire without a plug.

He went back out to the landing and opened another door. Airing cupboard, filled with sheets. Then bedroom three, a smaller bedroom at the back, crowded with cardboard boxes and books. "Looks like the boxroom," said Josh, peering around. But with a prickle of shock he suddenly caught sight of a dark figure standing in the corner, half-hidden behind the wardrobe.

"Jesus!" he said, jumping back, and jarring his shoulder against the door frame.

"Let's *go*!" shouted Simon, and launched himself down the stairs. But Nancy said, "Stop it! Stop it! What are you afraid of?"

Josh stopped, and took another look in the corner. The dark figure remained motionless. It was nothing but a dressmaking dummy with a large felt hat tilted sideways on top of it. He covered his face with his hands and shook his head. "I must be letting this whole thing get to me. Scared of a one-legged dummy."

He closed the bedroom door and went across to the bathroom. Simon stayed where he was, halfway down the stairs. He didn't say anything: he had given up trying. But he remained poised, ready to run out of the house at the slightest suggestion of trouble.

"I just want to check that Julia didn't leave anything personal here," said Josh. "If she left a toothbrush or a razor or something, we could have that checked for DNA."

"Who by? The police in this world won't be able to do it. Even if they have the inclination, I doubt if they have the technology."

"I just want to gather as much proof as possible," said Josh. "I'll worry about the way we're going to use it when I've got it."

"You're the boss," said Nancy, and it was then that Josh opened the bathroom door.

Sixteen

It was the smell that hit them first, and all three of them cried out in a chorus of disgust. Josh couldn't imagine how it hadn't permeated the whole house; and then he realized that he *had* been smelling it, all the way upstairs, and that he hadn't really registered what it was. And then there was the noise: the furious zizzing of hundreds of glittering bluebottles as he disturbed them in the middle of their feasting and their egg-laying.

The smell was ripe and sweet and almost visibly green. All of the bathroom windows were closed and an electric wall-heater had been left on, which had increased the temperature inside the bathroom to well over eighty degrees. Above the bath hung a wooden drying-frame, intended for drip-dry shirts and pantyhose. But spreadeagled on this frame was what appeared at first sight to be a half-gutted animal.

It was only when Josh stepped closer, keeping his hand clamped over his nose and mouth, that he understood what he was actually looking at. The animal was a woman – a naked, gray-haired woman, her body split wide open from her chin to her pubic hair. It was impossible to see who she was, or who she might have been, because her face was crawling with bluebottles, as if she were wearing a living Mardi Gras mask.

On the green-tiled wall, a large cross had been marked in blood and excrement.

Josh pulled the door shut. Nancy was already halfway down the stairs, with Simon close behind her. Simon didn't bother to go back through the kitchen: he snatched open the front door and took three stiff-legged steps outside, gasping for air. Nancy leaned up against the porch, both hands clasped over her stomach, saying, "God . . . oh my God. That was appalling."

Josh said, "We'd better get out of here. Whoever did that to Mrs Marmion, they won't hesitate to do it to us, too."

"The Hoodies," said Simon. "Didn't you see the cross? They always do that."

They climbed back into the Austin. Simon swung the starting-handle and the motor chugged into life. Then he executed a fifteen-point turn, with a gladiatorial clashing of gears, and managed to point the car back the way they had come.

"They must have guessed that we were coming to see her," said Nancy.

"I doubt if it was a guess," put in Simon. "The Hoodies have people in the telephone exchange, they listen to everything. You can't even phone up your fishmonger without them knowing about it."

"Isn't that illegal?"

"Course not. It's all allowed under the God's Word Act. They can't allow people to talk a lot of popery, even in private."

They drove down St John's Hill toward Wandsworth. Josh glanced out of the rear window from time to time to make sure that they weren't being followed, but there was a convoy of three buses behind them which would have made it very difficult for anybody to keep them in sight.

Nancy said, "We can't stay here, Josh. It's much too dangerous. We have to go back."

"Not bad advice, guvnor," said Simon. "Even if it *was* Frank Mordant that topped your sister, how are you going to prove it? So far as *this* world's concerned, she never existed, so she couldn't have been topped; and so far as *your* world's concerned, Frank Mordant is gone without a trace, ain't he, and you try convincing your constabulary to come here and collar him."

"You're not suggesting I let him get away with it?"

"I don't see that you've got very much choice. You've

got a body in one world and a murderer in another, and never the twain shall meet. You *might* find proof enough to get him arrested, even without a body. But then there's the question of the Hoodies. It looks like he's come to some sort of arrangement with them; and if that's the case, you won't have a dog's chance of getting him convicted. One wink to the reeve and that'll be it, no case to answer, your worship. You saw that woman back there. They're a law unto themselves, the Hoodies. Do what they like, say what they like, kill who they like; and all in the name of God."

"Josh, we have to go back," Nancy insisted.

"The world's taken a turn around since you first arrived," put in Simon. "You can go back as soon as you like."

"I'm not sure," said Josh. "What if I can never find my way back here again? How can I spend the rest of my life knowing that the man who strangled Julia is going unpunished? And if he murdered John Farbelow's girlfriend, too, how many times has he done it before, and how many times is he going to do it again?"

"There are times in this vale of tears, guvnor, when we just have to admit that we're up against a brick wall."

"That's exactly right. We *are* up against a brick wall. But you and I know that if you have enough faith, you can jump right *through* that brick wall."

"Can't see your constabulary swallowing that. Even if they *did*, they wouldn't have any jurisdiction over here, now would they?"

"I wasn't talking about the cops. There are other ways of settling scores than calling the cops."

"Like what?" Nancy demanded. "Killing Frank Mordant yourself?"

"Of course not. But if he *did* do it, I can think of a whole lot of ways to make his life a misery. Mind you, if I *did* kill him, I wouldn't be caught for it, would I? Any more than *he*'s ever going to be caught for killing Julia. But it would be justice."

"Justice? If you killed him, then you'd be just as evil as he is. Besides, I can't imagine you having the nerve to kill *anybody*. You killed that dog and you can't stop blaming yourself."

"The dog was innocent."

"The dog was going to kill a man. You had to make a choice. Now you have to make another choice."

"You ought to think about going back, guvnor," said Simon, his eyes floating in the rear-view mirror. "You don't want to underestimate the Hoodies, believe you me; and if Frank Mordant really is their man they won't let you get away with giving him grief. You'll be looking over your shoulder for the rest of your natural. I'll tell you something else: don't trust that John Farbelow further than you can throw him. He's the kind of cove who gets everybody else to do his dirty work for him. For all you know, he's got a grudge against Frank Mordant for something quite different, and there never was no girl what he met on the number fifteen bus. What could suit him better than for you to do his topping for him?"

Nancy reached across and sandwiched Josh's hand between hers. She was looking tired and stressed, and he could see that the sight of Mrs Marmion had been just too much for her. He suddenly realized how tired *he* was, and how dirty he felt. They needed to get back to "real" London for a rest and a shower, if nothing else.

"OK, then," he said. "Take us to Star Yard. Do you know anyplace where we can buy some candles?"

"Ironmongers on the corner here, guvnor."

Simon parked the car and left them sitting in the back seat while he went to buy some candles. Nancy said, "You shouldn't come back here again, Josh. You've got an idea of what might have happened to Julia . . . you don't need to follow it up any further."

"I'm sorry, Nance, that's where you're wrong. There's no way that I can leave this unfinished."

"But what about the Hooded Men? Look what they did to that woman!"

"That's exactly my point. There have been Hooded Men all through history, of one kind or another. The day we let them intimidate us, that's the day we might as well get our dogs to dig us some graves, and scoop the earth back on top of us."

"Of everybody in the world, Josh, you're the only person I know who could persuade a dog to do that."

They drove through crawling traffic along the Embankment until they reached Charing Cross. The rain was even heavier now, and as they turned up Villiers Street the sidewalks were crowded with bobbing black umbrellas. Villiers Street was a steep gradient, and the Austin whinnied up it like a protesting old horse. On the corner of the Strand, a drummer was silhouetted, his triangular black hat dripping with rainwater.

"Keep your heads down," Simon advised them. "He's a Watcher. He probably won't recognize you, but you never know your bloody rotten luck."

It took them nearly twenty minutes to drive from Santa Cruz Square to the Aldwych. The road was clogged with buses and horse-drawn wagons, and two enormous horse-drawn drays were drawn up outside a half-timbered pub called The Battle of Winceby. The rain trickled down the Austin's windows and Simon kept tapping the thermometer gauge because the engine was overheating.

At last they turned into Chancery Lane, and then left into Carey Street. The torrential rain had forced a pieman to cover up his "Eric the Pie" stall with wet tarpaulins and wheel it away, and Simon was able to park in the space that he had just vacated. There was still a smell of hot coke and beef pies in the rain as Josh and Nancy and Simon climbed out of the Austin. They made their way up Star Yard, their collars pulled up, their heads ducked down.

They reached the niche, which was still clogged up with wet rubbish. Simon took the brown-paper package of candles out of his pocket, and set three of them down on the ground. He produced a cigarette lighter and flicked it, and managed to light two of the candles, but every time he tried to light the third it was instantly extinguished by the rain.

"Come on, you bastard," he snarled at it, and tried to light it again. It managed to flicker for a moment, but then the rain put it out again, and then another candle went out.

"Here," said Josh, and leaned over him, holding his coat out like an umbrella. Simon managed to light all three candles for a few triumphant seconds, but as soon as Josh stepped away, two of them went out again.

"How about finding someplace to wait this rain out?" Josh suggested. "A pub, maybe. I don't know about you, but I could sure use a serious drink."

Simon flicked his cigarette lighter yet again. "No good hanging around, guvnor. The forecast is, bucketing down till next Wednesday fortnight. Hold your coat up again."

Josh leaned over the niche once more, and Simon managed to light all three candles. This time, Josh stayed where he was, to give the wicks time to burn more strongly. But as he waited, he thought he heard a faint sound like a train approaching, over a jointed track.

He shook his wet hair. It was difficult to distinguish anything over the clatter of the rain and the roaring of buses and the sizzle of tires on the tarmac-covered cobbles. "Do you hear that?" he asked Nancy. "Kind of like a train."

Nancy lifted her head. Her forehead was decorated with beads of rain, and her eyelashes sparkled. She listened for a moment, and then she nodded. "*Drums*," she said.

Simon stood up, too. "They're coming nearer. They're definitely coming nearer."

"They don't know that we're here, do they? How do they know that we're here?"

"Perhaps that Watcher spotted us. Don't ask me, I'm not a per-sychic."

"Maybe they're not coming this way," said Nancy. But the *trat-a-trat-trat* was growing louder and louder; and it wasn't long before they could hear it quite distinctly over the grinding of the traffic.

"We're going to have to go," said Josh. "Simon . . . you'd better get the hell out of here. Tell me where to find you when I come back."

"*Josh . . .*" said Nancy. She wasn't only warning him to hurry, she was telling him that she didn't want him to come back, ever.

"Go to the British Museum. John Farbelow will know where to find me."

"OK," said Josh, and grasped his hand. "And, look, if I don't make it back . . ."

The drums were battering off the sides of the nearby buildings, and people were hurrying past them as fast as they could. Even if you hadn't lied or stolen or committed a blasphemy, even if you didn't have a Book of Common Prayer secreted under your mattress, it was better to keep well out of the way of the drums and the dogs and the Hooded Men.

"Nancy, you first," said Josh. Nancy took three steps back and said, "*Jack be nimble, Jack be quick, Jack jump over the candlestick.*"

As she ran forward, however, a rain-filled gust swept across the sidewalk, and all of the candles blew out. She struck the brick wall with her shoulder and almost fell over.

"There's no time to do this now," said Josh. "Let's get out of here and try it again later, when we can rig up something to keep the candles alight."

At that moment, however, dog-handlers came round the corner of Star Yard and Carey Street, and drummers appeared behind them, from the direction of Chancery Lane. The drumming was totally deafening now. It seemed to make the rain rattle and the paving slabs shake. And behind the drummers, Josh could see the silhouettes of Puritan hats and buckles, and heads that were covered in hessian hoods, and the shine of long sharp swords.

Simon was down on his knees, frantically trying to relight the candles. He lit one, then another, and then another. Josh put his arm around Nancy and held her tight, and she covered her ears to blot out the drumming. The first candle blew out, but Simon persisted and lit it again, just as the first of the dogs came barking and slathering up to him.

"*Jump*!" Josh shouted at Nancy. He seized hold of her fringed buckskin sleeves and almost threw her over the candles, toward the solid brick wall. She landed on the other side of the candles, and turned.

"*Josh, you too*!" she cried out, in a distorted, watery voice.

Josh took a step back, ready to jump, but as he did so one of the dogs seized the cuff of his pants. He swung his leg, trying to shake it loose. Simon, right next to him, gave it a kick in the ribs. But Josh knew that you could set one of these dogs on fire before they would open their jaws.

"*Josh*!" screamed Nancy. "*You have to jump*!"

Josh swung his leg again, hitting the dog against the sidewalk with a crunch that must have broken one of its legs, but it still clung on. Simon reached down to seize its collar, but as he did so Josh caught the shine of steel out of the corner of his eye. At the instant that Simon's fingers closed around the studded leather choker, a straight-bladed sword came down with a *chappp!* sound and cut right through his wrist. Simon didn't scream. He didn't utter a sound. But he fell backward on to the candles with blood jetting out of his severed wrist like water out of a garden hose.

Josh felt a powerful hand seize his hair and wrench his head back. He felt hessian scratch against the side of his head. A sword was held across his throat, and a harsh voice said, "You won't move a single muscle, sir, or else I'll have your head off."

In the niche, Nancy stared back at him in desperation. He wanted to yell, "*Go*!" but the sword was just touching his Adam's apple and he was afraid that his captor would cut his throat if he tried to shout out. All he could do was stare at her and *will* her to carry on.

One of the dog-handlers came forward and snapped, "Spit it out, Rancour," and the dog that had been gripping Josh's pants released its grip. It trotted back to stand by its master with Simon's hand still clutching its collar and Simon's blood still matting the fur on its back.

Down on the sidewalk, Simon had gone into shock. He was trembling like a run-over stag and his eyes had rolled up into his head. One of the drummers knelt beside him and looped a lanyard around his arm, just below his elbow, and knotted it tight. The blood stopped spurting across the yard, but it was still leaking all over the paving stones, and so the drummer wrapped a grimy-looking cloth around it and told Simon to press it against his stump as hard as he could.

"Jesus save me," Simon quivered, through whitened lips.

"Oh, Jesus will save you, mate," said the drummer. "Jesus saved Barabbas, didn't he?"

Nancy was still hesitating. None of the Hooded Men made any attempt to follow her, and of course they couldn't, unless they relit the candles. She was already through to the "real" London – a different existence altogether. With an expression of bewilderment and anguish, she lifted both hands, with the palms flat, as if she were pressing them against a window. Josh knew what it meant: I love you, and I'm not going to abandon you. She stood like that for three or four helpless seconds, before she turned and walked away. She turned right and then she was gone.

"Pity your poor lady," said the Hooded Man. "She's going to miss all the amusements."

"Call an ambulance!" Josh demanded. "If this man doesn't receive medical attention right now he's going to go into deep shock."

"He'll have his ambulance. Meanwhile, you can come with us."

"What am I supposed to have done?"

"Did I say that you'd done anything? We'd like to engage you in a little conversation, that's all."

"And supposing I don't want to?"

"Oh, you will, sir. Believe me, you will."

Josh was turned around and pushed firmly against the opposite wall. There was a broken guttering high above his head and the rainwater splattered against his shoulder. He tried to edge sideways but one of the Hooded Men prodded him with his sword. "Stay where you have been told to stay."

"I'm an American citizen. You don't have any right to hold me like this."

"Yes, I do."

"At least let me talk to the US Embassy."

"You're making no sense, sir."

The Hooded Man quickly searched through his pockets and

discovered his billfold in the back pocket of his jeans. He sorted through his credit cards and his driver's license and his photographs of Julia and Nancy.

"Joshua B. Winward, is that your name?"

"You can read, can't you? How about calling that ambulance?"

"If I were you, Mr Joshua B. Winward, I would concern myself more with my own welfare."

"But you're not me. You're just a goddamned sadist with a sack over his head."

The Hooded Man, unexpectedly, laughed. "You have a great deal to learn about life in *this* London, sir. A very great deal. Now, let's get you off and ask you some questions."

"I'm not saying anything."

"Wiser if you do, sir. We don't want to have to open you up, do we, and read what we want to know from the disposition of your vitals?"

"I see . . . you're going to cut me open, just like you cut open that woman in Lavender Hill."

"Keep your peace, sir."

They heard an ambulance bell approaching from Chancery Lane. Simon, without warning, began to wave the stump of his arm in the air and scream. He screamed so loudly that one of the dog-handlers slapped his face with his dog leash, but it didn't stop him. Two or three of the dogs began to join in his screaming with a mournful howling of their own.

What with that, and the rain, and the fact that he was now alone with the Hooded Men, Josh began to feel that – even if he hadn't really returned from Purgatory – he had certainly been sent to hell.

Seventeen

With their drums beating a fierce tattoo, the Hooded Men marched Josh to the end of Chancery Lane. There, a black van was parked, of the kind they used to call a Black Maria. They opened the back doors and heaved him inside, forcing him to sit on a varnished wooden bench, handcuffed to a rail that ran the length of the interior.

"You can't do this."

"I don't think you understand, sir. We can choose to do whatever we wish."

"Why don't you just let me leave? I didn't come here to cause trouble."

"Believe me, you've caused a bushel of trouble already."

With that, the Hooded Man stepped down from the van, slammed the doors, and locked them. After a few moments, the van's engine started up, and Josh was driven off at high speed. Every time the van swung around a corner, he was pitched against the side of it, bruising his shoulder.

He felt the van drive down a steep cobbled hill and then turn to the right. It swayed from side to side as if they were weaving through traffic, and every now and then it shrilled its bell. After less than five minutes it slowed down, turned again, and stopped. The doors opened and the Hooded Man reappeared, with a dog-handler and two police constables, both of them wearing high-collared tunics with silver buttons.

"Welcome to Great Scotland Yard," said the Hooded Man, as one of the constables unlocked Josh's handcuffs. He was led across a wide courtyard surrounded by towering red-brick offices. It was raining even harder, and the day was so dark that green-shaded desk lamps were dimly shining in almost every window.

Josh was escorted through black-painted double doors marked MORO ONLY, then marched along a narrow corridor with an echoing parquet floor. He was pushed into an elevator with clattering steel gates and he had to stand with the dog panting and slavering only inches away from him while it clanked its way up to the fifth floor. He tried to give the dog his famous "chill-out" look, which would have had any Marin County pooch rolling over on to its back and whining in pleasure; but the dog-handler was pulling the animal's choke-chain so hard that it was practically asphyxiated. The gates clashed open.

At the end of another narrow corridor, he was steered into a large room with a bare table and two upright wooden chairs. Outside the window there was a dreary view of the Thames, with the rain dredging down, and Waterloo Bridge. The tide was flooding in, so that lighters and pleasure boats rode high at their moorings, and an archipelago of driftwood and oil and nameless flotsam was being carried slowly upstream, in the same way that Julia's body had been.

They kept Josh waiting for over an hour, with the dog wheezing against its chain, as if it was waiting to take a bite out of his face. He developed an agonizing cramp in his left ankle, and began to feel sick with hunger and delayed shock.

"How about a cup of coffee?" he asked the Hooded Man; but the Hooded Man said nothing.

At last the door opened and a small, bald-headed man entered, dressed in a black Puritan tunic and breeches. He had the features of an ill-tempered doll. He had a tiny braided pigtail at the back of his head, tied with a thin black ribbon.

He sat down on the opposite side of the table, spread out a sheaf of papers, and unscrewed a fountain pen. Then he stared at Josh for a long time without saying anything, his pen poised as if he were deciding what he ought to write down.

"I insist that you call the US consul," said Josh. "You can't hold me here without making any charges."

The bald-headed man spoke very softly, punctuating each

phrase with a little suck of his lips. "My name is Master Thomas Edridge. You . . . I gather . . . are Joshua B. Winward . . . from Mill Valley, California."

"Are you the big cheese here?"

"I'm here to ask you some questions. That's all."

"Well, you're out of luck, Master Thomas Edridge, because I'm not about to answer. I'm very upset about what's happened today. Your people terrorized us and cut off that young man's hand."

"Cutter? He's a thrice-convicted thief."

"Maybe he is. But you're supposed to be Christians, not mullahs."

Edridge shrugged. "He knew what the risks were. I wonder . . . if you do."

"Listen, we didn't come here to stir up any trouble. My girlfriend's gone back. All I want to do is join her. I can guarantee that you won't hear from either of us, ever again."

"I'm afraid that it's not as easy as that. You've been causing ructions. To say the least. And I need to know what you're doing here. What mischief you had in mind."

"We didn't have any mischief in mind. We came here completely by accident."

"Come, sir. Nobody comes through any of the six doors by accident. You know very well that there are rituals involved. Synchronicity."

"My girlfriend and I were experimenting, that's all. We were doing a research project on Old Mother Goose rhymes for University of California at Berkeley. We thought we'd try the old 'Jack-be-nimble' trick. We jumped over the candlesticks but we never believed that it would actually work."

"How did you discover . . . where the door was?"

"What?"

"The door in Star Yard. How did you discover where it was?"

"What does it matter?"

"It matters because the precise location of the six doors is known to only a few in *this* world – and to even fewer in yours."

"I told you. We came here by chance."

"Nonetheless, you immediately associated yourselves . . . with thieves and other malcontents."

"They were the first people we met. We didn't know who they were."

"You expect me to believe that?"

"I really don't care what you believe. I want to talk to the US consul."

Edridge licked his lips and carefully adjusted the papers in front of him. "I regret that you have found your way . . . into a world . . . where America is a very different place. Oh, you'd have no trouble in recognizing it. It's a very prosperous country. Wealthy, well fed. Except that you'd find it rather less advanced scientifically. No atom bomb, for example. And socially more . . . stratified. There was no Civil War, for instance, and in many southern states slavery is still acceptable."

"*Slavery*?"

"A very benign form of slavery, Mr Winward. But it is far too profitable a trade for Britain to abandon altogether. And of what other use are the Africans, except to supply the civilized world with labor?"

"I don't believe what I'm hearing."

"What I'm trying to explain to you . . . is that history took a different course in this existence. Slavery persists because there was no War of Independence. What you call the United States of America is a British possession. And hence, there is no US consul."

"How come you know so much about my world?"

"Through interviewing people like yourself. Through books and films which have been brought through the doors. It is part of my duties to understand the history and the motivations of those who come through. Some of them, you see . . . represent a serious threat to the stability of our society."

"That doesn't alter the fact that you have no right to hold me here."

"You don't think so? You are a trespasser, sir, in a place where you have no business to be. You were seen to be associating with criminals and subversives. And what was the purpose of your visit to Lavender Hill?"

"Were your people responsible for that? For killing that woman?"

"We exact very severe punishments on those who attempt to undermine the social and religious structure of our society."

"You're nothing but a gang of butchers."

"I would watch my tongue . . . if I were you. You still haven't given me a satisfactory explanation of your presence here."

"I didn't come here to subvert anything. I don't have any interest in your politics and I'm definitely not interested in your religion."

"You should be. To publicly deny the Lord thy God is a very serious offense in itself."

Josh said, "I'm not denying the Lord my God. I just think it'll be simpler all around if you let me go back where I came from."

"And what guarantee could you give me that you wouldn't return?"

"Because, believe me, I wouldn't come back here for a million dollars."

"Easy to say. But perhaps you have some unfinished business here."

Josh shook his head. "Forget it. I'm not going to play along with this. I've told you how we came here and if you don't want to believe me I really don't mind."

Edridge pushed back his chair with a sharp bark of wood. He stood up and walked around the table until he was standing so close that Josh could smell the musty wool of his tunic.

"This is no joking matter, sir. I have the power to imprison suspected subversives without trial. In some extreme cases I may order them put to death."

"For Christ's sake, how many times do I have to tell you that we came here by accident?"

"Do you think I believe that? Do you think I believe that you accidentally jumped through the door, and accidentally met up with young Mr Cutter and his Burmese friend, and accidentally killed one of our dogs? My dear sir! What a terrible chapter of accidents!"

"Listen, kiss my ass."

Edridge was silent for so long that Josh began to wonder if he was ever going to speak again. But then he sat down again with his hands steepled in front of his face and stared at Josh with eyes that were utterly pitiless. "Tell me why you came here. Tell me the truth."

Josh said nothing at first. But it was becoming clear that Edridge would keep him here for ever, if necessary, until he came up with some kind of satisfactory explanation. "All right," he said. "You want to know the truth. A few days ago my sister's body was found in the Thames. Somebody had murdered her, cut all of her insides out. But nobody could discover where she'd been for the past ten months."

Josh told Edridge all about the letter from Wheatstone Electrics, and how Frank Mordant had arranged to meet Julia at Star Yard. But he purposely omitted any mention of Ella Tibibnia or Mrs Marmion's mother. He didn't yet understand the connection between Mrs Marmion and her mother; and he wasn't sure of the part that Ella was playing – was it really supernatural or was it some other trickery besides? For some reason he felt that he might be putting them in jeopardy if he told Edridge that they had helped him.

"I know Mr Mordant," Edridge nodded. "As far as I'm aware he's a very respectable businessman. Very God-fearing."

"Listen – I'm not suggesting that he had anything to do with Julia's murder. I just wanted to talk to him, to see if he could help me fill in some of the missing months."

"The Masters of Religious Observance don't look very kindly . . . on members of the public who try to investigate criminal matters on their own."

"Well, neither do the Metropolitan Police, but I believe that Julia was here during those ten months and I couldn't see any other way of proving it."

Edridge jotted a few notes on the paper in front of him. "It's not a bad story," he said.

"What do you mean, story? It's the truth."

"You still haven't told me . . . *why* you came to the conclusion that your sister might have gone through the door. What you say about Mr Mordant's letter . . . is plausible. But what reasonable person would come to the conclusion that she had entered . . . a parallel existence?"

"I don't know. I heard the rhyme and I guess it seemed like the only possibility. You know what Sherlock Holmes said."

"No. And I don't wish to know. The fact remains . . . that your story is fanciful and full of . . . unexplained discrepancies. I suspect that you are bent on crime or subversion or both and I intend to discover . . . exactly why you came here and what you intended to do."

"Then I'm sorry. You'll have a hell of a long wait."

"Oh, I don't think so." Edridge beckoned the Hooded Man, who came over to the desk and inclined his head so that Edridge could whisper in his ear. He nodded once, and then again, and Josh could see his eyes shining inside the torn-open gaps of his hessian hood.

"You have a last opportunity . . . to explain why you came through the door." Edridge slid a sheet of paper across the desk and offered Josh his fountain pen. "I want it all here. Names. Addresses. Meeting places. Dates."

"I can't help you."

"Is that your last word?"

"First and last. I've told you why I'm here. I'm trying to find out what happened to my sister, that's all."

"Have you heard of the Holy Harp?" asked the Hooded Man, harshly.

"Somebody mentioned it, yes. I don't know who."

"The Holy Harp sings with the voice of pure truth. As you will shortly discover."

Josh tried to stand up, but the dog leaped up at him so ferociously that he sat back down again. "Listen," he insisted. "I'm not a Communist or an atheist or a terrorist. All I want to do is go back home and leave you people to run your society the way you see fit. You want to cut people's hands off? Fine. You want to keep slaves? I'm not arguing. You want to deny everybody their basic religious rights? That's up to you. Just let me go and you won't see me again till Doomsday."

"Doomsday!" said Edridge. "What an appropriate word to conjure up! The day when everybody has to give an honest account of themselves in the face of God. Well, today is *your* Doomsday, Mr Joshua B. Winward. And may the Lord have mercy on you."

Eighteen

Nancy rang the doorbell three times before Ella answered on the intercom. "*Who is it*?" she asked, suspiciously.

"It's Nancy. Something terrible's happened. Please open the door. I didn't know where else to go."

The door buzzed and Nancy pushed her way inside. Ella was waiting for her at the top of the stairs, with Abraxas wagging his tail so hard that it slapped against the banisters.

"Have you been *swimming*?" asked Ella, when she saw Nancy's damp clothes and bedraggled hair.

Nancy shook her head. "It was raining in the other London."

"So you got through," said Ella, ushering her into her apartment. "Isn't Josh with you?"

"The candles blew out. I had to leave him behind."

"You look exhausted. Here – let me give you something dry to wear. You don't mind a caftan, do you?"

"I had to leave him behind," said Nancy, desperately. "I didn't have any choice. These terrible Hooded Men caught him. They have swords, and they cut a young man's hand off. I don't know what they're going to do to Josh."

"The Hoodies," said Ella. The sun was shining through the window, and outside the noises of Earl's Court traffic sounded reassuringly normal.

Nancy was tugging off one of her boots. She stopped, and looked up at Ella in astonishment. "You *know* about them?"

Ella nodded. "I've always known about them. I come from there. This isn't my London at all."

"You knew about them and yet you let us go there? They killed a man in front of us! They chased us all across the rooftops and we almost died!"

"I'm sorry. I was taking the chance that you wouldn't run into them. If I'd told you what it was really like there, would you have gone?"

"I can't believe this! You tricked us into going!"

"I didn't trick you, Nancy. You wanted to go. It was just bad luck that you ran into the Hoodies."

"Why didn't you *warn* us? For Christ's sake, Josh could be dead by now!"

"I couldn't warn you. I didn't know if I could trust you or not. If I'd have warned you, it would have been an open admission that I was part of the resistance network."

"*You* didn't trust *us*?"

"We can never be too careful. The Doorkeepers send all kinds of people through to infiltrate us, and they come in so many different guises. Some of them look so innocent you can't believe it. University students, council officials, widows who come to me because they want to talk to their dear departed husbands. You and Josh could easily have been planted by the Doorkeepers to find out how many of us there are, and where we live."

"You really believed that we were spies for the Hooded Men?"

"No, we didn't. But we had to be sure. Because you and Josh were a godsend. Almost too good to be true."

"Too *good*? Too damned gullible!"

"Please . . . I can understand why you're angry. But we've been trying to catch Frank Mordant for a very long time, and we thought that you might have better luck than us."

Nancy shook her head in disbelief. "You knew who we were even before you first met us at the subway station, didn't you?"

"Yes, I did. A whole lot of people have been keeping a very close eye on you, ever since you got here. One or two police officers . . . the receptionist from the Paragon Hotel . . . Ranjit Singh at St Thomas's . . . old Mrs Marmion. The resistance come in all creeds and colors and ages. The only thing they have in common is a hatred of the Doorkeepers."

"I don't understand this at all," said Nancy. "All of those people were *watching* us?"

"Watching and guiding. Now – why don't you change, and I'll make you a cup of tea, and I'll tell you about it."

"I have to go back. I have to go back and find Josh."

"I know. And we can't waste any time, either. The Hoodies probably won't hurt him until they find out why he came through the door. But they're not very patient. There are lots of stories about them cutting people open and eating their livers, but that's all they are, stories. The Hoodies don't discourage them, though. It makes them sound more frightening than they really are."

"You don't think they're frightening enough?"

"Come on, don't worry too much. Josh doesn't know anything about the resistance, so they can't charge him with subversion."

"We met John Farbelow at the British Museum. Josh knows about *him*."

"Yes, but how much? And John Farbelow is a totally wild card: even the Hoodies know that. His heart's in the right place, but he always follows his own nutty agenda. All the same," she said, "I'm glad you mentioned him. He has outstanding contacts in all kinds of places, including Scotland Yard. He could help us to get Josh free."

"So if I went back and got in touch with him . . . ?"

"*You* can't go back, not until tomorrow. The earth has to turn a full circle before you can go back the way you came."

"Or what? I just couldn't get through?"

"Oh, you'd get through, all right. But not to the world you'd just left behind. You'd get through to the next world in the sequence of worlds – and, believe me, you wouldn't want to do that."

"There are *more* Londons?"

"An infinite number, as far as anybody can tell. Some people have tried to go further, to see how different they are, but not many of them have ever come back." She spooned a powder of peony root into a blue china teapot and poured boiling water over it. "Here . . . peony is great for calming you down. It restores your sense of reality."

"That's good. Right now, I need all the reality I can get."

Nancy dropped the caftan over her head. It was pure silk, and it felt cool, soft and reassuring, like gently being stroked by an affectionate friend. Ella sat down next to her, cross-legged.

"I was born in the other world. It's hard to believe, isn't it, but I had no idea this London existed when I was a child. I was born in British Martinique and my mother was a slave. I would have been a slave, too, if I hadn't had the same psychic sensitivity as my grandmother. One day I used my sensitivity to find a small child who had been trapped down a well for three days. The slavemaster told the Hoodies what I'd done, and the Hoodies took me away from my family and brought me to London by Zeppelin. They trained me to find subversives and non-believers and Purgatorials."

"So how did you get here?"

"The Hoodies beat me and they abused me and they treated me so bad. So one day, when a subversive was running away from them, jumping over the candles and right through the door, I followed him. I've been here ever since. But I always swore to God that I would get my revenge on the Hoodies one day."

"What exactly *are* they, the Hoodies? Why do they wear those horrible hoods all the time?"

"They're sensitives, too. They're direct descendants of the Puritan witchfinders. They can actually *sense* when a man or a woman is an unbeliever. They can almost *taste* your lack of faith. That's why they all wear hoods . . . so that they're not distracted by what they can see with their eyes. They could find you blindfolded if they really wanted to. Where do you think the game of Blind Man's Bluff came from? It was children, pretending that they were the Hoodies, hunting for Catholics. Sniffing them out."

Nancy sipped her tea. Ella was right: she felt very much calmer now, very much more focused. The day seemed clear and sharp, and her panic was beginning to subside.

"Tell me about Frank Mordant."

"What a piece of work he is. About two years ago we discovered by accident that he was advertising for young girls here in this London; and that he was taking them through the doors to the other London. One of my friends saw him by the Tower of London, taking a girl through the door by Traitor's Gate. The same thing happened to Julia and it happened to John Farbelow's girlfriend, too. Frank Mordant always preys on girls who are lonely or distressed or looking for a new life. He gives them a job; but he doesn't touch them for weeks; or months; or even years. He doesn't touch them until he thinks that the trail has gone stone cold and hardly anybody in *this* London is looking for them any more.

"Then – without any warning – he kills them. He hangs them and he takes video pictures while they die. Snuff movies, which he sells for hundreds and thousands of pounds all over the world. He always mutilates them, too, in different ways, although we don't know why. Some of their bodies he dumps back here, but a whole lot more of them have disappeared for good. We don't know how many exactly, but we reckon he may have murdered as many as fifty or sixty."

"My God. Can't you *do* anything? Can't you talk to the cops?"

"We've tried more than once. We found a very sympathetic young detective inspector in Chelsea who was prepared to listen to us. But even he had to give up, in the end. He didn't want to jeopardize his career by sounding as if he was some kind of raving lunatic. And there's the burden of proof, too. We have to catch Frank Mordant red-handed, actually disposing of one of the bodies, or else we have to find fingerprints and fibers and DNA samples. And even if we do that, we have to catch him and physically drag him back here, without the Hoodies stopping us. And we know from bitter experience that he's very well in with the Hoodies. They never touch him, no matter how many times he goes backwards and forwards from one London to the next. I don't know why.

"*Then*, of course, we have to persuade the police *here* to arrest him and bring him up in front of a court of law. And do you seriously think that any jury is going to believe anything about nursery-rhyme doors or parallel Londons?"

"Couldn't you light the candles and *show* them? They'd have to believe!"

Ella gave her a wry smile. "Let's cross that bridge when we come to it. Let's just see if we can get Frank Mordant first. And before that, let's see if we can get Josh back."

"Don't the police in the *other* London suspect Frank Mordant of anything? I mean, if girls are disappearing . . . doesn't anybody wonder what's happened to them? Even there, they must have laws against abduction and murder."

"Don't ask me. Perhaps the Hoodies protect him. Perhaps he bribes them. Perhaps people from this London aren't entitled to the same kind of human rights. They don't have valid birth certificates or passports or any proof of identity. Strictly speaking, they don't exist. In that other London, they have slavery, don't they? What are they going to care about a few homeless girls?"

"So, what are you going to do?" asked Nancy.

"I'm going to go through this evening, probably through Bread Street. With any luck the Hoodies won't be looking for anybody to come through there. I'll find John Farbelow and see what he can do to help me. I'll do everything I can, Nancy, I promise. I'll be back tomorrow evening, and let's hope that Josh will be coming back, too."

"And what can *I* do?"

Ella grasped both of her hands, and gave her a smile of sympathy. "I'm sorry. Nothing. You'll just have to sit and wait."

When Nancy returned to their hotel room, a red light was flashing on the phone. She picked it up and the receptionist told her that they had been called by DS Paul. Could they call her back on her mobile?

"Detective Sergeant Paul? This is Nancy Andersen."

"Is Mr Winward with you?"

"He's – ah. He had to go out for a while. To buy some dental floss."

"Well, when he comes back, can you tell him that we may

have had something of a breakthrough. A young man called us today to say that he was down by Southwark Bridge on the night that Julia's body was dumped into the Thames. He was depressed because he had just split up with his girlfriend, and he was thinking of throwing himself into the river. That's why he's taken so long to come forward."

"He saw something?"

"Yes, he did. He saw three men carrying a bundle to the parapet and throwing it over. He swears that it was just like a body. One of the men was oriental in appearance, the other two were white, middle-aged. The young man says that he would be confident about identifying all of them. He's coming into New Scotland Yard in about an hour to help us prepare a photofit picture."

"This is amazing. I mean, this is real evidence, right?"

"Oh, we've got more than that. After the men had gone, our suicidal friend found a gold and brown enamel cufflink on the pavement, close to the place where they had thrown the bundle over. It was a monogrammed cufflink, with the initials FM."

Nancy felt as if her stomach had suddenly filled up with icy cold water. "FM?"

"That's right. Whoever it was, he could hardly have helped us more if he'd left a note stuck to the bridge with his name and address."

"That's good news. That's terrific news. So . . . all you have to do now is find the guy, yes?"

"There's more to it than that. We still have to prove that the bundle was Julia's body, and that whoever this man was, he killed her. But it's a very, very significant step forward. I don't have to remind you not to talk to the media about it, do I?"

"I won't say anything to anybody. I really appreciate all of the hard work you've put into this, I can tell you; and I know that Josh does, too. All you have to do now is find the guy, huh?"

"We'll find him," DS Paul assured her. "If he's still in London, I promise you, we'll find him."

It all depends on which London, thought Nancy, and put down the phone.

* * *

Late in the afternoon, as the shadows lengthened along Piccadilly, and swallows wheeled over Hyde Park, Nancy took a tube up to Berman's, the theatrical costumiers. In a huge upstairs room, dimly lit by a grimy skylight, she walked along rail after rail of period costumes. Flamboyant flouncy dresses from *The Three Musketeers*; crinolines and hobble skirts and flapper dresses made of beads. At last she found a tailored suit in gray Prince-of-Wales check, very fitted, with a skirt that came just below the knee. Very 1955 – a suit that nobody in Frank Mordant's London would look at twice. She found black high-heeled shoes and a white blouse with a frilly collar to match.

Back at the hotel, she filled a plastic carrier bag with anything she thought she could trade for money. Her watch, her hairdryer, Josh's alarm clock, even his Nike trainers. She was in bed by eleven o'clock, with a map of suburban London spread over her knees, and BBC's *Question Time* burbling in the background.

Before she slept, she said a prayer to the spirits that Josh should be safely rescued from the Hooded Men; and blessed Ella and John Farbelow and whoever might be involved in setting Josh free. Then she asked Gitche Manitou to give her strength to do what she needed to do. If she couldn't help to rescue Josh, she could at least avenge Julia's murder by bringing Frank Mordant back to this London, where DS Paul had enough evidence to hold him, and almost enough evidence to convict him.

She closed her eyes, and dreamed of running through twisting alleyways, colliding with the walls. She dreamed of echoing laughter and lashing rain. She dreamed that dogs were after her, and that men in masks were breathing harshly in her ear. They were urging her to go back. *Go back, Nancy, there's nothing here but horror and blood. Go back, Nancy, you don't know what you're getting yourself into. There's blood here – gallons and gallons of blood, and you wouldn't want to be drowned, now would you*?

Nineteen

Josh was jolted awake by the feeling that his jaw had cracked apart. He opened his eyes and the room suddenly tilted. His mouth was stretched wide open, and crowded with a whole array of tight steel wires. He tried to swallow and he almost choked himself in his own saliva.

He couldn't think where he was, or even *who* he was. All he knew was that his head was swimming like a lava lamp, and that he was shivering cold.

He tried to close his eyes, to deny that this was happening, but he was in too much pain to fall back into unconsciousness, and so he opened them again. Reality began to reassemble itself, like a broken mirror in a movie run backward.

He was bound upright in a cramped and very uncomfortable wooden chair. Not only that, his mouth hurt so much that his gums had started to throb. And his legs hurt, too. And there was a pain between his legs that was worse than that time that Sergeant Szymanski had kicked him in the crotch for refusing to climb up the scramble-nets.

He tried again to swallow, and this time he retched, with a horrible cackle. But it was all he could manage: he couldn't even manage a whimper. The wires that crowded his mouth were attached by screws to a triangular iron frame which stood on the floor just in front of him, a little over four feet high – a grotesque parody of a harp. The wires formed a fan shape as they entered his open lips, and each of them was attached to one of his molars. He must have been given a general anesthetic when they were fastened, because each molar had been drilled right down to the nerve. Every time he moved his head or accidentally tugged on one of the wires, he suffered a blinding spike-shaped surge of utter pain in every tooth. He would have shrieked out loud, if it had been humanly possible.

Shuddering with shock and cold, he looked down and saw that more steel wires had been screwed into his kneecaps and all along his thighs, seven or eight of them, right into the bone. These, too, were attached to the frame of the harp, so that every time he shifted his legs, they tugged at his nerve endings and gave him a kind of pain that he never could have imagined possible.

His penis looked as if it were half-erect, and it took him a few seconds to focus and understand why. A single steel wire had been inserted into his urethra, and he could feel something sharp and prickly deep between his legs. Blood was dripping from the end of his penis, and this alone would have been enough to make him weep.

But there was more. Wires had been screwed into his forearms and his shoulder blades. Wires had been driven right through his nipples, through his body, and attached by screws to the chair in which he was sitting. If he had tried to sit up, he would have sliced himself into a grisly *julienne* of Josh.

He waited, shaking like an epileptic. He was sitting in a bare cream-painted room, nothing exceptional about it, except a large portrait of a somber-looking man dressed all in black. A police officer was standing in the far corner, staring at the floor.

"Ah . . ." Josh choked. "Ahh . . . agghh . . . ah!"

The police officer lifted one finger, as if cautioning Josh to have patience. He picked up the phone, and said, "Yes, Master Edridge. Yes, he's come round. He seems well enough, yes."

When he had finished, the police officer hunkered down next to Josh and smiled at him for a while, as if enough smiling could compensate for what they had done to him. The police officer had pitted cheeks and a tiny gingery moustache, no bigger than a smoker's toothbrush. He could have been painted by Norman Rockwell, if there hadn't been such deadness in his eyes.

"Master Edridge is coming to see you. Take my advice. If Master Edridge asks you a question, answer it. Don't try to tell lies. The pain isn't worth it. You'll probably be dead by the end of the day, so don't worry about heroic gestures, if you know what I mean. And the rest of your lot, what are they worth? All you subversives. They'd sell you down the river, too, if it meant they didn't have to suffer the Holy Harp."

So this was the Holy Harp that Simon Cutter had warned him about. He tried to choke out some kind of reply to the police officer, but he was suffering far too much pain, and all he could manage was a gargling sound. He dropped his head down, but the wires tugged at the nerves in his teeth and he had to lift it up again.

"They'll execute you quick and clean if you confess," said the police officer, surreptitiously checking his watch. "The longer you mess them about, the more riled they're going to get, and the more they'll make you suffer. And let me tell you, some of the things I've seen them do . . . They're agents of the Lord, that's what they call themselves. And that gives them carty blanky."

The door opened and Master Thomas Edridge came in, with a loose black hood draped over his head. He was closely followed by a dog-handler with a vicious pink-eyed terrier, whose claws kept dragging up the rugs. Edridge approached the Holy Harp, slowly and almost prissily, and when he was standing close enough he dragged a long white handkerchief out of his sleeve and patted his face and his scalp. Josh saw his eyes glance for a split second between his legs, but then he coughed like the Bey in *Lawrence of Arabia* and said, "Ready to be cooperative yet, Mr Winward?"

Josh couldn't say anything. His lips were numb, his tongue was swollen, and his teeth felt as if they had been wrenched around in his gums.

"I don't expect you to talk," said Edridge. "We don't expect miracles, after all. But here is a pen and here is a sheet . . . of good-quality paper. On this paper you will explain exactly why you came here. And you will list the names and addresses of all of those you came to see, and what help you expected from them."

Josh hesitated for a moment, but then he took the pad and wrote the only word he could think of. *No.*

"You came here to make contact. With troublemakers. Come on. Admit it."

No.

"If that wasn't the reason for your coming through the door, then what was?"

I told you, Josh wrote. *I want to know who killed my sister.*

"To find out . . . who killed your sister. That's brilliant! What a cover. One of the very best that the subversives have ever come up with. It wouldn't surprise me if you killed your sister . . . yourself. In order to give yourself a watertight cover."

You're sick.

"Sick? You talk to me of sick? I'll show you a world where people no longer fear God. I'll show you a world where every one of the ten commandments has been crushed underfoot. I'll show you a world of such greed and licentiousness and lack of faith that it would take your very breath away. Except that it wouldn't. Because that is *your* world, my friend. And that is why we guard our doors, and hunt down subversives with such vigor. To prevent you from infiltrating us, from corrupting us, from undermining our faith and our moral fortitude. For let me tell you, Mr Winward, the world where you come from is the very definition of hell on earth."

Josh hesitated for a moment. He felt such pain that he could hardly keep the pen steady. Then he wrote, *Hell is made by bigots.*

Edridge stood up. He circled around the room for a moment, but then he leaned close to Josh and whispered in his ear, "You could have everything you wanted, in this world, if you helped us."

Josh flicked his eyes toward him. It would have been too painful for him to try to move his head.

"We reward those who help us to track down subversives. We reward them very well. You could find yourself with a very fine house in the country, and substantial money in the bank. Do you know the price on John Farbelow's head? Three thousand pounds. Think of it! A man could live like a king."

Josh wrote, *Don't know squat.*

"Squat? What's squat?"

Josh tossed the pen down on to the paper. Edridge suddenly lost his patience. He stepped away from Josh's chair and beckoned the policeman forward. "Show him how the Harp works. Play him a penitential hymn."

With a serious, wary look on his face, the policeman approached the Holy Harp and flexed his fingers. Josh stared back at him, sitting rigidly upright, hardly able to bear the idea of the pain that he was going to feel. The policeman hesitated for a moment, but then he dragged the tips of his fingers down the tightly-stretched wires. They made a plangent, harmonic sound, in a minor key, like the beginning of an avant-garde symphony. At the same time they tugged at the naked roots of Josh's teeth, so that he let out a hoarse, incoherent roar of total agony. They pulled at every ganglion in his shoulders. They dragged at his nipples and made his stomach muscles convulse. His knees shuddered; his thighs tensed in a vicious, vise-like cramp; and his penis felt as if it had been peeled inside out, and every single nerve exposed.

The pain was so intense that it was almost wonderful. Josh felt crucified, sanctified – lifted above his everyday existence into a world where there was nothing but dazzling red light and blinding white pain. He could almost believe that he was close to God.

The strings of the Holy Harp were rippled again, and he closed his eyes tight as the pain made every nerve ending in his body contract and flinch. It was his teeth that hurt him the most, though. His teeth hurt so much that he was far beyond weeping.

The policeman stepped back, and Edridge came up to Josh again.

"What a hymn that was," he said, softly. "Now do you think you might tell me what I have to know?"

Josh reached out for the pen but his hand was like a helpless claw. Edridge picked it up for him and placed it between his fingers, like a solicitous mother teaching her three-year-old to write. He pushed the paper nearer, and Josh was able to scrawl *I know 0.*

"Nothing?" said Edridge. "That can't be right. Young Simon Cutter has already told us that he took you to meet John Farbelow, and that you and he spent the evening discussing acts of sabotage and subversion. Don't tell me he was lying to us. If he was lying to us, he will have to die for obstructing our investigation – and very unpleasantly, too. The wicked must be permitted to see the evil of their ways before they are allowed to enjoy the comforts of the grave."

He waited for almost half a minute for Josh to answer. Then he beckoned to the police officer again.

It was then that Josh knew that he wasn't going to be able to take any more hymns on the Holy Harp. His training in the Marines had given him a high degree of tolerance to physical pain; and his studies of Zen and hypnosis had made him mentally able to detach himself from his immediate surroundings. But the agony of the Holy Harp had penetrated right through to the very root of his soul. It had taken away everything: his pride, his dignity, his endurance – and most of all, it had taken away his humanity. He had been reduced to the level of an insect, writhing in agony on the end of a pointed stick.

He scrabbled for the pen, picked it up, dropped it, and then made another desperate grab for it. As he tried to lean forward, the wires in his mouth tugged at the nerves in his teeth and his eyes filled with tears. Edridge watched him in amusement.

"You want to write something else, perhaps? Don't tell me that you wish to confess."

Wincing, Josh managed to scrawl, *Yes dont hurt Cutter*.

"You're sure of this? You're going to tell us everything you know? You won't change your mind once we release you from the Holy Harp?"

No. Josh didn't have any idea what he was going to tell them, but he knew that he would rather invent names and addresses and subversive secrets than face any more pain. At least it would give him time; and he knew that Nancy wouldn't abandon him here.

Edridge nodded to the police officer and the police officer picked up the phone. A few minutes later a thin young man in a white lab coat and wire-rimmed glasses came in, carrying a small leather wallet. He drew up a chair, sat down beside Josh, and opened the wallet to reveal a neat set of shiny little tools.

"Still as you can, please," he said. His breath smelled of spring onions. With the smallest of wrenches, he unfastened the tiny bolts that had been screwed into Josh's teeth. Josh breathed in through his mouth, and the cold air was sucked directly on to his nerves.

One by one, the dental wires were released and drawn out of his mouth. Then the thin young man unfastened the wires that went right through his body and were screwed to the back of the chair. He had to slide them right through Josh's muscles, and through the soft tissue of his abdomen. When he drew the wire out of his penis Josh had to bite his own hand.

He might have fainted. He remembered being helped out of the seat. He remembered somebody wrapping a coarse woolen bathrobe around him. But the next thing he knew, he was crouched up in the fetal position on a thin ticking mattress, on an iron bedstead, in a pale green cell. It must have been morning, because there was wishy-washy light coming in through the high barred window.

He eased himself gradually into a sitting position. His mouth was enormously swollen, and when he opened his bathrobe he saw that his whole body was peppered with tiny scarlet wounds, as well as dozens of purple and yellow bruises. The last time he had felt as bad as this was when he had driven his Firebird into a sofa-bed that somebody had dropped in the middle of the San Diego freeway, and rolled over three times.

Outside his door he heard whistling and laughter and the scratching of dogs' claws on linoleum flooring. His teeth ached so badly that he was almost tempted to bang his face against the bedrail and knock them all out. He tried to stand up, but the pain between his legs was unbearable.

He lay down again, and in spite of his pain, he managed to doze for a while. An image of Julia and her daisy kept spinning slowly through his mind, around and around. He hoped to God that she hadn't suffered as much as this.

He didn't hear Edridge and the Hooded Man come into his cell. He opened his eyes and there they were, standing over him.

Edridge said, "Feeling fit, Mr Winward? We're going for a little ride."

A black Ford V8 was waiting for them in the courtyard. The rain was lighter now, whirling down in a fine, prickling spray, but still enough to give them a soaking. One of the Hooded Men was already waiting in the front passenger seat, next to a uniformed driver with a haircut so short that the back of his neck bristled. But neither of them turned around as Josh was pushed into the back seat, sitting between a plain-clothes police officer in a brown double-breasted mackintosh and Master Thomas Edridge, in his hood.

"Let's get cracking," said Edridge. They drove out of Great Scotland Yard and headed east, along the Embankment. Josh was still feeling swimmy with shock, and every jolt was agony, but he kept thinking to himself that he still had a chance. What had they told him during his Marine training? "Every minute you're alive, that's an extra minute to take the advantage." And what had he read from the Chinese scholar Lao-Tzū? "The Way is an empty vessel that may yet be drawn from."

"Where are you taking me?" he asked Edridge, in a puffy voice.

"The Tower, you'll be privileged to hear. We have some people there who are very good with blasphemers and subversives."

"The Tower? Isn't that where they used to lock up traitors?"

"What do you think *you* are, Mr Winward?"

The Ford's transmission whined; the windshield wipers

flapped feebly against the rain. The plain-clothes policeman began an elaborate exploration of his right nostril with the tip of his index finger. In another time, in another place, in another world, Josh would have said something sarcastic.

They had almost reached Blackfriars Bridge. On their left, an exit ramp led up to New Bridge Street. As they approached it, Josh was sure that he could see headlights coming *down* it, in the wrong direction, and coming down it fast. Other vehicles were swerving to the side of the exit ramp to get out of the way. As they came closer, Josh could see that they belonged to a huge dray lorry, loaded with wooden kegs of beer.

"Bloody hell!" said the police driver. "What the bloody hell does he think he's—"

Edridge gripped the seat in front of him. Even the Hooded Man raised his arm to protect himself. But the dray came roaring straight down the ramp without slowing down at all, and collided directly with the front of their car. With an ear-splitting smash, they were spun around on their axis, and collided backward with the median strip. Josh was thrown forward, hitting his chin on the seat in front. The Hooded Man knocked his head so hard against the passenger window that it cracked.

"*Get out of here*!" Edridge screamed at the driver. "*Put your foot down*! *It's an ambush*!"

The driver must have broken his ribs on the steering wheel, because his face was gray and he was whining for breath. Next to Josh, the plain-clothes policeman reached into his coat and produced a large Webley revolver. He wound down the window and jabbed it wildly at everybody that he could see, shouting, "Keep your distance! Keep your distance! Police! That's an order!"

With a miserable slithering of tires, the driver managed to get the Ford moving. "*Go*!" screamed Edridge. But before they could cover more than fifteen feet, another car came hurtling toward them – a big black car like a Pierce-Arrow, its headlights blazing – and it crashed into them at nearly twenty miles an hour. They were hurtled backward, and the Ford hit the side of the Blackfriars underpass so hard that its trunk was flattened.

Josh, stunned, was aware of men in long flappy raincoats running across the road. The front passenger door was wrenched open and the Hooded Man fell sideways on to the tarmac. The plain-clothes policeman seemed to have lost his gun, because he was fumbling around on the floor, but then his door was pulled open, too. Josh saw an iron bar swing, and the policeman was cracked so hard on the side of the head that he dropped into the gutter, quaking.

Edridge was struggling to open his door, but it had been jammed by their last collision. He turned to Josh and both of his eyes were bloodshot, like a vampire's. "You will pay for this, you and your friends! You will burn in hell, for ever and ever, as Latimer and Ridley had to burn!"

He was still struggling when his window was smashed open with a hammer, and he was showered with glass.

"*I am Master Thomas Edridge*!" he screamed. "*You dare to touch me, on pain of execution*!"

Two hands in grubby gray mittens reached in through the window. One hand snatched at Edrige's little ponytail, and forced his head back, exposing his protuberant Adam's apple. The other hand held an upholsterer's knife, short-bladed and sharp. Edridge didn't even have time to protest before it sliced across his throat. It happened so quickly that Josh didn't understand what was going on; but the next thing he knew there was warm blood spattering his hands. The car door was heaved open, and Edridge tumbled out sideways, with a gargling noise.

The mittened hands took hold of Josh's arm and pulled him across the back seat. For a terrible moment he thought that he was going to be killed, too. But then an urgent voice said, "Come on, Mr Winward. We have to skip out of here quick!"

Josh managed to climb out of the car. He supported himself on the roof for a moment, his eyes half-closed against the drizzle. Then he staggered: he could hardly walk. A tall young curly-headed man in a gray raincoat helped him across the street, his feet tripping and stumbling. Four or five young men and women were keeping watch all around them, in poses that were almost heroic. They lifted him into the back of the Pierce-Arrow, and climbed in beside him. He heard doors slamming, and then they were roaring away down Upper Thames Street.

They swerved left, and then right, and then up through all the steep side-turnings between St Paul's and the river. The Pierce-Arrow was a huge car, with very soft suspension, and it collided several times with roadside bollards and parked cars and boxes of rubbish. But at last they skirted their way around St Paul's Cathedral, and the first police car they saw with its blue light flashing and its bell ringing was speeding off in the opposite direction, back to Blackfriars.

A black face appeared over the top of the front seat, and gave Josh a wide and toothy smile. Ella – with her hair knotted up in a scarf, so that she looked like a 1930s scrubwoman.

"How are you doing, Josh? You look like something the cat sicked up."

"*Ella*?" he said. He could hardly believe it.

"It's a long story, Josh. But don't worry. Everything's going to be fine."

Another face turned around from the front seat. It was John Farbelow, his thistledown hair concealed beneath an old black beret, his chin prickly with white stubble. "Welcome back, Josh," he told him. "That little exercise tested our resources, I'll have to admit. But we couldn't let the Hoodies have you, could we?"

"You've been here before?" Josh asked Ella. "You *know* these people?"

"I was born here, Josh. Brought up here."

"I don't get it. The séance . . . the letter . . . why did you bother with any of that?"

"I'm sorry," said Ella. "I have to confess that I put you both at risk. But like I told Nancy, I didn't really know how genuine you were. The Hoodies have agents and informers absolutely everywhere."

"Well . . . our informers aren't bad, either," said John Farbelow, with a satisfied smile. "We knew which car Josh was going to be traveling in; we knew approximately when;

and the rest was just a case of being totally violent." He paused, and lit a cigarette. "The dray was good, though, wasn't it? I mean, what's anybody going to do when they see eight tons of best bitter hurtling toward them?"

Ella playfully tugged his beret down at the back. "You know as well as I do that it was a fantastic piece of planning. You did well, John. And so did all the rest of you. Thanks."

They kept speeding north-westward – jolting down sidestreets, bouncing through mews and garage blocks and private driveways and parks. The rain was lashing down harder still, and it was so dark inside the Pierce-Arrow that they could hardly distinguish each other's faces.

"How's Nancy?" asked Josh. "She didn't come back with you, did she?"

"Nancy's great. She's back at your hotel, resting."

"How are we going to get back?"

"The Farringdon door," said John Farbelow. "It isn't used very often, because it's difficult to find. The Hoodies will probably think that you've gone back to Star Yard."

"I didn't tell them anything," said Josh. "They knew your name already; and they knew that Simon Cutter had taken us to see you."

"You can't keep any secrets in the resistance," John Farbelow replied. "There's too much bribery, too little faith. Anyhow, I wouldn't have blamed you if you'd blabbed. Nobody can take more than two or three hymns on the Holy Harp. My friend Michael died when they did it to him. Heart attack. And of course the Masters of Religious Observance never take the blame. 'Death by natural causes in the course of routine judicial questioning.'"

They reached the corner of Farringdon Street and Bowling Green Lane. It had suddenly stopped raining, even though the gutters were flooded and cars were still swishing past them in clouds of spray. Josh was helped out of the car and across the street, with John Farbelow and Ella following close behind. They passed a sandwich shop on the corner, with steamed-up windows and a sign advertising Craven A cigarettes – "the only cigarettes that don't hurt my throat". Just past the sandwich shop was a narrow alleyway which Josh would never have noticed if it hadn't been pointed out to him. It was less than three feet wide and looked like nothing but a crevice in between the sooty black buildings.

"Right to the end," said John Farbelow. They walked about thirty or forty feet, where the crevice came to an end. Bricked up. Blank. Josh leaned against the wall, his mouth throbbing and his whole body tingling with pain.

John Farbelow knelt down and took three stubby church candles out of his pocket. "They say that the doors go right back to the days of the Druids. They made them so that they could escape from the Romans."

Ella glanced nervously back along the alleyway. "Can we hurry, John? You never know who might have been following us."

"Oh, there's always somebody following us. Always somebody ready to sell their soul for seven-and-six." He lit the candles one by one, and crossed himself. "There – that should take you over. Good luck, Ella, and pray for us, won't you?"

Ella held him tight. "You don't know how much I appreciate what you've done, John."

"It was nothing. It was time that we shook them up a bit, anyway. Time we drew some blood. They won't be so damned complacent now that we've given Master Thomas Edridge an extra smile."

He grasped Josh by the elbow, supporting most of his weight, and led him toward the candles. Josh felt so weak that he didn't know if he was going to be able to stumble, let alone jump. But John Farbelow picked him up bodily, held him a foot off the ground, so that his legs dangled, and then physically threw him over the candles into the end of the alleyway. He fell heavily on to the ground, in a mess of wet leaves and pigeon-droppings. He didn't shout out, because of masculine pride; but he lay on his face for a moment, biting his tongue so hard that he could taste blood.

"Come on, Josh! Up!" John Farbelow shouted at him. "Ella's coming through!"

Josh managed to grip the brick wall and drag himself on to

his feet. As he did so, Ella came bounding across the candles and almost collided with him.

"Let's go, quickly," she urged.

Josh lifted his hand in greeting to John Farbelow; and John Farbelow, as he turned his back, gave him a wry, dismissive salute.

"Where do we go from here?" he asked Ella, looking around. "This still looks like a dead end."

"Oh, there's always a door, everywhere," said Ella. At the very end of the alleyway there was a narrow crevice in the brickwork, barely wide enough for a cat to squeeze through.

"We can't go through there."

"It's the only way. Well, it's not the *only* way. You could jump back over and give yourself up."

"Ella, confined spaces give me panic attacks. I mean, serious panic attacks. How far does it go, this gap in the wall?"

"Fifteen feet, not much longer."

"Fifteen feet, Jesus. What happens if I'm wedged?"

"You won't be wedged. I'll push you out ahead of me."

"What happens if *you* get wedged?"

"What are you trying to tell me here, that I'm overweight?"

"I didn't mean that. But you have to admit that you're curvy."

"Oh, I see. Now my ass is too big."

"Your ass is perfect. But that's a real narrow gap there. And I don't want to end up a skeleton, jammed solid between one world and the next."

Ella took hold of both of his hands and kissed him. "You're making excuses, Josh. You're hurt. You need to get back to reality. Just force yourself through. Don't panic, it'll make you breathe more deeply, and your lungs will expand. Take shallow breaths and tell yourself that you're going to keep on going, and that nothing's going to stop you."

Josh took two or three very deep breaths, then a succession of shallow breaths. "OK . . . I think I'm ready."

He pressed his back flat against the brick wall and pushed himself into the crevice. Now that he was in it, he could see the end of it, but it looked a very long way off, as if he were viewing it down the wrong end of a telescope. More like fifty feet than fifteen. All the same, he pushed himself sideways, his clothes scraping harshly against the brickwork, almost hopping with his feet to keep himself going.

Ella followed him, and the two began their slow, arduous journey from one side of the universe to the other. It didn't take long before their knuckles were scraped raw, their feet ached, and they were gasping for lack of oxygen. For Josh, the struggle was even worse, because his teeth ached and his body ached, and he could barely find the strength to move himself along.

"Don't give up," Ella panted. "It's not far now."

But Josh was suddenly overwhelmed with a terrible feeling that he was going to be trapped between these two brick walls for ever. He was only six or seven feet from the end of the crevice. He could see daylight, and hear traffic, and he knew that it was the real world, *his* world, where there were no Hoodies and no Holy Harps and the skies didn't grind with the sound of Zeppelins. But he couldn't move any further. He was exhausted, agonized, and he simply couldn't find the will to continue.

"*Move*!" Ella urged him. "Come on, Josh, you have to move!"

He shook his head. It was strange, but he almost felt like going to sleep, pinned between these walls. Anything was better than trying to scrape his way through. Anything was better than carrying on.

"*Move, Josh, you bastard*!" Ella screamed at him.

"I can't," he told her.

"Oh yes, you can. Because Nancy's waiting for you; and your parents are waiting for you; and, most of all, because Julia wants you to catch the man who killed her, Josh, and you won't be able to do that if you're stuck here between these two brick walls."

Josh looked at her. He had never seen a woman's eyes look so fierce.

"You're right," he said. "God, I hate you. But you're right." And, inch by inch, he began to drag himself further along the crevice, until at last he reached the end. Ella followed him, and the two of them walked along the narrow alleyway until they reached Farringdon Road.

Outside, on the street, there was a blast of noise. Buses, trucks, taxis, trains. Hundreds of hurrying pedestrians. The air was thick with pollution, but at least the smell was familiar. He had left behind the oily diesel of the other London's buses, and the stench of horse manure. He looked up in the sky and saw a small private jet whistling on its way to London City Airport. The sky was streaked with cloud, but the day was bright, and it was *his* sky.

They took a taxi back to west London. Josh was beginning to tremble uncontrollably, and Ella wanted him to get to bed as soon as possible.

"Do you want me to call you a doctor?" she asked him, as they went up in the hotel elevator.

"What am I going to say to a doctor? All of my teeth have been drilled right down to the nerves and there are holes in my body. He's going to think I'm some kind of sado-masochist."

"Just watch out for infection, that's all."

"I'll take a salt bath. But I need sleep, more than anything else. And I need to see Nancy."

He opened the door of his hotel room. "Hallo?" he called. "Nancy?"

He knew that she wasn't there, the moment he stepped inside. The television was blank, the bed was neatly made. He walked through to the bathroom and switched on the light, but she wasn't there either.

"Maybe she's gone round to your place," he suggested. He opened the closet. She didn't seem to have taken any of her clothes. There was a beige cardigan lying across the bed which he had never seen before.

Ella held up a note that she had found on the dressing table. "I don't think so. You'd better read this."

Josh sat down on the bed. The note was written in big, loopy writing, the kind that Nancy used for love letters.

Don't be mad at me, Josh. I pray that Ella has brought you back safely and that you're able to read this note and I want you to know that I love you so much. But there's only one way to finish this, and that's to catch Frank Mordant. I knew you wouldn't let me go, so I've kind of made a unilateral decision. I'm one hundred percent sure that I can handle this, so please don't worry about me. I'll be back before you know it, and I'll be bringing Frank Mordant back with me.

Twenty

"Did you *know* that she was going to do this?" Josh demanded.

"I didn't have a clue, Josh. Honest. But it sounds to me like she's got some kind of a plan."

"How the hell does she expect to catch Frank Mordant single-handed? The goddamned Hoodies will have her before she's gotten anywhere near him!"

"She probably stands a better chance alone," said Ella. She picked up the cardigan that Nancy had left on the bed. "It looks like she bought herself some period clothes, too, so she shouldn't attract too much attention."

"I have to go after her," said Josh. "She doesn't have any idea what kind of danger she's in!"

"I think she does," said Ella. "I told her all about Frank Mordant. Well, the little we know. Obviously she's decided that she can deal with him better if she deals with him alone."

"Deal with him? *Deal* with him? How do you deal with a guy like Frank Mordant in a world where the Hoodies are loose? You might as well deal with your broken sink disposal unit by sticking your hand down it."

"Josh, there's nothing that you can do. You're injured; you're in shock. You need to sleep for twenty-four hours just to get your head back together. Besides, you can't go looking for Nancy because you've only been back here for less than an hour."

"I'm not tired, Ella. I'm going after her."

"Josh, it's impossible. You have to wait for at least one full rotation of the earth before you can go back to *that* London. Otherwise, you'll carry on to the *next* London, and the next."

"But it's only a door, right? You come in, you go out."

"We call it a door but it's not like a normal door. If you go through it again and again, all on the same day, you'll take yourself further and further away from the London you left. We're talking about parallel worlds here, Josh. Worlds within worlds, like one of those Japanese ivory balls, with another ball inside it, and another ball inside that. To put it in words of one syllable, things have to line up."

"Ella, I can't let Nancy wander around alone in that other London. She's not *sightseeing*, for Christ's sake – she's trying to find a serial murderer!"

"Hasn't it occurred to you that she might know exactly what she's doing?"

"Oh, sure. And maybe bears go into the woods and dress up as women."

Ella laid her hands on his shoulders and looked him directly in the face. "You cannot go after her, Josh. Neither can I. Right now, all we can do is to give her some time, and wait to see what happens. If you really want to go and find her tomorrow, then we'll talk about it. But you're a wanted man now, and you won't be able to do it unaided. If the Hoodies catch you again, they'll kill you, no doubt about it."

That evening, Josh ordered a turkey club sandwich on room service, and after he had eaten it, he poured the entire contents of the salt-cellar into the bathtub, to make a healing saline solution. He had a long and painful soak, and several times he nearly fell asleep. When he managed to haul himself out of the bath, he stood in front of the steamed-up mirror. He hardly recognized himself. He looked like an amateur boxer after an unsuccessful fairground challenge; or the victim of a head-on traffic accident.

It was so tempting to creep between the clean white sheets of his hotel bed and fall asleep. After all, hadn't Ella told him that there was nothing he could do until tomorrow? But he wasn't sure that Ella had been telling him the truth about the rotation of the earth. Simon Cutter had said the same thing, but both he and Ella had shared a vested interest in him not going immediately back through the door. Ella, because she obviously cared about him, and wanted him to rest; and because she didn't want him causing any more trouble for the resistance movement. Simon, because he had wanted to exploit him for all of the watches and laptop computers and bottles of whisky that he could get.

But Nancy was out there someplace. Nancy was out there, all on her own. And it didn't matter to Josh how independent she was, how self-sufficient. It didn't matter if she was one hundred percent sure that she could handle herself. All that mattered was that he wasn't able to stand beside her and protect her.

He wondered if he was jealous of her, for having had the courage to go looking for Frank Mordant on her own, and for trying to solve the mystery of Julia's murder for him. All his adult life, people had come to *him* for help, and he wasn't used to the idea of being looked after.

In spite of his anxiety, he slept for nearly an hour, although when he woke up he felt worse. He read a few pages of a John Grisham novel that somebody had abandoned in the nightstand, folded over at page twenty-three. Then he watched the television news. Serbs and Muslims were killing each other in Kosovo. Catholics and Protestants were killing each other in Northern Ireland. A famous television chef had suffered a heart attack. England's cricket team were all out for eighty-seven. Tomorrow's weather: humid, with thundery showers. No hijacks along the Embankment; no Hooded Men killed; no Masters of Religious Observance found in the road with their throats cut. But what was the difference?

Did that other London really exist? Or did *this* London really exist? What did existence mean? If nobody knew that you existed, would you still be there?

The phone rang. It was Ella. "Are you OK?" she wanted to know. In other words: you're not going to try anything rash, are you?

"Sure, I'm fine. I'm just trying to catch some zees."

"Well, make sure you do. Abraxas will never forgive you if you do anything stupid. He'll come around and bite your balls off."

"I'd like to see him try."

When he woke up again it was half past midnight. He went into the bathroom and splashed his face with cold water. He still felt stiff and pummeled, but he was much steadier on his feet, and his head was clear.

After cleaning his teeth, he went to the closet and took out a pair of dark blue chinos, a pale blue check shirt, and a tan linen coat. Maybe it wasn't exactly period costume, but it was reasonably inconspicuous. He had seen three or four people in the other London wearing linen coats. Admittedly, they had all been clerics, but that was a chance that he was prepared to take.

He left his room and went down to the lobby, to the night porter's desk. The night porter was a gray-haired black man, who was sitting comfortably in his chair with the cryptic crossword in *The Daily Telegraph*.

"Morning, sir," he said. "Looking for a drink?"

"No, no. I . . . uh . . . I wondered if you had any candles."

"*Candles*?"

"It's a religious thing. Every fourth Tuesday I light a candle for my father, and a candle for my mother, and a candle in memory of John Lennon."

The porter took off his glasses and gave Josh a long, unfocused look. Then he said, "Are you serious, sir?"

"Do I look as if I'm joking?"

"No, sir, you don't. But then different people have a different sense of humor."

"Listen, I'm serious. I'm looking for candles."

The porter rummaged in the bottom drawer of his desk and eventually produced four wax nightlights, in little aluminum-foil cups.

"That's the best I can do, I'm afraid. But you're welcome to them."

"They're great," said Josh. "Absolutely ideal."

"They're nightlights, that's all. I only keep them here in case of power cuts. You're not going to light them in your room, are you?"

"No, no. I'm going to do this outside."

"Well, that's OK. We don't allow candles in the rooms. Not even for religious purposes." He picked up his glasses and said,

"You could help me with this clue, though. 'It's disgusting that hell is so elegant.' Eleven letters."

"Don't ask me. I was never any good at cryptic crosswords."

Josh left the hotel and hailed a passing taxi, reaching Star Yard at about twenty after one in the morning. His footsteps echoed against the buildings on either side. The only background noise was the harsh brushing of a roadsweeping truck as it made its way slowly up Chancery Lane.

As he knelt by the niche that led to the other London, he thought he saw a brief shadowy flicker, further up the passageway. He turned his head, and saw a gray cat running around the corner. He stood up, wondering if he ought to go after it. It meant something, he was sure, but he didn't know what. But he waited and waited and it didn't reappear, so he knelt back down again, and set out three of the nightlights, and lit them.

Jack be nimble, Jack be quick, he breathed to himself. He waited until he was sure that the nightlights were burning properly, and then he jumped into the niche.

Putting out one hand to steady himself against the wall, he looked back at the London he had left. The nightlights were still burning, their flames dipping in the breeze; and beyond the nightlights, with the flames reflected in its eyes, stood the gray cat, staring at him.

"Ladslove?" Josh challenged it.

The cat continued to watch him with the solemnity that only cats can muster. Then it turned away and disappeared.

Josh turned left, and then right, and then left. It was very dark between the buildings, and when he looked up he couldn't even see the stars. He was beginning to feel very tired, and the wounds of the Holy Harp were feeling sore. What was worse, he had to make sure that he breathed through his nose, because the slightest flow of air across his deeply-drilled teeth was agony.

He saw light up ahead – not as bright as the sodium lights that he had left behind him, but the same distinctive orange. He stepped out of the niche, back into Star Yard. He heard traffic, and the distant clanging of bells. There was a strong smell of burning in the wind, and another smell, like dust.

Cautiously, he walked as far as Carey Street. It was deserted, except for three parked trucks and an old-fashioned-looking automobile. There were no streetlights anywhere, and not a single light in any of the buildings all around him, but there was a glow in the sky above the rooftops, and so he guessed that this part of the city was suffering from a power blackout. He heard a woman's high heels walking very quickly down a side alley, but he couldn't see her.

It *felt* like the same London that he and Nancy had first ventured into. He recognized the Law Society and the Public Record Office – and down at the end of Chancery Lane, although it was closed for the night, he saw the same newsstand where they had tried to buy a paper. But as he walked down to Fleet Street, the smell of burning grew stronger, and before he could reach the corner, a firetruck drove past, with a silver bell clanging on its front bumper, and firefighters standing on its running-boards.

He soon saw where it was headed. Less than a mile away, the great dome of St Paul's Cathedral was surrounded by fires. Thick gray smoke was billowing up into the night sky, and powerful searchlights were criss-crossing through it, as if they were fencing with each other. The air was filled with distant shouts and panicky bells and the deep, soft rumbling noise of buildings burning.

There was hardly any traffic around – only one or two small private cars speeding along Farringdon Street with their headlights shuttered – and not a soul on the sidewalks. No sign of the Hooded Men, thankfully, or their drummers, or their dog-handlers. Josh didn't have much of a plan, apart from finding Nancy, but he knew that he was going to need help. He started to walk toward the British Museum, keeping close to the walls, and stepping back into the shadows whenever he heard a vehicle approaching.

He was walking along a narrow alley off Drury Lane when a voice called out, "What's your hurry, darling?"

He stopped. A woman was standing in a doorway opposite. All he could see was the glow of her cigarette and the light shining on her stockinged leg.

"Got a spare ten minutes, darling?" she asked him.

"I'm sorry, I'm in kind of a hurry."

"You won't regret it, sweetheart, I promise you. Five pounds and you can do anything you like."

"Thanks for the offer, but no thanks."

There was a pause, and then the woman said, "Here, you're not a *Yank*, are you?"

The way she asked him, Josh was suddenly aware that he ought to be careful what he said. "I'm just on my way to meet some friends, that's all."

She stepped out of the doorway. She looked much younger than she sounded. Nineteen or twenty, not much older. She walked in an odd tilting way because her shoes were too high. She had upswept blonde hair and she wore a purple satin dress with padded shoulders, a deep décolletage, and a handstitched hemline that finished just above her knee. She was heavily made up, with thin plucked eyebrows, but she hardly needed it. She had a pretty, almost elfin face and huge dark eyes.

"Come on, darling. You can spare a fiver, can't you? I'm starving."

"I'm sorry. I don't have any money at all. If I did, believe me, you could have it for nothing."

She came up to him, lifted her hand, and turned his face to the side so that she could see him better. "You sound like a Yank. You didn't get shot down, did you?"

"Shot down? No. You've got to be kidding me. I can't even fly."

"So what are you? A spy? I could make a lot of money out of you, if you're a spy."

"Listen," said Josh. "I came here looking for a friend of mine, that's all. I'm not a pilot and I'm not a spy. If you really want to know I'm an alternative veterinarian."

"What's that when it's at home?"

"I don't really have time to explain. Now, if you'll excuse me."

"You *are* a spy, aren't you? A Yank spy. They give you fifty quid if you turn one in."

Josh heard the distant *crump-crump-crump* of anti-aircraft guns. More searchlights played tic-tac-toe in the sky.

"This may sound like kind of a dumb question," he asked the girl. "But . . . is there a *war* going on here?"

"Oh, no. It's fireworks night, that's all."

"God, you British and your sarcasm. There's a war on, isn't there?"

She came up close to him, and gripped the lapels of his coat, and pouted at him, and licked her lips, and lifted her thigh up against his leg. "Where have you been?" she asked him, with a smoker's catch in her voice. "How come you don't know there's a war on? You're not a loony, are you?"

In the far distance, Josh heard the droning of aero-engines. Not jets – piston engines, and there were scores of them, by the sound of it. The whole night started to throb, and the *crump-crump-crump* of anti-aircraft fire grew deafening.

"Second wave," said the girl, in a matter-of-fact voice. "We'd better get under cover."

She opened the door behind her and stepped inside. Josh stayed where he was, unsure whether she wanted him to follow her. "What are you waiting for?" she asked him, from the darkness. "You don't want to get blown to bits, do you?"

Josh entered the shadows. The girl closed the door behind him and switched on the light. He found himself standing in a narrow, cabbagey-smelling hallway. On the right, there was a gloomy flight of stairs covered in old brown linoleum. On the left, there was a door which obviously led down to the cellar. "Come on," said the girl. "We'll be safe in here. Unless we cop a direct hit, that is." Josh hesitated, but he suddenly heard a shrilling chorus of whistles in the air high above them, followed by seven or eight deafening bangs. They couldn't have been more than half a mile away, and Josh felt the jolt through the soles of his feet.

"Don't hang about. My Aunt Maisie hung about, and got her head blown halfway down the garden." The girl led the way down the steps. Josh closed the cellar door behind him and followed her. "See . . . look," she said. "I've got it quite homely, really." The cellar walls were limewashed white. Two brick arches supported the ceiling, and formed three separate rooms: a makeshift bedroom at the far end, which was curtained off with a thick gray blanket, a living area with two old armchairs and a sagging sofa, and a kitchen with a paraffin stove and a few cans of food – corned beef, peas and carrots and a box of Shredded Wheat.

The cellar smelled of damp and stale cigarette smoke and unwashed sheets, but the girl was wearing a strong, cheap lavender perfume, which mostly overwhelmed it. She sat down in one of the armchairs, crossed her legs so that her dress rode high on her white, bruised thighs, and held out a packet of Senior Service cigarettes. "Gasper?"

"No, thanks."

"Come on, it'll do you good. Look at the state you're in."

"Are you kidding me? Don't you know how bad for you those things are? You don't want to survive all this bombing and die of lung cancer, do you?"

"Lung cancer, darling? What are you talking about? My doctor *told* me to smoke. He said it was good for my nerves." She lit a cigarette and inhaled it deeply, blowing out twin tusks of smoke from her nostrils. "I think I'd die if I couldn't have a fag."

Above them, Josh could hear the pulsing of engines coming closer and closer, punctuated by dozens of ground-shaking explosions. It sounded as if somebody were stalking along a corridor, violently slamming one door after another. After each explosion, dust sifted down from the ceiling, which the girl nonchalantly brushed off her knees with her hand.

"It's murder on your hair, all this dust. They said it was going to be bad tonight. I reckon we'll have to throw in the towel if it goes on like this."

There was another immense explosion, very close by. The lights went out for a moment, and they could hear masonry and glass dropping on to the ceiling.

Josh held out his hand. "Guess I'd better introduce myself, if we're going to die together. Josh Winward."

The girl said, "Petty Horrocks. Stupid name, isn't it, Petty? Better than Petunia, though."

"How long have you lived here, Petty?"

"Three months, give or take. My mum and dad moved out to the country when the war started, but I couldn't stand it there. Lincolnshire, do me a favor. Nothing but sugar beets and lads as thick as shit. I told them I'd rather be blown to bits than die of boredom. So I came back to London; and this place was empty; and that was that."

"And you survive . . . ?"

"By screwing anybody who's got a fiver. Or two pounds ten for a blow job. Sorry if that offends you. But at least I can go dancing in the evenings and have a laugh."

"I guess we all have to survive the best way we can."

Another five or six bombs fell, but this time they sounded further away. All the same, the droning of aero-engines continued, and Josh guessed that there must have been nearly a hundred airplanes passing overhead.

"We won't be able to put up with this much longer, you know," said Petty, in a matter-of-fact voice, tapping her cigarette ash on the floor. "The docks is all gone, Covent Garden's gone. They even dropped a bomb on the Odeon in Leicester Square. Fifty-eight people killed, right in the middle of a Ronald Shiner film. Serves them right for going to see it, that's what I say. Still, I won't be sorry when it's all over."

Josh said, "Listen, I know it all looks pretty bad at the moment. But you guys are going to win this war. I promise."

"Oh, yes, and how do you know that?"

"I just know it. Trust me."

"I bet you're a loony. Where did you escape from? It's all right. You can tell me. I won't grass on you, promise."

"I'm not a loony. I happen to have . . . privileged information, that's all."

"So you *are* a spy!"

"I told you. I came here looking for a friend of mine, that's all. But you shouldn't worry about the war. Once the United States gets involved – that's going to be the end of it."

Petty looked baffled. "You just said we were going to win."

"Of course you're going to win. We'll be sending over planes and ground troops and tanks and you name it."

"Oh, great. How are we going to stand up to that? We've got

hardly any air force and most of our army got killed in France and the *King George V* was sunk last week and that was our only battleship."

"I don't understand. We're sending more of everything. The Germans are going to collapse."

Petty blew out smoke and shook her head in bewilderment. "The *Germans*? What have the Germans got to do with it?"

"They're bombing you to hell, aren't they?"

"The *Germans*? That proves it, you need locking up. The Germans wouldn't bomb us. They've done nothing but send us ships and tanks and food. They're our *allies*, the Germans. Same royal family, same blood. Why would the Germans want to bomb us?"

Josh was speechless at first. Then he pointed a single finger upward, and said, "Those are not Germans?"

"Of course they're not Germans. They're bloody Yanks."

"Americans? *Americans* are bombing London?"

Petty sucked on her cigarette and tugged her hemline up a little higher. "Do you know something, I believe you. You can't be a spy. You're too bloody stupid to be a spy. In fact you're too bloody stupid to be a loony."

"Jesus. Americans are bombing London. But why?"

"Don't ask me, darling. They call it the War of Independence. They don't want to be part of the good old British Empire any more. And of course the bloody French are helping them, letting them base all their bombers in France. But, you know, what can you do? I don't think there's any point in fighting. They're going to win anyway, aren't they? The sooner they invade, the better, as far as I'm concerned. Life is going to be ten times better, under the Yanks. All cocks and chocolate."

It was then that Josh knew for sure that Ella had been right, and he was wrong. The world needed to turn through a complete twenty-four hour cycle before you could venture through the doors again. The first parallel London was the London of Frank Mordant and the Hoodies. This must be the second London. And who knew how many infinitely different versions of London lay beyond, like the endless reflections in a dressing-table mirror?

* * *

The bombing eased for a while, although Petty said that they should stay in the cellar until they heard the "all clear".

"Cup of tea?" she asked him.

"No thanks. You don't have anything stronger, do you?"

She produced a half-bottle of Gordon's gin from under her chair and poured two large measures into teacups. "What shall we drink to?" she asked.

"Peace," Josh suggested.

"I don't know. How about clean knickers?"

"OK, then." He lifted his cup. "Peace, and clean knickers."

"That's what I'm really looking forward to, when it's all over," said Petty. "Clean white cotton knickers, with a lacy frill."

Josh said, "How long has this been going on? This war?"

"Do you know, I can't make out if you're having me on toast."

"I promise you, I'm serious."

"Well, all right, then. But I still think you're kidding me. The war's been going on for nearly a year now. The bloody Government said it would all be over by Christmas. I don't know why they didn't just let the Yanks go off on their own. But, oh no. Treason, they called it, and then the Navy sank that big American aircraft carrier, and that was it. All bloody hell broke loose." She looked at Josh for a long time, playing with one of her earrings. It was a plastic poodle with green glass eyes. "I like you, you know," she said, after a while. "I know you're supposed to be the enemy and everything. But you've got something about you, you know? You're thoughtful."

"I'm confused, if that's what you mean."

"I just don't understand how you don't know nothing about the war. The Yanks have been bombing us for months and months. It's not exactly something you wouldn't notice."

"I haven't been here. I've been . . . away."

"Bloody hell, where? Mars?"

Josh leaned forward. "If you want to know the truth, I came from another London."

Petty gave him a smile of bewilderment. "*Another* London?"

"I know it's hard to believe, but there are probably hundreds of Londons, all of them different, all with a different history. There are doors between them – ways to get through – and if you know how to do it you can get through these doors, from one London into the next. In the London I came from, there's no war, no bombing, nothing. There's plenty to eat and drink. There are restaurants, nightclubs, you name it. Clean knickers, too."

Petty blew out smoke. "If that's true, what did you come here for? To see how miserable we all are, and have a good old laugh about it?"

"I came here by accident. I was trying to find another London, but not this one."

"So what are you going to do? Listen to me! I'm talking like I really believe you."

"I'm going to try to get back to the London I started from, and have another crack at finding the right one."

Petty didn't say anything for a while, but she didn't take her eyes away from him, either. She started to gnaw at the side of her thumbnail. At last she said, "You're having me on toast, aren't you?"

"Why should I do that? If it's a joke, it's a pretty goddamned stupid one, isn't it?"

"Perhaps you're expecting to have your wicked way with me, without paying for it."

"I don't want my way with you, wicked or otherwise. I'm involved with somebody else."

"What, engaged, are you?"

"Kind of."

"Would she mind if you took me back with you?"

"Say what?"

"Your fiancée or whatever she is. Would she mind if you took me back with you? To *your* London, with the restaurants and the nightclubs and everything?"

"So you *do* believe me?"

"I don't know. Either you're completely bonkers or else you're telling the truth. But you don't *talk* like you're bonkers. You meet loads of people with shell-shock and that, and they talk about their families like they're still alive, and stuff like that, and then you find out that they all got bombed. I had one bloke who thought he was an angel. But you don't talk like one of them."

Josh checked his watch. It was a quarter after three in the morning, and he was exhausted. "Do you mind if I get some sleep?" he asked. "I have to wait a full twenty-four hours before I can go back to my own London. Otherwise I'll end up in another London like this. Or worse."

"Couldn't be worse, darling," said Petty, finishing her gin. "Why don't you and me lie down for a while?"

"I'll take the couch. No problem at all."

"Oh, rubbish. Let's go to bed. I'm too knackered to rape you anyway."

She stood up and tugged her satin dress over her head. Underneath, she was wearing nothing but a grubby white bra. Josh had thought that she was wearing pantyhose, but she had simply colored her legs with foundation cream, which ended just above her hemline, where she was startlingly white. She was plump and full-breasted, with a rounded tummy, and she wasn't unattractive, but there were bruises all over her – finger-bruises mostly, where men had gripped her thighs and her buttocks and her breasts. Josh felt powerless and sad, and he cursed all men for everything they do, their wars and their religions.

He watched her as she cleaned her teeth with an old, splayed toothbrush. She drew back the blanket that separated the "bedroom" from the rest of the cellar, and climbed into bed. Josh waited for a few minutes, but tiredness was overwhelming him, and eventually he stood up, took off his coat, and stripped down to his shorts. He climbed into bed next to Petty and lay there staring at the limewashed ceiling.

She turned over and touched some of the reddened scabs from the Holy Harp. "Are you all right?" she asked him. "Who did those?"

"It's a long story."

"I don't mind. Everybody says that I'm a very good listener. You have to be, when you're on the game. That's what they come for, you know. The listening, more than the sex."

She kept on stroking him, but the effect was more soporific

than erotic. She played with his nipples, and then ran her fingertips down his sides. His eyes closed. He wasn't quite asleep, but he was very close to it. Her fingers trailed lightly across his stomach muscles, almost as lightly as butterflies. He saw darkness and thought that he was back in bed in Mill Valley, in the middle of the night. He was sure that he could hear cicadas, and the wind-chimes jangling out on his verandah.

"Wouldn't it be lovely if there *was* another world?" said Petty, as she inserted her finger into his navel. "No war, no bombing. Everybody being nice to each other. Imagine."

Josh slept. He was very far away. He was sitting in the bookstore coffee house in Mill Valley, trying to discourage a little mongrel called Duchovny from jumping up and annoying people. Nancy was there, and she was laughing. He could see her eyes sparkling and the sun shining through the feathers in her hair. He reached out to take her hand, but she wouldn't let him, even though she was still laughing. Somehow her laughter began to sound tinny, and false.

"They're coming," she said. "Can't you hear them drumming?"

Twenty-One

He opened his eyes. The cellar was shaking. The whole world was shaking. It sounded as if thousands of airplanes were flying overhead, thousands of them. Their droning made the door rattle and the brickwork crack and the cheap aluminum saucepans drop off their shelves. Josh looked at Petty: she was fast asleep, lying on her back with her mouth open. He shook her and shouted, "Petty! Petty, wake up!"

She opened her eyes and blinked at him. "What's the matter? I was having a good dream then. I was dancing, and all these blokes were clapping and throwing me money." She looked around, almost as if she expected to find the bedspread strewn with five-pound notes.

"It's another raid!" Josh shouted at her.

The roaring of aero-engines was enormous now. It seemed to blot out everything: sight, hearing, smell, touch, and any sense of logic. Josh felt as if he were drowning in it.

"There's nothing we can do!" Petty screamed at him. "This is as safe as anywhere else!"

They heard whistling, not far away. That dreadful, triumphant *wheeeeeeee*! Then the sticks of bombs began to land, fifteen or sixteen at a time, running up St Martin's Lane and Charing Cross Road in a series of minor earthquakes. They heard a gas main explode. They heard tons of masonry falling into the road. They heard bells, and bells, and more bells.

"Oh Mary Mother of God protect us," prayed Petty.

"Are you a Catholic?" asked Josh.

She frowned at him. She was still naked, and there were red wrinkled marks from the sheets on the side of her left breast, where she had been sleeping.

"Yes, I'm a Catholic. What difference does it make?"

"It doesn't."

A huge explosion at the lower end of Drury Lane made the whole house shake. Josh heard windows bursting and bricks collapsing, and it sounded as if a whole truckload of bricks had been unloaded on the floor right above their heads.

"Oh please God don't let us be buried alive," begged Petty.

Josh didn't say anything, but was thinking the exact same thought. Of all the deaths that he could imagine, being buried alive was the one that filled him with the greatest dread.

Another bomb hit Drury Lane, much closer this time. The impact made Josh's ears sing, and almost threw them out of bed. Josh lay on top of Petty and pulled the blankets over his head, while even more masonry dropped on to the floor above them, and brick dust sifted down from every crevice in the ceiling.

Under the blankets, they clung to each other, sweaty and hot, but both of them praying to survive. They heard another whistle, much louder this time, and growing louder, as if a train were hurtling toward them, and Petty held him so tight that she almost suffocated him. "Whatever happens," she breathed in his ear, "remember that I love you."

"How can you love me? You don't even know who I am."

"I know. But you're going to be holding me tight when I die. I can't ask any more than that, can I?"

She lifted her head and kissed him. Her mouth tasted of gin and cigarettes, but all the same it was warm and soft and she obviously wanted him. At the same instant the world seemed to come to a stop. Josh felt an enormous compression in his ears, and the next thing he knew he was flung out of bed across the cellar, hitting his head on one of the armchairs and landing upside down in the kitchen, scattering cans and cartons and cutlery. Petty was hurled against the cellar steps and lay hunched up with her head in the corner as if she were playing turtles.

Tons of rubble dropped on top of the cellar. The lights went out, and they were left in choking darkness. Josh stayed where he was for a while, his feet up in the air, trying to get his breath back. Then he called out, "Petty?"

Petty didn't answer. Josh managed to roll himself sideways, bringing down another clatter of pots and pans, and crawled on his hands and knees across the grit-strewn floor. "Petty, can you hear me, is everything OK?"

He caught his hand on a protruding nail, and he could feel the blood running down his forearm. "Petty?" he called. "Petty, for God's sake, talk to me."

Groping sideways, he managed to find the bottom of the stairs, and then Petty's right foot. He felt his way up her body until he reached her head. Her hair was thick with dust and thousands of tiny fragments of glass. She might have been bleeding, but it was impossible for him to tell because his own hand was bleeding, too, and everything felt sticky and wet.

"Petty," he urged her, turning her over on to her back. "Petty, for God's sake say something."

She remained floppy and cold and unresponsive. Josh could feel a pulse, but it was very thready. He felt for her mouth and stuck his finger into it, to make sure that it wasn't obstructed. Then he leaned over and gave her mouth-to-mouth. A huge explosion like that could have compressed her lungs, or filled them with dust.

"Petty," he said, between breaths. "Listen to me, Petty, you're going to be fine. The worst of it's over. They won't be coming back. Not tonight, anyhow. Come on, Petty, you have to breathe here, baby. You have to use your lungs. There's one thing for sure, I'm not going to let you die, whatever it takes."

He kept up mouth-to-mouth for nearly twenty minutes. He massaged her heart, too. The cellar remained totally dark and he couldn't see her at all.

"Petty, you're going to make it. You're going to be fine. If you don't die, I'll take you with me when I go back to London. I promise. And you'll have all the food you want and all the dancing you want and enough clean knickers to stretch from here to Sausalito."

There was still no response. Josh leaned over her and gave

her one last kiss of life – and then gave her a kiss. "I'm sorry, baby. I did what I could. Take care of yourself, wherever you're going. I love you."

He stood up, reaching for the handrail to steady himself. As he did so, he thought he heard movement. A slight shifting, nothing more.

"I was waiting for you to say that," said Petty, her voice clogged with dust. "Those are the magic words."

Feeling around in the darkness, Josh managed to find her arm, and then her shoulders, and lift her on to her feet. "I'm OK," she said. "I was knocked out, that's all. That was a bloody close one, wasn't it? Must have hit the building next door."

"We need some light," said Josh.

"That's all right. I've got loads of candles. Under the basin, there's a whole box of them. Christ, my head. I feel like somebody's been sitting on it."

Josh groped his way around the room until he located the sink. Underneath it, he found a brown-paper package filled with candles. He took out two to light up the cellar, but he also took another six, cramming them into his coat pockets, just in case he needed to cross through any of the doors, looking for the London he had left behind. In the darkness, he damned Nancy's independent spirit. He loved her, and he was proud of her, but where had it got them both? He didn't even like to think what she was doing right now, while he was trapped in this bombed-out cellar with Petty.

He flicked his butane lighter and lit one of the candles. Petty looked like a ghost, a voodoo duppy, her face white and her eyes black and her lips blood-red where Josh had been kissing them. Her hair had turned into dreadlocks, crammed with dust and debris, but glittering with glass. She had a crimson lump on her forehead, and superficial cuts and bruises, but no serious injuries. The blood that was criss-crossed all over her naked body was Josh's.

Josh looked down at his own hand. The cut was L-shaped, deep in the muscle just below his thumb. He picked up a tea-towel from the kitchen floor, snapped it in the air to shake off the dust, and wrapped it tightly around his wound.

Petty managed to climb to her feet. Josh helped her across to the bedroom area and sat her on the bed. She coughed and spat dust, and sat with her shoulders hunched, wheezing like an asthmatic, trying to get her breath back. But at last she reached for her bra and her dress, and painfully began to dress herself.

Josh heard an ominous lurching sound from the ceiling. "We have to get out of here, Petty. It sounds like the whole goddamn house is coming down."

Petty nodded, but she was too choked up with dust to say anything. Holding the candle high, Josh led her back across to the stairs, and the two of them climbed up together, until they reached the door. Josh took hold of the door handle and tugged it, but the door was jammed solid.

Not only that, they could both hear the deep droning noise of another wave of approaching bombers.

"Oh shit," said Petty. "They're really going to give us a pasting tonight."

Josh gave the door another tug. It might be more dangerous outside, with fires raging all across London's West End, but he couldn't stay buried in this cellar any longer. He was beginning to hyperventilate already.

"We'll be safer here," said Petty, but he shook his head. He didn't want to admit to his rising panic.

He heard more bombs falling, only a few streets away, and that gave him the strength to wrench at the door again and again, until he had pulled it half-open. Outside, the hallway was blocked with debris. The staircase had collapsed, and the banisters covered the cellar like a fence. Huge blocks of broken brick were piled on top of each other, some of them still plastered and wallpapered.

"We're going to have to move some of this stuff if we're going to get out," said Josh. "Come on up here and give me a hand."

He managed to twist three uprights out of the banisters, backward and forward, until they eventually came free, and toss them out of the way. Crouching down like Quasimodo, he climbed out of the cellar, underneath the banister rail, and into the hallway itself. His shoes slid down a heap of pulverized dust and glass and broken china. He saw half a willow-pattern teacup and a doll's face with staring blue eyes, as well as a vegetable-strainer and a diary with all of its pages singed at the edges.

"Come on, Petty," he insisted. "You too."

Awkwardly, she climbed out after him. "God, look what the bastards have done to my house!" she wept. "This is my house, this is where I live! What right have they got to come and smash it all to pieces? What right? I don't care if they're part of the bloody Empire or not!"

Outside, the sky was growing lighter.

They looked around, in that gray hallucinatory light just before the sun comes over the horizon, and they could have been standing in a stage set, meant to depict the end of the world. Drury Lane was nothing more than two parallel heaps of bricks, with fires burning everywhere. It wasn't even recognizable as the same street that Josh had been walking up earlier this morning. The theaters had gone, the shops had gone, the houses had gone. There was nothing but rubble and slates and broken chimney pots and twisted fire escapes and skeletal roof timbers. And fires everywhere, and acrid smoke.

"Are you OK?" he asked Petty.

Petty was shivering, but she nodded. "I'm all right. I wish it was over, that's all."

Josh put his arm around her. "Cocks and chocolate?"

She managed a smile. "That's right. Cocks and chocolate."

"I guess we'd better find ourselves someplace to hole up."

"What about your friend? The one you came here to find?"

"John Farbelow? I'm not sure that he even exists in *this* London. Even if he does, he may not even be the same guy."

"Well, we've got to do something. Can't we go back to your London?"

"We can. Well, I hope we can. But not yet. We have to wait until one o'clock tomorrow morning."

"Oh, wonderful. And what do we do in the meantime?"

Josh stopped, and listened. "Do you hear something?" he asked her.

She wrinkled up her nose. "Like what?"

"Like a sort of drumming noise."

"Don't ask me. I can't hardly hear nothing after that last bomb went off."

Josh listened even harder, gripping Petty's wrist so that she was sure to stand still. They could hear fire engines racing around London, their bells frantically ringing. They could hear the diminishing drone of scores of heavy bombers, circling around East London on their way back to their bases in Normandy. But they could hear something else, too. They could hear drumming. *Ratta-tat-tatt*! *Ratta-tat-tatt*! And they could hear barking, and the piercing whistles of dog-handlers.

"Oh God," said Josh. "I don't believe it. It's the Hooded Men."

"The Hooded Men? Who the hell are the Hooded Men?"

"Ask me later. Let's just get the hell out of here."

He grasped Petty's hand and started to jog northward, up toward High Holborn, where automobiles were burning. But Petty said, "I *can't*, Josh. I can't go any further."

"You have to. Don't you realize what these people can do to you?"

She slowed down to a walk. "I don't care what they do to me. I'm not going to run any further. I can't."

Josh stood beside her. The drumming sounded louder, and sharper. The dogs began to bark more enthusiastically, because they had obviously picked up the scent.

"Come on," he urged Petty. "They'll kill us if they catch us."

He pulled her behind him with her bare feet reluctantly slapping on the ground. Up ahead of them, the street was filled with billowing black smoke from a burning office building. "Come on, we can use the smoke to get away from them."

As they neared the smoke, however, Josh heard more drums, right in front of them. He stopped, and turned around. The drums were still following them. He turned back, to see four men approaching through the smoke. A drummer, with his side-drum, beating out an endless and terrifying rattle. Two dog-handlers, with bull terriers wheezing at their leads. And a tall man wearing an angular black hat, his face covered by a hessian mask. As he walked toward them, he swung his shining sword from side to side, as if he were cutting off wheat stalks.

"Is that a Hooded Man?" asked Petty, gripping Josh's arm.

Josh nodded. Behind them, the drums came closer and closer, and he could hear the dogs yapping in a frenzy of excitement.

"Who are they? What are they going to do to us?"

"I don't know. It's me they want. They must have followed me here."

There was no point in trying to run. Josh knew that the dogs would catch them before they had covered less than fifty feet. All they could do was stand and wait as the Hooded Man walked up them; two more Hooded Men appeared from behind.

"Well, Mr Winward," said the first Hooded Man, in a harsh, muffled voice. "We have you."

"What the hell are you after me for?"

"Isn't murder enough?"

"I never murdered anybody. What those guys did when they rescued me, that was nothing to do with me."

"Come now, Mr Winward. The murder was committed in effecting your release from custody. That makes you a co-conspirator."

"I told you that I wasn't interested in making trouble. If you'd let me go—"

The Hooded Man lifted his sword and prodded Josh in the chest with it, again and again. He didn't prod hard enough to penetrate his shirt, but Josh could feel the point against his ribs.

"You are a liar and a subversive and a murderer, sir. You are one of the rats that run in the sewers beneath our society, spreading the plagues of dissent and faithlessness. Believe me, you will suffer for what you have done."

Another of the Hooded Men came up to Petty, and took hold of the sleeve of her dress. "And who is this whore?"

"Don't touch the girl. Let go of her. She has nothing to do with this."

"I can find that out for myself, thank you. Both of you are coming with us."

"Well, sorry about that. I've only been here since one o'clock this morning. I can't go back to your London. Not for seven hours yet."

"We're not taking you back *there*," said the Hooded Man. "We have a house here, just as we have houses in every reality that we can visit. Now, let's be moving on, shall we?"

The Hooded Man prodded Josh again, in the shoulder this time. Then he prodded him yet again, and again, and this time the point actually broke the skin. Josh stepped back, covering his shoulder with his hand. The Hooded Man stabbed him in the forearm.

"I said, let's be moving on, didn't I? So let's be moving on."

He stabbed Josh twice more, but this time Josh held his ground. He had never been physically brave, even when he was training in the Marine Corps. Suddenly, however, he felt an extraordinary rush of power – a power that was totally overwhelming, like nothing he had ever felt before, ever. It was partly anger, and frustration, and a sense of injustice. But it was much more than that. It was a complete absence of fear. He wasn't afraid of the Hooded Men. He wasn't afraid of their swords, or their dogs, or anything.

Without hesitation, he ducked forward and seized the Hooded Man's wrist. He twisted his arm around and pulled the sword right out of his hand. Then he elbow-punched him very hard in the chest. Beneath the black tunic he could feel a deep, bony ribcage, and he was sure that he felt something crack.

The Hooded Man dropped to his knees in front of him. The two other Hooded Men drew their swords and one of them shouted, "*Dogs*! *Let the dogs have him*!"

But Josh lifted the Hooded Man's sword and shouted back, "*Stop*! You let those dogs go and I'll take his head off! I swear to God!"

To his own amazement, he realized that he meant it. And the

Hooded Men must have realized it, too, because they stayed where they were, and one of them lifted a cautioning hand to the dog-handlers.

Josh gripped the Hooded Man's white Puritan collar and pulled him on to his feet. The Hooded Man felt bulky and disjointed, as if he had all of the components of a human body, all the bones and liver and intestines, but all thrown together willy-nilly. He had a smell to him, too – a sweet distinctive smell that reminded Josh of rotting apricots. He pressed the sword-point into the Hooded Man's back and said, "Now it's your turn to be moving on, pal. And I warn you I'll kill you if you give me any problems."

He stepped backward, away from the Hooded Men and their dog-handlers and their drummer. Petty hesitated, but Josh said, "Come on, Petty. Let's get out of here."

Petty followed him, and together they began to retreat along the street toward the smoke that still poured out of the burning offices. The Hooded Men remained where they were, but the drummer started up a single, threatening beat, like the beat that used to accompany condemned men to the scaffold.

"You can never escape us," said the Hooded Man. "We can follow you to the ends of the earth. We can follow you to the ends of *every* earth."

"Just shut up," Josh told him, and pulled at his collar even harder.

They walked into the whirling smoke, and the other Hooded Men were gradually blotted out of sight, although they could still hear the persistent drumbeat. The smoke was hot and filled with flying sparks. It smelled strongly of burning varnish and their eyes filled up with tears.

Petty started to cough, and even the Hooded Man began to wheeze for breath.

"As soon as we're clear, I want you to run," Josh told Petty.

She coughed and nodded and waved her hand.

"You will suffer for this," the Hooded Man grated. "You will beg to be put out of your misery, I swear it."

Josh ignored him. He dragged him as far as the end of the

office block, where the smoke began to thin out, and then he released the grip on his collar, pushing him away.

The Hooded Man took two or three steps back, apparently staggering, and for a moment Josh thought that he was going to fall over. But then, without warning, he pulled a long dagger out of his tunic and lunged at Josh from the right-hand side, trying to catch him underneath his sword. He was so quick that it was almost unnatural, like a special effect in a movie.

His dagger sliced at Josh's side, but Josh dipped to the left and swung the sword over his head. The Hooded Man tilted back, and feinted, and tried to stab Josh's wrist. There was a clash of steel on steel – one cutting edge against another. The Hooded Man spun around and kicked at Josh with his buckled shoe. Josh swung at him, again and again, and the sword-blade whistled through the smoke.

The Hooded Man dodged to the right, and then to the left, and then he suddenly rolled over on the ground and stabbed at Josh's knees. Josh jumped back and whirled his sword in a great circular sweep. He was only trying to protect himself, but at that instant the Hooded Man tried to stand up. The sword hit him in the side of the neck – *knock*! – cutting right through his hessian hood and almost taking his head off.

He dropped backward on to the road, with blood squirting out of his neck like a crimson geyser. He tried to reach up to his neck, to stop himself from hemorrhaging, but the wound gaped open so wide that there was nothing he could do. He let out a horrible gargling, his hands shaking and his feet kicking, and then he lay still.

"Oh my God," said Petty. "I think I'm going to be sick."

Josh stood back, the smoke still swirling all around him. Christ almighty, he had killed a man, and killed him with a sword. He didn't know whether he felt like a medieval hero or a homicidal maniac. The feeling was completely primitive.

"We should run," Petty told him, glancing back anxiously in the direction of the single drumbeat. "Don't tell me they won't be looking for us."

"Yes," said Josh. "You're absolutely right. We should run."

"Then *run*, for fuck's sake!"

Josh nodded. But for some reason he couldn't bring himself to leave the still-shuddering body on the ground. He approached the Hooded Man, and stood over him. His hessian mask was almost completely soaked in blood, and his head was tilted sideways at an impossible angle. One more swipe from his sword would have beheaded the Hooded Man completely.

"Please," begged Petty. "Let's get out of here!"

Josh prodded the Hooded Man's chest with the point of his sword. Then, carefully, he started to cut at the side of his hessian hood.

"What are you *doing*?" Petty fretted.

"I want to see," said Josh. "I want to see what these bastards really look like, underneath their hoods."

He carried on cutting. The hessian was old and fragile, so he cut through it quite easily. Then, still using the point of his sword, he pulled it off the Hooded Man's head, and flung it aside.

"Oh, my God," said Petty; and even Josh could only look for an instant before he turned away.

Twenty-Two

Nancy walked into the echoing lobby of Wheatstone Electrics and briskly approached the reception desk.

"Can I help yew?" asked the girl behind the marble-topped desk. She wore a tight beige cardigan and brown plastic combs in her hair.

"I don't have an appointment. But I wonder if Mr Mordant could spare me a minute."

"Mr Mor-*dant*? I don't know about thayt. Mr Mordant only sees people by appoint-munt."

"All the same, maybe you could tell him I'd like to see him."

The girl looked Nancy up and down, and then sniffed. "I suppose I could try. You're wasting your time, though. Mr Mordant's always up to his eyes."

"He's up to his eyes?"

"Oh, yace. If he's not here he's somewhere else."

"You know," said Nancy. "That's been happening to me lately, too."

The girl plugged in the telephone line, and rang it, and after a few moments she said, "Mr Mor-*dant*? Yace. Brenda here in reception. I've got a young lady here to see yew."

"Nancy Andersen."

"Her name's Nancy Andersen. That's right. No, I haven't asked her. No."

The receptionist covered up the mouthpiece with her hand and said, "What's it about?"

"Tell him I'm a friend of Julia Winward."

The receptionist rolled her eyes up into her head. "She says she's a friend of Julia's."

She listened again, and then she said, "He'll be right down. If you wouldn't mind taking a seat."

Nancy sat in a large brown art-deco couch, next to a glass-topped table on which there was a fanned-out display of *Advanced Electrics* and *Grid & Generators Monthly*.

She didn't have to wait long, though. Frank Mordant came down almost immediately. The elevator chimed and he stepped out into the lobby, wearing white shirtsleeves and pinstripe pants and very shiny black Oxford shoes. *So this is the terrible Frank Mordant*, thought Nancy. This ratty little gent with his clipped moustache and his Brylcreemed hair. Mind you – who would have thought, looking at pictures of Ted Bundy, or Son of Sam . . . ?

"Miss—?" he said, crossing the lobby with a grin, and holding out his hand.

"Andersen. Nancy Andersen."

"Well, well," he said, sitting on the couch beside her and resting his arm along the back of it, so that she couldn't miss the whiff of body odor. "So you knew Julia. What a smashing girl she was. I was very sorry when she went."

"You don't know what happened to her, do you? I expected to hear from her weeks ago, but – you know, nothing."

"I don't know. One day she was here, happy as a skylark. The next day, nothing. She didn't turn up for work, and that was that. I tried to ring her at home but her landlady said that she had moved away. Perhaps she had personal problems. I simply don't know."

"You didn't report her missing?"

"What for? She was a grown-up girl, after all."

"You didn't think that anything might have happened to her?"

"Such as what?"

"Well, anything. Julia was one of my best friends. She would never disappear without telling me where she was going."

Frank Mordant examined his well-buffed fingernails. "You're American, aren't you?"

"Hey, full marks."

"What could we see by the dawn's early light?"

"Old Glory, of course."

Frank Mordant looked up at her with a chilling smile. "You don't come from here, do you?"

"I'm sorry?"

"Oh, you've tried hard. The tweed suit. The shoes. But I can always tell. The hair's not right. You haven't tweezered your eyebrows. You smell too good and you're too damned self-assured. This is like Britain in the 1930s. Women aren't *confident*. There hasn't been a war, remember. They haven't been driving ambulances and making munitions and looking after their families on their own."

He looked at her for a while, still smiling, and then he said, "In this world, my dear, Old Glory doesn't exist, and never has. The United States of America is nothing but a rather prosperous part of the British Commonwealth. You'd recognize it, if you took the Zeppelin over and had a look around. Similar accent, similar culture. They make cars in Detroit and films in Hollywood. Perhaps they're rather more class-conscious. You know, they have dukes and earls, just like we do. And nobody's invented the hamburger, thank God."

Nancy said, "Look, I'm really worried about Julia. I was hoping you could help me."

"Of course." Frank Mordant had such a sinister aura about him that Nancy felt her skin prickling. It was the kind of personal darkness that her grandfather used to call "crow-feathers." It was the aura of carrion-pickers, those huge black birds that tear at the corpses of rabbits and gophers on the highway, and only lazily flap away when you're almost about to run them over. Greedy and cheap and contemptuous, with a kind of throwaway evil about them.

"I met Julia two or three times in London," Nancy lied. "She told me all about Wheatstone Electrics, and you, and how much she liked her job."

"Really? You met her? She didn't tell me that she'd ever been back."

"Oh, sure. She told me all about the doors, and the candles. Of course I didn't believe it at first, but the second time we met, she showed me."

"She showed you."

"That's right. She lit the candles and recited the rhyme, and she was gone."

"Well, she never told me that, I must admit. She never told me that she'd been back. But then, I was only her employer, wasn't I? So long as she was happy and she did her job."

"Oh, she was happy, all right. She really enjoyed working here. She said that it helped her get over all kinds of traumas. It was like starting all over, you know? That's why I'm so worried about her."

"I'm not sure that I can help you. She seemed perfectly cheerful to me. But one morning she didn't turn up, so what could I do? I couldn't tell the police, could I, because she didn't actually exist, not as far as this world's concerned. I just assumed that she'd sorted herself out, packed her bags, and gone back home to the bosom of the family."

Nancy said, "She hasn't been home, and nobody's heard from her."

Frank Mordant tugged at each of his fingers in turn, popping the knuckles. He didn't take his eyes away from Nancy for a moment. "This looking for Julia . . . it's just an excuse, isn't it?"

"What do you mean?"

"You're running away, too, aren't you? Julia was running away from some rotten relationship, and she wanted some peace and quiet and gainful employment. What are you running away from, darling?"

"I'm not your darling."

Frank Mordant reached over and patted her thigh. "Oh, you are in this world. Especially if you want to get ahead. They haven't heard of women's liberation, and they probably won't, not for another forty years. A woman's place is in the home, cooking the meals and changing the nappies and clearing out the hearth. Either that, or typing."

Nancy tried to smile, even though she felt that her lips were anesthetized. "You're right, I guess. I'm just looking for a kind of retreat. Someplace to heal my wounds and get my head back together again."

"Well, you've come to the right place for that. And if you want a job . . . I think I can find you a vacancy in a day or so. I gather you can type? And use a rotary-dial telephone? And what do you know about circuit-breakers?"

"You'll really give me a job?"

"That's what you came for, isn't it? All this sob story about Julia. I'm sure that Julia's all right, wherever she is. And you'll be the same, once you've worked here for three or four months. It's a different life, believe me. Slow, sedate. And the money's not bad. I can help you to find a flat, if you want me to."

"I don't have any money. Well, I do. I have an Amex gold card. But nothing that anybody will accept over here."

"Yes. Very jolly."

Frank Mordant took hold of her left hand, lifted it up, and examined her watch. "That's a Maurice Guerdat. What do you think that's worth?"

"I don't know. Two or three thousand dollars."

He reached into his trouser pocket and produced a brown snakeskin wallet. "Here you are . . . I'll give you thirty quid for it." He took out two ten-pound notes, a five-pound note, and five ones.

"You're going to give me thirty pounds for a three thousand dollar watch?"

"Barter, we call it. I had to do the same, when I first came here. I flogged off everything I owned, practically. Watches, clocks, rings, you name it. And don't turn your nose up at thirty quid. Don't forget that you can buy a nice little semi-detached house for three hundred and fifty."

Nancy wasn't sure. Josh had bought her this watch when she first agreed to live with him. But she guessed that he would understand, especially if she managed to bring Frank Mordant back with her. Reluctantly, she took it off, and handed it over.

"Right, then," said Frank Mordant. "All you have to do now is find yourself somewhere to live. I've got a little place of my own, on top of a pub in Chiswick. My current secretary, Sandra, is living there at the moment, but she's leaving us the day after tomorrow. So, if you're interested . . ."

"It sounds perfect. Do you know where I can stay in the meantime?"

"Here." Frank Mordant took out a pen and wrote "The Sheffield" on a corner of *Electronics News*. "It's a small hotel halfway along Drogheda Street in Fulham. I know the owner, Mrs Watson. She'll take care of you."

"You're very kind."

"Don't mention it. I always like to think of myself as something of a Good Samaritan." He stood up, and held out his hand. "Meanwhile, I'll see if I can find out anything more about Julia for you. It would be rather jolly if you were reunited, wouldn't it?"

"Yes. Very jolly."

The receptionist rang for a taxi. "Fulham, is it?" the cab driver asked her, as she climbed into the back.

"No. Take me to the British Museum."

"You're the boss."

Cromwell Road was heavily congested with traffic and it took them nearly forty-five minutes to reach Bloomsbury. The morning was warm and windy and in the middle of London the air glittered with golden needles of dried horse manure. Nancy saw two Watchers along the way, one of them standing on the corner in Knightsbridge and the other in Leicester Square. She raised her hand across her face in case the Hooded Men had issued a description of her.

She paid the cab driver and he gave her a handful of big bronze pennies and chunky little threepenny bits. She crossed the street to the British Museum and walked around to the entrance where Simon Cutter had taken them to see John Farbelow. As she approached it, however, she saw that there was some kind of commotion going on. The street was crowded with people, and five white ambulances were drawn up along the curb.

She slowed down. Over the heads of the crowd she saw the tall black hats of Hooded Men and their dog-handlers. There were seven or eight of them at least. Her heart beating quickly, she crossed back over to the opposite side of the street and hid herself behind a postbox. It was difficult to see what was happening. Somebody started shouting and screaming and then abruptly stopped. The Hooded Men came through the crowd and everybody shrank out of their way. They stood together, surrounded by their dog-handlers, as if they were waiting for something.

An old woman in a yellow floral print dress came and stood close to Nancy and shook her head. "That's the way to deal with them," she said. "Show them the sharp end, that's what I say."

"What's going on?" Nancy asked her.

"Subversives, that's what I heard. The Hoodies went in to arrest them, and they put up a fight."

Nancy felt a growing sense of dread. She had come here to make sure that Josh had been successfully rescued. She prayed to every spirit of life and good fortune that he hadn't still been here, with John Farbelow's people, when the Hooded Men arrived.

There was a murmuring from the crowd, and then a spontaneous burst of applause. Two ambulancemen came up the steps from the museum basement, carrying a canvas stretcher. At first Nancy couldn't see very well, but then the crowd parted a little, and she caught a glimpse of a young man, his clothes drenched in blood. One hand swung loose, and blood dripped from his fingertips and made patterns on the pavement.

Two more ambulancemen appeared, carrying another body, a girl this time. Nancy's first impression was that her hair was ginger, but then she realized that it was blonde, and soaked in blood. The girl had been cut with a sword across the bridge of the nose, so that her face had almost been sliced in half.

The procession went on, and after twenty minutes the ambulancemen had brought up eighteen bodies, each grisly new appearance greeted by more applause, and even shouts of "hooray!" Nancy still hadn't seen anybody who looked like Josh, or John Farbelow, but she thought that she recognized the Chinese-looking girl who had first opened the door for them, and one or two others.

After all the ambulances had driven away, their bells shrilling, the Hooded Men dispersed the crowd and went marching off to a sharp, aggressive drumbeat. Nancy walked down to Oxford Street, where she hailed a taxi to take her to Fulham.

She felt seriously frightened now, and physically sick with guilt. Of course she had understood that John Farbelow and his band of young subversives had been running a risk, trying to rescue Josh – but she had never thought that the Hooded Men would react with such savagery.

But right now, there was nothing she could do. She couldn't even go back to the "real" London until tomorrow afternoon. Her courage began to fail her. Far from being daring and clever and independent, her plan to capture Frank Mordant now seemed ridiculously dangerous.

The taxi drew up outside a shabby four-story building, yellow London brick with red-painted front steps. "This is it, miss. The Sheffield."

Inside the Sheffield, there was a red and gold carpet so swirly-patterned that it almost gave her motion sickness, and gilded mirrors, and vases filled with dried honesty, all sprayed gold, and a pervasive smell of disinfectant. A blond young man in a green blazer was sitting behind the reception desk, working on a cryptic crossword. He didn't look up as Nancy approached, but licked his index finger and turned the page.

Eventually, Nancy said, "Frank Mordant said I should come here. He said you could find me a room."

The young man blinked at her as if he couldn't understand how she had managed to walk right up to the reception desk without him seeing her. "A room?"

"This is a hotel, isn't it?"

"Of course. What sort of a room?"

"Something pretty basic. I only want it for a couple of nights."

"Hmm," the young man pouted. "I don't know whether we've got anything *basic*."

"Well, whatever. So long as it has a bathtub."

The young man pushed a registration card across the counter.

"If you fill in your particulars. Do you want breakfast in the morning? You have to order porridge the night before."

"No, thanks. No porridge."

"Is that all the luggage you've got?" he said, nodding toward Nancy's overnight case. "We're not supposed to accept single ladies without a full-size suitcase. It's the law."

"Oh, Frank Mordant has my bags. He's bringing them around later."

"Room eleven, then," he said, handing over the key. "Top of the stairs, third on the right."

Nancy climbed the swirly-patterned stairs. When she was halfway up, the young man said, "Excuse me!" and she stopped. "You can't think of an eight-letter word meaning 'banned church service on the field of slaughter'?"

"No, I'm sorry. I can't. I'm not very good at cryptic crosswords."

"Oh. All right, then. Just thought I'd ask."

She let herself into her room. It was large and airy, with a high Victorian ceiling, but it was so crowded with chairs and occasional tables that it was more of an obstacle course than a bedroom. The walls were hung with more gilded mirrors and prints of white horses dancing through the surf; and the bed was covered with a swirly-patterned bedcover in brown and white.

Nancy took off her shoes and sat down at the fussy little onyx-topped dressing table. Her reflection looked completely composed, quite unlike the way she actually felt. She stared into her eyes. How can you appear so calm, when you're so scared? How can you look so remote, when they were carrying up the bloodied bodies of all those young people, and it was all your fault?

She was beginning to feel hungry but she knew that she wouldn't be able to eat. She took off her coat and hung it in the wardrobe. Then she lay down on the brown and white bedcover and tried to rest. She told herself to stop panicking. She had a well worked-out plan to entice Frank Mordant to return to the "real" London with her, and if she managed to pull it off, Frank Mordant would be arrested and charged, Julia would have the justice she deserved, and Josh would be able to take her back to Mill Valley, where they could forget all about Hooded Men and dogs and drummers and Doorkeepers. Early this afternoon, she had felt like giving up, and going back to the "real" London as soon as the world had turned around. But now she felt determined to finish what she had started. Her grandfather had once put his arm around her and told her that a hunter never returns home empty-handed. "No matter if it takes all winter, you never return to your family without carrying your kill over your shoulder. That is why the hunter hunts. That is why the family waits."

She was still thinking of her grandfather and his gentle, finely wrinkled face when she fell asleep, and the world turned even further.

She was woken up by the phone jangling. It was light, but she didn't have any idea what the time was. The phone was a white Regency-style affair with a gold revolving dial. She picked it up and said, "Yes? Who is it?"

"Miss Andersen! It's Frank Mordant. I didn't wake you, did I? Do you know what time it is? Ten past nine!"

"What? I must have overslept."

"Well, not to worry. I know what it's like, coming through the doors. Knocks you for six, bit like jet lag. The thing is, though, I might need you to start work with me a little earlier than I expected. Like, today."

"*Today*?"

"I hope that's not inconvenient. The problem is, Sandra phoned in this morning and said that she wasn't coming back. Sandra, that's my secretary. You know what these young girls are like. Boyfriend trouble, more than likely. But she's really left me in the lurch. I was wondering if you could come in A.S.A.P. and help me out. I'm absolutely snowed under."

"I don't know, Mr Mordant. It's kind of sudden."

"Yes, quite. I do appreciate that. But it's pretty straightforward work and I'm sure you can cope. Especially since the flat's free now, and you can move in any time you like."

"You mean that Sandra's moved out completely?"

"Upped sticks. Didn't even leave me a forwarding address. Inconsiderate, or what? But if you come in now, we'll have time to take a look at it."

Nancy sat up. She hadn't expected to have the opportunity to put her plan into action so quickly; but now that the moment had come, she felt a sudden rush of adrenalin. "Listen, give me an hour," she said.

"Chop-chop, then. I'm having lunch with a chap from the Coal Board at twelve thirty, and I'd like to get things weaving before then. Take a taxi; Wheatstone's will pay for it."

Nancy dressed in her suit and the cream silk blouse that she had brought in her overnight case. She knew that she could chicken out now, if she wanted to. All she had to do was wait for three and a half hours and she could go back through the door and forget that Frank Mordant and the Hooded Men had ever existed. But that would mean that Julia's murder would go unpunished and that she would never be able to stop Josh from coming back here and trying to make sure that Frank Mordant got what was coming to him.

She had seen for herself how vengeful the Hooded Men were: they wouldn't let Josh escape a second time. Not only that, if she went back to the "real" London now, who could tell how many more vulnerable young girls like Julia would be killed and mutilated? To say that Sandra's sudden disappearance was deeply suspicious was the understatement of the century.

She hailed a cab on the corner of Munster Road. It was one of those strange hazy mornings when everything seems out of focus. The taxi driver never stopped talking, all the way to the Great West Road. He thought that all the colored people ought to go back to where they came from, and that Parliament ought to bring back beheading. "Stick their heads on a spike, that's what I say. Make an example of them."

They were delayed for almost twenty minutes at the Chiswick Flyover. A private autogiro had crashed on to one of the carriageways. As Nancy's taxi crept past it, she saw the pilot still trapped in the wreckage. It was almost impossible to tell where the man ended and the machine began.

"Never get me up in one of them things," remarked the taxi driver.

Frank Mordant was on the telephone when she arrived at the office but he beckoned her in.

"No, Malcolm," he was saying. "It's absolutely out of the question. Well, tell him that's the lowest I'll go. Ninepence a unit? Who does he think I am? Father Bloody Christmas?"

He cradled the phone and leaned back in his chair. "Well, then," he said. "You managed to get here all right."

"I'm looking forward to it."

"As I say, the work's pretty humdrum. Pretty run-of-the-mill. Typing, filing, all the usual. Have you ever used a manual typewriter? Good exercise for the fingers, I can tell you."

"I'm sure I'll pick it up."

"Jolly good." He looked at his wristwatch and said, "We've just got time for me to show you the flat. If you like it, you can move in today. If you don't – well, don't feel embarrassed to tell me. I can always help you find diggings somewhere else."

He ushered her downstairs, and out into the car park, opening the door of his Armstrong-Siddeley for her. "By the way," he said, as they drove out of the factory gates, "I made one or two enquiries about Julia for you."

"That's kind of you."

"I talked to her landlady, in case she'd been back to pick up any more of her stuff, but no joy there, I'm afraid."

You liar, thought Nancy, picturing Mrs Marmion's body hanging over her bathtub. She must have been discovered and buried by now.

"I talked to some of her chums in the office. One of them said that Julia was always keen on going to Scotland, so we might have a lead there."

"I see," said Nancy. "Scotland's a pretty big place, though, isn't it?"

"You never know. If she took the train from King's Cross, somebody in the ticket office might remember her."

"Kind of a long shot."

"I suppose so. But I got back to an old pal of mine at Scotland Yard yesterday afternoon, to find out if he had any ideas."

They reached the Sir Oswald Mosley pub and Frank Mordant parked outside. "It's like I tell all the girls . . . it's a little noisy here, but it's cheap, and it's close to the office."

"*All* the girls?"

"They come and they go. Little boats bobbing past on the river of life, if you don't mind me being poetic."

He opened the front door and led her up the steep flight of stairs. "It's very private . . . I put down a nice thick underlay so that you couldn't hear too much noise from the pub underneath. In fact I think you could scream your head off in here and nobody would hear you."

He led the way past the kitchenette and into the living room. "It's a great place," said Nancy. But she wasn't telling the truth, either. The second she walked into the room, she could feel a wave of desperation, and pain, and cruelty. People had been killed in this room, and monstrously killed. This was more than a crow-feather aura. This was an atmosphere of sheer terror that she could almost *smell.*

With a salesman's grin, Frank Mordant opened the bedroom door. Strangely, there was nothing there, no bad karma at all. Everything evil that had happened in this flat had happened in the living room.

"What do you think?"

"I like it. How much are you asking for it?"

"To you, £1.15s.0d a week."

"Out of a salary of how much?"

"Seven pounds fifteen shillings. So you'll have plenty of money left over for all of the things that girls like to buy. Brassieres, frilly garter belts, that kind of thing."

"I don't wear frilly garter belts, Mr Mordant," she replied, sharply. "Frilly garter belts went out with the Ziegfeld Follies." She knew that she shouldn't have said it. She wanted him to go on thinking that she was weak and pliable. But Frank Mordant didn't seem to notice; or, if he did, he didn't take exception.

He went into the kitchenette and started opening and closing the cupboard doors. "Sandra's left a few things. Tea. Packet of sugar. Couple of jars of raspberry jam."

"You were saying about some friend of yours at Scotland Yard."

"Oh, yes. So I was. Not Scotland Yard *here*, though."

"You mean Scotland Yard back through the door?"

"That's right. New Scotland Yard. I've always made a point of cultivating friends in the Met."

Nancy felt her heartbeat slow down. "I guess you have to wait twenty-four hours for an answer. You know, wait for the world to turn around."

"Oh, no. I sent a lad over with a message and a couple of hours later he sent another lad back. That's how we communicate through the doors. Give a lad a couple of quid and a cheap digital watch, that's all you have to do. Almost as good as e-mail."

Nancy didn't say anything. Frank Mordant came out of the kitchen. He was still smiling but there was an odd, vindictive look in his eyes. "My pal's only a woodentop. Not CID or anything. But you can't beat him when it comes to inside information. Police Constable Bob Smart – smart by name and smart by nature. Mind you, I don't know why I'm telling you this, darling. You met him yourself, when you and Julia's brother went to the hospital to identify her mortal remains."

He stayed where he was, blocking her escape route to the stairs. "Do you know what I ask myself?" he said. "I ask myself why you came to see me, pretending to be looking for Julia, when all the time you knew she was dead? Now, why did you do that?"

"I thought you might know how she died," said Nancy, with a dry mouth.

"What are you saying? You're not saying *I* did away with her, are you?"

"If you didn't, why did you lie about her landlady? Mrs Marmion's dead, you know that. And why did you say that Julia might have gone to Scotland?"

"Because I knew you knew. And I just wanted to see how far you were prepared to keep up this little act of yours. What were you going to do? Trick me into making a confession? Rifle through my desk for incriminating evidence? Try to get me back through the door, and hand me over to Detective Sergeant Paul? You must think I was born yesterday."

"You murdered her and you murdered her right here, in this room. You hanged her, I've seen it for myself. Seen her legs kicking."

"You couldn't have done."

Nancy touched her fingertips to her temples. "The Hoodies aren't the only people in this world with psychic powers, Mr Mordant. I saw Julia Winward die, and I know that you did it. Just like you murdered John Farbelow's girlfriend Winnie and who knows how many others. Where's Sandra, for example? Isn't it amazing how she conveniently managed to disappear as soon as I arrived on the scene?"

Frank Mordant let out a snort of amusement. "Actually, darling, Sandra didn't disappear. I gave her the day off. After I heard from Police Constable Smart I wanted to find out what you were up to. And now I know."

He slowly rubbed his hands together, around and around. "The only trouble is, you've put me in a bit of an awkward spot. If I let you go back through the door, who knows what mischief you'll get up to. If I keep you here . . . well, I can't do that, either. You're wanted by the Hoodies, you and Mr Winward. Subversion, conspiracy and murder. It's been in all the papers. Lucky for you they didn't publish a very good likeness. Made you look like Daryl Hannah."

"What murder? I haven't been involved in any murder."

"Oh . . . a very serious murder. Master Thomas Edridge, chief proctor of the Masters of Religious Observance. His throat was cut when John Farbelow and his scruffs managed to rescue that chap of yours."

"Josh escaped?"

"According to the news, yes – although the Hoodies are still hunting for him. Mind you, having you here . . . that's going to make their job a lot easier, don't you imagine? Because I'm sure that your chap won't just leave you here to face the music on your own, will he?"

"Get out of my way," said Nancy, approaching him.

"You don't stand a chance, darling. You might as well resign yourself to the fact that you and your chap are going to have to give yourselves up."

"I said, get out of my way."

Without any warning at all, Frank Mordant slapped her across the face. Then, before she could recover, he punched her in the stomach. Nancy had trained in uyeshiba aikido but she had never been attacked so hard and so fast. She dropped on to her knees, gasping for breath, and as she did so Frank Mordant seized her hair and banged her head against the floor. She blacked out for an instant, and when she opened her eyes again she was seeing stars.

"You stupid bitch, did you really think that you were going to get me arrested?"

Nancy couldn't answer. She was doubled up on the floor, coughing. Frank Mordant strutted around her, first one way and then the other. "You don't have a bloody clue, do you?" he demanded. "You don't have a bloody clue who you're dealing with. The only thing I'll say is, you're very privileged. You're going to be the first girl who's ever left this flat alive."

Still stunned, Nancy lifted her head.

"Yes," said Frank Mordant. "I admit it. I did kill Julia. But you have to look at it this way: sometimes a single human life is worth sacrificing for the greater good."

"A *single* human life?" coughed Nancy. "What about Winnie? And don't tell me there haven't been others!"

Frank Mordant snorted impatiently. "Look, darling, we're not talking about a few stupid secretaries here, we're talking about the bloody cosmos. If I had my way I'd hang you the same way I hung Julia, and all the others, and make a fortune out of the videotape. They love it, those Japanese. But you are about to discover for yourself what keeps the six doors open, day and night, twenty-four hours a day. That takes power, believe me. That takes power like you can't even imagine.

"Think about it. Bloody well *think* about it. Whoever keeps the doors open controls every single alternative existence to which they give access. And there are thousands of them, believe me. Probably an infinite number. You could never visit them all, not if you lived to be a million."

"But all these murders?" Nancy retorted, almost hysterical. "I don't understand all these murders! Innocent girls! What did you have to kill them for?"

Frank Mordant smoothed back his Brylcreemed hair. "You're about to find out."

Twenty-Three

It was well after two o'clock before John Farbelow woke up. He opened his eyes and the sun was shining in through the dormer window, so he dragged the Indian durry up over his face. His hair – what was left of it – stuck up like a white cockatoo's.

"You can't hide, John," said Ella. "You managed to run away, but you can't pretend it never happened."

"They murdered them," said John Farbelow, his face still covered by the durry. "Those Puritan bastards. Christ almighty, they were only children, some of them. Ralphie had just turned sixteen."

Abraxas came over to John Farbelow's couch and started to lick at his hand, his tail slapping against Ella's legs. "Shit. Just what I need. Dog spit."

"Abraxas is very hygienic, aren't you, Abraxas? I give him licorice root to chew. It's good for his breath and it's a wonderful laxative."

"They killed my children, Ella."

Ella handed him a steaming blue-decorated mug. "Here, drink this. It'll make you feel better."

"It's not more of your stinking ragwort tea, is it?"

"No. Black coffee with a double vodka in it."

John Farbelow eventually pulled the durry away from his face and managed to sit up. There was a diagonal sword-cut across his left cheek, and his right eye was swollen up like a plum.

"They killed my children, Ella. How can I live with myself?"

"You have to. We all have to. It's the price we pay for fighting against the Lord Protector and the Doorkeepers. You seem to think that it's wonderful, living here. But this isn't home, is it? This is exile. Who cares if they know how to cure TB and they can fly to the moon? Home is where your heart is, John, and nobody can ever take that away from you."

Abraxas gave a sharp bark of agreement. John Farbelow tugged at his ears and rubbed him under his chin. "What a price, though, Ella. What a price to pay. We rescued one man and where is he now?"

"I don't know. But I suspect he's gone back, looking for his girlfriend."

John Farbelow reached into the pocket of his shirt that was hanging on the chair beside the couch and took out a pack of cigarettes. He lit one, and coughed like a dredger.

"They'll kill you, those things."

"Not where you and I come from, Ella. They haven't discovered the connection yet, between smoking and lung cancer. And even if they have, they're keeping really, really quiet about it."

Ella said, "I had a very strong feeling that we ought to rescue Josh Winward. I saw it in my tealeaves and I saw it in the Sybil. I also saw it in the ordinary deck. Every time I asked if we should take the risk of rescuing Josh, it came up with an ace. You know what that means, don't you?"

"Of course. You haven't shuffled the deck properly."

"It means that Josh is the chosen one. I've seen this before. It means that no matter what you think of him, or how much you question his importance, or his good sense, or his courage, he is the chosen one. Some people are just like that. They're chosen by fate, no matter what their aptitudes are. Joan of Arc. Toussaint I'Ouverture. Lawrence of Arabia."

John Farbelow swallowed coffee and sucked at his cigarette and blew smoke out of his nose. "I don't know, Ella. All this occult shit."

"Julia Winward's lung came out of her brother's mouth during my séance and that was psychic evidence that somebody had stopped her from living and breathing, and a guide to how to find them. If I did the same to you, who knows, you might even find yourself holding Winnie's hand."

"Just her hand?"

"Of course. Spirits only materialize in little pieces. To bring a whole person back . . . that would probably kill the medium, and everybody else in the room. How do you think the Hoodies found you, underneath the British Museum?"

"Somebody grassed us up, that's all. It doesn't take much, does it? A few packets of fags and a bottle of this world's whiskey."

"They found you because you were all excited, after you rescued Josh Winward. The Hoodies could feel your excitement, and their dogs could, too. Especially since you killed that Thomas Edridge. I know Thomas Edridge, and I'm glad he died. For your own safety, though, you should have let him go."

"Yes," said John Farbelow, wearily.

Ella held his hand. "I feel guilty, that so many of your young people were killed."

"Well, I feel guilty, too; and sometimes I wish that the Hoodies had killed me, instead of any one of those young people. But that's not the way life works, is it? Life is unfair. Life is full of surprises. All of those clichés."

At that moment, there was a pummeling knock on the apartment door. Abraxas barked wildly and ran over to it. John Farbelow swung his legs off the couch and said, "Ella? Are you expecting anybody?"

"No, I'm not. And even if I was, they'd always press the downstairs bell first."

John Farbelow went over to the kitchen area, tugged open the cutlery drawer and took out a chopping knife.

"It could be Nancy or Josh," said Ella.

John Farbelow shook his head. "It could be. But I'm not taking any chances, that's all." He went over to the door and listened. There was silence for a long, long while – so long that Ella thought that whoever it was had given up and left. But then there was another thunderous knocking, and something that sounded like a kick.

"For Christ's sake, that's my door!" shouted Ella.

"*Open up*!" a voice demanded, in a muffled roar.

"Oh, Jesus," said John Farbelow. "It's the Hoodies. They're here."

"Oh, shit. How good are you at abseiling?"

"Abseiling – what are you talking about?"

"I'm talking about climbing out of the kitchen window and sliding on a rope down to the sidewalk."

"Without anybody seeing us, or shooting us, or bursting into this room and cutting the rope when we're halfway down?"

"We don't have any alternative, do we?"

John Farbelow looked at her, and for the first time Ella saw beneath the ravages of age and pain and grief, saw the kind of hopeful young man he must have been once. Never striving to be anything important, but chosen all the same.

She climbed on to the kitchen sink and opened up the window. "The rope's here. I think it's safe. The fire brigade insisted that the landlord put it in."

There was another kick at the door. The architrave splintered, and lumps of plaster fell down from the sides. Ella wriggled herself backward out of the window, gripping the rope with her left hand. "Abraxas!" she called. "Come on, boy! Come on, Abraxas!"

Abraxas hesitated but then he jumped up on to the draining board. John Farbelow shouted, "What the hell are you doing? You can't take the dog down with you!"

"He's my dog," Ella insisted, just as the door was kicked again, and the two lower panels splintered.

"You can't! You'll kill yourself!"

Ella pulled Abraxas by his collar and dragged him out on to the windowsill. Abraxas whined and his claws scrabbled reluctantly against the stone, but Ella snapped, "Come on, stupid! You have to! You want to be *sancoche*?"

She managed to wrap her right arm around Abraxas' chest. Then she edged her way backward, over the sill, and began to inch down the wall, gasping with the effort. John leaned out of the window and watched her in desperation. It was nearly seventy feet down to the sidewalk, and in front of the block of flats stood a row of spiked cast-iron railings. Behind the railings there was a deep area crowded with metal trash cans and pieces of rusty corrugated iron and pieces of timber.

"Take it slowly, Ella," John Farbelow cautioned her. "Don't worry about me. I can take care of myself."

Behind him, the lower door panels were kicked out, and the central bar splintered. John Farbelow looked around, anxiously. Two or three more kicks and the lock would give way.

Ella managed to reach the windowsill of the flat below. She was still clinging on tight, but when she stepped off, she began to spin around, so she had to pedal desperately to get her feet back on the sill again. Abraxas began to panic, and thrashed his legs, and so Ella had to wedge herself tight against the window frame to stop herself from losing her balance.

"Calm down, Abraxas," she soothed him, even though her voice was shaking. "Come on, boy, calm down!" But Abraxas struggled even more wildly, and barked, and bit her hand, so that she almost let go of the rope. She looked down and the whole world seemed to tilt.

"Drop the dog!" John Farbelow shouted at her. "You don't have any choice, Ella! Drop the damn dog!"

"I can't!" she screamed. But at that instant, Abraxas struggled out of her grasp and jumped toward the ground. Ella twisted around to see what had happened to him, and it was then that the rope broke.

She snatched at the wall, trying to find a handhold. Her fingertips momentarily caught the top of the sash window, but then they slipped. The next thing she knew she was plunging to the ground, her arms and legs frantically waving, as if she were drowning, rather than falling. She went on swimming until she hit the railings.

There was a dull ringing sound, like a leaden bell chiming. John Farbelow looked down and saw her lying crucified, her arms lolling on either side, both shins penetrated by the same cast-iron spike. She was staring up at the sky with her eyes wide open, as if she were surprised that this had happened.

Abraxas had hit the sidewalk on all fours. It looked to John Farbelow as if he had broken one of his legs, but he managed to limp back to the railings, and stand looking up at Ella's body, whining in pain and perplexity.

The door opened with a crash. John Farbelow turned around as three men entered the room, all of them dressed in burnouses, like Arabs. Their faces, however, were completely masked with hessian hoods, with ragged holes torn open for their eyes.

He raised his hand and said, "I don't know who you are, or who you're looking for, but you're making a mistake!"

One of the Hooded Men drew a long saber out of his robes, and approached John Farbelow with the confident crouch of a trained swordsman. John Farbelow could hear him hissing to himself, hissing in triumph.

"This is all a mistake. None of us had anything to do with Edridge."

"Perhaps you did, perhaps you didn't," said one of the Hooded Men. "But, in history, even the innocent must pay for the sins of the guilty. It's the law."

John Farbelow looked away from him; and took in the positions of the other two Hooded Men. One of them was opening every one of Ella's herbs and spices and tipping them on to the floor. The other was pulling all of her gewgaws off the wall, all her crucifixes and mirrors and necklaces and voodoo dolls, all of the pictures of her family and friends, and all of those people who had helped her to believe that she didn't have to be enslaved.

"What are you going to do with me?" asked John Farbelow.

"We're going to give you justice," said the Hooded Man. "Isn't that what you were always fighting for?"

"Without freedom, my friend, justice doesn't mean anything."

"So that's what gives you your excuse to murder anybody you like?"

John Farbelow moved slowly sideways. If he was quick enough, he could dodge between the two Hoodies who were ransacking Ella's apartment and make it to the broken-down door. The third Hooded Man half-turned away from him for a second. "Look at this heathen trash. And to think this woman thought that she had some divine right to subvert our society."

"Well . . ." said John Farbelow, as if he were going to say something in reply. But then he ran for the door, jinking from one side to the other like a football player.

Before any of the three Hoodies could turn around, he had made it to the door, and on to the landing. He seized the banisters and swung himself down the first flight of stairs. He heard the Hoodies shouting and running after him, their boots drumming on the cheap-carpeted treads. He threw himself down the next flight, and the next, and he was galloping down the last flight at full tilt when another Hoodie appeared in front of him, as black as the shadow of death, and he ran straight into his upraised sword.

He reached out with both hands, trying to grasp the Hoodie's shoulders to support himself. He knew what had happened to him. He could feel that the steel had penetrated his lung and come right out of his back.

"Winnie," he whispered; and he made a conscious effort to picture her, the way he had first met her, on the number fifteen bus. Because all of his subversion, after all, had been nothing more than his rage and his grief at losing Winnie.

The Hoodie, in turn, grasped *his* shoulder, and slowly tugged the sword out, and it was a hundred times more painful than it had been, going in – especially the way it slid against his ribs. John Farbelow collapsed on to his knees and tumbled down the last six or seven stairs into the hallway, next to the bicycle.

He lay with his cheek against the grimy green vinyl, watching his blood creep away from him. He saw the Hoodies' boots stepping over him, as they left the apartment block and made their escape. By this time tomorrow, they would be back in the other London, and nobody would ever know who had murdered him. Worse still, nobody would ever know who he – or Ella – was.

Outside, in the street, Abraxas sat patiently on the sidewalk, while Ella lay spreadeagled on the railings, and the hazy afternoon air was filled with the whooping of ambulances and police cars.

Twenty-Four

Josh and Petty ran down Kingsway, their footsteps echoing against the derelict buildings. Fires were still burning in the offices all around Aldwych, and they could hear the ringing of fire-engine bells and the crackling of broken glass. All the same, they could still hear the penetrating tattoo of the drums that were following them; and the yapping of the dogs.

"Down here," said Petty, and they turned left into Sardinia Street. In the open gardens of Lincoln's Inn Fields, six or seven air-raid wardens were battling with a punctured barrage balloon, which filled up almost the whole square like a maddened but half-deflated elephant. They were tugging at ropes and trying to tie it down. "Your end, Reg! What the 'ell are you up to? Pull *your* end!"

They reached Carey Street and turned into Star Yard. "Listen," said Josh. "If we go through the door now, we're going back to the world of the Hooded Men. Another London, nothing like this."

More anti-aircraft guns coughed in the distance, over by the Surrey Docks. "There can't be anywhere as bad as this," said Petty. "And if we don't go, they'll catch us, won't they, and kill us?"

"All right," Josh agreed. He put his arms around her and gave her a hug.

They walked up Star Yard to the niche in the wall. Josh took three candles out of his pocket and set them on the ground.

"Is this all you have to do?" asked Petty.

"You have to recite a Mother Goose rhyme, too," said Josh, touching each candle with his butane lighter, his hand shielding the wicks until they were all well alight.

"A Mother Goose rhyme? What's that?"

Josh stood up. "You Brits call them nursery rhymes. Like Humpty Dumpty. This is a real old one, one of the oldest. 'Six doors they stand in London Town . . .'" And then he said, "Jack be nimble, Jack be quick . . ."

Petty stared at him in growing disbelief. "That's *it*? And that gets you through to this other London?"

"Try it," said Josh.

Petty held back. Exhausted and grimy and shocked as she was, this was enough. She couldn't cope with madness as well.

"I don't believe you," she said.

"You saw the Hooded Man. You saw his face."

Petty covered her eyes with both hands. "I don't want to think about it. I don't want to have nothing to do with it. I don't want to stay. I don't want to go. I don't know what I want to do."

Josh put his arm around her plump shoulders, in her cheap satin dress.

"Petty, I can't make you any promises. If we go through this door now, it may be worse. But right now these guys are after me *here* and because of me they want you too."

"I don't know what to do," Petty wept, and the tears poured down her cheeks and made dirty streaks in the dust.

But it was then that they heard the crackling noise of side drums, only two or three streets away. "It's them," Josh told her. "They won't give up, not until they track us down. I'm sorry."

"You're sorry? How do you think I feel? Why did I bloody well have to meet *you*, of all people?"

The three candles were burning strongly now. There was very little wind in Star Yard, and the flames scarcely nodded at all. They reminded Josh of the candles that used to burn in church, when he was a boy. "Maybe you met me because you were always meant to," he coaxed her. "Come on, Petty, these things happen. Some people get together whether they like it or not."

"Oh, I see. You were always meant to save me from a

life on the streets, were you? By frightening the *shit* out of me with that man's face. You *knew* he looked like that, didn't you? You knew! That's why you cut his hood off, you bastard."

"Petty, I swear to you I didn't know. I never saw one of those guys without his hood, ever. Not without his hood."

The drumming was nearer now, and much more frantic. The Hooded Men were probably turning into Carey Street. They knew where he was going. They knew that he was trying to escape. Underneath those harsh hessian hoods they could probably sense everything that he was thinking.

"Petty, if we don't haul ass out of here now . . ."

Petty lifted her face to the sky, and pressed her hands in front of her in prayer. Although she was so grimy, and her dress was so torn, Josh thought that she looked beautiful. More than beautiful, almost divine.

The drums racketed closer and closer but she kept her eyes closed and her hands pressed together. "Amen," she said at last, and crossed herself; but when she turned to him her face was wild with worry. "I bet it doesn't work."

"If you think it doesn't work, why did you pray?"

"I wasn't praying for me. I was praying for all the poor sods we're leaving behind."

"So you'll give it a try?"

"I don't know. I don't want to die, that's all."

Josh recited the rhyme again, just to make sure. The drums were very close now, and he could see the flickering lights of lanterns on the buildings opposite: shadows that jumped and danced like devils.

"Go," he told Petty. "Jump over the candles, that's all you have to do."

"That's all I have to do? Jump? But there's nothing *there*!" she suddenly panicked. "Only a wall!"

"Come on, you just said you were going to do it."

"*But it's only a bloody wall*!"

Josh gripped hold of her dress and stared her wildly in the eyes. "Remember that face? Remember what that thing looked like, when I cut off its hood? There are more of them coming!

They're going to be here before you can count to ten, and then we won't have any options at all!"

"But his *face* . . ."

Josh, tired as he was, bent his knees and picked her up and practically threw her over the line of candles. With a screech of Cockney indignity, she landed on her bottom on the other side. He glanced to his left and saw four dogs pelting toward him, four of the Hoodies' dogs, their tongues flapping and froth flying out of the sides of their mouths. He heaved himself over the candles, rolling over into the rubbish. He climbed to his feet, blew out the candles and took hold of Petty's arm. "Come on, we have to get out of here fast. I wouldn't be surprised if they come after us."

"Hey . . . there's a way *through* here!" Petty exclaimed. "I didn't see that before!"

"You have to look, that's all."

"What? Meaning I'm blind, as well as stupid?"

"Meaning you have to *look*, that's all."

They hurried through the dark, dripping passageway between the buildings. Pigeons fluttered from the windowsills high above their heads. From time to time, Josh glanced back worriedly, but it seemed as if the Hooded Men had chosen not to follow them. Not today, anyhow. But he had no illusions that they wouldn't go on hunting him down until they found him.

"Slow down," he panted. His teeth were aching so much that he could hardly think, and every wound that had been inflicted by the Holy Harp was prickling with pain. Petty slowed down, and leaned against the wall, trying to catch her breath.

"They're not coming after us, are they?"

Josh shook his head. "Maybe later. Maybe tomorrow. Maybe they're waiting for us in this world."

They turned the next corner in the passageway. Petty said, in bewilderment, "We're back where we started from."

"That's right. That's the way the doors work. You're not going from one *place* to another. You're going from one reality into another."

They stepped out into Star Yard. It was raining hard and

there was almost nobody around. Josh took Petty to the derelict building in which he and Nancy had first escaped from the dog-handlers, and they hid themselves in a corner office, listening all day and all night to the rain beating on the ceiling above their heads, and cascading down the stairs.

Petty fell asleep, her head resting against Josh's shoulder, one clogged-up nostril whistling. Josh was exhausted, reality-lagged, but he still found it almost impossible to sleep. He kept thinking of the Hooded Man's head, when he had torn his hood open. The sight had overwhelmed him. More than that, it had dropped open a trapdoor beneath his feet, so that he could no longer be sure of what was believable and what wasn't. It was just as if his father and mother had suddenly dragged latex masks off their heads when he was thirteen years old, and shown themselves to be two hideous-looking strangers.

Petty stirred and touched his shoulder. "What time is it?" she asked him, without opening her eyes.

"Seven and a half hours to go. Don't worry about it. Go back to sleep."

An hour later, he heard drums rattling. The Hooded Men, on patrol. They came up Chancery Lane toward Holborn, but they didn't stop. If Josh knew anything about dogs, they wouldn't have stopped to sniff them out, not in this weather. All they wanted was a dry kennel and a bowl of food.

The rain stopped. Josh fell asleep at last, with his head tilted back. He woke up at five o'clock in the morning with a raging sore throat and a crick in his neck.

"Have we got any food?" asked Petty.

Twenty-Five

Nancy opened her eyes and was aware at once of the utter silence. Complete, flawless silence. She was lying on an iron-framed bed in a hospital room with cream-painted walls and a light green dado. She knew it was a hospital room because it smelled of hospitals: antiseptic and boiled vegetables. The only other furniture was an oak-veneered nightstand with a glass of water on it, an oak-veneered closet, and a green armchair. For some inexplicable reason, she felt that somebody had recently been sitting in the green armchair, watching her.

Her head felt thick, as if she had been drinking too much red wine. She tried to lift her head but she felt swimmy and nauseous, so she lay back on the pillow again. It was a big pillow, with a starched pillowcase, and it reminded her of staying in hospital when she was a child. Homesick, and alone.

She turned toward the window. Outside, she could see the upper branches of some tall elm trees, and some angular rooftops, and chimneys. Even if she had been familiar with London, she wouldn't have been able to tell where she was. The sky was clear blue, with only a few high clouds in it, unraveling themselves in the upper atmosphere like skeins of white cotton. And it was silent. She couldn't even hear any traffic.

She tried to think what had happened to her. The last moment she could remember was Frank Mordant hitting her. After that, all she could recall was a jumble of voices and a kaleidoscope of faces.

An hour went past. The sun moved across the window. Still

there was silence. She tried to keep her eyes open but she couldn't, and she slept. She had a dream that she was walking along a desolate seashore, with the tide gradually coming in. It was foggy, and she knew that it was getting late, and that it was time for her to turn back. But up ahead of her she could see a hooded figure, and felt that she had to catch up with it, and ask it if it could tell her where Josh was. She was deeply afraid of it, this figure, the way it walked through the fog with its robes curling and flapping, but she knew that there was no alternative. She hurried across the hard, ribbed sand, even though the water was already starting to surge across her shoes.

The figure stopped. She slowed down, and cautiously circled around it, until she was facing it.

"I know what you want," the figure said, in a hollow whisper. "I know what you've *always* wanted."

It reached inside its robes and drew out a yard-long poker, the tip of which was red-hot and crackling with tiny sparks. "You want the Five Holy Cauterizations, don't you? Eyes, tongue, and ears – the greater to seal your purity."

She wanted to turn and run, but she couldn't. All she could do was sink slowly to her knees in the chilly seawater as the figure slowly approached her, the poker held aloft. She could actually smell the overheated iron.

"The supplicant always has a choice," the figure whispered. "You can decide which cauterization you will enjoy first, and which last. You'd be surprised how many leave the tongue till last, so that even when they're deaf and blind, they can still curse the Lord that made them."

The figure was standing right over her now, its robes stirring in the breeze. The seawater swilled around her knees. She lifted her head and stared defiantly into the blackness of its hood. "You can do whatever you damn well like," she told it.

"Well, that's jolly generous of you," said another voice. She opened her eyes. She wasn't on the seashore at all, but lying in her hospital bed. Frank Mordant was standing not far away, his hands in his pockets, beaming. Two other men stood much closer, both of them dressed in starched white collars and black coats and gray pinstripe pants, like bankers. One of them had wiry gray hair and gold pince-nez that were perched on a bulbous, port-wine-colored nose. The other was young, with a neck like a heron and a dark, downy moustache.

"What am I doing here?" asked Nancy, thick-tongued. She tried to sit up but the older man gently reached out and pushed her back on to the pillow.

"You ought to rest," he told her, with an avuncular smile. "Conserve your energy."

"I want to get out of here, that's all. I want to go back to where I came from."

"You *did* go back to where you came from," said Frank Mordant, still beaming. "But then you decided to return, didn't you, and make a nuisance of yourself. Your choice, darling. You can hardly put the blame on me. We all have to cover our asses – as you Yanks put it – don't we?"

"So what are you going to do? Are you going to murder me, the way you murdered Julia?" She turned to the two men in black coats. "Did you know that? Did you know that he was a murderer? He admitted it to me. He confessed."

Frank Mordant stepped forward and laid one hand on each of the men's shoulders. "Perhaps I ought to introduce you, Miss Andersen. This is Mr Brindsley Leggett, senior surgeon here at the Puritan Martyrs Hospital, and this is Mr Andrew Crane, his junior."

"He confessed to me," Nancy insisted. "He told me that he's been hanging women and making goddamned videos while they die!"

"Come on, now," said Mr Leggett. "You've been through a very disturbing experience. I'm not at all surprised that you've been suffering from misapprehensions. My goodness, if it had happened to me . . . !"

"You're trying to say that I'm sick? If there's anybody who's sick around here, it's Frank Mordant! He's a killer, I tell you! I can prove it!"

"You can prove it, can you? Now, how can you do that?"

"If you let me take him back to where I come from, I have DNA evidence."

Mr Leggett shook his head. "DNA evidence? What's that, when it's at home?"

"Irrefutable scientific proof that Frank Mordant killed a woman called Julia Winward."

"And where did you say this evidence was? Do the police have it? Or the Doorkeepers?"

"It's back in the other London. It's back through the door."

Mr Leggett turned to Frank Mordant and shook his head. "Poor dear. 'The other London.' What a way to speak of Purgatory."

"I didn't come from Purgatory, you superstitious asshole!" Nancy shouted at him. "It isn't Purgatory on the other side of those doors! It's another London, that's all – just like this London, only different. It has people and houses and hospitals and cars. It's real – not some goddamned medieval never-never-land!"

Mr Crane looked quite pale. "I've never seen a Purgatorial so . . . deluded."

"Well, she's certainly the liveliest we've ever had," said Mr Leggett. "Mr Mordant usually sends us those who are so close to meeting their Maker as makes no difference; and the Doorkeepers have usually been having a bit of a chat with the others."

"The Doorkeepers wanted this one kept as she is," said Frank Mordant. "They have their reasons, apparently."

Nancy said, "If you're not going to believe me, then I just want out of here."

"Oh, you can't *go*," said Mr Leggett, benignly. "We have plans for you, after the Doorkeepers have done whatever they want to do. You want to make a contribution to society, don't you, before you finally make your peace with God?"

"What the hell are you talking about?" Nancy demanded.

Mr Leggett laughed. "This is so interesting, isn't it? I wish they could always send me Purgatorials in this condition! From the way she talks, though, I don't know whether she's going up . . ." he pointed to the ceiling, "or you know where . . ." and pointed to the floor.

He turned to Frank Mordant and shook his hand. "Very

good to meet you again, Mr Mordant. I particularly enjoyed that brandy you brought me the other day. Where did you say you found it?"

"Oh . . . just on one of my business trips," smiled Frank Mordant.

Mr Leggett and Mr Crane left the room. Nancy was left on the bed, frustrated and enraged. Frank Mordant came over and stood beside her, but he wasn't smiling any longer.

"I'll tell you something, darling, you made a serious error coming after me. I've got too many contacts in too many different realities. Too many friends in high and low places."

"Why won't you let me go?"

"Because you're wanted by the Hoodies, that's why. Do you know what the Hoodies would do to me, if I sprung you from here? I was tempted, I must admit. I think you're a very lovely girl, and I wouldn't like to see anything . . . you know, *ugly* happen to you. But then you had to blurt it out that you had evidence against me. So you can see that I wasn't quite so tempted after that."

"You bastard."

"Sorry, darling. You should have stayed where you were, and forgotten about Julia, and that would have been the end of it. But as it is . . ."

"What do the Hooded Men want me for?"

"They wouldn't say. But my guess is, they want that boyfriend of yours, and you're the Judas goat. That's why they wanted you alive and well; and that's why they haven't touched you so far – although they probably will."

"So what are those two going to do to me? Those surgeons?"

"You'll find that out in the morning, so I'm told. But I think you can safely assume that they're going to be carrying out one or two operations on you. Major operations."

"Operations for what? What the hell are you talking about?"

Frank Mordant leaned over her, so close that she could see the hairs in his nostrils. "You seem to have forgotten that you came from Purgatory. People who come back from Purgatory are dead already. They don't have any rights to their life or property. That's what the Lord Protector teaches us, anyway. So gentlemen surgeons like Mr Leggett and Mr Crane feel quite unconcerned about cutting them up and taking whatever organs they require."

"You're crazy, all of you. You're all stone crazy."

Frank Mordant stood up. "You know that it's tommy-rot. *I* know that it's tommy-rot. But men like Mr Leggett and Mr Crane have been brought up to believe it, as do ninety-nine point ninety-nine percent of the rest of the population. You took the chance and came back here, my darling; and now you're going to have to pay the price."

"You, Frank Mordant – you are the most disgusting piece of slime that ever slid across the earth."

Frank Mordant's left eye twitched. "It depends on your yardstick, my darling. I do have a heart, you know, whatever you think. I had a dog once. I loved that dog. I really, really loved that dog."

Nancy had never spat at anybody in her life, but now she did, hitting Frank Mordant on the cheek. The saliva slid down to the corner of his mouth. He stared at her for a moment and she thought that he was going to hit her, but then he took a carefully-pressed handkerchief out of his pocket and dabbed at his face.

"Don't you blame me," he told her. "You're the one who came back."

Nancy had another night of appalling nightmares. She saw dark crablike shapes leaping and hopping across the ceiling. She heard her grandmother screaming her name. When she woke up, the sun was shining through the window again, and a nurse was setting out her breakfast on a tray. Toast, solidified scrambled eggs, and a grilled tomato. The nurse was young, with a long pale face and freckles, and she stared at Nancy anxiously all the time that she was serving her.

"What's the matter?" Nancy asked her. "I don't bite, you know."

The nurse gave her a quick, nervous smile.

Nancy said, "Haven't you ever seen a Purgatorial before?"

"Not one like you."

"What's different about me?"

"You're awake. You talk."

"That's because I'm still alive. Here, you want to take my pulse?"

The young nurse shook her head.

"So what goes on here?" Nancy asked her. "What kind of a hospital is this?"

The young nurse didn't answer, but gave her a nervous shrug.

"Come on," Nancy urged her. "What do they do here? Heart surgery? Orthopedics? Pediatrics?"

"We look after – you know. We look after *her*."

"*Her*? Who's her?"

"*Her*, that's all."

"Does she have a name, this *her*?"

"I suppose she must have done once, but nobody ever mentions it."

"You're not telling me that she's the only patient here?"

"Oh, no. She's not a patient. She's . . . well, she's . . ."

The young nurse was obviously struggling for the right words. Nancy sat up and said, "Are you *frightened* of what goes on here?"

"Of course not. It's a privilege."

"Then why can't you tell me all about it?"

"I'm not allowed to. Not to you. Not to anybody."

"Don't you trust me?"

"You're a Purgatorial. You're dead."

"You're a nurse and you think I'm dead? If I'm dead, why are you feeding me scrambled eggs and grilled tomatoes?"

"I don't know. I was told to."

"So where are you going next with your breakfast trays? Down to the mortuary? Wake up, boys, come and get it while it's good and hot!"

"Don't. You're confusing me."

"I'll bet I am. I am absolutely and positively not dead. I never *have* been dead. I have never been to Purgatory. Everything that you've ever been told about Purgatorials is a lie. When people are dead, they stay dead, they don't come back. But when people come from another world – when people come from another reality – now, that's something different."

The young nurse stared at her for a long time, and then she brushed a strand of hair away from her face.

"What's your name?" Nancy asked her.

"Sophie."

"Well, Sophie, thanks for the breakfast. And all I can say to you is, never believe what you read in books. Especially *A Child's Book of Simple Truth*."

Sophie, still staring at her, crossed the room, opened the door, and walked out. Nancy lay back on her pillow. She didn't know what to think. All she knew was that she had very little time. Josh probably would have given her twenty-four hours to come back – but when she didn't, there was no question in her mind that he would come after her. He could arrive in this reality any time today. It might take him a few hours to find her here at the Puritan Martyrs, but she knew how resourceful he was.

She closed her eyes and said a prayer to her ancestors, to protect her. But here, in *this* existence, she wasn't at all sure that she could still feel their closeness.

Early in the afternoon, when she was halfway between sleeping and waking, she heard the door swing open, and the sound of boots on the polished linoleum floor. She opened her eyes and saw two Hooded Men, one on either side of her bed, with their tall Puritan hats and their black tunics and their long swords and their grotesque hessian masks. She sat up in bed and tugged the blanket up to her neck. She was too frightened to say anything.

"You believe that your friend will come looking for you?" asked one of the Hooded Men, in the softest of rasps. It was like somebody sawing a velvet cushion in half.

Nancy still couldn't speak.

"You don't think he's going to abandon you, do you? Especially when he discovers what fate we have in store for you."

"I don't know what he's going to do."

"Oh, he'll be here. In fact, we've given him a little guidance, so that he knows where you are, and how to find you."

"He's not stupid, for God's sake. You think he'll walk right into a trap?"

"I think he loves you," said the Hooded Man, and it sounded as if he were smiling.

"Why can't you just let me go? We only came here to find out who killed Josh's sister."

"So you keep telling us. But what mayhem you created, you and your subversive friends. And this morning we learned that your precious Josh has killed one of our number. Taken his head off. You don't think that we can turn a blind eye to murder, do you?"

"You're lying! Josh couldn't murder anybody!"

"There were more than enough witnesses, I promise you."

"Where did this happen? Was it here? Is Josh in *this* London?"

"It happened in another London. At this particular moment, we think we know where your partner is, but we can't be certain. He could be hiding in any one of a million Londons, and we could never find him. That is why *you* are so valuable to us. When he discovers that we have you here, and what we intend to do with you, don't worry, he'll be here as fast as the turning world will allow him. We'll give him three or four days. We're not in any hurry."

Nancy said, "You'll be damned for this. Call yourself religious zealots? You'll be damned for this and you'll all burn in hell."

The Hooded Man leaned forward. Nancy could see something moving behind the eyeholes in his hood. She was aware of a strange smell, too, that reminded her of something that had happened to her long ago, when she was a child. Something cold and unpleasant. Something that she had tried to forget.

"You, lady," the Hooded Man rasped. "You don't know the meaning of hell."

Josh and Petty took a taxi from Chancery Lane to West

Kensington. Petty was amazed to see London undamaged, and crowded with traffic and people.

"I can't believe it," she kept on saying. "Look at that girl's dress! Look at it! There's nothing of it, is there?"

The taxi driver's eyes watched them in the rear-view mirror. They were both filthy and bruised, and they smelled. Their clothes were thick with dust and their hair was matted. Josh saw his reflection in the taxi window and realized that his cheeks were gray and his eyes were rimmed with red, like a zombie.

When they reached Josh's hotel, he gave the driver a ten-pound tip. "That's for stopping, and for cleaning up the seats, if you have to. I can tell you that we don't normally look like this."

"Doesn't bother me, mate," said the taxi driver. "At least you didn't throw up."

They walked into hotel reception and headed toward the elevators. Petty's head went around and around in astonishment. "I've never seen nothing like this. This is incredible. And, look, what's that? Is that a television? It's huge! And it's in *color*, just like a film!"

"Mr Winward?" called one of the receptionists, dubiously.

"That's me."

"There's a message for you, sir." She reached into one of the pigeonholes behind her and took out a folded slip of yellow paper.

Josh opened it up. It read: *Mr Joshua Winward, your lady frend wos cort by the Hoodiz, I no where they are kepin her cum back to Star Yd as soon as U can excuss my riting on a/c of havn no rit han. Yor frend Simon Cutter.*

"Josh, I love this place," said Petty, taking hold of his arm. Her eyes were bright with delight. "It's de-luxe, isn't it? Really de-luxe."

Josh took hold of her arm and propelled her toward the elevators. "Here, steady on," she protested. "What's your rush?"

"I have to leave. Something I have to do."

"But we've only just got here!"

"I know. But it's urgent. I'm going to take a shower, change, and then I'm going to have to go out. I may not be back until tomorrow."

"So what am I going to do?"

"You can stay here. You can order meals on room service. You can watch color television. You can do whatever you like. I'll give you some money so you can buy yourself cigarettes or candy or pantyhose or anything else you need. You'll survive."

He hurried her into the elevator and pressed the button for the third floor. "But I don't know anybody here!" she protested. "How do I know that you're going to come back? Supposing you don't come back?"

He took hold of her hands and squeezed them. "I'll be back, I promise you."

When they entered the hotel room Petty dubiously sat on the bed and bounced up and down a few times. Josh went into the bathroom, stripped off and took a shower. He was exhausted, but Simon Cutter's note had filled him immediately with fresh determination. You have to be strong, he told himself. Nancy needs you, and you have to be strong. He just hoped that he didn't have to face up to the Hooded Men again. He stood with the water spraying at full blast directly into his face in the hope that he could wash away the image of the Hooded Man's head. But the tighter he closed his eyes, the clearer the picture came back to him, and in the end he had to open them again, wide.

There are times in your life when you think, *oh, Jesus, what have I done*? And this was Josh's moment.

He stepped out of the shower to find the bathroom door wide open and Petty standing naked in the doorway. He wrapped his towel tightly around his waist and gently maneuvered his way past her into the bedroom.

"You don't have to go, you know," she told him, reaching out for him. "Not straight away, anyhow."

"I'm sorry, it's something I have to do."

"Couldn't we have a rest first? You and me? This bed's ever so comfortable."

Josh put on a clean blue checkered shirt. "Petty . . . I like you. Believe me, I really like you a whole lot. But this is a matter of life and death."

"So where are you going?"

"It's safer for you if you don't know. Really."

"Those geezers in the hoods aren't coming after you, are they?"

"I don't know. But whatever happens, you haven't seen me, and you don't know where I've gone."

She lay back on the bed, twisting her hair around her finger, and giving him a coquettish look that reminded Josh of a 1940s movie star. "Sure I can't tempt you?"

It took him only ten minutes to walk to Ella's flat. A gritty wind blew newspapers across the streets of Earl's Court. He pressed the doorbell again and again but there was no reply. He clenched his fist and thumped the door frame in frustration. This was a time when he really needed some support. More than that, he desperately needed some insight into what the Hooded Men might be thinking of doing next.

He gave the doorbell one last, long ring, in case Ella had taken one of her own sleeping potions. He still had his thumb on the bellpush when Abraxas came hobbling around the corner.

"Abraxas! What are you doing out here, boy? Where's your mom?"

Abraxas came up to him and Josh hunkered down on the sidewalk and took hold of his ears and stroked him. He was streaked with dirt and his eyes were dull. He had lost weight, too. Josh reckoned that he hadn't been properly fed for three or four days.

"Where's your mom, Abraxas? Where's Ella? She hasn't left you, has she? She wouldn't do that."

At that moment, the front door to the apartment building opened and a tall middle-aged woman came out, carrying a Harrods shopping bag.

"Oh, that *poor* dog!" she exclaimed. "He's been hanging around for three days now. I've called the RSPCA twice, but when they arrive he's never here. I feel so sorry for him."

"Where's his mistress?"

"Why, she's dead. Didn't you read about it in the papers?"

"Dead?" Josh felt a sensation in the pit of his stomach like dropping fifty feet in an airplane. "When was this? What happened?"

"It was quite awful. She fell out of the window of her flat and landed right on the railings. I'm so glad I wasn't here when it happened. And a man friend of hers was stabbed right here in the hallway. I almost decided to move out. I still would, if I could find a decent flat around here for the same sort of rent."

Josh kept on stroking Abraxas' head and looking directly into his eyes. "You must be grieving, boy. You must be feeling your loss so bad."

Abraxas came up closer and rested his chin on Josh's knee and looked up at him with his sad amber eyes. "You certainly have a way with animals," the woman remarked.

"I'll take him and get him cleaned up," said Josh. "He needs some emotional care, too. He's going to be feeling very confused about Ella disappearing so suddenly."

"I've got the number of the RSPCA if you want it."

"That's OK. Right now, the last thing he needs is a kennel, with a whole lot of other distressed dogs. He needs calm. He needs reassurance."

He walked back toward the hotel with Abraxas gamely limping after him. The woman watched him go, slowly shaking her head.

Petty watched Abraxas wolfing down a bowl of milk and dog biscuits and shook her head. "Looks like you're picking up all the waifs and strays, doesn't it?"

"I couldn't leave him wandering the streets like that."

"So what are you going to do with him? You can't keep him here, can you? And if you're going away tomorrow, don't expect me to look after him. I don't like dogs."

"Look, I'll take him with me, if I have to."

"That's all right, then." She lit a cigarette and blew out a long stream of smoke. "So you're going to be staying here tonight, after all?"

"I'll have to, won't I, now that my friend's been killed."

"Well, don't expect any hanky-panky. Not with that dog in the room."

Josh couldn't help smiling. He was exhausted and he couldn't think about anything else but Nancy, caught by the Hooded Men – but he was still amused by Petty's unshakable conviction that men were only interested in one thing. Hanky-panky? he thought. You wish.

It was another gusty day, and Josh had difficulty in lighting the candles. Abraxas stood beside him, patiently panting. Josh had made a lead for him out of a suitcase strap. One or two passers-by stopped to watch him, and one old woman asked him if he was making a shrine.

He told her yes; and in a way he was. This niche in the wall was a shrine to Julia, and to Ella, and all of those who had been killed or tortured at the hands of the Hoodies.

At last the candles were burning strongly. Josh hefted Abraxas up in his arms and recited the words of the Mother Goose rhyme. There was hardly anybody around – only a girl with a basket of sandwiches walking up from Carey Street – and so he stepped over the candles and into the niche. Abraxas barked three or four times as they turned the corner out of this Star Yard and made their way through the passageway.

The other Star Yard was almost deserted. Josh peered around the corner of the niche, to make sure that there were no Hoodies or Watchers waiting for him. Then he tugged at Abraxas' lead and said, "Come on, boy. Let's go find Nancy."

He had almost reached Carey Street when a hand seized his left shoulder. "'Ere! Don't go beetling off! I've been waiting for you for days!"

It was Simon Cutter, although Josh could hardly recognize him. His face was swollen and scratched, both his eyes were black, and his two front teeth were missing. His right arm was wrapped in filthy bandages and held up in a sling. His long coat was covered in mud and straw and the lining dragged along the paving stones.

"God almighty, what happened to you?" Josh asked him.

"The Hoodies gave me a going-over, didn't they? They wanted to know all about John Farbelow and the rest of his subversives. They wanted to know all about you."

"What did you tell them?"

"I didn't tell them nothing. What could I tell them, I didn't know nothing. They were going to scrag me, and then they were going to transport me, but in the end the reeve said that since I'd lost my hook and feeler, that was punishment enough."

"Where's Nancy?"

Simon took hold of Josh's arm and pulled him back up Star Yard. "I heard from one of my street arabs that they took her to the Puritan Martyrs Hospital in the City. That's not a hospital for sick people, guvnor. It used to be a plague hospital, so they say, but it's closed these days. The windows are always lit up at night, and there's coming and going, but nobody ever says what goes on there."

"Can we get in there, do you think?"

"Why do you think I sent you that note? It so happens that I know a lad who works in the kitchens at the Puritan Martyrs. Me and him used to do a little business together. Leather goods." He hesitated for a second, and then he added, "Wallets, purses, that kind of thing. He can let us in through the scullery, ten o'clock sharp."

"OK . . . do you know someplace we can stay until then?"

"There's a room up over the Old Cat & Ninepence. We can use that."

The Old Cat & Ninepence was a seventeenth-century pub wedged in the corner of Gough Square, between two glass and concrete office buildings. Outside, it was tile-hung, with a crazily tilting chimney. Inside it was all dark paneling and tobacco-stained plaster, and the ceiling beams were so low that Josh had to duck his head as they went in through the front door.

Simon led the way up a flight of narrow, sloping stairs, and then along to the back of the building, where there was a small sitting room with a chintz-covered sofa and two armchairs, a large radio set, and a magazine rack stuffed with yellowing copies of *Radio Times* and *The People's Friend.*

"We'll be snug enough here," said Simon, easing himself stiffly into one of the chairs. "The Hoodies may have sensed somebody coming through the door, but they won't think to look in a gaff like this."

Josh went to the window. It was made up of small octagonal panes of yellowish glass, with bubbles and inclusions in them, so that when the sun shone through it on to his face he looked as if he were suffering from leprosy. Abraxas sat down at his feet and yawned.

"You're sure you don't have any idea why the Hoodies might have taken Nancy to the hospital?"

"Search me, guvnor."

"You see, what worries me is that Julia was mutilated. When they found her body in the Thames it was empty, all of her internal organs taken out. And apparently it had been done by experts. Frank Mordant may have hung her, but what happened after that?"

Simon coughed, holding his right arm close to his chest.

"You sound pretty sick," said Josh.

"It's my stump, isn't it? It's infected. I kept it in a bowl of salty water but that still didn't stop it from turning rotten."

"Can't you ask your doctor to prescribe you some antibiotics?" Josh asked him, but remembered almost at the same time that this was a world that was medically equivalent to the 1930s, before penicillin had been discovered.

Simon coughed again, and this time he brought up a handful of blood. "I'm bloody dying," he said. "You don't know what those bloody Hoodies did to me."

Josh said nothing. He couldn't quite understand why, but he felt uneasy. Why had the Hooded Men let Simon go so readily? After all, they had slaughtered all of John Farbelow's people, in revenge for Master Thomas Edridge's murder. And if they were holding Nancy prisoner, they must have guessed that he would come looking for her. So why hadn't they been keeping a constant watch on the doors?

Unless they wanted to be absolutely sure that they had

him trapped, where he didn't have any chance of escape whatsoever. Josh remembered Ella's tarot card with the man snaring songbirds. "You're not setting me up, are you?"

Simon looked up at him, the whites of his eyes still stained with blood, like a broken vampire. "You can trust me, guvnor. You know that."

Josh sat down next to him and pointed a finger directly at his nose. "If this is a trap, I swear to God that I will kill you first."

Twenty-Six

Josh and Simon reached thc rear of the Puritan Martyrs Hospital through a narrow alleyway that led from the side of a parade of shops on Bunhill Row. On the far side of an overgrown allotment stood a high corrugated-iron fence with its top cut into serrated saw-blade points. There was a gate in the middle of it, but it was locked.

"How do we get over this?" Josh demanded.

Simon checked his watch, and at the same time the bells of a nearby church struck ten o'clock. "Whippy should be here any second. He's always dead reliable, Whippy."

Abraxas was snuffling around the weeds, searching for interesting smells. He was still whuffling when they heard a padlock clanking, and the sound of bolts being drawn back. The gate was opened, and a short, stocky young man appeared, with black curly hair and a Roman nose and eyes as bright as a badger's. He was wearing a long white apron and he was carrying a large bowl of vegetable peelings.

"Simon! Christ almighty! Look at the state of you!"

"I'm all right, Whippy. Don't make a song and dance about it. I'm lucky I'm still living and breathing. This is Mr Winward."

Whippy wiped his hand on his apron and held it out. "Pleased to make your acquaintance," he said, in a strong Manchester accent. "Any butty of Simon Cutter's is a butty of mine. Taking your dog for a walk, are you?"

"He'll be OK, don't you worry."

"I hope so. If those Hoodie dogs get a smell of him, it'll be mutt chops for breakfast."

Whippy tossed the vegetable peelings on to a compost heap,

and then he beckoned that they should follow him through the gate and into the grounds.

The hospital was set amongst wide, well-trimmed lawns, and was illuminated by floodlights, which gave it an appearance of unreality, as if it were constructed of nothing more substantial than cardboard. It was a large three-story Victorian building built in the shape of a cross, with four Gothic towers at each end. There were lights shining in almost every window, but there were no ambulances here, no staff walking around. Beyond the hospital walls they could hear the sound of buses and horse-drawn wagons clattering along Bunhill Row; and in the distance they could make out the mournful drone of a Zeppelin as it flew toward London Airport. But inside the hospital grounds it was oddly quiet, and windless, as if the whole world were holding its breath.

Whippy led them along a gravel path to the kitchen entrance, his feet noisily scrunching. "I'm cleaning up now, that's all, so there's only me." The kitchen was large and bright, with white enamel worktops and a wide green-enamel range. There was a faint smell of steak-and-kidney pie in the air, but a very much stronger smell of pine disinfectant.

"Do you have any idea where Nancy is?" asked Josh.

"Oh, yes. I have to cook her tea in the evening and send it up. Room three-thirteen, on the third floor."

"Is the room guarded?"

"Doesn't have to be. It's locked."

"Have you seen her? She isn't hurt or anything?"

Whippy lifted a casserole dish out of the sink, rinsed it under the faucet and wiped it with a tea-towel. "I haven't seen her myself, but Sophie has. She's the nurse who takes her food up for her. She says she's amazing, for a Purgatorial. She talks, she eats. You'd have never credited it, would you, a dead person talking and eating? But I suppose that's the way it happens, isn't it? If God doesn't want you, and the Devil sends you back, what else can you do?"

"What has she eaten?"

"Eggs, bacon; a nice cheese omelet; steak-and-kidney pie; gooseberry fool."

"Has it occurred to you that somebody who eats like that can't possibly be dead?"

Whippy clattered saucepans. "I'm a cook, mate. Not a fucking philosopher."

"She's alive and I have to get her out of here."

"Come on, Whippy," said Simon. "You said you would. You owe me that much after everything I did for you. Your kid brother would be brown bread by now, if it wasn't for me."

Without another word, Whippy reached into his apron pocket and produced the key to a five-lever lock. "I lent it off Sophie. Whatever happens – if you get caught – don't you say where you got it from. Otherwise it's both of us heads."

Josh said, "What kind of security do they have in this place? Any Hoodies? Any patrols?"

"There's only a skeleton staff. You shouldn't have any worries, so long as you're quick."

"Right, then. Let's get going."

Simon sat down behind the kitchen table. "I'm sorry, guvnor. This is as far as I go."

"What the hell do you mean?"

"I mean that I've got you into the hospital, and given you the key, and they could scrag me for either of those. I can't risk going any further."

"Simon, you're beginning to give me a very bad feeling about this."

"I've lost my hand. I've had three ribs broken. My balls have been burned to buggery. I don't want to lose my bonce, that's all."

Josh stared at him narrowly. "You're telling me the truth here, right?"

Simon shrugged, and looked down at the kitchen floor.

"You're telling me the truth here, right? There are no Hoodies waiting for me up on the third floor? Nancy's safe and well?"

"I brought you here – what more do you want? I almost died, because of you!"

Josh went up to him and laid his hand on Simon's shoulder.

Under his coat, his shoulder felt like chicken bones. "Yes, you did, and I'm sorry."

He took Abraxas and walked out of the kitchen, into the corridor beyond.

It wasn't difficult to locate the third floor. The corridor led to a huge, high-ceilinged hallway with a highly-polished floor of white and tawny marble. A sweeping flight of stairs led up to the first-floor landing, with nude bronze figures holding up torches on the newel-posts. Abraxas had difficulty crossing the hallway: it was so shiny that his paws kept slipping, and he made a loud scrabbly sound until he managed to reach the other side. "You should wear Keds," Josh admonished him, and he let out a thin, suppressed whine.

They climbed the stairs to the first-floor landing, where huge dark oil paintings hung: portraits of famous benefactors and doctors. Abraxas was panting again. Ella had kept him in her apartment for most of the day so he wasn't very fit. Josh almost had to drag him up the next flight of stairs, and at the bottom of the third flight he refused to move, and sat on his haunches whining.

"Come on, Abraxas, you can't stay here. We have to go find Nancy."

He heard echoing voices in the hallway below. Footsteps, and people laughing. "Come on, Abraxas, for Christ's sake! We have to go find Nancy!" The footsteps began to mount the stairs, and there was even more laughter.

Abraxas still refused to budge. Josh tried pulling the leash, but he sank his shoulders lower to the floor and frowned up at him, defying him to try to pull him bodily up the next flight of stairs. The footsteps were climbing higher, and the voices were so clear that Josh could actually hear what they were saying.

"*. . . plenty of new supplies, and without any risk whatsoever . . .*"

"*. . . don't have to be squeamish . . .*"

"*. . . who's squeamish . . . ?*"

Josh came back down the stairs and sat close to Abraxas. "You are going to come up these stairs with me, and you are going to be alert and hot and ready to trot whenever you're told. Do you understand that?"

There was a moment when he knew that Abraxas had agreed to do what he was told. It was hard to tell exactly how he knew; but he felt something pass between them – not spiritual perhaps, but certainly empathetic. That weird understanding between one species and another.

"Come on," he said, and climbed the stairs, and Abraxas came bounding up after him.

He walked along the third-floor corridor, looking for 313. The corridor was decorated with Regency-striped wallpaper, maroon and cream, and it smelled like a stuffy, second-rate hotel. There were crystal wall-lights all the way along, but two out of three of them had broken, or needed new bulbs, and so the corridor was filled with occasional pools of darkness.

Room 309, Room 311 . . . He turned the corner and it was only then that he realized what a fool he had been. Right ahead of him, silhouetted against the next wall-light, were three Hooded Men and two dog-handlers. Another man was standing behind them, right under the light – pale-faced, with greased-back hair, wearing a navy-blue blazer with brass buttons. He laughed out loud as Josh appeared.

"Look at this! Didn't I tell you! Here he is! Aren't the Yanks the stupidest race on earth! He trusted Simon Cutter! He bloody well trusted him! And here he is!"

The Hoodies' dogs jumped against their chains and barked at Abraxas in hysterical fury. Abraxas barked angrily back, tugging Josh forward. But Josh managed to heave him back, and grab hold of his collar, and pull his head back.

"I'm going to let you off the leash," he said. "You're going to run, and you're going to save yourself. Now, go!"

Just then, he heard the steel-sliding sound of a sword being drawn, right behind him. A sharp point jabbed into the back of his neck.

"You are under arrest," said one of the Hooded Men. "You are charged with heresy, treason, murder, conspiracy to murder, subversion and insurrection."

Josh didn't move, but he unbuckled Abraxas' collar, and before the Hooded Man could stop him, Abraxas went tearing off along the corridor with his claws scrabbling on the floor.

"Send a dog after it?" asked one of the dog-handlers, his own dog straining at the chain so hard that it was standing up on two legs, and whining like an acute asthmatic.

"Forget it," said the Hooded Man. "We have what we wanted – don't we, Mr Winward?"

"Screw you," Josh retorted. "You don't have any jurisdiction over me or anybody else who doesn't live in this screwed-up London of yours. I want to see Nancy. I want to see her now. If you've hurt her – by God, even if you've even *touched* her – I don't care what you do to me, I'm going to murder all of you, one by one."

"I think you're being a little optimistic, don't you?" asked the Hooded Man. "There are many of us, and there is only one of you. And besides, this is *our* world, not yours. You have nowhere to run to. No friends, no hiding places. Ella Tibibnia is dead – we killed her. John Farbelow is dead – we killed him. Fifteen more subversives were eliminated on the very same day. Mrs Marmion's mother, Ranjit Singh – many, many more. We rule all of these different existences, Mr Winward, and we keep very good order."

"I want to see Nancy," Josh insisted. He felt hopeless and exhausted and his teeth ached furiously, but his sole purpose was to find Nancy. Even if she were dead already.

The man in the blue blazer came up to him and offered his hand. "Allow me to introduce myself. Frank Mordant. You and I could do business together."

"What?" Josh retorted. "You've got your fucking nerve. You murdered my sister. You personally murdered my sister!"

"Oh, come on, Mr Winward, it wasn't like that at all. We were fooling around a little. You know what it's like, the boss–secretary relationship? She said she wanted to try this restricted breathing thing."

"I don't believe a goddamned word of it. You murdered her."

"I'm sorry. I know you don't want to believe it, but it's true. One minute we were going at it hammer and tongs. The next minute, she went all blue and I had to call the ambulance. Dead on arrival, I'm afraid."

"You're out of your mind. Julia would never try anything like that."

"I know she was your sister, and you knew her very much better than I did. But our brothers and sisters don't always tell us everything about their private inclinations, do they?"

"So who mutilated her? Who emptied her out?"

"It was all in a very good cause," said Frank Mordant, taking his arm. Josh immediately twisted himself free. "When your sister Julia died, another was able to carry on living."

"You took all of her organs without any kind of permission, and then you just dumped her body in the river."

"Actually, no permission was required. Living here, in *this* London, she was subject to all of our laws. Vital organs can be taken from the dead at the discretion of the surgeon in charge. It's quite humane, when you think about it. And don't tell me it doesn't happen in *your* world, too."

"You think it was humane to throw her in the Thames?"

"That was undignified, I'll admit. But we wanted you to have her body back. There can't be anything worse than losing somebody and never discovering what happened to them."

They walked together along the stuffy corridor with the Hooded Men and the dog-handlers following close behind them. One of the Hooded Men caught up with Josh and said, "I want you to call that mongrel of yours."

"I can't. He's not even mine."

"If you don't call it, I'm going to send our own dogs after it, and have them rip it apart right in front of you, and eat it."

"I can't call him. He just won't answer. And he could be anyplace by now."

The Hooded Man turned to the dog-handlers and said, "Let them off the leash. I want that animal found and destroyed."

"Yes, sir," they said, and unclipped their animals' leads so that they could follow Abraxas' scent.

The dogs immediately ran off, but they were only thirty feet down the corridor when Josh called out, "*Hey*!" and gave them a piercing birdlike whistle. Both dogs skidded to a stop and turned around and stared back at him in expectation.

"What are you waiting for?" one of the dog-handlers screamed at them. "Go and track down that other damned dog! Kill!"

Josh said, "There's no point in yelling at them. You should appeal to their better nature."

The dog-handler had a blue-shaved head and his face was scarred like a patchwork quilt. "None of my dogs has a better nature."

"Yes, they do," said Josh. He put out his hands and the dogs came trotting up to him. He rubbed their heads and tugged at their ears. The dog-handler was furious and astounded at the same time.

"Did you ever hear of the Montenotte Method?" Josh asked.

"No, I didn't."

"The Montenotte Method says that you can teach a dog to be aggressive by appealing to its sense of loyalty."

"This dog is aggressive because I'll strangle him if he isn't."

Josh rubbed the dogs' muzzles and let them go. They walked uncertainly toward the staircase, paused, and looked back at their handlers, bewildered.

"*Go*!" screamed the bald handler. "*Kill, or I'll feed your bollocks to the cats*!"

The dogs scampered off down the stairs and out of sight.

"I see you have a very special talent, Mr Winward," said Frank Mordant.

"Anybody who cares about animals can do it," Josh told him. "And I care enough about Abraxas to buy him a little more time to get away."

Frank Mordant smiled. Then he said, "You wanted to see Miss Andersen? Come along, and I'll show you."

He stood beside Nancy's bed and he hardly knew what to say. She was pale and drugged, and her eyes were puffy, but he could see that they hadn't hurt her.

"Josh," she whispered, reaching out her hand for him. "I'm so sorry. I thought I could find Frank Mordant for you . . . I really thought I could do it."

He took a step closer to the bed, but the Hooded Man said, "That's near enough."

Frank Mordant said, "As you can see, she's a little sleepy, but we've kept her in the best of health."

"What are you going to do with us?" asked Josh.

"Me, personally, nothing. I'm only a minion, I'm afraid. I brought Nancy here because the Doorkeepers had a warrant out for her arrest, and yours, and I really didn't have a choice. If it had been up to me, I would have let her go. My conscience is clear about Julia, I promise you. She died by accident. But Miss Andersen came after me, and you came after her, so what was I to do?"

The Hooded Man said, "Tomorrow at noon you will hear the judgement of the Masters of Religious Observance; and then you will know what punishment you will suffer."

"You can't do this. You don't have any right."

"I wouldn't worry about it too much, old man," put in Frank Mordant. "They'll probably decide to exile you, that's all – on pain of imprisonment if you ever come back."

"Oh, you think so? If that's what they're going to do, why don't they let us go now?"

"It's all a question of ritual. You know. Keeping up appearances."

"Follow me," ordered the Hooded Man, and led him out of the room. Josh turned back just in time to see Nancy raising her hand to him in the Modoc sign meaning *Hope*.

Twenty-Seven

The Hooded Man locked Josh in a bare room with a view of the hospital lawns. In the distance he could see the glittering lights of London, with autogiros swarming over it like fireflies. He lay on the iron-framed bed without undressing and tried to rest, but his mind was teeming with fear and worry.

At eleven o'clock a burly male nurse unlocked the door of his room and escorted him along the corridor to the toilet.

"What if I try to make a run for it?" he asked, as he stood in front of the urinal.

The male nurse let out a sharp, humorless bark of laughter.

Josh was allowed to pour himself a Bakelite beaker of water, and then he was escorted back to his room. "Breakfast at seven," the male nurse told him. "Don't let the bed bugs bite."

He sat on the edge of his bed with his head in his hands. He almost felt that if he squeezed his eyes tight enough, he would open them again and find himself back in Mill Valley, in his own bedroom, with the wind-chimes tinkling on the verandah outside. He tried to wish this world into disappearing, by the power of mind alone. If somebody had wished the six doors into existence, maybe he could wish that he had never heard of them, and that time could turn backward.

He was still sitting there when he felt something nudging his left leg. Something alive. Instantly – shocked – he opened his eyes. It was Abraxas, with his eyes bright and his tail slapping wildly against the frame of the bed.

"Abraxas! How the hell did you get in here?" But then he remembered that the male nurse had left his door ajar while they went along to the head. There wouldn't have been any point in him locking it, after all – he wouldn't have imagined that anybody wanted to get *in*.

"How're you doing, boy? Hungry? I don't have any food, sorry. But here, you can have a drink of water."

Abraxas thirstily slurped from Josh's beaker, and then he shook himself and sat down beside him, as if he were waiting to be told what to do next.

"You're a good dog, you know that. You must have the best-tuned nose I ever came across. A Stradivarius of noses. And you didn't let those mangy hounds find you, did you?"

Abraxas gave a whine of appreciation in the back of his throat.

Josh said, "I'll tell you what I'm going to do now. I'm going to teach you the Montenotte Method. I'm going to teach you how to be fearless and brave and a little bit crazy. I'm going to teach you to fight your way out of here. You're going to be the fiercest dog that ever was. That's the least that Ella deserves."

He started to stroke the top of Abraxas' smooth, well-boned head. "Now you listen to me," he began. "This is the last time I'm going to stroke you like this, because you and me, we're equals." He pressed one hand flat against his chest, and then he pressed it against Abraxas' chest in exactly the same way. "We see with the same eyes," he said, pointing to his own eyes, and then to Abraxas' eyes. "We hear with the same ears, and we feel with the same heart. You wait. By the end of tonight, you and I are going to be so physically and mentally attuned to each other, you'll be wondering why I'm wearing pants and you're not. We're going to be symbiotes, you got it? And more than that, we're going to be friends."

All through the night, until a ghostly gray dawn began to reveal the trees and the lawns and the hospital buildings, and the streetlights began to wink out, Josh talked and touched and trained Abraxas to understand everything he was thinking and everything that he needed from him.

It was almost a dreamlike experience for both of them, a Zen master and his pupil, and Josh found that he could ask Abraxas to do things that he had never asked of a dog before, such as growling to order, and walking around the room seven times, and jumping in the opposite direction whenever he jumped himself.

He taught him more than tricks, though. Josh taught Abraxas to look at him and know what he wanted him to do next. Sometimes he needed the slightest of winks, or an almost-imperceptible nod of the head, but by morning he was sitting and lying down just because Josh was thinking *sit* and *lie*.

At five after seven, the male nurse came into his room with a tray. He set it down on a folding table, and gave Josh a Bakelite knife and fork. "There you are. Better make the most of it."

Josh lifted the aluminum cover off his plate. Underneath lay four rashers of fatty bacon, two sausages, two fried eggs, and two soggy slices of fried bread.

"Is this the punishment? Execution by cholesterol?"

"Very funny," said the male nurse, as he walked back toward the door.

Josh waited until the door was closed and locked. Then he set his breakfast plate down on the floor. "Abraxas? Come and get it."

Abraxas shuffled out from under the bed and wolfed down the entire plateful in less than twenty seconds. "Now, get back under there and grab yourself some zees," Josh told him. "I can't take you out for a walk, not just yet, so you'll have to hold it."

The Hooded Men came for him at five after twelve. There were five of them, with three dog-handlers and two drummers. As they escorted him along the corridors, the drummers let out an intermittent *bang!-bang!-bang!* that almost pierced his eardrums.

They went down the main staircase and across the hallway. Ahead of them stood two huge double doors, clad in polished copper. Two of the Hooded Men produced keys, and unlocked them. Two more pushed them open.

"Come on, now. This is your time," said one of the Hooded

Men, pushing Josh forward. They marched him down a long corridor, lit only by dim greenish skylights. Josh could feel a faint draft blowing along it, and the draft carried with it the pungent smell of camphor, mingled with the dry aroma of herbs. It reminded him of hiding in his grandmother's closet when he was very small, and how he had once been accidentally locked inside it for a whole afternoon, crying and calling out for help.

They reached another pair of double doors, and swung these open, too. Inside, it was darker still, and it took Josh over half a minute for his eyes to become accustomed to the gloom. He looked around and saw that they were standing in the entrance to a Victorian operating theater, with a hexagonal floor, and tiers of balconies rising up on three sides. Right at the very top, there were six clerestory windows, but they were glazed with dark blue glass, so that only the inkiest of lights could penetrate the theater itself.

As his eyesight improved, Josh saw that the balconies were occupied by Hooded Men, with their Puritan hats and their black tunics; and by other men in Puritan costume, their pale faces gleaming in the darkness like Hallowe'en lanterns. There was a murmur of conversation and a thick rustle of clothing, as well as the clank of scabbards.

The theater must have been very poorly ventilated. Apart from the smell of camphor and herbs, there was an overwhelming smell of stale sweat and tobacco. Josh found it suffocating, and had to steeple his hands in front of his nose.

Out of the shadows, Frank Mordant came forward, dressed in a black double-breasted suit with dandruff specking his shoulders. "The moment of truth," he grinned. "I don't know whether you're going to enjoy this very much, but it's going to be an experience like you've never had before, I promise you."

"Where's Nancy, you bastard?"

"Oh, she'll be here in a minute, don't you fret about that. In fact – look – here she comes now."

Two doors at the rear of the theater opened up, and a high surgical trolley was wheeled in by two hospital orderlies. A figure lay on it, draped in a white sheet, one arm dangling. As it was wheeled nearer, Josh saw that it was Nancy, very pale, her hair tied back and covered by a white surgical cap. She looked like Saint Joan, on her way to be martyred.

Josh tried to step forward, but one of the Hooded Men immediately grasped his arm with a gloved hand that felt like a bag full of crushed bones. "Stay here and observe," the Hooded Man breathed. "Your turn will come soon enough."

Now the two surgeons entered the theater, Mr Leggett and Mr Crane, both of them dressed in white surgical robes. There was a spattering of applause, but they stayed in the background.

One of the Hooded Men raised his arm and called out, "Pray silence for Master Gordon Spire!"

The theater became suddenly hushed. A thin man in Puritan costume descended from his place on the tiers, and stalked stiff-legged into the center of the theater. He had a sharp, ratlike face, with a hairy wart next to his nose, and when he took off his hat he revealed a mane of steel-gray hair, curled up at the back.

"What we have come here to do today is historical," he said, in a sharp, penetrating voice. "We have come here to judge, yes. We have come here to punish, yes. We have come here to uphold the law. But we have also come here to perpetuate the consciousness that gives us rule and dominance over every manifestation of our Lord's creation.

"This man that stands before you, Joshua Winward, stands accused of heresy, conspiracy, subversion and murder. We have deliberated and found him guilty. This woman who lies here, Nancy Andersen, is similarly accused of heresy, conspiracy, subversion of the Commonwealth, and deception. We have deliberated, and we have found her guilty as charged."

"On what evidence?" Josh shouted out. "Where are your witnesses? Where is your proof? You didn't even give us a chance to speak in our defense!"

The Hooded Man gripped his upper arm even tighter. "Quiet," he insisted. "This is a court of law."

"This isn't any goddamned court of law! Where's our

defense? Where's the goddamned jury? This is a total travesty, and you know it!"

"*Quiet*," ordered the Hooded Man, and crushed his arm harder.

Now Mr Leggett stepped forward. He paused for a moment, for effect, and then he said, "What you will witness here today will be a miracle of modern surgery. Out of justice, comes perpetual life. This woman who lies here on this trolley is convicted of mortal offenses against the Commonwealth. But now she will have the opportunity to give the greatest contribution possible to its welfare and its survival."

"What's he talking about?" Josh wanted to know. "What the hell's he talking about?"

"Shh," said Frank Mordant, lifting one finger to his lips.

Mr Leggett said, "The six doors which we all have sworn to protect for all eternity were created by one woman. Out of this one woman's mind, out of this one woman's consciousness – a flame that has been kept alight for two thousand years.

"She has outlived kings and emperors, uprisings and rebellions, invasions and conquests. She has survived so long because of the pharmacological skills of the Druids, and by mystical influences which we still cannot fully understand, even today, for all of our scientific advances. For century after century, she has been cared for by the finest doctors and surgeons and herbalists – still conscious today, where she is sustained by the latest in surgical techniques.

"This, gentlemen, will guarantee her survival through this new millennium, and into the next, and probably for ever. The six doors will never close!"

Josh tried to pull himself free, but another Hooded Man grasped his other arm, and all he could do was kick and twist.

Mr Leggett turned to Mr Crane, and said, "Shall we begin?" Then he looked around at the audience in the theater and shouted out, "What you are about to see now is a miracle! Praise the Lord!"

The doors at the back of the theater opened again, and a paler blue light suffused the auditorium.

"Gentlemen," said Mr Leggett, his voice cracking with emotion. "I give you the queen of all queens. I give you Boudicca."

Six hospital orderlies slowly pushed a black-draped carriage in to the center of the operating theater. It looked like a moving tent, because it was completely covered, so that only the lower half of its wheels were visible.

After the tent came a stainless-steel trolley, laid out with dozens of surgical instruments – saws, clips, scalpels, and some extraordinary devices which Josh had never seen before, and whose purpose he couldn't even begin to guess.

The theater fell completely silent as one of the orderlies pushed Nancy closer to the tent-like affair. Then, like a waiter whipping off a tablecloth, he removed the sheet that covered her. Josh struggled again, but the Hooded Men were holding him far too tight for him to break free. Nancy was completely naked, her pale skin shining blue in the light from the clerestory windows. The orderly secured her wrists and ankles with leather straps, and tightened them.

Now – on a signal from Mr Leggett – another orderly tugged a string at the side of the black tent. It resisted for a moment, but then it abruptly dropped to the floor. Josh looked at what was underneath, and felt a prickling sensation of utter horror, like centipedes running up his back.

The carriage was an elaborate construction of slings and pulleys and supports. Suspended on all of these slings were layer upon layer of coarse dried-looking fabric, the color of rotten linen. Out of these layers hung scores of gnarled sticks, hundreds of them, like the legs of long-dead spiders crushed between the pages of an ancient book.

At first, Josh couldn't understand what he was looking at, but gradually he realized that the layers of fabric formed a pattern, like a huge dead chrysanthemum. Toward the center of the chrysanthemum, the layers appeared to be thicker, and paler, and the sticks much less gnarled. Josh peered at them more intently, and then he saw that they weren't sticks at all, but human arms, their skin dried out, their flesh desiccated.

Between them, there was a distorted, twisted torso, thick with ribbons of scar tissue, and another torso attached to it, at an angle, and a third torso beneath them.

This enormous flower was nothing less than the mummified bodies of literally hundreds of people, all sewn together to form a single, immense being. And most terrifying of all was the face that lay in the very center of it. A woman's face, as white as if she had been powdered with flour, her red-rimmed eyes staring out of this concatenation of arms and legs and bodies as if she were right on the point of screaming. Yet the minutes passed, and she didn't scream.

She blinked, and that frightened Josh even more, because that meant that she was alive. She was actually alive, in the middle of all of these layers of atrophied skin and time-brittled bone.

There was no smell of decay, only a haunting mustiness. As each new organ was attached to her body, she must have drained it of all of its blood and all of its mucus, until it became nothing more than human paper. So this is why Julia had been emptied; and why all of the girls that Frank Mordant had murdered before her had been selectively dismembered. Their mutilations had depended entirely on this creature's particular needs. New heart, new lungs, new stomach – whichever had been drained of all of its nourishment, and started to fail her.

Her face was both alarming and remarkable. It wasn't the face of a modern woman at all. It was broad, with a heavy jaw, and the faintest trace of freckles across the bridge of a small, straight nose. A wide black band of cloth had been tied around her forehead, but underneath it Josh could still see traces of reddish-gray hair.

Mr Leggett stepped forward and raised his hand for attention. "Today you will witness the removal of the donor's legs, arms and head, and the attachment of her entire body to the queen. At the moment, the queen is breathing with only one lung, the other having been misplaced during her most recent transplant. Today's operation will strengthen her respiration, her digestion – and something more.

"We have been planning for over a year to give her reproductive capabilities. Ovaries, and a womb. Today we are going to attempt to make it possible for her to have a child. It is possible that – if she can do this – her child will eventually be able to carry on her conscious existence in her place. In other words, she will have an heir to keep the six doors open for her."

"You're crazy!" Josh shouted at him. "All of you! You're all fucking crazy! How can you think of killing anybody to keep that thing alive? How can you do it? And you call yourselves men of God!"

One of the Hooded Men clamped his hand over Josh's mouth. Josh tried to bite into his glove, but it was too thick, and it tasted of sour, untanned leather.

"We will commence by removing the donor's legs," said Mr Leggett. "You will remember that this is a punishment as well as a surgical operation, so it is the law's requirement that this young lady should suffer as much pain as possible. If she screams and begs for mercy from the Lord, then you will know that Master Spire's judgement was true."

Mr Crane handed him a black surgical crayon and he drew circles around Nancy's upper thighs, as close to her pelvis as possible. Josh wrenched himself from side to side, almost blind with anger and fear, and with the Hooded Man's glove clamped so tight over his mouth that he could scarcely breathe. This was a nightmare. It had to be a nightmare. He felt that he must have gone mad, and that he was hallucinating that he was here in this operating theater, with all of these faceless men and this grotesque thing that was lying in front of him, staring out at nothing with her death-white face.

Josh dropped to his knees, but the Hooded Men heaved him upright again. He tried to turn his head away so that he wouldn't have to watch what Mr Leggett was doing, but they seized his hair and made him look straight toward the operating trolley.

Nancy herself said nothing at all – just lay on the trolley making no attempt to struggle. Josh guessed that she had put herself into a medicine-trance, which badly-wounded Modocs used to do to numb their agony. Whether it would be enough to anesthetize her when Mr Leggett started to saw through her thighbones, he couldn't tell. *God, please help her*, he said to himself, with tears in his eyes. *This one time, God, please help her.*

Mr Leggett held out his hand and Mr Crane slapped a scalpel into it. "Now," said Mr Leggett, "you should watch this closely. It's always fascinating how quickly the human body protects itself against massive injury – how rapidly the bleeding stops of its own accord."

He leaned over Nancy and started to cut. A thin rivulet of blood ran across her thigh. Because of the dim blue light, it looked almost purple. Nancy shuddered, but she didn't cry out.

Josh raised his eyes to the tiers surrounding the operating theater. He couldn't watch any more, even if the Hooded Men were gripping his hair. He saw tier after tier of faces, the Masters of Religious Observance, and apart from the hessian hoods with their torn-open eyes, all he could see were lit-up expressions of ghoulish curiosity, almost a sexual excitement.

He lifted his eyes to the very top tier, which was empty. He tried to remember a prayer that his mother had taught him and Julia when they were children – a prayer that we would all find Jesus one day, and that when we did, He would pick us up in His arms and comfort us for ever.

And then he saw Abraxas.

The dog was standing in the middle of the tier, alone, staring at him through the railings. Josh couldn't believe his eyes. He must have gotten bored and restless in Josh's room, and decided to find out where he was.

The theater was gloomy, and Josh couldn't even be sure that Abraxas had seen him. But he stared up at him hard; and he tried to convey with every ounce of his will that he wanted Abraxas to jump down into the center of the theater. *Jump, Abraxas! Jump, you stupid bastard! Jump!*

Abraxas' ears pricked up, but he stayed where he was. Josh heard Nancy cry out, but he didn't take his eyes away from the topmost tier. *Jump, Abraxas! For God's sake, jump!*

Abraxas turned and started to trot away. In desperation, Josh twisted his neck violently to the right, and then to the left, and cleared the Hooded Man's glove away from his mouth.

"*Abraxas*!" he yelled, and gave a high-pitched, curling whistle. "Here, boy! Here, boy! Jump!"

The Hooded Man fumbled his glove over Josh's mouth, but Josh managed to twist his head sideways again and shout, "*Kill*!"

Abraxas came leaping down from tier to tier, until he landed with a scrabble of claws in the middle of the operating theater. There were cries of surprise from all around. Some of the Masters started to laugh. Mr Crane shouted, "Get that dog, somebody!" and Mr Leggett looked up from the operating trolley in alarm.

Without any hesitation, Abraxas launched himself at the Hooded Man holding Josh's right arm. He sank his teeth into his leg and furiously tussled his head from side to side. The Hooded Man fell backward, knocking over another Master. He grabbed Abraxas' front legs and tried to pull him off, but Abraxas was part bull terrier, and once his jaws were locked, they stayed locked.

"*Get it off me*!" roared the Hooded Man, smacking and punching at Abraxas' head. "*Get this infernal mutt off me*!"

The other Hooded Man released his grip on Josh's left arm and drew his sword. But Josh – his adrenalin fired up – was even quicker. He grasped the Hooded Man's wrist and forced it violently backward, snapping all his tendons. The Hooded Man dropped his sword and Josh picked it up.

Now he went mad with rage. He grasped the sword in both hands and swung it around, hitting the Hooded Man across the chest. It cut through cloth and leather and bone, and the Hooded Man collapsed on to his knees. Next he thrust the point of the sword straight into the hessian face of the second Hooded Man. It went right into his head and stuck in the back of his skull. Abraxas looked up from the man's leg.

"Come on, boy, kill!" Josh urged him.

"*Seize that man*!" shouted Master Spire. "*Seize him at once*!"

But Josh yelled out, "*Yaaaaaaaaaaaaaaaa*!" and advanced into the center of the operating theater with his sword whirling over his head and nobody was ready to take him on – not even the Hooded Men. Mr Leggett dropped his scalpel and pushed his way toward the rear doors. Mr Crane came hurrying after him, knocking over the trays of surgical instruments.

One-handed, Josh unbuckled the straps that held Nancy's wrists and ankles. Her thigh was bleeding but it was a clean, sharp wound and Mr Leggett had only just started to cut.

"Come on," Josh told her, and helped her off the operating trolley. He reached down and grabbed the sheet which had covered her and said, "Here – wrap yourself in this."

Two more Hooded Men had drawn their swords and were climbing down from the tiers, but Abraxas rushed at them, barking wildly, and all they could do was circle around, cautiously prodding at him.

Josh crossed over to the wheeled carriage where Boudicca lay. She watched him from the middle of her dried layers of human flesh as he lifted his sword and pointed it toward her neck.

"*What are you doing*?" screamed Master Spire. "*If you kill Boudicca, the six doors will close for ever*!"

"I'll tell you what I'm doing," said Josh. "I'm making sure that Miss Andersen goes free, and that you give her safe passage through the nearest door. If you don't, I'll cut your precious Boudicca's head off. And don't think I'm joking."

Frank Mordant stepped forward. "You're an idiot, Mr Winward. I always said that Yanks were idiots. If you kill Boudicca, then you'll be trapped in this world for the rest of your life – which probably wouldn't be very long, if the Doorkeepers have their way."

"That's a risk I'm prepared to take."

"My, my! You *are* selfless! But, you see, I'm not going to let you hurt one wrinkle of our lovely Boudicca's skin, because you won't be the only one who's trapped here. *I* will be, too. And without the doors, I won't be anything more important than the sales director of an electrical company out on the

Great West Road. So you see – I can't possibly have that, now can I?"

Nancy said, "Josh, I'm not going without you. There's absolutely no way." There was a wide bloodstain on the sheet that she had wound around herself.

"Honey, it's the only way. I want one of these people to take you to Star Yard. When you're there, and when the candles are lit, I want you to call me from the phone booth down on the corner of the street. Tell me that the Hoodies are staying at least a hundred feet away from you, and that you're ready to go. Then run, and jump, and get yourself back to the real world."

"I can't live without you, Josh."

"You'll have to. We don't have any choice. Now, go."

Nancy still hesitated. Josh said, "Please, Nancy. Don't make it any harder than it is already."

He held out his left hand for her. At that instant, however, Frank Mordant ducked and feinted like a boxer, and snatched Josh's sword. With a grunt of exertion, he lifted it like a giant dagger and aimed it directly at Josh's heart.

But Abraxas was even faster. He bounded from the floor, landing right on Frank Mordant's shoulders. Frank Mordant shouted out, "*Shit*!" and stumbled forward, catching his foot on the frame of Boudicca's carriage.

Josh saw it happen almost as if it were in slow motion. Frank Mordant's expression, wide-eyed, horrified. Boudicca's ghostly face, staring at him in an extraordinary mixture of fear and relief. And the sword breaking through the layers of dried skin, crumbling and cracking, deep into her many-layered abdomen.

The silence in the theater was overwhelming. Boudicca's eyes looked down at the sword that was piercing her many bodies, almost up to the hilt. She let out a thin, reedy whine, and a trickle of watery blood ran down the side of her chin.

"You've killed her," said Master Spire, rigid with shock. "You've killed Boudicca."

Frank Mordant stepped back, licking his lips. Boudicca's chest rose and fell, rose and fell. One of her desiccated hands twitched up, its fingers curled like an autumn leaf. Nobody moved. Nobody seemed to know what to do. Boudicca coughed, and it sounded as if she were trying to say something.

"She's not dead yet," said Frank Mordant. He turned and stared at Josh. "*She's not dead yet*!"

Josh suddenly understood what he meant. As long as Boudicca was still alive, the doors would still be open. He seized Frank Mordant's sleeve and said, "Get us all out of here! Now! The nearest door you know!"

"What? So that you can have me arrested?"

"If you get us back through that door I'll forget I ever heard of you."

Two of the Hooded Men approached them, their swords held high. Without hesitation, Josh bent down and swept up the sword of the first Hooded Man who had fallen, and stalked toward them, swinging it wildly around his head. Abraxas jumped at the Hooded Men, too, snarling and barking. They backed away, confused, and as Nancy and Frank Mordant and Josh retreated out of the operating theater, they made no attempt to come after them.

Josh said, "They're not even following us."

"They don't think they have to. The second Boudicca dies, that's it – we're going to be trapped here, and they can hunt us down at their leisure. And you can imagine what they'll do to us then."

They reached Frank Mordant's car in the hospital parking lot. He fumbled with the keys, but he managed to open the doors and start up the engine. Josh sat in the front. Nancy sat in the back with Abraxas. The dog was quivering with excitement and Nancy had to stroke him to calm him down. He obviously couldn't understand why he wasn't allowed to continue biting Frank Mordant's head off.

Frank Mordant was sweating now, and he backed out of the hospital gates with a jarring clash of gears.

"Candles?" asked Josh. "Do you have any candles?"

"Glove box," said Frank Mordant. Josh opened it and took out a carton of six.

They sped through the City, weaving in and out of traffic, running red lights. They drove across Ludgate Circus at nearly fifty miles an hour without stopping. A double-decker bus had to swerve to avoid them, and two other cars slewed around and careered up on to the pavement. "We may be too late already," said Frank Mordant, as the Armstrong-Siddeley squealed around the corner of Carey Street. He hit the curb, switched off the engine, and yanked on the handbrake. They scrambled out and ran up Star Yard as fast as they could, dodging in between passing pedestrians.

Frank Mordant knelt down and lit the three candles with trembling hands. "Oh God, don't let her be dead yet. Please God don't let her be dead."

He and Josh recited the rhyme between them. "Now, *go*!" Josh urged Nancy.

Nancy jumped awkwardly over the candles and started to walk into the niche. Abraxas jumped after her.

"Please God, let it still be there," prayed Frank Mordant.

Nancy limped to the end of the niche. She stopped. Then she turned around and said, "It's OK! It's still here! I'm going through!"

She disappeared from sight. Frank Mordant stepped back in preparation for following her. As he did so, Josh punched him hard in the face, and then in the stomach. Frank Mordant gasped and dropped on to his knees.

"I'm going to keep my promise," Josh told him. "I'm not going to hand you in to the cops. But you deserve to be punished, you bastard. You murdered my sister and God knows how many other girls. You would have stood there today and watched us die, and enjoyed it. Well, this is your punishment. Staying here with the Hoodies. I hope you live a long and miserable life."

With that, he punched Frank Mordant again, so that he fell backward on to the pavement, and lay there, stunned.

Then, with a last quick look at the world of the Doorkeepers, Josh jumped over the candles and started to make his way through the dark brick passage between the buildings.

He was only on his second turn, however, when he realized

that the passage seemed much narrower than it had before. His shoulders were actually scraping against the walls. By the time he reached the next turn, he had to turn sideways, and even then it was difficult to force his way through. With a rising feeling of panic and claustrophobia, he realized what was happening – Boudicca was dying, and as she died her consciousness was fading, and the door was closing up. With him still inside it.

He dragged himself through the passage faster and faster, his knuckles scraping against the brick. He managed to maneuver himself around the last corner, and ahead of him he could see daylight, and Star Yard, and Nancy waiting for him, still wrapped in her sheet.

He stopped, and tried to calm himself down, and exhaled. *Don't panic, whatever you do. Take it steady, take it easy, and you'll get out safely.*

Inch by inch, he edged himself nearer the opening. Now he could hear traffic, and Nancy shouting out, "Josh! Hurry! It's getting smaller and smaller!"

He was nearly at the opening when his left shoe caught, wedged in between the walls. No matter how he twisted it, he couldn't dislodge it. The walls were so close together now that he could hardly breathe, and he felt his ribs cracking.

"*Josh*!" screamed Nancy, and seized hold of his arm. She pulled him as hard as she could, and gradually she managed to inch him out. His foot came out of his shoe, and he fell sideways on to the pavement, gasping for breath. Nancy lay beside him, oblivious to the stares from passers-by, sobbing and laughing at the same time.

"We made it. We made it. I can't believe we made it. What happened to Frank Mordant?"

Josh lifted his bruised knuckles. "I kind of discouraged him from coming with us. I think he'll get quite enough punishment for killing Boudicca."

They slowly stood up. As they did so, however, Abraxas started to bark at the last narrow crack in the wall.

"What's the matter, Abraxas? What's wrong, boy?" Josh tried to pull him away, but he stayed where he was, still barking. "Come on, Abraxas. I want to get the hell out of here. Nancy needs to see a doctor."

It was then that he heard a gasping sound, and then another. He shaded his eyes and peered into the niche.

"Don't let it close!" choked a voice from inside. "For Christ's sake, whatever you do, don't let it close!"

"My God," said Josh. "Frank Mordant's in there."

They could just see him, trying to make his way around the last corner in the passageway. He was thinner and much less muscular than Josh, but it seemed almost impossible for any man to be able to squeeze himself through such a tight crevice.

"Let your breath out!" called Josh. "Try and wriggle like a snake; that'll help you get through!"

"Don't you think I'm fucking wriggling?" Frank Mordant gasped back at him.

There was nothing they could do but watch in horror as Frank Mordant pulled himself painfully toward them. The passageway was now so narrow that his face was scraping against the brick, and as he came nearer he stopped, and let out a breathless cry of agony. A few seconds later, they heard his ribcage crack.

Somehow, his face lacerated and his fingernails bleeding, he managed to drag himself right to the opening. "I'm sorry," he panted. "I'm sorry for what I did. Just get me out of here."

Josh took hold of his sleeve and tried to pull him out. The sleeve tore from shoulder to cuff, so he had to grip his bare arm. He wedged one foot against the wall and leaned backward, tugging Frank Mordant out of the niche inch by scraping inch.

Frank Mordant's head was out, and half of his chest. "Come on," said Josh. "One last pull and we'll have you out of there."

But it was then that Frank Mordant turned to look at him with an extraordinary expression, almost sad. The bricks closed completely together with a soft, suppressed crunch, and the top half of Frank Mordant's body dropped into the niche, among the leaves and the candy wrappers and the empty cigarette packets. He stared up at Josh and for three or four seconds he was still alive.

"Sorry, old man," he repeated, in a small bubble of blood.

DS Paul sat and listened to Josh and Nancy's explanation of Frank Mordant's death without interrupting. When they had finished, she closed the file in front of her and said, "We'll be making a press announcement later today."

"Saying what?" asked Josh. "You're not going to charge us, are you?"

"Saying that the mutilated body of a man was discovered in Star Yard by two American tourists. The man is thought to be the victim of a drugs war in South-East London."

"That's all?"

"That's all that anybody needs to know."

"I don't understand," said Josh. "Are you telling me that you *believe* us?"

"Let me just say that to a very few people, you are one of the greatest heroes of the century." DS Paul gave a secretive little smile. She dropped the file into her desk drawer, closed it, and stood up. "I hope you feel that you found justice here in London, Mr Winward. It's the very least that you deserve."

"I think I found a whole lot more than I bargained for."

DS Paul shook their hands and showed them to the door. "By the way, your friend Petty. Nice girl, even if she is a little . . . well, idiosyncratic. We passed her case on to Kensington & Chelsea social services. They've found her a job at Burger King."

"Thanks," said Josh. "I don't know what else to say."

"Have a safe journey home," said DS Paul, and closed the door behind them.

Epilogue

A week later, Josh woke up at two o'clock in the morning in a shivering sweat. He climbed out of bed and groped his way along the corridor toward the bathroom. He didn't switch on the light, in case he woke Nancy, but trailed his hand along the wall to find his way.

As he passed the living-room door, he thought he saw something dark lying on the couch. He stopped, and peered at it through the gloom. It was his brown leather bowling-ball bag. What the hell was that doing there?

He went into the living room and crossed over to the couch. He distinctly remembered storing his bag away in the shoe closet by the front door. Nancy wouldn't have moved it – what was the point?

He was about to pick the bag up when he heard a faint buzzing sound. He leaned forward, listening. There was no question about it. A soft, rattling whirr was coming from inside the bag. Yet all that was in it was his favorite ball.

Taking hold of the handles, he tugged the zipper down a little way. There was something inside the bag, something round and heavy, but somehow it didn't feel like a bowling ball. He took a deep breath and tugged the zipper all the way down.

It was too dark to see what was inside, but he was sure that he could see movement. He leaned over toward the reading-lamp behind the couch and switched it on.

"Oh, shit," he said, and stepped back in horror.

Inside the bag was the severed head of the Hooded Man. His hessian hood was ripped open, so Josh could see his face. His eyes stared out at him with sightless resentment, and his mouth was stretched wide open, as if he were shouting in silent protest. And he was crawling with blowflies, hundreds of them, glittering and green. They poured in and out of his mouth and his nostrils, they walked across his unflinching eyeballs. The Hooded Man was living putrefaction, decay without end, amen.

Josh opened his eyes. He was still in bed. Nancy was lying close to him, breathing softly and evenly. Sweat was trickling across his chest, so he dragged back the sheet to cool himself down. He lay on his back for almost five minutes, staring at the ceiling.

After a while, he eased himself out of bed. He stepped over Abraxas, who was sleeping on the floor on his favorite Indian blanket. Then he shuffled along the corridor toward the bathroom. As he passed the living room, he made himself look inside, just to reassure himself that he had only been having a nightmare.

But the bowling-ball bag was still there, lying on the couch.

Josh stood in the darkness, looking at it. Then he slowly approached it. Whatever it contained, he was going to have to open it, and confront it. He leaned over and listened to it. He couldn't hear any buzzing. He took a deep breath and tugged the zipper all the way down.